NEVER VOLUNTEER

Showing on the large wallscreen facing one end of the conference table was the *Valentina Tereshkova,* more than a mile in diameter and housing over twelve thousand people.

"About a year ago, a defector appeared in Austria who claimed to have worked on the station's construction," Kehrn said to Paula. "He described X-ray lasers, a giant accelerator track, parts for launching ejectable eggbuster lasers."

"To cut a long story short," Foleda said, "we succeeded in recruiting one of their people who collected a package of information. Then he got caught. But the file is still up there inside their own databank. We have the access code, but don't have somebody up there who would know how to break into a Russian computer system and use it."

Paula stared hard at him as the meaning of it all became clear. She swallowed and shifted her gaze from one to another of the faces staring back at her questioningly. "Now wait a minute," she began.

By James P. Hogan

Inherit the Stars
The Genesis Machine
The Gentle Giants of Ganymede
The Two Faces of Tomorrow
Thrice Upon a Time
Giants' Star
Voyage from Yesteryear
Code of the Lifemaker
The Proteus Operation
Endgame Enigma
The Mirror Maze
The Infinity Gambit
Entoverse
The Multiplex Man
Realtime Interrupt
Minds, Machines & Evolution
The Immortality Option
Paths to Otherwhere
Bug Park
Rockets, Redheads & Revolution
(*forthcoming*)

ENDGAME ENIGMA

JAMES P. HOGAN

BAEN

ENDGAME ENIGMA

Copyright © 1987 by James P. Hogan

A Baen Books Original

Baen Publishing Enterprises
P.O. Box 1403
Riverdale, NY 10471

ISBN: 0-671-87796-8

Cover art by Doug Chaffee

First Baen printing, August 1997

Distributed by Simon & Schuster
1230 Avenue of the Americas
New York, NY 10020

Printed in the United States of America

To EDWARD JOSEPH, my third son in a row, who, after three daughters in a row, restored my faith in mathematics by proving that the law of averages does work in the end, provided one gives it long enough.

ACKNOWLEDGMENTS

I would like to express my gratitude to the following people for their help and advice in writing this book:

Brent Warner of NASA's Goddard Space Center, Maryland, who spent many hours thinking about pendulums, gyroscopes, vortexes, and rotating geometries, and gallantly placed his sanity at risk by sharing for a while the weird kind of world that science-fiction writers inhabit. Jim Waligora of NASA's Johnson Space Center, Houston, for information on the physiology of low pressures and spacesuit design. Steve Fairchild of Moaning Cavern, Murphys, California, for thoughts on just about everything and his invaluable penchant for devil's advocacy. Lynx Crowe of Berkeley, California, for suggestions on security methods. David Robb of Applied Perception Technologies, Minneapolis, for lots of data on space colonies. Cheryl Robinson, who helped hatch Lewis and his companions from a pile of barren notes. Owen Lock of Ballantine Books, for sharing some of his immense knowledge of the world of military intelligence. Kathy Sobansky, for her assistance with Russian language translations. And Takumi Shibano, for his guidance in penetrating Oriental inscrutability.

And then there was Jackie, who doubled as electrician, plumber, handyman, auto mechanic, gardener, chauffeur, and carpenter, as well as being a mother to three small, rowdy boys—and never once complained about the hours a writer works. She made the book possible; they made it necessary.

PREFACE TO BAEN BOOKS EDITION

The original Bantam "Spectra" hardcover edition of
Endgame Enigma was published in August 1987. When
I conceived and wrote the book, which would have been
in 1985 through 1986, neither I nor very many others—
if any—guessed that the Soviet empire, which had
withstood through the best part of a century so many
predictions of imminent demise, was indeed tottering into
its final few years, and by 1991 would be in the process
of becoming history.

The speed with which these events overtook the
astonished world may be gauged from my own experience
as a guest of the annual European science-fiction convention, which was held that year, 1991, in Volgograd (the
former Stalingrad), in the USSR. A few days before I was
due to leave on an Aeroflot flight from Dublin, an agitated
travel agent called me to ask if I still wanted to make the
trip.

"Well, of course I do," I replied, surprised. "Why
shouldn't I?"

"Because of everything that's going on there?"

"How do you mean? What's going on?" I should explain
that I haven't owned a TV for longer than I can remember,
and seldom open a newspaper—and then usually just to
do the "Crossaire" cryptic crossword in the *Irish Times*.
I regularly have to call the phone operator to check what
day it is, and I've gone a week past the summertime clock
adjustment without being aware of it.

"There's a civil war going on," she told me, astounded.
"Tanks in the streets, people getting shot."

"And the planes are still flying?"

"Well, yes. . . . I suppose so.

I was thrilled. It was happening—ordinary people
actually standing up to one of the most brutal regimes of
modern times. "Well, if they can face tanks, the least I
can do is be there," I said. "Sure, I still want to go."

But so swift were the events that by the time I got there it was all over. When I checked in for the flight, the board behind the desk said DUBLIN-LENINGRAD-MOSCOW. By the time I returned, the flight announcement read MOSCOW-ST. PETERSBURG-DUBLIN. There were already pictures of the former Czar in windows and adorning souvenirs and gifts. There's something reassuring in looking at the march of history and noting how consistently it seems that the oppressors end up being buried by their intended victims. Nero's Rome has crumbled, but Christianity flourishes worldwide. The Nazis are gone, but the Jewish people prosper. And now Stalinism and the horrors of the gulag are no more, and Russia is again becoming a part of European culture.

So what's the point of reissuing a book set in circumstances that will never, now, come to pass? Well, for one thing, obviously, the story is still the same, and as the whole realm of science-fiction, fantasy, myth, and legend attests, the setting doesn't have to be factual or even plausible for a story to do its job and be enjoyable. But beyond that, this is a story involving political realities that remain constant beneath the superficial ebbs and flows of the particular power rivalries that happen to constitute the present, and which it pays to remain mindful of precisely because they are no longer reiterated in every other morning's headlines.

The prime reason for forming government has always been to protect individuals from the violence they inflict on each other when each is left to face the prospect of survival as a law unto himself. Today's democratic nation state—which appears, from the struggles witnessed in the twentieth century to be the most successful form of social organization to have emerged so far—seeks to achieve this through the establishment of one system of law before which all are judged equally, to which each individual forfeits the right to make and execute his own law privately. However, no such arbitration applies to affairs between governments, and the state of war that was once the lot of tribal groups everywhere reemerges periodically as collisions between nations. The authority of God is no longer compelling as a restraining influence—and was never all that notably effective, anyway—and those of us raised in the tradition of individualism and freedom are suspicious of moves toward an international order with all its socialist underpinnings and ramifications.

What, then, will contain passions and excesses on the global scale? I have no glib formula to offer. Some place their faith in reason (is there not a certain attendant irony in such a phrase?), others in the spread of better understanding as modern communications dissolve barriers of prejudice and misunderstanding, while some have hope in the ability of technology and industry to eradicate the differences in wealth that they believe are the causes of strife. But the question needs to be asked, especially in these comparatively tranquil times, for it can never be repeated too often that those who forget the past are doomed to repeat it.

As half a century of ferocity has shown, ideologies in conflict will stop at nothing. In *Endgame Enigma*, it is Lew McCain's grasp of human nature and the constancies of political reality that enable him to see through deceptions that others would have followed them to disaster. What deceptions? Well . . . that would be giving away too much. But as a gentle hint let's just say for now that in keeping with any spy thriller that involves political intrigue and some out-at-the-edge technological ingenuity, nothing is quite what it seems.

James P. Hogan
Bray, County Wicklow
Ireland
April 1997

PROLOGUE

The Mig-55E fighter-bomber, code-named "Grouse" in Western military parlance, was rugged, easy to maintain, and equipped for a variety of ground-attack roles, making it popular for counterinsurgency operations among rulers of the Third World's teetering Marxist regimes. Western military intelligence was interested in it, too, because it carried the first production version of the Soviet OC-27/ K target-designating and -tracking computer, which the countermeasures experts were anxious to learn more about.

Like most Soviet aircraft, ships, and ground units, the MIG carried a black box that could compute its position accurate to a few feet anywhere on the Earth's surface with respect to an electronic navigation grid laid down by Soviet satellites. What Pilot Officer Abel Mungabo didn't know when he took off on a training flight from Ziganda, one of the two Madagascar states into which the former Malagasy Republic had fragmented, was that aboard the Australian destroyer cruising fifty miles offshore was a group of professional mischiefmakers with some highly classified equipment, which in conjunction with transmissions from the USAF high-altitude bomber that just happened to be passing over at the time, was causing Mungabo's black box to come up with wrong numbers. He turned back after becoming hopelessly lost over the ocean, but missed the tip of Madagascar completely and ended up off the coast of the South African mainland. There he ran out of fuel and bailed out.

What happened after that was never cleared up officially. Mungabo swore upon his return that he saw the plane go down in the sea. The South Africans said he must have been mistaken: the plane crashed on the shore and exploded.

1

They even produced pieces of twisted wreckage to prove it. But the Soviet engineers who arrived in Ziganda to examine the remains were suspicious. The damage, they said, was more consistent with demolition by explosives than with a crash. And it seemed strange that not one piece of the more sensitive electronics devices aboard the aircraft had been recovered. The South Africans shrugged and said that was the way it was, and the ensuing diplomatic accusations and denials continued for a while longer.

But by that time, specialists in several Western military laboratories were already acquiring some interesting new toys to occupy them. The OC-27/K target-designating and -tracking computer found its way to the US Air Force Systems Command's Cambridge Research Labs at Hanscom Field, near Bedford, Massachusetts.

CHAPTER ONE

Dr. Paula Bryce brushed a curl of blond hair from her forehead and studied the waveforms on one of the display screens surrounding her desk. She tapped a code into a touchpad, noted the changes in one of the pulse patterns and the numbers that appeared alongside it, and commanded a reconfiguration of the circuit diagram showing on another screen. "That's better," she said. "D-three has to be the synch. E-six is coupled capacitively to the second-stage gate."

On a bench a few feet away, the Russian computer had been stripped down into an assortment of frames and subassemblies that were now lying spread out amid tangles of interconnecting wires and test leads. Ed Sutton, another Air Force communications scientist, peered through a microscope at a detail of one of the boards and repositioned a miniature probe clipped to it. "That's it again with the input on both," he said. "Anything now?"

Paula looked at the waveforms again. "Aha!"

"Bingo?"

"It's triggering. . . . Threshold's about point two of a volt."

"So it is differential?"

"Come and look."

"But not for noise rejection?"

"Uh-uh. That wouldn't figure."

Sutton straightened up from the microscope and sat down on the stool behind him. He pivoted himself to look across in Paula's direction. "It's starting to look the way you guessed," he said. "Initialization for a smart missile with its own inertial reference, updating from the aircraft's grid-fix."

Paula nodded. "Air-to-ground fire-and-forget."

"That was a pretty good hunch you had."

"Not really. It's a modification of something I've seen before. This version would permit tighter evasive maneuvers while attacking." Paula shifted her gaze to a screen displaying text, and began updating her notes. As she tapped deftly at the pad, glancing intermittently at the display of the reconstructed circuit and the data alongside, she was aware of Sutton staring over the cubicle between them. Almost thirty, she was slimly built—bony almost—beneath her lab coat and jersey, with fair, wavy hair, which although cut to neck-length and battened down with a clip, broke free into unruly wisps wherever it got the chance. Her features were clear, but somewhat sharp with a prominent bone structure, and her nose a shade too large and her chin too jutting to qualify her as glamorous. Nevertheless, men found her candid, light-gray eyes and the pert set of her mouth attractive in a way that derived from her poise and the self-assurance that it radiated, rather than from looks. "Challenging," was how many of them said they found her. She didn't find that especially complimentary. If they meant formidable as an object of conquest, it wasn't exactly flattering, while if it referred to something ego-related in themselves that they saw her as potentially instrumental in resolving, well, that wasn't her mission in life or reason for existing. The real challenge was to recognize that the challenge was to avoid being placed in either of those categories. It was too subtle to be articulated, for the whole purpose of the game was to divine its rules, but the few who could pass—those were the really interesting ones.

"Good reason to celebrate, maybe," Sutton ventured after a while.

"Really?" Paula continued entering her notes. Typically, he was waiting for her to put the proposition. Just for once, why couldn't he simply say straight out what was on his mind?

He skidded off along the tangent. "Cher's away this week—gone to the Catskills. We've got relatives and a vacation lodge up there, you know. Good skiing area in winter. Ever get up that way?"

"No, I never did." Paula sighed inwardly with exasperation. The stupid thing was that Sutton wasn't too bad a guy. His being the man had nothing to do with her refusing to help him out, or with any hangup about who was supposed to make a first move to whom. It was simply that the matter seemed important to him, while it wasn't especially important to her. Therefore the game required him to do something about it. That was what the challenge was all about.

"Did you ever try skiing?" he asked. Before Paula could reply, a call-tone sounded from the flatscreen terminal on the desk. She touched a key to accept, and as she swung the unit toward her, a picture appeared of a pinkish, heavy-jawed face with crinkly yellow hair combed back from its forehead. It was Colonel Raymond, who headed the section. He was framed against a background that included part of a picture hanging in a conference room two floors up from the lab.

"Paula, I'm with some people here in G-eighteen. We've, ah, got something we'd like you in on. Can you get up here right away?"

"Sure thing. . . . Oh, will you want the latest on Squid?"

"Squid" was the code word for the OC-27/K computer.

"No, it's nothing to do with that. But how's it going?"

"We're progressing."

"That's good." The screen blanked out.

Paula closed the log on the other screen, got up from her chair, and tidied together the papers she had been using. "I've updated the log for Charley and Bob when they get back from lunch," she called back from the door as she left. "And yes, skiing's okay."

Sutton shook his head and looked back at the disemboweled Soviet computer. He wasn't sure why he persisted in making a fool of himself from time to time like this. It made him uncomfortable, and he was always secretly relieved inside when she turned him down or the subject changed. But somehow he felt better for going through the motions of having tried. God alone knew what he'd do if she ever took him up on it.

The picture showing on the large wallscreen facing one end of the conference table was a prototype habitat designed to test ideas and technologies for living in space. It housed over twelve thousand people, in an immense torus more than a mile in diameter. Six spokes—three thick, major ones alternating with three thinner ones—connected the torus to a central hub structure. Part of the image was shown in a cutaway to reveal miniature cityscapes and residential areas alternating with multilevel agricultural sectors and parks. At intervals around its exterior, the colony carried the Red Star emblem of the Soviet Union. The Soviets had named it *Valentina Tereshkova*—after the first woman to go into space, more than fifty years previously. They claimed that it symbolized the peaceful goals of their space program and would stand as a showpiece to the world of what a Marxist economic system could achieve. Completion of "Mermaid," as the structure was code-named by the Western intelligence community, was targeted for the following year, to coincide with the centenary celebration of the Russian Revolution.

Gerald Kehrn, from the staff of the assistant secretary

of defense for international security, was more concerned about the colony's suspected hidden function, however. He was an intense, restless man with a bald head and a heavy black mustache, who radiated nervous energy and paced agitatedly below the screen as he spoke. "Then, about a year ago, an East German defector appeared in Austria, who claimed to have worked on construction of *Tereshkova* from 2013 to 2014. He was brought back to the States, and in the course of further interrogations described some of the hardware that he'd seen, and in some cases helped install."

Dr. Jonathan Watts, a civilian adviser with the decade-old US Space Force, who had come with Kehrn from the Pentagon, interjected for Paula's benefit, "Big-mother X-ray lasers. Nuclear-driven microwave pulses strong enough to melt metal. A giant accelerator track buried inside the main ring—what you'd use to feed batteries of matter-zappers." He tossed up his hands and shrugged. His face was constantly mobile, changing expression with each thought progression behind black, heavy-rimmed spectacles. "Other parts of the place seemed to be for launching ejectable modules, probably fission-pumped eggbuster lasers. And according to other reports, certain key parts of the structure are double-shelled and hardened against incoming beams."

"Yet nobody else has seen a hint of all this," Paula remarked. "Enough visitors have been through the place, haven't they?"

"Just on the standard tour," Colonel Raymond said from his seat opposite Watts. "They only see what they're allowed to see. The place is over three miles around, not counting the hub. There'd be enough room backstage to hide the kinds of things we're talking about."

Paula nodded and looked again at the image on the screen. Except for its inner surface—the "roof" facing the hub—the main torus was not visible directly; it moved inside a tire-like outer shield of sintered lunar rock which, to avoid needless structural loading, didn't rotate with the rest of the colony. The shield was to exclude cosmic rays. Supposedly. Or was that another part of the defensive hardening? The question had doubtless occurred to other people too, so she didn't bother raising it.

In the center of the group, informally chairing the proceedings, was a broad-framed, craggy-featured man with a dark chin, moody eyes, and gray, wiry, short-cropped hair. He was Bernard Foleda, deputy director of the Pentagon's Unified Defense Intelligence Agency, and had arranged the meeting. The UDIA was essentially an expanded version of the former Defense Intelligence Agency, now serving the intelligence needs of the Space Force in addition to those of the traditional services. He had said little since Paula's arrival, tending instead to sit back for most of the time, watching and listening impassively. At this point, however, he leaned forward to take charge of the proceedings again.

"Obviously this was something we had to check out." Foleda spoke in a low-pitched, throaty voice that carried without having to be raised. "We put a lot of people on it. To cut a long story short, we succeeded in recruiting one of the people who worked on *Tereshkova*—a Russian, who was code-named 'Magician.' "

Paula's eyebrows lifted. "As a source? You mean you actually got yourselves an inside man up there?"

Foleda nodded. "Luck played a part in it. He was someone we'd had connections with for a while. The details don't matter. Magician was an electrical maintenance supervisor, which meant he moved about a lot—exactly what we wanted. He worked there for almost six months. But as you can imagine, it wasn't the easiest place to extract information from. The snippets he did get out to us were tantalizing. He indicated that he'd collected a whole package together, but he couldn't get it down to us. The security checks on everybody who came back for leave or whatever were too strict. He wouldn't risk it. But what he said he had up there sounded like dynamite. We christened it the 'Tangerine' file."

"Dynamite," Jonathan Watts repeated, tossing up his hands again. "Weapons specks, pictures, firepowers, ranges, configuration data, parts lists, blueprints, test data, installation dates . . . the works."

Foleda resumed, "Then somebody had an idea." He stopped and then looked at Colonel Raymond. "It might be better if you explain the technicalities," he suggested.

Raymond turned his head toward Paula. "It involved the packet-header and checksum protocols used in the Soviet communications link down from Mermaid." Paula nodded. The terms related to data-communications networks.

In many ways, communications networks are like road systems: their purpose is to move traffic quickly from one place to another with minimum congestion. They therefore present similar problems to their designers. Speed is important, of course, and so is safety, which means essentially the same in communications as it does on highways: what arrives at a destination should bear as close a resemblance as possible to whatever left the departure point.

Also important in both fields is using system resources efficiently, which means avoiding situations in which some channels become choked while others are not being used at all. Thus, morning commuters seek out alternative routes for getting to work, which spreads traffic out over all the available roads, to come together at a common destination. A standard technique for sending large files of information from one computer to another through a communications network works the same way. The sending computer breaks the file up into data "packets," which follow different routes through the network to the destination, with different computers along the way deciding from moment to moment which way to route any given packet, depending on the conditions at the time.

To guard against errors due to interference, equipment faults, or other causes, the computer at the sending end uses the data content of a packet to compute a mathematical function known as a "checksum," which it sends along with the message. The receiving computer performs the same calculation on what should be the same data and compares its checksum with the one that has been sent. If they match, then the message is clear; or more precisely, the chances against it are astronomically remote.

Raymond went on, "We figured out a way to transmit Magician's Tangerine file down, using the Russians' own Earthlink. Basically the idea was very simple: rig the packets to carry a bad checksum, which means that the receiving Soviet groundstation throws them out as garbage. But NSA is watchlisting the mismatches. Get it?"

Paula was already nodding and smiling faintly. It was neat. When the checksums failed to match, the receiving computer would simply assume that the message it had assembled was corrupted, disregard it, and signal for a repeat transmission. What Colonel Raymond was saying was that the checksums for the packets containing the Tangerine file would be *deliberately* miscalculated. Therefore they would, in effect, be invisible to the message-processing computers at the Soviet groundstation. But the computers in the US National Security Agency's receiving posts in Japan, Australia, Britain, and elsewhere, which eavesdropped on the Soviets' communications all the time—and just about everyone else's, too, for that matter—would be programmed to look for just those mismatches. Thus they would be able to intercept the information that the Soviet system ignored. (It went without saying that it would be a simple matter to abort the retransmission attempts for each packet after a couple of tries, to avoid getting the system into a loop that would otherwise go on forever.)

"Tricky, though," Paula said. "Magician would have to get inside the communications center up there."

"He was a maintenance supervisor," Raymond reminded her. "That part was okay."

"Yes, but it would involve actually getting into the system

software somehow, and tampering with it. Was that really Magician's field?"

Foleda gave a heavy sigh. "You've hit it, right on the nail."

Paula glanced around quickly. "I take it from the way we're talking that this didn't work out."

"We worked with what we had," Foleda said. "Magician wasn't an expert on Soviet software. But we got the job down to what seemed like a straightforward procedure, and he was confident he could hack it. . . . But something went wrong. He got caught. The last we heard he was back in Moscow—in the Lubyanka jail."

"The Tangerine file wasn't transmitted?" Paula said.

Foleda shook his head. "Nothing ever came through."

"Presumably they got him first," Kehrn said, still below the wallscreen. He came back to the table and sat down at last.

Paula looked away and gazed at the image of *Valentina Tereshkova* again while she thought over what had been said. So, if it was a disguised battle platform, in combination with the other weaponry that the Soviets were known to have deployed in space, it would outgun everything the West had been putting up for the past decade. But why did that call for the meeting in progress now, and in particular her presence at it? Then it came to her suddenly what the meeting was all about. She jerked her head away from the screen to look at Raymond and Foleda. "That file is still up there," she said.

"Right on the nail, again," Foleda confirmed. "Magician managed to get a message through to us after he was arrested—it doesn't matter how—saying that as a precaution, he created a backup copy of the file. Apparently the Soviets never found out about it." Foleda gestured at the screen. "It's up there right now, inside a section of Mermaid's databank, stored invisibly under a special access code. We have that code. What we don't have is somebody up there who would know how to break into a Russian computer system and use it."

Paula stared hard at him as the meaning of it all became clear. They had risked using a nonspecialist, and the gamble had failed. But by a small miracle, the prize was still waiting to be claimed. This time they wanted an expert.

She swallowed and shifted her gaze from one to another of the faces staring back at her questioningly. "Now wait a minute . . ." she began.

CHAPTER TWO

"Now wait a minute," Paula had repeated in the privacy of Colonel Raymond's office an hour after the meeting ended. "My degrees are in electronics and computer communications. I'm a scientist. If I wanted to get mixed up in this kind of business I'd have joined Foleda's outfit or the CIA, not the Air Force."

"But this job needs your kind of expertise," Raymond had said. "And the way they've got it figured out, it wouldn't really be that risky."

"Tell that to the last guy who tried. He's in Lubyanka prison."

"This approach would be different. You wouldn't have to get inside the computer center—or anywhere that'd be all that difficult."

"Except a Soviet space station nearly two hundred thousand miles out."

"Kehrn explained how that could be arranged. . . . Paula, just promise that you'll take a few minutes to think over how important this is, would you, please? It's not only the potential military value of getting detailed intelligence on those weapons. The political implications are monumental. The unaligned great powers that we've seen emerging in this century—Japan, China, Brazil, the Southeast Asian alliance—have tended to regard both us and the Russians as equally crooked in the long run, and played us off against each other. But *this* would prove to the world, irrefutably and finally, that all the assurances we've been hearing about how the Soviets have changed but nobody understands them are just as much horseshit as everything else they've told us over the years. It would show that we are not victims of paranoia . . . that our suspicions all along have been grounded in reality, and their aim is still to spread their system worldwide, by force or otherwise, as much as it ever was. But against the lineup of global power that this could generate, they'd be powerless—ruined politically. This 'Pedestal' operation that Foleda's people are talking about could do it, Paula, the end of the line for them—*kaputski*. That's what this job could mean."

That was when she had made her first mistake, she decided: she'd agreed to think about it.

A male voice that incongruously blended an American twang with a guttural Russian accent spoke from a loudspeaker somewhere overhead and interrupted her reverie. "Ladies and gentlemen, we are now approaching *Valentina Tereshkova* and should be docking in approximately twenty minutes. Arrival formalities will be minimal, and there will be refreshments while we hear a short address in the hub reception lounge before commencing our tour. The Soviet Ministry of Space Sciences hopes that despite the limited space aboard the transporter craft, your journey has been comfortable. Thank you."

On the viewscreen at the front of the cabin, *Tereshkova* was almost a full circle, highlighted as two brilliant crescents slashed in the black background by the Sun off to one side. Around Paula, the other passengers were stirring and becoming talkative again, and those who had been asleep were stretching, yawning, patting hair back into shape, and refastening ties and shirtcuffs. There were a hundred or so altogether—mainly political and military figures, scientists, and reporters from Western and Asian nations—invited on a special visit to the colony to commemorate the Soviets' centennial May Day. The voyage from the low-Earth-orbiting transfer platform where they had boarded the transporter from surface shuttles had taken over fifteen hours. Although this was probably the first spaceflight for most of them, the initial excitement had lasted only so long, even with receding views of Earth coming through on the screen periodically to relieve the unchanging starfield. Now there was something new to see.

"Time to wake up," she murmured to the man sprawled in the seat next to her, a still-open magazine resting loosely between his fingers. "We're here. Welcome to Orbitskigrad."

The man whom she still knew only as Lewis Earnshaw stretched against his restraining belt, held the pose for a few seconds, while emitting a long-drawn mixture of a yawn and a groan, and relaxed. Then he rubbed his eyes, sat up in his seat, and looked around. "Home, home at Lagrange?" he murmured.

He was in his late thirties, solid but athletically built, and had straight dark hair parted conventionally, brown eyes that were alert and humorous most of the time but could be reflective when the occasion demanded, and a clean-cut, square-jawed face with a tight, upturned mouth. This kind of thing was his business. He was a civilian agent from a department that Bernard Foleda ran somewhere in the murkier depths of the UDIA, known nebulously as the "Operations Section." Like Paula, he was wearing a badge that identified him as representing Pacific News Services of California, USA.

"Quite an experience, eh, General?" someone inquired in the row behind them.

"More boring than driving across Texas," another voice drawled loudly in reply.

"The people don't seem exactly wild with excitement," Earnshaw said, closing the magazine and slipping it back in the pouch in front of him. "That's what you get when a generation raised on electronics grows up. Gotta have new stimulation all the time."

"Reality can be a good substitute," Paula answered dryly. "So long as you don't get hooked on it."

She had met him before their first briefing together

by some of Foleda's spooks from the Pentagon underworld. After Colonel Raymond finally talked her round, transfer orders had come through with amazing rapidity, assigning her to temporary duty with the UDIA. She had moved from Massachusetts to Washington within a week, and after a crash course in regulations and procedures for offplanet duties, she found herself in orbit aboard a USSF manned platform as one of a dozen trainees undergoing practical familiarization with a space environment. Talk about personal backgrounds had been discouraged, so she had learned little about her classmates, including Earnshaw. At that time, before their cover identities had been invented, she had known him only by his class pseudonym of "George," and had herself been known to the rest simply as "Joyce." It only occurred to her later that the entire class had probably consisted of final candidates for the same mission. She wondered how many people that last dozen had been selected from. Foleda certainly wasn't taking any chances this time.

Earnshaw had struck her as capable and self-assured, which she respected, and the two of them had worked well together on group tasks, despite her stubborn independent streak and his perennial skepticism and refusal or inability to trust anyone, which at times exasperated her. On the other hand, he didn't talk when he had nothing to say, and he wasn't especially bothered about maintaining an image and having to be popular all the time. It was a pity he was in a profession that·bred such cynicism and suspicion, she remembered thinking. He might have made a good scientist.

"What attracted me into science as a career?" she had answered once to a question he'd asked her. It was something they'd talked about during time off and breaks between classes aboard the space platform. "I guess because the challenges were demanding intellectually. It doesn't leave room for pretentiousness or self-delusion, as you get in a lot of other areas—I've never been able to stand phoniness. It deals in facts and truth, its conclusions are unambiguous, and it tests them against reality."

"The rest of the world has a lot to learn, eh?" he'd said, in the way he had of talking absolutely neutrally when he wanted to—usually when they drifted into something controversial—with no discernible expression or intonation, neither approving nor disapproving, agreeing nor disagreeing, encouraging nor discouraging. Somehow it always had the effect of opening her up more. She'd wondered if it was a result of gumshoe training.

"The rest of the world runs on deception and manipulation—what else can you say?" she'd answered. "It's what people perceive and believe that matters. Whether or not the perceptions and beliefs happen to be true has nothing to do with it. What matters is that everyone buys the product, votes the right way, and behaves themselves. I don't know who I blame most—cynical leaders, or the gullible people who listen to them. The irony of it all is that I should end up here, working for this outfit." Yet, here she was.

On another occasion, while they were having lunch together in one of the Pentagon's cafeterias during the three-week preparation period after they were selected, she had said, "You see, the whole problem with the world is that fools and fanatics are always so certain of themselves, but wiser people so full of doubts."

"Who said that?" Earnshaw had asked.

"Bertrand Russell." She'd waited a moment while he thought it over. "A philosopher."

"Philosopher, eh?"

"Sometime back in the last century."

"Just like that?"

"What do you mean, 'just like that'?"

"That's how he said it, just like that?"

"I guess so."

Earnshaw had eyed her skeptically, then asked, "So how come he didn't put 'I think' at the end of it?"

The pressure of the seat against her back increased as the transporter came round and decelerated into its sternfirst final approach. The image on the screen had enlarged noticeably. Then the view cut to a close-up of the central part of the hub structure with its array of communications antennas, and the docking port's outer doors swinging open to admit the ship. The sight of the bay inside loomed larger, ablaze with arc lamps, provoking a twinge of nervousness inside her. Her second mistake, she decided, had been to go ahead and think about it after she'd promised to.

A quarter of an hour later, the passengers collected their coats, bags, and other belongings, and exited through the forward door, moving awkwardly and using handrails for assistance in the low-gravity conditions near *Tereshkova's* axis. They emerged onto a carpeted ramp, where smiling attendants in gray uniforms were waiting to usher them through to the reception lounge.

CHAPTER THREE

"*Dobro pozalovat v Valentinu Tereshkovu,*" the Russian official said when they came to the front of the short line at one of the reception booths. There had been a baggage check when they transferred from the surface shuttle in Earth orbit. He peered at their badges and switched to English. "Welcome to *Valentina Tereshkova.*" Earnshaw handed him their two document holders. The Russian extracted a plastic card from Paula's, passed it through a reader, checked the information and picture that appeared on a screen in front of him, and entered a code into a keyboard. Then he repeated the process with the other folder. "Ms. Shelmer and Mr. Earnshaw, both from Pacific News Services, Los Angeles, California." He studied the screen again for a moment. "Yes, these are correct. What is the purpose of your visit?" His tone was one of personal curiosity rather than of officialdom.

"Special coverage for a consortium of West Coast agencies," Paula replied. "We've scheduled a number of special-feature items on this for the next few weeks."

"I see. Well, we must be sure to take good care of you. Can't afford any bad publicity, eh? I'm sure that Americans know all about that." The Russian passed across two preprepared ID badges in red frames. "Wear these at all times for your own convenience and safety, and remain within the designated visitor zones, which are clearly indicated. The stewards wearing red armbands are at your service if you have questions or need assistance." He indicated the camera and other equipment that Earnshaw was holding. "Pictures are permitted anywhere within the visitor zones. Thank you, and enjoy your stay with us. Next, please."

Still loping in bounds more than walking—because of their negligible weight near the spin axis—they followed a short ramp to a gate that led from the arrival area into the reception lounge. Groups of people were already forming around tables set, cocktail-party style, with assorted hors d'oeuvres, breads, meats, and cheeses. Earnshaw's wrist unit, which looked like an ordinary computer-communicator, beeped almost inaudibly as they passed through the gate. He stopped a few feet into the lounge to press something on it and consult the readout.

"That Russian was quite civilized," Paula said as she stopped along side him. "Are you sure we're in the right place? I thought they were all supposed to be monsters."

"Today, they're all on their best behavior," Earnshaw said. "Shop window to the world. Come on, let's get a drink and eat." They began moving toward the bar that had been set up by one wall. "Oh, incidentally" —he made it sound like an afterthought— "you've just been X-rayed." Fortunately the special equipment they were carrying had been designed with that kind of possibility in mind, and would have shown nothing unusual.

For the next half hour or so, the guests munched on snacks and stretched their legs as guests of the Soviet press agency *Novosti*, while two speakers delivered a double act that alternated welcoming remarks and a preview of the coming tour with a lament for misunderstood Marxism. Then the party moved on out of the reception lounge into a large, brightly lit gallery with corridors leading off in all directions, railed catwalks above, machinery bays below, doorways everywhere, and a confusing geometry in which verticals converged overhead and the floor was visibly curved.

As they waited to board elevators for the half-mile "descent" to the rim, Paula looked around to reconcile the surroundings with the published construction plans that she and Earnshaw had spent hours memorizing. She wondered if it was significant that the tour didn't take in any part of the hub system. The same thought seemed to have occurred also to a woman behind them, who was wearing a European Space Agency badge. "Excuse me," the ESA woman said to the red-armbanded steward by the door as the group began shuffling forward into the elevator.

"Madam?"

"Are we going straight down to the ring now? We're not going to see anything up here first?"

"There is really nothing of special interest to see up here."

"Nothing? That's surprising. What's behind that far bulkhead, and the pipes back there, for instance—between here, where we're standing, and the next spoke?"

"Only storage tanks—fuel for the Earth and lunar transporters, various agricultural and industrial chemicals, and water.

"You must store an enormous amount of everything. There's nothing else?"

"Just storage tanks, madam."

Earnshaw glanced at Paula and raised an eyebrow. That was where the launchers for some of the ejectable modules that Jonathan Watts had talked about were supposed to be located.

❖   ❖   ❖

After the long flight up from Earth orbit, the return to normal bodyweight as the elevator moved out to the rim felt like a debilitating heaviness creeping through their bodies; but in another respect, it was reassuring to emerge walking naturally again.

Valentina Tereshkova contained three built-up urban zones inside its main torus, which in the official bureaucratese of the predistributed literature were designated, mind-bogglingly, "high-density residential-occupational social units." The bureaucrats didn't have to live there, however, and the Russian guides who accompanied the visitors down from the hub referred to them simply as "towns." Each was clustered around the base of one of the major spokes, which formed a central tower disappearing through the roof to connect to the hub. Alternating with the three major spokes were three slimmer ones, which terminated in the middle of the agricultural zones between the towns at built-up transportation and processing complexes known simply as Agricultural Stations 1, 2, and 3.

The town that the party arrived in was called Turgenev, and constituted the administrative and social center. The tour began with a stop high up on the central tower above the main square, where the guides led the visitors through from the elevators onto an outside terrace for a general view of the colony. Paula judged the roof to be fifty to a hundred feet above where they were standing. The cross-section of the rim was not circular as in a true torus, but flattened like a wide automobile tire, with the roof stretching away horizontally for a distance on either side before it curved over and down to become the sides. Illumination came from two rows of what looked like immense, golden-glowing, venetian-blind slats receding upward and out of sight with the sweep of the roof—louvered reflectors that admitted light from an external mirror system. Power for the colony's industries came from nuclear reactors located at the hub.

Below the terrace, a ribbonlike miniworld curved away and upward between enclosing walls a little under a sixth of a mile apart. The nearer buildings were higher, merging into a monolith of tiered plazas, ramps, pedestrian ways, and bridges around the tower to form the town's center. Architectural styles were varied and followed light, airy, clean designs incorporating plenty of color and glass, intermixed with screens of natural greenery. The strangest thing was the geometry, or lack of it—for everywhere and on all levels, walls met at odd, asymmetrical angles, passages branched between buildings, roadways curved beneath underpasses to emerge in a different direction, and nothing seemed to run square to anything else, anywhere. Presumably the intention was to break up the underlying continuity and dissolve the sense of living inside a tube. If so, it worked.

"The architect who designed this must have had a fetish about rhomboids," Paula remarked as they looked out from the terrace.

There were many figures moving about; below, a vehicle emerged from behind a building, moving along some kind of track. Farther away, the townscape gave way to a more open composition of public buildings and residential units, trees, and parks, with glints of water in several places. The terrain climbed on either side to form a roughly U-shaped valley about a central strip, with buildings giving way to terraces of crops and pasture strips for animals farther away in the agricultural zone. Due to unanticipated difficulties with maintaining the ecological balance, which the Russians freely admitted, the general scene was not as idyllic as their public-relations releases had enthusiastically promised when construction commenced. In some places the metal shoring walls stood bare between tiers of barren, grayish-looking soil formed from processed moondust, and in others the vegetation was yellowy and limp. Their official line now was that this was only the first phase, and aesthetics would be attended to later; and most reactions were to concede that that was what experimentation was all about. This was a prototype colony, after all.

"Conventional enclosed dwellings are not functionally necessary, of course, since the climate can be controlled at all times," the Russian guide was saying. "As you can see, however, familiar styles and arrangements into neighborhood groupings are used, to give a feeling of normality as far as is practicable. The designers of *Valentina Tereshkova* took the view that the forms of houses which people have evolved on Earth over long periods of time best reflect the kinds of surroundings they prefer to live in. There seemed no reason to change it—at least, until much more is known about how people adapt to living in space."

"What materials are used for construction?" somebody asked.

"Of the buildings? Mainly aluminum, titanium, and other light metals processed from lunar ores. Currently the ore is catapulted magnetically up from the lunar surface, but we are constructing an experimental facility on Mare Cognitum to test high-power lasers as a launch mechanism. The Moon is not rich in hydrogen or carbon. You will find many things fabricated from ceramics and metals here, but few plastics. That will change, of course, when technologies for transmutation of elements are developed on an industrial scale."

"What's outside the town?" someone else wanted to know.

"A recreation area that includes sports fields and a lake. Beyond that is the region called Ukraine: one of the agricultural sectors where we raise food and livestock to feed the colony. We will be taking a look at it when we leave Turgenev. Past Ukraine, at the bottom of the next major spoke, is the town of Landausk, *Valentina Tereshkova*'s scientific and industrial center. We will have dinner in Landausk, and accommodation will be provided there tonight before we tour the town in the morning. Now let me point out some of the more interesting things that are visible from where we are now . . ."

Paula tried to take her mind off the mission that had

brought her here. She found herself envying the other people around her, wishing that she, like them, could enjoy the experience without apprehension. She went through the mission plan once again in her mind, mentally rehearsing every step as she had a hundred times, like a nervous, first-time actress muttering her lines while waiting backstage for her entry cue. She thought of the crew back in the lab in Massachusetts, secure in their familiar day-to-day routine. Her third mistake, she decided, had been rationalizing to herself that she could use a little more excitement in her life. If she ever got out of this, an occasional dabble in sin with the likes of Ed Sutton would be just about all the excitement she'd need.

"The six-sided building behind, with the glass frontage, is the university gymnasium, with courts for squash, tennis, and volleyball, a swimming pool, a weight-training room, and a general arena with seating for fifteen hundred people. The students come from . . ." The guide's voice droned on interminably. Wouldn't they ever get on with it?

She glanced at Earnshaw, who at that moment was doing a convincing job of panning slowly sideways to record the view with his camera. He lowered the instrument from his face to let the shoulder strap take the weight, and looked around casually, if anything seeming slightly bored, like someone passing a slow Sunday afternoon at the city museum. But as always, his eyes were constantly mobile, missing nothing, checking everything. She tried to tell herself that if there had been anything unsound about this mission, someone like him would never have let himself be talked into coming on it.

". . . transportation around the ring, as we shall see later. Good. Well, if there are no further questions for the time being, we will board the elevators again and complete our descent to the central concourse, and from there come out into the central square of Turgenev. Actually it's not square really, but an irregular polygon, as you'll see. I suppose we call it that through convention. So, if you would follow the stewards at the back, ladies and gentlemen . . ."

And then they were all moving back inside the tower. One of the voices around her commented that the place was artistic as well as functional, showing spontaneity and individualism. Surprising. Not at all the staid, crushing conformity you came to expect from Russian bureaucracies. Another voice explained it was because the Russians had copied it from a Japanese design.

Despite her resolve, Paula found her chest thumping. Now it would be only a matter of minutes.

CHAPTER FOUR

Russians had been mistrusting and spying on each other for centuries, long before the abdication of the czar in March 1917 and the subsequent seizure of power by Lenin in November. Largely as a result of this kind of tradition, their officials worried about anything they couldn't predict. They worried especially about behavior by their subordinates that they couldn't explain to their superiors. Hence, all the way down the lines of command, the overriding formula for survival came to be: follow orders, don't ask questions, never volunteer, and always behave predictably. One consequence was the stifling of innovation and creativity. Another was that they never—well, hardly ever—deviated from precedent. The operations analysts in Bernard Foleda's covert section of the UDIA had established from records of previous tours of *Valentina Tereshkova* that the schedule, the route, and the procedures followed were always the same. This fact had been of great help in drawing up the mission plan.

As the party of a hundred or so visitors assembled from the elevators in the main central concourse at ground level, the guides divided it into a number of special-interest groups according to preferences which had been indicated in advance. Thus, all the visitors would be able to see what they wanted to without being wearied by overload and without taxing any one location unduly. Furthermore, in a way that was uncharacteristically flexible for Russians, people were allowed to change their minds and switch groups at the last moment. Invariably some did. On this particular tour it was certain that quite a few would, because they had been asked to. They didn't have to know why.

Hence, for a while the compositions and sizes of the various groups would be uncertain. The Russians could have kept track precisely if they wanted to, of course, but not without subjecting the visitors to a lot of cattle-like herding and head-counting, which on previous occasions they had refrained from doing. It was certain, however, that the total would be verified when the whole party came together again for lunch two hours later. Thus, Paula and Earnshaw would have somewhere in the region of an hour and three quarters to complete their task and reappear by the time the groups reassembled in the central concourse before proceeding through to the restaurant.

The plan required them to leave the zone that visitors were free to move in, and the first problem was with the badges they had been given on arrival. As anyone conversant with security practices would have assumed—and checking with various intelligence sources had confirmed—the badges contained electronic microchips, which when triggered by a particular infrared transmission would transmit back a code uniquely allocated to the wearer. When sensors detected somebody about to pass through a doorway, say, the badge would be interrogated and its response forwarded to a computer that knew who was authorized to go where, and which would raise an alarm if it detected a violation.

Earnshaw and Paula drifted to the side of the central concourse. For the moment conditions were disorderly, with people milling around between the various groups, some splitting away into the short corridor nearby that led to the rest rooms, and others coming back out. Earnshaw looked around, saw nothing to arouse suspicion, and nodded. They moved on into the corridor. It was fairly broad, with the entrance to the men's facilities lying to the right, the women's to the left, and some doors to storage closets on both sides. Facing them at the far end was a second exit, which they knew from their briefings led to a foyer interconnecting various machinery rooms, technical workshops, and offices. A large sign above the far exit announced in several languages, NO VISITORS PAST THIS POINT. There were no physical guards—shipping people from Earth was too expensive a business for them to stand around all day doing nothing—but it was clear that anyone setting off the alarm wouldn't get very much farther before being apprehended. That was the way Earnshaw and Paula needed to go.

Earnshaw entered the men's room and unslung his camera and satchel of accessories. A half dozen or so other men were inside, and some of the cubicles were occupied. To one side of the entrance was the white, louvered door of a janitor and maintenance technician's closet. He looked around and overhead but could detect no sign of surveillance. According to a CIA report that he'd seen, the Soviets resorted to such extremes of snooping as concealing lenses in rest rooms only in top-security locations. This was hardly a top-security part of *Valentina Tereshkova*—indeed, according to the Soviet claims, the whole place was just a civilian experiment in space colonization. But on the other hand, if it really was a disguised battle platform . . . But there had to be some risks.

"Long way to come to see Disneyland, huh?" the ruddy-faced man wiping his hands by the mirror said.

"I guess this has to be the real Space Mountain," Earnshaw answered. The ruddy-faced man laughed and left.

Earnshaw locked himself in one of the cubicles and commenced his transformation. A touch of facial cream to dull his skin, some shadow to enhance wrinkles, a graying, ragged, Stalinesque mustache, and a modest application of hair whitener added a dozen years to his age. His vest, turned back-to-front, became a worn crewneck sweater;

his suit reversed into a dark green, grease-stained work uniform; and a pair of false uppers changed his shoes into crumpled boots. The satchel that he was carrying wasn't as rigid as it appeared. With its stiffening frame removed it could be turned inside out, and when the frame was put back again it became a toolbox of the kind issued to mechanics all over the colony, large enough to hold the dismantled "camera." Finally, he rubbed a trace of grime into the creases of his hands and under his nails, added a streak to his forehead, and pulled on a cap.

When the Russian steward stuck his head in the door of the rest room to check, all the visitors had left. "No stray sheep left in here?" he said to the maintenance engineer in the green uniform, who was rummaging in the closet near the door.

"They're all gone," Earnshaw mumbled in Russian without looking round.

"It's chaos out there this time. You know, I swear our schoolchildren make less fuss than some of those people."

"No discipline. That's what it is."

"You're right. Although, mind you, I wouldn't say no to some of those American women out there. How do they afford such clothes?"

"Well, if they don't do anything that's worth enough to pay for them, then somebody else must pay for them. That's capitalism."

"Give me a break. You sound like a Party hack."

Earnshaw finished putting tools into his box and turned from the closet, holding a reel of electrical wire. He had hidden his red-framed visitor's badge in the closet and had exchanged it for an imitation blue-framed one, as worn by general workers and inhabitants of the colony. "I don't know you," he said to the steward. "You might be KGB."

"Do me a favor! I transferred here from Landausk a few days ago."

"I see. Landausk, eh?" Earnshaw lifted a stepladder out from the closet. "I suppose we'll be seeing more of you around here, then."

"Yes, I suppose so. Well, I'd better be getting back. See you around."

"Sure."

The steward disappeared. Earnshaw waited for a few seconds, and then carried the ladder out into the corridor. He positioned it in the center of the floor underneath the translucent panel covering the light, climbed up, and had just begun undoing the fastenings when Paula emerged from the ladies' room. She was wearing a maintenance engineer's uniform, too, now. Her face had shed its makeup, and she had acquired dark hair.

When a tubby man in a blue shirt came through from the off-limits direction a minute or so later they were hard at work, with several of the lighting tubes removed and wires trailing down from the opened panel in the ceiling. They said nothing, and the tubby man went through into the rest room. Earnshaw reached into his toolbox and handed down one of the subassemblies that the camera had come apart into. Superficially it looked like an electrician's test meter. Recessed into it at one end, however, was a tiny lens sensitive to infrared. When the tubby man came out again and went back through the doorway, Paula aimed the unit to read the interrogation signal emitted by the transmitter above the door. It also read the response code from the tubby man's badge, which reflected invisibly off the surrounding wall. A moment later, a sign appeared in the unit's readout, confirming that the computer inside was set to mimic the tubby man's code. Paula glanced up at Earnshaw and nodded.

Earnshaw came back down the ladder, and Paula plugged a lead from the unit into another meter to program it from the first. Then she disconnected it and handed it to Earnshaw. Now they each had a device that would mimic a valid response signal. Earnshaw picked up his toolbox and approached the doorway. A light on his unit flickered as he went through, indicating that it had been interrogated and had responded. Paula came after him, and hers did the same. Now they were committed. They followed the

wall on the far side of the doorway for a short distance
and stopped at a switch panel, where they set down their
equipment and tools. Paula removed the coverplate and
began loosening connections inside, while Earnshaw
squatted down and made a play of searching in the toolbox
while he checked the layout of the surroundings against
what they had been led to expect. Two men walked by,
talking, then turned a corner and disappeared. A woman
came out of a door and went off in the other direction.

Paula fought to keep her hands steady and look as if
she were working normally. The method they had used
was far from foolproof, and it was possible, even now,
that they had triggered an alarm, although there were no
whooping sirens or flashing lights to indicate the fact. If
the computer that the badge-readers talked to was
programmed to check each individual's movements from
place to place, for example—which it possessed all the
information to do—it would just have deduced that the
same person had passed through the same point three
times without going back again. Or perhaps the system
used a one-time code for every badge, where the response
changed according to a predetermined formula every time
it was used. In a top-security environment, precautions
like that would be routine. But the whole essence of the
new plan was to avoid having to penetrate into such areas,
and this location had been selected for the operation
precisely because nothing of other-than-domestic
significance went on there. In those circumstances, the
Washington experts had pronounced—probably keeping
their crossed fingers out of sight behind their backs, Paula
had come to suspect only when it was too late—automatic
tracking would be unlikely. As long as there was nothing
to indicate that anyone had gone where they weren't
supposed to, and that no visitors were about to wander
off and get lost, the computer would be happy.

Earnshaw seemed satisfied after surveying the
surroundings. "Let's go," he whispered. They had an hour
and fifteen minutes.

Leaving a sign saying, in Russian, DANGER—HIGH VOLTAGE, below the opened switch panel, they picked up their things again and followed a corridor out of the foyer to a metal-railed staircase. A flight down brought them to a landing overlooking a machinery bay, with a catwalk leading off and running along above it on one side. They went on down to where a narrow passage led the other way at the bottom of the stairs. A man in a white coat appeared out of the passage, stood aside and nodded perfunctorily as they passed, then went on up without giving them a second glance.

They entered the passage. After a short distance, one side opened into a gallery full of ducts, piping, structural members, and cable runs, with a bank of electrical cabinets standing in a line along one wall. The passage continued on, but they left it and picked their way through the gallery to a set of steps leading down into a shallow bay, partly screened from the corridor by the clutter of machinery they had climbed through. Three sides of the bay consisted of banks of plain metal boxes containing environmental monitoring and control computers, along with conduits bringing in signals from sensors and instruments in thousands of different locations. Although the place was normally unmanned, it contained a bench for use by service engineers when they came to perform checks or repairs. At one end of the bench was an instrument panel containing test meters, switches, a keyboard and display screen, and fitted with various supply sockets. One of these sockets was a standard type provided for the engineers to plug portable computers into to access the maintenance department's database for reference data—with the complexity of modern systems, carrying the requisite manuals around would have required a wheelbarrow. And it was inside the maintenance department's section of the databank that Magician had hidden the backup copy of Tangerine—the file that the whole operation was aimed at recovering.

Earnshaw took out the final section of the "camera"

from his toolbox. It was, in fact, a specially designed microcomputer, with a plug that matched the standard Russian data socket. Paula pulled a stool from under the bench and sat down. She plugged in the set, connected the power lead, and activated a search routine to begin testing access routes into the system. She worked quickly, nervously, pausing to study a response on the set's miniature screen, thinking for a second, entering a command—wanting to get it over with. Earnshaw stood behind, silent, watching the approach into the bay. There were maintenance points like this all over *Tereshkova*, but this one was more secluded than most. That was why they had picked it.

Paula bit her lip with suppressed tension as a hunch yielded a positive response. The maintenance department's system used a fairly straightforward method of access codes, which was to be expected, since it contained relatively insensitive information. As another line of code appeared, opening the executive level of the file manager, she breathed a silent prayer of gratitude for Magician's presence of mind in choosing *this* system to hide the file in. Or had it been simply because he worked in the maintenance department? Breaking into one of the higher-security systems, such as the research department's, or the information bank kept by *Tereshkova*'s branch of the KGB, would have been impossible in the time available.

She attempted a direct request for the file. It failed. The initiating address pointer had been erased to make it invisible. She obtained a sector table, located the header she wanted, and commanded a forced read. The system acknowledged that it had the file, but demanded an access validation to release it. She supplied the code she had been given. There was a pause. Then a new line appeared, requesting an output-destination spec. "I think we're getting there!" Paula hissed up at Earnshaw.

He turned and hunched down to peer over her shoulder. She entered another line and sat watching the screen tensely. A delay of perhaps two seconds dragged by. Then a confirmation appeared. In the same instant a line in English appeared below:

GP700 "TANGERINE"; STAT OK: READY TO READ. MEM DES? FILE DES? READ ACC?

Paula shifted the keyboard from Cyrillic alphabet to English and complete the dialogue. A final, single-word line confirmed:

COPYING

She sat back, closed her eyes, and exhaled a long, silent breath of relief. Earnshaw's fingers closed around her arm and squeezed reassuringly. She blinked and peered at the screen again, as if to make sure. The word was still there, glowing solid and jubilant. It meant that Magician's file was being copied through to create a duplicate inside the high-density memory-crystal arrays contained in their portable device. The copying would take just a matter of seconds, and then the original inside the maintenance department's databank would be destroyed. All that would be left then would be to get the copy home.

COPYING COMPLETED AND VERIFIED

CONFIRM SOURCE ERASURE?

Paula leaned forward to enter a reply . . .

She wasn't sure what it was that registered—a sound, something glimpsed from the corner of her eye, an unconsciously perceived sense of movement? Earnshaw was still down next to her, watching the screen. She turned her head suddenly to look up past him . . . and gasped out loud in sudden dismay.

"Remain as you are!" the Russian officer snapped, pointing his pistol. Earnshaw's head jerked around. Paula could do nothing but stare up numbly.

There were four more uniformed guards behind, two of them holding leveled submachine guns. The officer moved a pace forward to the edge of the bay, and looked down. He had a Tartar face beneath the peaked cap, olive-skinned, with narrow eyes and high cheekbones. "Keep your hands in sight," he instructed. "Now, back slowly against the far wall. Make no sudden moves."

CHAPTER FIVE

The night's rain had freshened the air after a week of early summer heat that had become oppressive, and the scattered clouds left over Washington, D.C., by morning promised a spell of cool relief. Bernard Foleda let the drape fall back across the bedroom window with a satisfied "pom, pom, pom, pom, pom-pom-pom-pom-pom" to the tune of Mozart's overture to *The Impresario,* and finished knotting his tie. He took the jacket of his suit from the closet, and, draping it over an arm, pom-pommed his way in a gravelly bass-baritone downstairs to breakfast. There was no reason for him to be humming to himself, considering the disaster that had befallen the department in the past week—it was simply a habit born of years. And besides, he had learned a long time ago that when people in his profession started letting the job get to them personally, they tended not to last very much longer.

Myra was sitting at the kitchen table with a cup of coffee in her hand, studying selected items from the morning's news offerings on a flatscreen pivoted to face her from the worktop opposite. Like him in her fifties, she was a tall, normally full-bodied woman, with a face that had managed to retain its composure and humorous set despite eyes and cheeks still sunken from a five-month illness that had lasted through winter. The skin on the backs of her hands was still loose from her not having fully regained her weight yet, and her dark, neatly trimmed hair showed gray streaks which she hadn't attempted to disguise by tinting. They had been married for almost thirty years, and unlike the mysterious, withdrawn spy chiefs of the popular movies, Foleda discussed his work with her regularly. He didn't understand how scriptwriters could expect people like him, on top of everything else, to carry on being furtive and secretive after they got home. Maybe they did it to give themselves an excuse for introducing beautiful women into their plots—usually Chinese, for some obscure reason—who made their livings by coaxing secrets out of semicomatose government officials in between bouts of frenzied lovemaking. If so, Foleda had no objection—the image was good for recruiting.

"The rain's stopped," Myra said as Bernard came in and hung his jacket over the back of one of the kitchen chairs. "It looks as if it's going to be cloudy today. Nice and cool for a change."

"Yes, I already looked. We could use it." Bernard walked over to the chef, took out two plates of scrambled eggs, ham, and a hotcake, and pressed a button to start the toaster. His wife poured the coffee while he sat down. The item on the screen was about a Japanese astronaut who had scored a first by achieving escape velocity under his own power with a series of hops and a leap off the surface of Deimos, the smaller of the two moons of Mars. "So maybe the old nursery rhyme isn't so silly after all, if we just change it slightly," the commentator babbled cheerfully in a way that Bernard found indistinguishable from banal at that time of morning. "The cow jumped *off* the moon, ho-ho!"

Foleda snorted. "What else do we have?"

Myra touched a button on the handpad lying beside the coffeepot, and a yellow light on the wallpanel by the stove came on to indicate that the house-manager was active. "Cancel," she said in a slightly raised voice. The picture vanished and was replaced by a selection of options. "Five-three," Myra instructed, and a new list appeared. "Poland," she said. A headline replaced the list: MORE WARSAW DEMONSTRATIONS. Myra glanced at Bernard. He nodded. "Yes," she said at the panel. Then, "X-out, out." The yellow light went off.

The item concerned Soviet responses to the latest round of protests and strikes in Poland and East Germany. As usual the media were emphasizing the military aspect, with dramatically narrated scenes of troops confronting crowds, NATO units being put on alert—Foleda recognized one shot of rolling tanks as being months old, with no connection to current events at all—and snippets of military and political spokesmen being questioned about the risk of a general European escalation. That was the kind of material that delivered audiences to advertisers, and was only to be expected. Western intelligence had been following the developments behind the present situation since long before the public became aware of them, however, and opinions were that the likelihood of any real shooting was remote.

The Soviets had accelerated their military buildup in the final decades of the previous century. Their intention had not been so much to provoke war, for they had no more desire than anyone else to be devastated again if they could avoid it, but, taking their cue from the woeful performance of the democracies at Munich in response to Hitler's aggressions, to gamble that, as before, their adversaries would back down without a fight from the *threat* of force. And for a time, as Western pacifists howled for appeasement and rediscovered moral outrage with the realization that every pulpit, podium, lectern, and armchair was just twenty minutes from somebody's launch site, it had seemed to work. But in the crucial early years of the twenty-first century, the Soviets had wavered when they found themselves faced by the prospect of having to take on not only the West's military technology, but the larger part of the numerically overwhelming population of Asia as well. Originally the Bomb had redressed the balance between sides whose different political systems resulted in unequal commitments to conventional forces. The irony was that when both sides drew even in terms of Bomb-power, *people* should become the deciding factor to tip the scales. And as Marxism's original appeal waned in the face of Asia's rising affluence, the Soviets fell farther behind in the competition for minds and souls. Their moment had gone.

Paradoxically, it was just this that made the present situation so precarious in a different kind of way. At one time, before Khrushchev, communist dogma had held that the capitalists would launch a last, suicidal war rather than submit to the final triumph of Marx's immutable laws. Now it seemed more likely to happen the other way around: that in desperation, an irrational element in the Soviet leadership might decide to take everyone else down with them if they perceived all to be lost anyway. It was Asia's armies that stabilized the situation; in turn, their protection was the West's "Starshield" orbital defensive system. If that shield were destroyed, the entire system of deterrence and containment around the Soviet bloc would disintegrate and set the stage for exactly the kind of last-ditch gamble that the West's strategic analysts feared most. That was what made knowing the true nature of *Valentina Tereshkova* was so important.

That something big was in the wind, the various intelligence agencies of the US, Western Europe, and Eastern Asia were agreed. Also, it would happen some time within the current year. But what or exactly when, nobody knew. In the eyes of many, the game was nearing its end. But endgames have a perplexing tendency to suddenly go either way. At this stage of this particular endgame, there was no latitude for error.

"I'll take a copy to read when I get a chance," Bernard said. Myra activated the audio again and directed the text to be hardcopied in the den. Bernard washed down the last of his toast with some coffee, and rose from his chair. "How are we for time?" he asked.

Myra went to the window and looked down over the tree-lined avenue outside, normally peaceful but busier at this time of the morning with people leaving for work. There was a black Chevrolet parked halfway along the next block. "They're here," she said matter-of-factly.

"Damn," Bernard muttered as Myra helped him on with his jacket. That meant he was running late. The two KGB agents from the Soviet embassy who tailed him every morning always arrived punctually and circled the block three times before parking. He bustled through to the den, picked up the sheets of hardcopied text, and slipped them into his briefcase. When he came back out, Myra was waiting in the hallway with his raincoat.

"You'd better take this," she said. "It might start raining again later."

"Thanks, I will." Bernard took his hat from the stand.

"Oh, and if nothing pressing comes up, remember that Ella and Johnny are coming this evening. I know you wouldn't want to miss your grandson's birthday if you can help it."

"I'll try not to. What have we bought him?"

"A junior spy kit, of course. It has invisible ink, false beards and mustaches, a codebook and some software to go with it, and a miniature camera. You see, just like the real thing."

"You mean they haven't got something for kids to tap into phone lines?"

"Give them time, dear."

"Okay, I'll see you later tonight."

"You too. Have fun today." Myra kissed him lightly on the cheek and watched from the door at the top of the stairs leading down into the garage as he descended and climbed into his maroon Cadillac. The outside door opened, and he backed out.

Minutes later in the thick of morning traffic streaming toward the Beltway, he caught sight of the KGB car, sitting solidly four places behind him as he swung right off an overpass to take the ramp down to the freeway. Several cars farther back still, just coming across the overpass, was the blue FBI Ford that tailed the KGB every morning. Foleda shook his head as he turned on a piano concerto to relax himself before the working day started. It was all sure as hell a crazy way to run a planet.

Gerald Kehrn was a born worrier. When he was younger he had worried about the things he read that said resources were about to run out. And then when they didn't run out and scientists began convincing the world that the whole problem had been exaggerated, he had worried that too many resources would produce too many people. When right-wing administrations were in power he worried about conservative fascists and fundamentalists, and with left-wing administrations he worried about liberal fascists and regulators. And of course, he had always worried about a war breaking out; the more time that went by without there being one, the more he worried that because weapons were constantly getting bigger and deadlier, it would be so much the worse when it did. He worried especially about things he didn't know about, and so tried to keep himself informed about everything. That made him good with details and a useful person to have around, which helped explain how he had made it to a senior position on the staff of the defense secretary. And the position suited him, for if worse did come to worst, he would prefer to be right there in the center of the action—not able to influence the course of events very much, perhaps, but at least knowing what was going on.

As he drove toward the Potomac on his way to the Pentagon on the morning of May 4, an inner foreboding told him that this was the beginning. He wasn't sure why, for there had been enough diplomatic goofs and intelligence screwups before, and this was hardly the first time the Soviets had nailed a couple of agents. Maybe it was the involvement of Mermaid, which had been taking on such big proportions in everyone's thinking lately. But something about the situation filled him with the dull, cold certainty that this was the first tripping over the edge into the scrambling, steepening tumble that would take them all the way to the Big One.

Because he worried about being late whenever he had an appointment, he always left early. Hence, none of the others had arrived yet when he got to Foleda's office. He found Foleda's operations assistant, Barbara Haynes, a tall, graying but elegant woman in her late forties whom he knew well, and Rose, Foleda's personal secretary, discussing something being displayed on a screen in the outer room. The strains of some piece of classical music coming through the open door at the rear—Kehrn had no idea what it was; he preferred jazz himself—indicated that Foleda was already ensconced within.

"We heard there was a snarl-up on the George Mason Bridge," Rose said. "Didn't think you'd make it so soon."

"A vegetable truck decided to unload itself there," Kehrn said. "But I left in good time. It wasn't so bad."

"Well, at least the rain's stopped."

"I'm glad I came in the other way this morning," Barbara said.

"Who's out there?" Foleda's voice called from inside.

"Gerry Kehrn," Barbara called back.

"Tell him to come on in. And you might as well come too, Barb. Let's get our thoughts together before the others start showing up. And now Volst" —who was the secretary of state— "has just been on the line saying he wants a report on the whole thing personally over lunch before the big meeting starts this afternoon. I've got the feeling this is gonna be a long day."

Kehrn went on through, and Barbara followed after, exchanging a few final words with Rose. Foleda touched a button below his desk to cut the music and pushed aside some papers he had been reading. "Hi, Gerry."

"Good morning, Bern. Or is that the wrong thing to say today?"

"Why should it be?—It's stopped raining. Sit down. Relax. You look worried."

Kehrn pulled out one of the chairs at the meeting table set at a tee against Foleda's desk and sat down, placing his briefcase in front of him. Barbara shut the door. "Who wouldn't be worried?" Kehrn said. "What a goddamn mess."

"A million years from now it won't matter," Foleda assured him.

"Who else have we got coming this morning?" Kehrn asked.

"Pearce and somebody else from State. Zolansky from Operations. Do you know him?"

"We've met."

"Uh-huh. And Uncle Phil will be coming in at around eleven to see where we're at." Philip Borden was the UDIA director. Foleda sent an inquiring glance at Barbara.

"Zolansky's deputy will probably be coming too," she said, sitting down at the far end of the table.

"But keep your party-joke book in your pocket, Gerry," Foleda advised. "They won't be in the mood."

Kehrn fiddled with the lock of his briefcase and began taking out notebook, compad, and several files. "So what do we have?" he asked. "Anything new?"

Foleda shook his head. "Nothing."

"What's the story with Pacific News Services?"

"Forget them. They're out of it. PNS agreed to being used as cover for a government operation. If our operatives haven't come back, it's our problem. The Soviets haven't lodged any protest with PNS, and PNS isn't going to go out of its way to pick a quarrel with the Soviets."

"The Soviets know they were our people, and they're letting us sweat for a while," Barbara said. In other words, the Soviet reaction would come via the official channels.

"And there's been nothing so far through State?" Kehrn checked.

"As Barb says, they're letting us sweat," Foleda said. "In fact, I wouldn't be surprised if they let us stew for a lot longer and don't do anything."

"You mean, like waiting until we bring the matter up with them."

"Sure. Let us come crawling. We have to do something. Two of our citizens have disappeared, who were last heard of heading for a Soviet transfer station. Presumably they were caught red-handed committing espionage. Why should the Soviets be in any hurry to come to us?"

"How much trouble are we in with the Air Force?" Kehrn asked Foleda.

"None yet. Bryce was assigned to us for the duration. So far they don't know bout it."

Kehrn shuffled some papers aimlessly for a few seconds and fidgeted in his chair. "What, er . . . what about the two people up there?" he asked at last. "Do we know what to expect?"

"I imagine they're still up there, and possibly will be for a while. Is that what you meant?"

"I was wondering more, how much are they likely to give away?"

"You're worried?"

"I'm worried."

"Well, Lew McCain's an old hand. You needn't worry about him," Foleda said. "He's worked for me for years. He won't tell them anything. Even if it's something that's obvious and undeniable, he won't confirm it. That's the way he is. That's the way they're trained." Foleda's brow creased and his expression became more serious. "I wish I could say the same about the girl, though. This kind of thing isn't her specialty. She's from a different world. I don't know what to expect there."

"It's one of the things we'll try and get an opinion on from Colonel Raymond up at Hanscom when we've figured out how to break the news," Barbara said.

Kehrn nodded and looked uncomfortable while he wrestled with some new thought. Finally he said, "What are the chances of the Soviets using . . . well, let's say, 'extreme methods' of interrogation?"

"I can't see it," Foleda said. "This whole business has big propaganda potential if the Soviets decide to go public, and they know it. This one they'll want to play clean for the world to see. They wouldn't jeopardize their advantage by risking bad counterpublicity."

"But threats, maybe," Barbara said.

"That's something else," Foleda agreed, nodding. "Threats, implications of nasty things . . . McCain would read the situation and not be intimidated. But again, with the girl . . . who knows?"

"We shouldn't have used her," Kehrn said. "There had to have been someone else, with the right background as well as the technical know-how. It was a bad decision from the start."

"Maybe," Foleda conceded with a sigh. "Somehow I think we're gonna hear that said a lot of times today."

A tone sounded from the screen by the desk and Rose's face appeared. "They're arriving," she announced. "Zolansky and his partner are on their way up, and Pearce has checked into the building."

Foleda glanced at the other two and raised his eyebrows. "Okay, Rose," he said resignedly to the screen. "You'd better start breaking out the paper hats and squeakers."

CHAPTER SIX

There was a subdued humming sound, and buried within it a periodic resonance that came and went. Lewis McCain lay listening to it with his eyes closed, allowing the preoccupation to keep other thoughts from entering his mind for a few moments longer. He was aware that he had just woken up. The hum, with its rising and falling undertone, was not something familiar. He was not in a place that he was accustomed to waking up in.

He opened his eyes and saw a white ceiling with an air-conditioner vent off to one side of his field of vision. He moved his head to look at it. His head felt muzzy; the image was blurred, and swam. An ache shot between his temples and down the back of his neck as he strained to rise. He abandoned the effort, letting his head fall back on the pillow, and lay for a while until he could breathe more easily. Then he rolled over onto his side and opened his eyes again.

The cot was in a small, windowless, sparsely furnished room containing a plain table and a single upright chair with his clothes draped over them. Above the table was a shelf with some books and a few other oddments. The walls were dark blue up to a black strip running at half height, and cream from there to the ceiling. Slowly his head cleared, and the surroundings registered as the cell he'd been occupying for—how long had it been? three days? four days?—inside the KGB Internal Security Headquarters at Turgenev. The door was solid, with a small grille and sliding panel on the outside, and led out to the corridor. In the opposite corner was a partition screening a tiny washbasin and toilet.

Moving slowly and cautiously, he raised himself onto an elbow. Pain stabbed through his head once more. He held the position this time, and after a few seconds the pain eased. He sat up, pushed the single blanket aside, and lowered his legs over the side of the cot. A wave of dizziness swept over him, then nausea. He braced himself for the effort of having to make a sudden dash to the toilet, but the feeling passed. He pulled on the baggy, beltless pants and canvas shoes he'd been given in place of his own clothes, stood up gingerly, and moved to the table. One of the books on the shelf above was a travelogue about nineteenth-century life among the Yakut hunters. McCain took it down and opened the back cover to reveal three small notches cut into the edge, about an eighth of an inch apart near the top. He pressed a fourth notch with his thumbnail, replaced the book, and went behind the partition to the washbasin to rinse his face. He felt unusually lead-limbed and sluggish when he walked.

He had seen nothing of Paula since their arrest. The interrogations had been constant and relentless, but so far he hadn't been treated improperly. That wasn't necessarily grounds for comfort, however. No doubt the Soviets intended to exploit the propaganda opportunities of the situation to their fullest, and had no intention of compromising their advantage by laying themselves open to counteraccusations. But how long that political condition might persist was another matter, he reflected as he wiped cold water from his eyes and peered at his reflection in the polished-metal mirror cemented to the wall. Certainly the Russians would be in no hurry to ease the pressure on the US, which probably had something to do with his not being permitted to communicate with his own authorities back on Earth. In fact, he had been told nothing to indicate even if the incident was public knowledge yet.

He had just emerged from the washroom and was about to put on his shirt, when the panel behind the grille on the door slid aside and voices sounded outside. A pair of eyes scrutinized him for a moment, and then came the sound of the door being unlocked. It opened, and a tall, lean man with gray hair and a pointed beard entered, followed by a younger, darker-skinned companion. Both were wearing white, hip-length physician's smocks and gray-white check pants. There were also two uniformed guards, who remained outside in the corridor when the bearded man swung the door shut. McCain tensed, but the manner of the two was not threatening.

"Well, how do you feel this morning?" the bearded man inquired. His tone was intermediate between genial and matter-of-fact, as if he presumed that McCain knew what he was talking about. McCain looked at him and said nothing. "Fatigued? Not quite coordinated? A little hazy in the head, eh?" He sat back against the edge of the table and folded his arms to look McCain up and down. The younger man put down a black medical bag that he had been holding. "Well, come on," the bearded man said after a short pause. "The patient can hardly help us look after his interests if he won't say anything, can he?"

"What interests?" McCain asked. "What are you talking about?"

The bearded man regarded him curiously. "You don't know who I am, do you?" he said.

A pause. "No."

"Oh, dear." The bearded man glanced aside at his colleague. "I think we may have a complete block here." Then, back at McCain, "My name is Dr. Kazhakin. We have met before, I assure you—several times, in fact. You've been a little sick, you understand." He gestured nonchalantly. "It's not uncommon among people unaccustomed to an offplanet environment. Space-acclimatization sickness. The weightlessness during the trip up plays a part, and so does the excess of cosmic rays, but primarily it's an upset of the balance mechanism caused by adapting to a rotating structure. The effects can be quite disruptive until the nervous system learns to compensate."

"Really?" McCain sounded unconvinced. "And that causes amnesia?"

"We put you under a rather strong sedative," Kazhakin explained. "You've been out for a couple of days. What you're feeling is the aftereffect. Sometimes the memory can be impaired slightly—rather like a bump on the head."

Although McCain's expression didn't change, inwardly he felt alarmed. Kazhakin was trying to justify memory loss and symptoms of the aftereffects of drugs. As McCain knew well, some extremely potent substances were available to psychological researchers and therapists, and to military and police interrogators. Although there was no truly reliable "truth drug" of the kind beloved in fiction, combined chemical assaults of different stimulants and depressants affected different individuals in different ways, and in general anything was possible. Suddenly he had the worried feeling that perhaps his interrogation mightn't have been so gentlemanly after all.

"Let's have a look, then," Kazhakin said. He motioned for McCain to sit on the edge of the cot, then inspected both his eyes, his tongue and mouth, and dabbed around on his chest and back with a stethoscope while the assistant prepared a blood-pressure gauge. "And we'll want sample bottles for some blood and urine," Kazhakin told him.

Tattered remnants of recollections were beginning to float back. He saw the image of a man in a Russian major general's uniform, with black, crinkly hair showing gray streaks, bright, penetrating eyes beneath puffy lids, and a craggy, heavy-jowled face. "Of course it's obvious you're not a journalist . . . Did you know what the file contained? . . . Which organization sent you? . . ." There was another Russian there, too, inseparable from the general as part of the image swimming in McCain's memory, but the details remained obscure.

Kazhakin was watching McCain's face as he inflated

the bulb of the sphygmomanometer. "Brain starting to function again now, is it? Some things coming back?"

"What day is this?" McCain asked.

"May fourth. You abused your guest privileges on the first, you fell sick the day after, and you've been out for two days, as I said."

If that were so, there ought to have been one notch in the book, not three, McCain thought. It was strange that he had woken up remembering to update his tally of days— or at least awakenings—and yet had no recollection of having done it before. It pointed to his having been out of control of his faculties for longer than Kazhakin was claiming. That would have been consistent with potent drugs, which was not exactly a reassuring thought.

"You probably feel a bit heavy and weak, but in fact you've lost a little weight," Kazhakin said. "I'll give you some pills to pick you up—no tricks, I promise—and we'll put you on an enrichment diet to build up your strength. I'm sure that General Protbornov wouldn't want you thinking of us as inconsiderate hosts." He saw an involuntary flicker in McCain's eyes. "Ah, so you remember the name, eh? That's good." Kazhakin unwound the bandage from McCain's arm and smirked at him with undisguised sarcasm. "Yes, we'll soon have you back to normal, *Mr. Earnshaw* of Pacific News Services, California. I do hope your readers won't be too upset if they have to put up with your being out of circulation for a while."

McCain watched expressionlessly as Kazhakin handed the sphygmomanometer back to the assistant and wrote some numbers onto a chart. It was obvious from the circumstances of his and Paula's capture that the cover story had capsized immediately. He wondered how much more—that he didn't even know about—might have started taking water since, or already have foundered completely to join it.

CHAPTER SEVEN

"You were apprehended in a place you had no right to be, in the act of obtaining misinformation fabricated to discredit the Soviet Union—and not trivially, but on a scale that would have had the gravest international repercussions. You were in possession of specialized espionage equipment, and you came here under assumed names, carrying false papers." Major General Protbornov paused to allow the gravity of his words to sink in. The action was for effect—this was hardly the first time he'd been through this. He continued, "We can all admire loyalty—indeed, we take justifiable pride in our own—but there is a point beyond which it turns into unreasonable stubbornness. At least tell us who you are and the name of the organization that sent you. You must agree that we are entitled to know that much."

Paula Bryce squinted against the light at the vague form outlined on the far side of the desk. At least they had turned the brightness down from the blinding level it had been at all through yesterday. And Protbornov's restraint was a relief after the shouting and impatience of the other general who had interrogated her initially, before she'd gotten sick a few days earlier. It was all part of a game they played, she told herself. The problem was trying—against fear, fatigue, and a numbing lack of sleep—to tell which of the roles and threats that she had been exposed to were for effect, which were real, and which, depending on expediency, might be interchangeable.

The bruises on her body still ached from the roughing up she'd been given on arrival at Internal Security Headquarters by two female Russian guards with sow faces and the physiques of weight lifters—a ritual doubtless intended to set roles and establish for future reference whose place was whose. Then had come the ordeal of hour after hour of demands, threats, and the same questions repeated over and over, always with the implication of further possibilities that her treatment by the two guards had represented a first taste of.

But she hadn't given away anything. That was the most important thing that she'd forced herself to recite in her mind, as had been drummed into her by Foleda's people. "Clam up, deny everything, never admit or confirm anything, even if it's obvious to everyone and staring you in the face," one of the UDIA men in the Pentagon had told her. "Because one thing leads to another. The first admission is a step onto a slope that gets slippier all the way to the bottom. It's like after quitting cigarettes: the only way to stay off is to stay off completely. You don't fool with even one, because there's a whole world of difference between *no* cigarette and *some* cigarettes. But there isn't a lot of difference between one and two, or between four and five, or nineteen and twenty. Okay? It's the same with revealing information: once you make that first slip, there's no place to dig your heels in and stop."

Or could she have given away a lot more than she thought, without knowing it? She had fallen ill for a couple of days—so they'd told her—with an acclimatization problem that affected some people on going into space. She couldn't remember much about it, but from the way she'd felt when she started seeing things coherently again, she concluded that she'd been under some kind of drug. The doctor told her it was a sedative. But she had been told something about drugs, too, before leaving on the mission . . . she couldn't remember what. She didn't have clear recollections of anything right now. All she wanted to do was rest and sleep . . . Everything was too muddled and took too much effort to think about.

"This is getting nowhere," the figure next to Protbornov complained—a colonel, younger, businesslike, projecting the image of being ambitious and unprincipled. His name was Buvatsky. "Give us just half a day. I guarantee everything you want to know." Bluff, Paula told herself. Nice guy-bad guy. Part of the act.

"Let us hope that extremes won't be necessary," Protbornov rumbled. "You agree that you came here to

Valentina Tereshkova under a false identity, and with the intention of committing acts of espionage?" His voice was louder this time, evidently directed at Paula.

She shook her head, feigning even greater fatigue than she felt. "What?"

"You agree that you came here under a false identity, intending to commit espionage?"

"I don't agree anything."

"But that much is obvious."

"I wish to communicate with a representative of the United Sates government."

"You know very well that there is no such person for you to talk to here."

"I didn't say talk to. I said communicate with. That can be arranged."

"That is impossible."

"Why?"

"For now, it is impossible. And besides, you are hardly in a position to be making demands. I ask you again, Do you not agree that you came here under a false identity?"

"I agree with nothing."

"What is your name?"

"I wish to communicate with a representative of my government."

"Do you still claim to be this person, Paula Shelmer?"

"That's what my papers say."

"Do you still claim to be an employee of Pacific News Services, California?"

"I'm not claiming anything. You'll believe what you choose to, anyway." Wrong, a part of her mind groaned. She was starting to talk back to them. Whether or not she revealed anything that mattered wasn't the point: it was just as much a first step.

"Common sense dictates that such is not the case. The equipment that you had with you was purpose-designed— hardly the kind of gadgetry that a news agency issues its staff, you have to admit." Protbornov's tone was casual now, almost chatty. He turned down the lamp, as if making a

symbolic gesture to stop all this unnecessary unpleasant-
ness. She needed to talk, it seemed to acknowledge. "It's
clear you were employed by the American government.
That much is true, at least, isn't it?" His voice held a note
of regret that sounded almost genuine. Or was she projecting
into it something that a part of her deep down needed to
hear? There was a short pause. Her head nodded down
onto her chest, and her thoughts swam. "It is true, isn't it?
You are not with Pacific News Services, are you?"

"No," she heard herself whisper, even as another voice
inside her head woke up, shouting too late in protest.

"But you are with the American government. Is that
not correct?"

From somewhere long in the past she remembered
hearing about the way salesmen were taught to begin their
closing pitch with a series of statements that the prospect
could do nothing but agree with. Once begun, the pattern
was difficult to break out of and made it easier to go along
with the salesman's proposal than refuse it. She had just
made her first slip, not by telling Protbornov something
he already knew, but by agreeing with him. She shook
her head and said nothing.

"Which department of the American government are
you with?" A pause. "The CIA?" Another pause. "The
UDIA?" Silence. Then, "I should remind you that it is
possible to ask these questions again, but utilizing
physiological monitoring instruments that will make
concealment of the truth impossible. . . . Very well, we've
established that you are not Paula Shelmer of Pacific
News Services, and that you are employed by the
American government. Now, purely for our records and
to enable us to furnish information to your own people
and to the various human-rights organizations who
concern themselves with the welfare of those in your
kind of predicament, what is your name?"

"I wish to contact a representative of the United States
government."

Buvatsky got up with a snort and paced impatiently away

to the side of the room, outside her field of vision. Protbornov raised a hand to massage his brow with his fingers, and leaned back with a heavy sigh. "Look," he said, "it is clear from the contents of the computer file you were in the process of copying that your mission was to obtain misinformation created to support the propaganda campaign which your government has been waging concerning the true nature of *Valentina Tereshkova.*" Protbornov looked up and shot at her with sudden sharpness, "Have you ever heard the name 'Magician'?" Even before the word registered consciously, Paula knew with a sinking feeling that her face had supplied the answer. Protbornov went on, as if the fact were too evident to be worthy of mention, "Magician was a traitor, who was uncovered by our counterintelligence operations, as you well know. He has recanted and gone on record voluntarily to confirm that the information he planted in the file was false. He was working in league with American propagandists as part of a plan to mislead world opinion at a time when the newly emerging great powers remain unaligned. We can show you a video recording of his admission. It was made quite freely, I assure you." Paula looked skeptical. "We could arrange for Magician to be brought here from Earth to tell you to your face, if that would convince you," Protbornov offered.

Paula frowned down at her knees. The significance escaped her. Or was she just confused? She looked up wearily. "Why do you care whether I believe it or not?"

Protbornov sat forward, and Paula sensed Buvatsky turning in a corner of the room. Too late, she realized that she'd said the wrong thing again.

"Don't you understand? That is what this whole issue revolves around," Protbornov said. "Your people told you that this colony is a disguised war platform, is that not so? They described various weapons that they claimed were concealed here, yes? And their proof was to be in the package that Magician had compiled. Oh, don't look so horrified—it was an elementary deduction from the facts that we possess. . . . But what matters is that you understand they were lying to you . . . lying, just as they have been lying to the world. As I said a few minutes ago, I admire your loyalty, but don't allow it to blind you to the possibility that the United States can be less than perfect sometimes, and that perhaps we of the Soviet Union are not always wrong." He allowed a moment for her to reflect on that, then continued, "You see, where Colonel Buvatsky and I differ is that I believe all of us are basically the same beneath the surface—all unfortunate victims of the mistakes of history and our own, unnecessary, mutual suspicions.

"I don't have to spell out the tragedy that could result from this paranoia. . . ." Protbornov raised a hand as if to forestall her reply. "Yes, on our side as well as yours. The world has been trembling for over half a century. But don't you see what an opportunity this represents? For once, the delusions that the paranoia is based on can be exposed for what they really are. It wouldn't put an instant end to all the tensions that have plagued our two nations for so long, of course, but it would be a solid step in the direction of defusing them. Every withdrawal from a brink has to begin with a first step somewhere. Don't you owe the peoples of that world down there that much—a chance to hope?"

Paula had been blinking her eyes, trying to follow. "I'm not sure I understand," she said. Her voice was dry and cracked. Protbornov poured water from a pitcher in front of him into a glass and set it down across the desk. Paula stared at it. Whether it was the wrong thing to do or not, she suddenly didn't care. She picked up the glass and gulped down the water gratefully.

"We are prepared to take you, in person, to all the places in *Tereshkova* where you were told these weapons were supposed to exist, and let you see for yourself that the accusations are simply not true." Protbornov threw up his hands. "What could be fairer than that? We want the truth to be known." .

Paula replaced the glass on the edge of the desk, noticing as she did so that her hand was shaking. "Why not open the whole place to international inspection, if that's what you want?" she asked. "Let everyone come and see for themselves."

Protbornov tossed up his hands again. "I agree! And if I were First Secretary of the Party, that is precisely what I would do. But I am not Comrade Petrokhov. And for reasons which I do not make it my business to criticize, our policy is that we will not strip ourselves naked before the world on demand, just to prove our good intentions."

"You've already demonstrated your good intentions," Paula said, massaging her stomach tenderly.

"I apologize for that incident. It was an accident. The guards responsible were transferred only recently from one of our military punishment units, where procedures are different. They have been reprimanded and removed."

Having served their purpose, Paula thought. "I'm still not sure what you're saying. . . ." Despite her resolve, she heard herself getting talkative. . . . But, dammit, stuck out here, two hundred thousand miles away from everything, she needed somebody to talk to, even a Russian general. That sounded a little like the beginnings of self-pity, she reflected idly. It wasn't like her at all to feel that way, but she found that the thought didn't really bother her very much. She had reason to feel sorry for herself—oh God, had there been something in the water?

"All we want you to do, after you've satisfied yourself that what I've said is true, is simply to make a public statement confirming what you've seen with your own eyes. If we can show you that our country has been slandered before the world, is it unreasonable that we should ask this? It is, after all, the truth which is supposed to matter, isn't it, even when it inconveniently fails to support preconceived notions? Isn't that what you were trained to think as a scientist?"

"Yes," Paula answered automatically, even as she saw the mistake.

Protbornov gave a satisfied nod. "So, we have established that you are a scientist. With whom? A private corporation, perhaps? But then, how would you come to know so much about Russian equipment? It was you who was operating the device. More likely one of the services, then, yes? . . . Yes. Very well, which one? Army, maybe? . . . Navy? . . . US Air Force, perhaps? We can run physiological tests, you know."

It was all being recorded by concealed cameras, Paula guessed. Afterward, Protbornov and his specialists would play the recordings over and over, studying her every response. Probably other hidden devices were measuring changes in her skin temperature and reflectivity, muscular tensions, eye movements, and other giveaways, at the very moment. Suddenly she found herself weary of it all, helpless against forces that she didn't comprehend and didn't know how to resist. It was all pointless. In the end they were bound to win. And in spite of herself, what Protbornov was saying *did* sound only fair and reasonable.

"Maybe," she said. She wasn't sure what she had said it in response to. Every thought that started to take shape dissolved away again.

"You will agree to consider making a statement, if we can show you that the allegations concerning weapons are false? This would not have to be a public declaration. It need only be for the information of certain Western and Asian governments. In fact, we could arrange for the recording to be vetted by your own people before it was shown to anyone else. That would relieve you of any personal responsibility, and it would cause no unnecessary embarrassment in international circles. You see, our aims are quite honorable. A wrong has been committed, and we simply wish to put it right." Protbornov paused and looked across the desk.

Paula rubbed her eyes. All she had to do was agree to a request that sounded reasonable, and she would be able to sleep. How could she be wrong for simply telling the truth about what she saw? God alone knew how much trouble throughout history had been caused by people refusing to. Protbornov waited a few seconds longer, then added, "It goes without saying that your cooperation in this small matter could make a big difference to eventual agreement between our governments concerning your future. We understand the regrettable necessity for the kind of work you were drawn into. Given a suitable incentive, we can find it very easy to let bygones be bygones over such things. Otherwise . . ." He shrugged.

Paula stared at the glass on the desk. A distorted, inverted image of Protbornov's face peered back at her out of the thick curve of its base. As she stared, it took on the appearance of a grotesque parody of a spider, watching from the center of its web for its prey's struggles to die away before it moved. She shook herself out of the stupor that had been creeping over her. Then it came to her that the Russians would have known far more than they seemed to if Earnshaw had given away anything to them at all. She wondered suddenly what he might be going through at that moment.

And gradually a feeling of self-disgust overcame her at the thought of what had almost happened. She drew in a determined breath and shivered as she fought back visions of what she might be letting herself in for. She looked up, clasped her hands together between her knees to prevent them from shaking visibly, and steadied her gaze across the desk.

"I wish to communicate with a representative of the United States government," she said.

CHAPTER EIGHT

The air conditioner hummed, and the resonating undertone came and went. Lewis McCain lay on the cot, staring up at the ceiling. Now that his head was clearer, isolated recollections from the hazy period following his arrest would appear suddenly in his mind in a seemingly patternless fashion. Lying here, staring up at the air-conditioner grille, was one of them. It had a gray-painted metal escutcheon surrounding it, with a scratch by one of the corner screws where a screwdriver had slipped. The sound hadn't contained that distinctive resonance then. Something must have loosened itself in the ducting fairly recently, he thought idly.

McCain didn't trust Russians. In his experience, whenever they started behaving reasonably, they were up to something. They'd been giving him too easy a time. Why? What were they after? From what he knew of Soviet interrogation practices, it was likely on two counts that Paula was having a tougher time: one, she was a woman, and therefore more easily intimidated, according to standard KGB thinking; and two, she would quickly have been identified as a technician rather than an intelligence professional, and hence more vulnerable through knowing less of what to expect.

So why were they playing a restrained game with him? Probably because they anticipated international ramifications and had no intention of compromising their own position by showing less-than-spotless hands. If they saw the affair as eventually being made public, they'd probably be putting pressure on Paula to make a signed statement. In his case, seeing there would be little chance of getting anywhere with a similar demand, they might simply have decided to work on convincing him that they weren't such bad people after all, and see what accrued benefits they might be able to squeeze from the results later. Yes, he thought, nodding up at the air-conditioner grille, that would be consistent with the way they had been acting.

He thought about how he had come to find himself here at the age of thirty-six, a prisoner in a Soviet space habitat hundreds of thousands of miles from Earth.

When people asked what had induced him to make a career in military intelligence, he usually told them it was ideological: that he believed the Western way of life was worth defending. Despite its faults, a democracy based on free enterprise allowed him to be himself, to believe and say what he chose, and, apart from a few not-unreasonable constraints, made how he preferred to lead his life none of anyone else's business. That suited him just fine. So, the answer was true as far as it went; it was the kind that people expected, and they accepted it. But there was another side to it, too, which involved more personal things.

McCain had been born in Iowa, but his mother, Julia, was Czechoslovakian. She had escaped during the anti-Russian uprising of 1968. He remembered her telling of the Czechs' disgust over the sellout by the British and French to Hitler at Munich in 1938 of the nation which they themselves had created a mere twenty years previously and pledged solemnly to defend. Instead, at the very moment when Czechoslovakia was mobilizing to defend itself, they had surrendered it to six years of Nazi barbarism. The story had made a deep impression on the developing mind of young Lewis McCain. It had convinced him that tyrants and dictators could not be appeased. The lure of easy pickings merely excited them on to greater excesses. As with people, nations able to defend themselves, and prepared to do so if they had to, were left alone.

Julia retold stories that her parents had told her of listening around an illegal radio to reports of Hitler's armies storming eastward, apparently overwhelming the Russians as effortlessly as they had overwhelmed the Poles. Czechoslovakia, left hundreds of miles behind the front, had surely been consumed in a nightmare that would lie across Europe for generations to come. But then the news began to change. The Russians counterattacked from the very gates of Moscow. They held at Leningrad. They stopped, then encircled and annihilated the Germans at Stalingrad. In the years that followed, the Germans were driven back remorselessly, until eventually the Red Army entered Czechoslovakia. On the day their T-34 tanks rumbled into Prague, Lewis's grandfather had strode into the house and announced in a voice shaking with pride and emotion, "I am a Communist!" And for a while Czechoslovakia became perhaps the most faithful of the Soviets' allies.

But the elation was short-lived. Ironically the Russians, like the Nazis before them, became oppressors of the people who had welcomed them as liberators. Instead of the independence they had promised, they imposed a Moscow-controlled puppet regime and brought in the familiar Bolshevik apparatus of ruthless persecution, midnight arrests, trumped-up charges, brutally extracted confessions, deportations, and executions to eliminate potential opposition. And, fanatically pursuing their socialist ideals, they seized land, property, and all small businesses, which henceforth were to be owned by the state.

The foundry and engineering shop that Lewis's grandfather had worked strenuously to build up through the worst years of the thirties was taken from the family and handed over to be managed by a Party bureaucrat who had never seen a lathe or a grinding machine, had no comprehension of taking pride in excellence, and who was incapable of thinking in any terms other than of quotas. Within six months the business was ruined, and Lewis's grandfather lost his income, which was replaced by a subsistence wage. Later, when years of anger at corruption, incompetence, and lies finally boiled over into open rebellion in the streets, he was shot in the fighting when the Red Army's tanks returned to Prague. That was the last thing that Julia remembered seeing before she and her companions fled for the border. She ended up in Holland, where she met her first husband, an American marketing executive. They moved to the US, but the marriage didn't work out, and Julia spent some years raising a son, Ralph, on her own before she remarried, this time to a widowed Iowa farmer of Scottish descent: Lewis's father, Malcolm. That was in 1981, during the latter years of what had been a confused period for America.

After emerging as the most powerful among the war's victors, the nation had gone on to enjoy two decades of growth and prosperity unprecedented by any society in history. Uninterested in the creeds and passions responsible for turning half the rest of the world into rubble, the generation that had grown up through the lean and threadbare years of the Depression turned to Sears, General Electric, General Motors, and the loan officer at the local bank for fulfillment. In their own eyes they were overcoming the problems of poverty, disease, hunger, and ignorance which had devastated human populations for as long as humanity had existed. They were proud of their achievement and of the society that had made it possible. They assumed their children would be grateful. They tried to export their system to other peoples and assumed they would be grateful, too.

Pendulums swing, however.

The next generation, watching the rest of the world's problems on color TV over refrigerator-fresh steaks after driving home from school in air-conditioned automobiles, instead of feeling grateful, felt guilty. By some curious twist of logic it became America's fault that the rest of the world still had problems at all. Through a sweeping extension of the "Eat-up-your-potatoes-because-the-children-in-China-are-starving" syndrome—as if, by some natural law of protein parity, every uneaten potato on a plate in Minnesota mysteriously induced the symmetric disappearance of rice from a bowl in Peking—America's enterprise in putting its own house in order was to blame for the disorder that persisted everywhere else.

The result was a moral crusade against the American system and the institutions that gave it substance: capitalism and the business corporations, the technological industries that supported them, the science that made technology possible, and ultimately the faculty of reason itself, which was the foundation of science. The weapon was fear. Wreathed in clouds of acid rain, radiation, and carcinogens, buried under indestructible plastics, deluged with genetically mutated microbes, and stripped of its ozone, the planet would ferment in swamps of its own garbage—if the Bomb didn't get it first or bring on a Nuclear Winter. And America had provoked the Soviets by refusing to disarm unilaterally and thereby ensure world peace—as the European democracies had ensured peace by disarming *them*selves unilaterally in the 1930's.

The greater the contribution to the success of the system, the greater the guilt. It followed that, along with the chemist, the auto maker, the pharmacist, and the nuclear engineer, one of the most persecuted victims of the process should be the American farmer. He had, after all, raised productivity to a point where three percent of the population could not only feed the country better than seventy percent had been able to a century earlier, but could also export a hefty surplus—freeing lots of intellectuals to write in comfort on the evils of production and to campaign for the civil rights of the malaria virus while treating people as pollution.

Consequently, after putting up with years of harassment from inquisitorial regulators and political activists seeking to ban everything from fertilizers to farm mechanization, Malcolm sold the farm and moved the family to California, where he invested the proceeds in an agricultural-machinery business that provided a reasonable living. Throughout Lewis's teenage years, Malcolm had continued to rage about "corporate socialism"—by which he meant the agribusiness giant that had bought the land in Iowa—as much as Julia warned against collectivism. It no more represented the spirit of America, he used to fume, than the liberal-socialist element in Washington, and had played as great a part in bringing about the economic mess and cultural negativism of the seventies.

Thus, one of Lewis's parents was a refugee from a tyranny that had destroyed the worth of a lifetime's labor; the other had been a victim of legalized witch-hunting in the name of ideology. Reflection on these things produced a deep sense of resentment and injustice in Lewis as a youth. He concluded that there were no such things as inalienable "natural" rights. The only rights that meant anything were those that could be defended—by custom, by law, and, if necessary, by force.

McCain graduated from UCLA at twenty-two with BA degrees in Political History and Modern Languages. These qualifications, along with his innate skepticism and desire to preserve his individuality, added up to a good grounding for work in the intelligence community. Hence, when, desperate to escape from the tedium of California farm-country life, he attended on-campus interviews for entry into the armed services, a recruiter from another department of the government pounced on him instead. So, he'd ended up back at school, this time with the UDIA at its training center in Maryland. Upon completion of the course he went to its headquarters to work as an administrative assistant, which he fondly assumed would be a cover title for more exciting and glamorous things. But the job turned out to be just what it said—clerk—and for two boring years he proved his loyalty by shuffling papers, filling in forms, sorting incoming material, and checking facts . . . and checking them again, and then rechecking them. The experience turned out to be vital to becoming an effective agent.

Since then he'd spent some years in Europe with NATO intelligence, which was followed by six months back in the US for intensive training on such things as codes and communications, observation, security, concealment and evasion, weapons and self-defense, breaking and entering, lock picking, safe cracking, wiretaps, bugs, and other noble arts. After that he'd gone back to Europe to be introduced to counterintelligence directed against Soviet espionage into NATO weaponry, and then back to the States for courses in Eastern languages and advanced Russian—he'd spoken Czech and German, which Julia and Ralph had often conversed in, since he was a boy. From there he'd been sent on a series of assignments in the Far East, beginning with a position at the US embassy in Tokyo. His last job before being recalled to Washington for the Pedestal mission was developing a network of intelligence contacts and sources in Peking. And through all of it, everything he'd seen reinforced his original conviction that the Western way wasn't such a bad way to live. Yet there were lots of people out there who for one reason for another, real or imagined, were ready to bring the West down if they got the chance.

The key sounded in the door, and McCain sat up. It was too early for lunch. Protbornov entered, accompanied by a major called Uskayev. Behind them was a guard carrying a canvas bag. Protbornov looked around, his dark eyes moving casually beneath their heavy lids. He took a blue pack of Russian cigarettes from one of the pockets in his tunic, selected one, and almost as if it were an afterthought offered the pack to McCain. McCain shook his head. "You must be feeling almost at home here by now," Protbornov rumbled. "Well, how would you say we have treated you? Not unfairly, I trust?"

"It could be worse," McCain agreed neutrally.

Protbornov lit his cigarette and lifted one of the books from the shelf to inspect its title. "A pity that it requires so much to convince you that we really are not so uncivilized. You do have an extraordinarily suspicious nature, you know, Mr. Earnshaw—an impediment for a journalist, I would have thought. Your female companion thinks so, too. I'd imagine that many people you've met in life have said the same. Have you ever thought about that? Is it possible, do you think, that you could be wrong on some things, and that the consensus of others might have some merit?" He flipped casually through the pages of the book, and then, either accidentally or making the motion appear so, ran a finger down the edge of the back cover. From the corner of an eye McCain saw Uskayev watching him closely, and forced himself to suppress any flicker of reaction.

"I don't think it's a good idea to be too influenced by other people's opinions," McCain said.

"Your Air Force scientist friend would agree with you on that," Protbornov replied, searching McCain's face as he spoke. "A most obstinate woman. But be that as it may, she recognizes the importance of the present situation and its relevance to world security, and she has agreed to cooperate responsibly by making a public statement of the kind we have requested." Protbornov gestured in the air with his cigarette and shrugged indifferently. "So now you don't matter to us so much. The only issue you need concern yourself with is your own fate. If you adopted a more reasonable attitude than the one you've been showing, well, anything is possible. If not . . ." he shrugged again, "what happens then will be up to the Kremlin. But as I said, it is no longer of primary importance to us."

McCain looked at him almost contemptuously. "I expected something better than that. Don't tell me you're slipping."

Protbornov seemed to have been prepared for as much. "Policy decisions are not my concern," he said. "My job is simply to carry them out. For whatever reason, orders have come through for you to be moved to another location. You should find it more congenial—at least you will have company . . . and the opportunity for more stimulating conversations than ours tend to be." He indicated the bag that the guard had placed on the table. "Collect your belongings. You are to be transferred immediately."

McCain began gathering together the clothes and personal effects that he had been given. "With a personal sendoff by the general? Why so honored?"

"Why not? I feel we have come to know one another a little in the course of the past three weeks, even if your attitude has been less than candid. A common courtesy from the host to a departing guest, maybe? Or simply a way to indicate that we desire no hard feelings?"

McCain went around the partition to retrieve his toilet articles. So far the whole thing had been an exercise in testing and probing for weaknesses, to be exploited later— and probably the same with Paula, too. What for? he wondered. There was a lot more behind it all than he had unraveled so far.

"So, where to?" he asked as he came back out, closing the bag. "Earthside?"

"Nothing so exciting, I'm afraid," Protbornov replied. The guard was holding the door open. "It's expensive to ship people between here and Earth. Why should we pay the bill for returning one of the United State's spies to them? They can come and collect you when the time comes—assuming, of course, that Moscow decides to let them have you back. Until then, you remain here on *Tereshkova*, at a place called Zamork." A guard went ahead. Protbornov walked by McCain, with the major a pace behind, while the guard who had held the door brought up the rear.

"Oh, you mean the gulag that you've got up here," McCain said. Zamork was on the edge of the town known as Novyi Kazan, and was labeled vaguely on the maps as a detention facility. "I always admired how faithful a copy this is of the Mother County."

"Oh, don't think of Zamork as a gulag," Protbornov said breezily. "Times are changing. Even your Christian heaven needed somewhere to keep its dissidents."

"I take it that means we're unlikely to be seeing the last of each other."

"I'm sure the Fates have it in store for us to meet again."

"What about Paula Shelmer? Will she be moving too?"

"We have received no orders concerning her." There was a short silence. Then Protbornov added, "However, she is in good health and spirits. I thought you might like to know."

"Thanks."

Ten minutes later, McCain, accompanied by two armed guards, boarded a magdrive car at a monorail terminal underneath the Security Headquarters. Soon afterward, they departed around *Tereshkova*'s peripheral ring, bound for the town of Novyi Kazan.

CHAPTER NINE

According to the Soviet publicity material, Novyi Kazan was a center for arts, sports, and education, intended to provide rest, relaxation, and a contrast to Turgenev's administrative bustle and the scientific-industrial concentration at Landausk. The travel guides made little mention of its including a prison. Maybe, McCain thought as he looked out of the speeding monorail car, that was what the Russian interpretation of rest and relaxation meant.

The car seemed to be a standard model containing three pairs of double seats facing each other on either side of a central aisle, but its only other occupants besides McCain were two armed guards.

Evidently this one was not for public use. It had left the jumble of Turgenev's high-rise core and moved out along the valley that he and Paula had viewed from the terrace high over the town's square on the day of their arrival. On one side, the central strip was an irregular ribbon of green, wandering among grassy mounds, clumps of shrubs, and occasional trees, with a stream threading its way from pool to pool between rocky banks as it collected cataracts tumbling in from the valley sides. Farther away beyond the green strip, wheeled vehicles vanished and reappeared at intervals on a hidden roadway roughly matching the monorail's route. There were plenty of people, alone, in pairs, and in groups, talking, walking, or just sitting and watching the water; a woman was feeding ducks, and two boys were sailing a boat. Above it all, the twin ribbon-suns curved away out of sight in their artificial sky.

In an earlier century, the Russian empress Catherine the Great had decided to tour the countryside to observe the living conditions of the people for herself. Her chief adviser, Grigory Potemkin, sent advance parties ahead of the royal entourage to erect a whole make-believe world of fake villages with gaily painted facades to conceal the poverty and misery that the peasants had to endure. The people were forced to put on new clothes, loaned for the occasion, and dance, wave, strew flowers, and cheer to maintain the illusion. Afterward, scores of Western observers who had traveled with the royal party returned home filled with enthusiasm and admiration by the scenes they had witnessed. As McCain stared out of the window of the monorail car, he thought back to the reports he'd read by excited visitors to *Valentina Tereshkova,* bringing to the world their revelation of the changed face of communism. Just as others had come back with glowing accounts of Hitler's Germany in the 1930's.

Halfway along the agricultural zone outside Turgenev, the line passes through the clutter of processing plant, freight elevators, storage silos, and handling machinery piled around the base of the minor spoke, which was known as Agricultural Station 3 and possessed a geometry every bit as irregular and disorienting as that of the town. The roof here was clear for some distance on either side of where the spoke passed through, giving a breathtaking glimpse of the spoke's entire length, soaring away to the hub structure a half mile overhead. Another half mile above that was the far side of the ring, and beyond, an endlessness of space and stars. The sight made the enclosing walls of *Valentina Tereshkova* suddenly seem very thin and fragile. For a while, McCain had almost forgotten he was in space at all.

Beyond the spoke, the car passed through more of the agricultural zone, all pretty much as before, and finally entered the outskirts of Novyi Kazan. Houses and apartments appeared strewn down the valley sides as at Turgenev, but with more greenery and water; a sports field came and went, with figures playing soccer, and the view ahead became one of buildings merging and rising toward another chaotic downtown center. Then the track entered a tunnel. The car slowed, and McCain watched through the front window as it lurched to follow a branch tunnel off the through-route.

One of the guards moved forward to the console under the window, which appeared to be the driver's position when the car was being operated manually, and the car halted before a sturdy-looking metal door closing off the track ahead. A tone sounded, and an officer's face appeared on the console screen. "Prisoner two-seven-one-zero-six for admission," the guard said. The officer consulted something off-screen, then leaned forward to operate a control. A camera mounted inside the car pivoted slowly to survey the interior, pausing for a few seconds when it came to McCain's face. Then the door ahead slid open. The car moved through and stopped beside a platform. The guards motioned to McCain to get out. When they emerged, the door across the track behind had already closed.

They were in what looked like a loading and unloading bay, with the track branching into two lines that ran parallel between service platforms for a distance and then merged again before disappearing through another door at the far end, also closed. More guards were standing on the platform that McCain and his escorts had stepped out onto. With them was a group of a dozen or so men in plain gray jackets and matching pants with scarlet stripes, who began filing into the car. They were of various colors and races, and McCain guessed them to be from the place that he was on his way to. Several of them glanced curiously at him as he passed. They seemed healthy enough and alert. At least it didn't look as if he were about to join a house of zombies, he reflected as he walked between the guards toward the door opening off the platform.

Behind the door was a guardpost, inside which McCain saw the officer who had appeared on the screen within the car. A short corridor brought them to a stairway and elevator. They took the stairs up a level and crossed a hall containing rows of seats to enter a room with a counter running along one side, where the senior of the two escorts from Turgenev produced papers for the duty sergeant to sign. Then a captain came out of a room at the back to take charge, and the escorts departed. The captain asked the routine questions, and McCain gave his routine fictitious answers, which the sergeant duly entered into a terminal on the counter. Then McCain was conducted through to an examination room, where he waited forty minutes for the doctor to be found to perform a physical check. At last, after being fingerprinted, voiceprinted, blood-sampled, facially scanned for computerized mug-shotting, typed, tested, measured, and weighed all over again, he was given an outfit like the ones he had just seen in the monorail terminal. The captain handed back the bag he had brought with him, along with another containing a spare change of clothes. Finally he told McCain to hold out his left arm.

"Why?"

"You are not here to ask questions."

McCain raised his arm. The captain pulled back the sleeve of his jacket, and the sergeant clipped an electronic unit on a red, plastic-coated band around his wrist, and then crimped and sealed it with a special tool. The captain pressed a button, and two more guards appeared from a door at the back of the room.

"This is your key to the areas which you are authorized to enter," the captain told McCain, indicating the wristband. "Security is mostly electronic at Zamork. Guards are too valuable here to stand around doing nothing, and the same applies to prisoners. Therefore you will be required to work a minimum-forty-eight-hour week. Your duties will be assigned by the foreman of the billet you're put in. Enforcement of discipline is firm, but not unfair. After an initial probationary period, a sensible attitude can earn privileges. Movement outside quarters after curfew, and attempts to cross the compound perimeter or to leave designated work areas in other parts of the colony are strictly forbidden—although escape from *Valentina Tereshkova* is, of course, quite impossible. Do you have any immediate questions?"

"What about communications with my government and messages home?"

"That does not fall within my area of authority."

"Whose area of authority does it fall in?"

"Such matters are questions of policy, decided in Moscow."

"So who's in charge of this whole place?"

"The governor is Lieutenant General Fedorov."

"So, how do I talk to him?"

"When *he* decides he wishes to talk to you. You will be interviewed by your block commandant later. Bring the matter up with him. In the meantime, you report to the foreman in billet B-three. The guards will take you there."

The guards took McCain back through the door that they had come from, and along a corridor to some stairs which led down to another door. A red light above the door came on as McCain approached, and a moment later went out again, accompanied by a beep. On the far side was a wide thoroughfare running crossways, with lime-green walls that were featureless except for welding seams and bundles of piping. There were large doorways opening off at intervals. It suggested, if anything, an enclosed street. Figures in gray tunics, singly and in pairs and groups, were walking on both sides, while in the center an electric tractor was hauling a trailer loaded with boxes. Just two guards were visible, pacing slowly together some distance away and looking more like street cops. McCain and his two escorts followed the road right to a corner, where it went left and continued, looking much the same as before. They passed an opening flanked on either side by sections of fixed bars, with a center section consisting of a sliding barred gate, which was open. A sign above read BLOCK A. Farther on they came to a similar gate, this time labeled BLOCK B. A red light came on as McCain followed the first guard through, then went out with a beep. McCain had the feeling that he could get really tired of red lights and beeps before very much longer.

They were at one end of a more-or-less square hall, with two rows of doors facing each other across a broad center space. On a higher level above, two more rows of identical doors looked down from behind railed walkways reached by metal stairs. Footbridges at both ends of the hall connected the walkways to complete a gallery overlooking the central floor area from all four sides. At the near end of the hall were several long tables with benches, at which men were loosely scattered, some in groups, others sitting alone. As with the group that McCain had seen boarding the monorail car, they were a mix of races and types. Some were reading, one writing, others playing cards, while many just sat. In the open area beyond the tables, more were standing talking, and others were gathered in a circle around some kind of game that involved tossing coins.

As he and his escorts moved on across the hall, McCain caught babbles of different languages. The voices dropped for a moment as he passed by the tables, and curious eyes followed him. They came to one of the doors on the right, which carried a large "3" painted in yellow. One of the guards gestured toward it. McCain stepped forward; the red light lit and the beeper beeped. He tried the door, and it opened. Without a word the two guards turned and left. McCain pushed the door wide and stepped through. The light was dimmer than in the area outside, and he paused for his eyes to adjust. Then he moved on inside, letting the door close behind him.

The room had an open area running all the way down the center, containing several tables with chairs pulled up on both sides. He moved forward and deposited the two bags he was carrying on the table nearest the door. To left and right, the space along the sides of the room was partitioned into a series of five or six bays, each of which contained two double-tier bunks, one alongside the partition on each side, separated by a narrow aisle containing kit lockers. There were pictures adorning the walls in places, some mugs and eating utensils on shelves, books, a long, carved wooden pipe resting in a bowl, and an unfinished game of chess on one of the tables. The place looked reasonably clean, but had a distinct odor of too many bodies living in too confined a space.

Whoever the bodies were, they were absent for the moment.

There was an open door at the far end of the room, and as McCain's hearing adapted to the quiet after the hubbub outside, he discerned sounds of movement. A moment later a figure appeared framed in the far doorway, holding a broom. McCain waited. The man shuffled out and approached around the farmost table. He was of Oriental appearance, lithely built, and wearing a black skullcap in addition to the regulation gray tunic. As he came closer, McCain found that he had an abstruse face that managed to both reinforce and contradict at the same time the impression of years conveyed by his physique. It was furrowed and wizened about the eyes, yet surprisingly smooth everywhere else. His chin sprouted a short beard that was turning gray, but his stare was bright and alert like that of a curious child.

"You must be the American," he said. "My name is Nakajima-Lin Kohmei-Tso-Liang." His voice and expression were neutral, carrying neither undue warmth nor hostility. McCain was instantly confused. The construction was typically Asiatic with the family name coming first, but the double name itself was a composite of Japanese and Chinese; the first of the given names following sounded Japanese, but the other two were Chinese. He watched McCain curiously, and McCain had the feeling that he was able to read if the contradiction meant anything to McCain or not. "Generally I am called Koh."

"Lewis Earnshaw," McCain responded. "Most people call me Lew."

Koh came to where McCain was standing and indicated the lower tier of the bunk by the first partition to the left. "Your place will be there," he said. He nodded toward the corner bunk behind McCain's right. As McCain had noticed with some of the other bunks, its upper cot was hinged upright out of the way. It suggested that the place was not occupied to full capacity at present. "I live across there. It seems, therefore, that for a while we are to be neighbors." Koh spoke English well, with slow and careful articulation.

McCain picked up his bags from the table and moved across. "Well, I guess that's fine with me. Does your name make you Japanese or Chinese?"

"A mixture of the two, which goes back many generations. Appropriate to this century."

"I've spent some time in both countries. It sounds as if you were expecting me."

"The billet foreman is usually notified when a new arrival is due."

"What exactly is a foreman?"

"You are not familiar with the system?"

"How could I be?"

"Aren't you transferring from another part of Zamork?"

"No, I only just arrived."

Koh nodded. "I see. Every billet has a foreman. It's a trusted category of inmates who are responsible for discipline, take complaints to the right quarters, and hand out work assignments. Ours is called Luchenko, a Russian." He gestured vaguely in the direction of the far end of the room with his free hand. "His place is back there. He'll talk to you when he gets back."

"So, what's he like?"

"Oh, some days good, some days not so good. Most times okay."

McCain looked down at his cot, which held just a bare mattress. "What do we do about getting blankets and stuff?"

"You pick up a kit at OI—dishes, eating implements, and so on."

"What's OI?"

"The Official Issue store, in the Core complex across Gorky Street."

"Gorky Street?"

"Outside the block mess area—where you just came along. If you wish, I will show you the way when I'm finished."

"Are you here all the time, Koh?"

"One half day each week is for cleaning. This week it's my turn. It provides a welcome opportunity to think in peace and quiet. One seldom gets time to be alone in Zamork."

"How long have you been here now?"

"A year, roughly."

McCain nodded absently and stepped back to survey the bunk above his, trying to gauge something about the person who would be his closest neighbor. There were several raunchily explicit pinups attached to the head end of the partition, a rock magazine cover showing a pop group in action behind a star-spangled logo in the shape of the letters "USA," and, folded on the pillow below, an Ohio State University T-shirt. "What are you in here for?" he inquired.

"*Vy govorite po-Russki?*" Koh asked suddenly from behind him—*Do you speak Russian?*

McCain turned and studied his face for a second, then nodded. "*Da.*"

"Where are you from in America?" Koh went on, still in Russian. "Have you been on *Tereshkova* long? What was *your* offense?"

McCain saw the point and nodded resignedly. "I don't know you," he agreed, switching back to English.

"Nor I, you. As you obviously already understand, one learns not to ask such questions of strangers."

"Would I have admitted to speaking Russian if I'd been planted here?" McCain asked.

"Unlikely," Koh conceded. "But then again you might, if you were being very clever."

"Are they often very clever?"

"No. But when they are, that's when they're at their most dangerous."

McCain sighed. There was nothing he could say to alleviate all suspicions instantly. It would take time and patience. He sat down on his bunk and turned his attention to transferring the contents of his bags into his locker. "Who's the guy upstairs?" he asked, changing the subject. "Looks like another American."

Koh gave a short laugh. "No, not an American. An Americophile. His name is Mungabo. He's Zigandan. The Russians have strange impressions of American life, especially with regard to racial tensions, which their propagandists exaggerate. They also have a strange sense of humor. Luchenko thought it would be funny to put the American under the black man." He turned and began walking back toward the far end of the room. "Toilets and washing facilities are through there. I'll take you over to OI when I'm through."

"So, what did this Zigandan guy do for America that caused him to wind up here . . . or is that something we don't ask about, too?" McCain called after him.

"Oh no, everybody knows about that. He gave them a top-secret Russian plane—a MIG-55. At least, that was what the court-martial decided. Mungabo claimed that his electronic navigation system malfunctioned, but the KGB refused to believe that the whole thing wasn't a put-up job."

"What made them so sure?" McCain asked.

"It was elementary. Equipment produced under a Marxist economy, they pointed out, cannot malfunction."

CHAPTER TEN

Dr. Philip Kress, from the Brookhaven National Laboratory on Long Island, stared out unhappily from behind the table of panel members at the rows of delegates to the Third Conference on Communications Physics, sponsored by the Japanese Science Council and being held at the "university city" of Tsukuba.

"There are no doubt several reasons why the underwater neutrino-detection experiments have given ambiguous results," he said. "The biggest problem all along has been statistical. We're talking about trying to separate out a very few real events from an enormous background noise. Whichever way you approach it, you end up subtracting one big number from another big number, neither of them guaranteed absolutely, to yield a very small number, which is the answer you're looking for. It's a tricky problem, and we're working on it. What else can I say?" He tossed up a hand to indicate that he was through and sat back in his chair to light his pipe.

The panel moderator, Jules Dupalme, from the French telecommunications corporation CIT Alcatel, looked from side to side for further comment from the others. "Okay? Any more questions from the floor? No? Good. Well, there is one announcement before we end the session for lunch. Would all those who—"

"One question." A Japanese about halfway back near one of the aisles stood up. In the fifth row, Dr. Melvin Bowers, from the Plasma Physics Institute at Livermore, California, sighed and looked at his watch. He was getting hungry, and speculations about communicating via neutrinos beamed through the solid Earth weren't his field. He shifted in his seat and tried to recall the name of the bar in the city that Sam and Max said they'd found the night before—the one with the underwearless hostesses that sat on the customers' knees. From behind him, the voice of the Japanese continued, "I see a difficulty with the data that have been selected as candidates. There is nothing that positively excludes every one of them from being an atmospheric muon, and not a neutrino-induced muon at all. For example, if the detected muon came from below, it would *have* to be neutrino-induced. But that is not so in a single case. All the once we have seen came from above. Even with a small sample, this asymmetry bothers me.

"Phil?" Dupalme invited.

Kress shook the match between his fingers to extinguish it and dropped it into an ashtray. "I agree, it's strange . . . not what you'd expect . . ." The answer wasn't satisfactory even to himself. He sighed. "But we have pushed the detectability threshold back an order of magnitude. Maybe we need to reexamine the sensitivity of the detectors. . . . It's difficult to say without further analysis."

"Thank you." Unenlightened, the Japanese bowed and sat down again. Dupalme glanced down to read the announcement he had been about to make.

Then, Professor Masaki Kurishoda from Osaka University, who had been curiously reticent throughout most of the proceedings, pulled a microphone across the table. Bowers in the fifth row groaned inwardly. Kurishoda had a pudgy, humorous face and shot a genial smile at the audience through his heavy-rimmed spectacles before he spoke. "Of course," he said, "another reason why you gentlemen are not getting unambiguous evidence for the existence of neutrinos might be that they don't exist." Somebody near the front started to laugh, then stopped abruptly with the realization that Kurishoda was serious. The professor regarded the audience calmly, shifting his eyes until sure that he had everyone's attention. Even Bowers had forgotten lunch for the moment. Kurishoda spread his hands expressively. "Explaining the unknown by means of the unobservable is always a perilous business. The neutrino was postulated by Pauli simply as a book-balancing device to preserve the conservation laws of momentum and spin in the beta decay of a neutron into a proton and an electron. Every subsequent interpretation since has merely extended that convention. We scientists, you see . . . we think we construct objective views as dictated by facts, but really we do not. Sometimes we seek solutions within a framework of ruling academic opinion." He paused and sent a broad smile around the room. Nobody interrupted.

He continued, "If we extend the conservation laws to include the *negative* energy states proposed by Dirac— and why should we restrict it to positive states only, except to satisfy convention?—then pair-production is explained without the need for a photon to mysteriously 'turn into' an electron-positron pair: the positron becomes simply the 'hole' left in the Dirac sea by the electron that has been promoted to a positive state as a result of absorbing the photon. The notion of a hole behaving like a particle might have been strange in Dirac's time, but today, in our world full of semiconductor electronics, we take it for granted. Now, neutron decay becomes such a simple pair-production event, with the electron escaping and the positron being captured. We no longer need a neutrino to carry away the missing energy, since the electron was raised from a negative energy level to begin with. And since three particles are involved in the process, spin conservation is also satisfied."

Kress was already spluttering farther along the table. "But . . . now wait a minute, I mean, what does that do to the weak nuclear force? You've just pulled the rug out from saying there is a weak force at all. I mean . . ."

Kurishoda shrugged. "I agree. And you are about to remind me of the theoretical work that has unified the weak and the electromagnetic forces since the 1980's. But I suggest that the 'weak' interactions are nothing more than electromagnetic forces acting between the dipoles of elementary particles and those of electrons in negative energy states. So, if the two forces were actually only one to begin with, then the whole thing will have to be reexamined."

A lot of muttering and head shaking was going on in the audience. "But it's been verified, hasn't it?" someone objected. "I mean, neutrinos are *detected* routinely. They have been, ever since the fifties."

"Cowan and Reines," another voice supplied. "Neutrino-induced transmutation of chlorine into argon."

"*Presumed* to be neutrino-induced," Kurishoda threw back, beaming, as if he had been waiting for just that. "The mechanism I have just described accounts for it equally well."

"Experiments have been conducted which suggest they not only exist, but possess mass," another member of the panel pointed out. "It's been measured."

"How else do you account for the missing mass in the universe?" somebody else in the audience called out.

"And other experimenters have found no indication of

mass," Kurishoda replied. "Some experimenters have reported that neutrinos oscillate among three forms, while others say they don't. As for the missing mass, well, maybe we just have to look for another kind of galaxy-glue." He half-turned, and motioned with his head. "Phil Kress himself has told us about the difficulty in observing anything, and then the ambiguity in deciding what it is. In short, it all relies on statistical methods that are questionable. There is nothing *conclusive* that proves neutrinos have mass, that the oscillate among three types, or that they exist at all. I contend that everything attributed to them can be explained more simply in terms that are already familiar. William of Occam would have approved."

The audience was clearly all set for a showdown on this. Dupalme raised a hand before anyone else could respond. "Ladies and gentlemen, lunch *is* waiting. Perhaps we could arrange a special session this evening to explore this subject further?" He looked down inquiringly to someone in the front row, who leaned forward to mutter something up at the dais. "Yes, we'll post details later this afternoon. . . ." He searched for something with which to wrap the topic up for the moment. "Maybe our speculations on neutrino-beam communications through the planet were a little premature, then, eh?"

Some of the panelists grinned, while others shook their heads. The atmosphere relaxed.

"Well, there's always tachyons to think about," someone quipped from the audience.

"How about that, Professor Kurishoda?" another called. "Do tachyons exist?"

The professor beamed back over the top of his spectacles. "But of course," he replied. "A tachyon is a quantum of bad taste."

Five minutes later, the attendees were spilling through into the central dining hall and dispersing among the tables, already set with a fish appetizer, fruit juices, and tea. Melvin Bowers headed for a quiet spot in a far corner of the room.

Jenny Hampden, a research manager from Bell Labs, joined him. They'd met the previous day at breakfast in the hotel, and talked briefly during some of the breaks between sessions. She liked caving, classical music, and cats.

"Well, there goes my favorite theory," Bowers said as they sat down.

"What theory?"

"My neutrino-bomb theory."

"*Neutrino* bomb? That's a new one."

"Think about it," Bowers said. "It meets all the requirements for the perfect strategic weapon. It keeps defense contractors profitable and employs people. It justifies the jobs of Pentagon generals and defense analysts. And it gives the media a new scare-word and the peaceniks something to howl about." He smoothed his napkin across his knees and turned up his palms. "*But,* it has no undesirable side effects: it doesn't damage property or kill people. The perfect bomb!"

Jenny laughed. "Maybe we could have neutrino-power reactors, too—something to divert the oppositionists away from fusion. Then maybe it could all come on-line, and they mightn't even notice."

"Hm, there might be something in that, too. I wish somebody'd thought of it back in the seventies."

Jenny put down her fork suddenly. "Oh, Mel, there's something I forgot. Look, I have to see Takuji right now. I promised him some slides for the talk he's giving this afternoon. Would you excuse me? I'll be back in five minutes."

"Sure. I'll have them hold the entree."

"Thanks." Jenny got up and disappeared in the direction of the door.

Bowers carried on eating alone. Was it called the Yellow Dragon? Red Dragon? . . . No, not Dragon, but Red something . . . He didn't notice the tall, elegantly groomed figure approaching from among the bodies still milling about to find places in the middle of the room. "Ah, Dr. Bowers, good day to you."

Bowers looked up. "Igor Lukich," he said, using the Russian familiar patronymic.

"Do you mind if I join you?"

"Not at all. Sit down, please. Oh, not there. That side's taken."

It was Professor Dyashkin, the director of a Soviet communications-research establishment in Siberia. Dyashkin's name was known internationally, and he and Bowers were friends from previous professional gatherings in Moscow and Bombay. They had both been involved in an informal spontaneous discussion that had taken place the night before among a group of scientists at one of the hotels in which the conference attendees were staying.

"An interesting notion of Kurishoda's," Bowers said after Dyashkin had sat down. "I was just saying to the friend I'm with—Jenny Hampden of Bell, I don't know if you've met; she'll be back in a few minutes—neutrinos would make the perfect bomb. Then all of you and all of us could stop worrying, eh?"

Dyashkin smiled automatically, but he didn't ask Bowers to elaborate and was evidently not in the mood for small talk. He scanned the surroundings constantly with his eyes, and seemed nervous. Bowers became serious and looked at the Russian inquiringly as he continued eating. "We know each other from several years now, yes, Dr. Bowers?" Dyashkin said. He spoke guardedly, with an elbow resting on the table and a hand covering his mouth.

Bowers nodded. "I guess so—in a formal kind of way, anyhow."

"Even so, sometimes we must take risks and trust our judgment. I judge you as someone who can be trusted."

Bowers wiped his mouth with a corner of his napkin and resumed chewing slowly. When he spoke, his voice had dropped to match Dyashkin's. "What are you driving at?"

"When are you due to go back to the USA?" Dyashkin asked.

"Well, I'm on a one-year exchange here in Osaka. But

I was planning to go home for a vacation right after this conference is over. Why?"

"Anyone might join us at the table, so I come straight to the point while we are alone." Bowers waited. Dyashkin drew a long, shaky breath. "Look, Dr. Bowers, it is possible that I might be interested in coming over, if the conditions were right. You understand?"

It took Bowers a moment. "To us, you mean? Over to our side?"

Dyashkin nodded almost imperceptibly. "Yes. Personal reasons—too much to go into now. But what I want to know from you is, would you be willing to convey my proposition to the appropriate authorities?"

"Proposition? But I don't know anything about what it is. How would—"

"I can arrange that. What I have to know now is, would you be willing to help me?"

Bowers chewed in silence for a while. "I'll have to think about it," he said finally.

"How long will you need? Please understand that we constantly risk being under observation when we travel abroad. The KGB even infiltrate their people into conferences such as this."

"Give me until tonight. I'll meet you in the bar of our hotel at, say, eight. Do you think it would be safe to talk there?"

Dyashkin shook his head. "I don't want to talk. All I need at this stage is a yes or a no answer."

"Okay, I won't say anything. If I offer to stand the first round of drinks, the answer's yes. Okay?"

"As you say, a deal."

Two more figures materialized at the table. "Gustav and Sandy," Bowers greeted. "It's about time—we were starting to get lonely here. Say, did I ever tell you my theory about the perfect bomb? . . ."

That afternoon, Bowers called the US embassy in Tokyo for advice. Later, back at the hotel, he went through into the bar for an after-dinner drink. Precisely at eight o'clock, Dyashkin appeared and joined him. "Hi," Bowers said. "Quite a day today, eh? What are you having, Igor? The first one's on me." The Russian asked for a vodka and soda.

Later, while they were talking, Dyashkin pointed to the orange document folder that Bowers had placed on the seat beside him. It was one of the packages issued to each attendee, and contained the conference agenda, copies of the papers being presented, and other information. "Obtain another package from the registration desk," he said. "Tomorrow there is a paper on laser solitons scheduled for three o'clock. Be there, and place the folder on the floor by your chair. I will exchange it for one I'll be carrying, which will contain details of the proposal that I wish you to carry to the American authorities."

CHAPTER ELEVEN

"'The fractional Fourier-Brown-Wierner series with independent Gaussian coefficients converges to a sum for all H greater than zero, you see. But above H-equals-one, the sum becomes differentiable . . .'"

The end of the day was approaching. McCain lay on his bunk in the billet and listened to Rashazzi expounding vigorously to Haber over a pile of books and papers strewn across the table in the center aisle. They had introduced themselves to McCain earlier, when they returned from the day work-shift. Rashazzi, or "Razz," as everyone called him, was an Israeli, young, handsome, dark-eyed, and of boundless energy and enthusiasm. Haber was a West German, with a pink, crinkled, bespectacled face and thinning white hair, who was getting on somewhat in years and gave the impression of belonging more in a sanatorium than a prison camp, although McCain already half-suspected this could be an act. They were both scientists of some kind, obviously. Rashazzi said he was a biologist from the University of Tel Aviv. Maybe, McCain had conceded. Maybe not.

Each pair of bays facing each other across the central aisle along the length of the billet constituted an eight-man "section"—two double bunks in each bay. The front section—i.e., the one immediately inside the door—housed Rashazzi, Haber, and Koh in the bay on the far side, and on the near side, McCain, with Mungabo the Zigandan above, and opposite them, occupying a single bunk by the end wall like Koh, an Irishman called Scanlon. Koh and Scanlon were elsewhere for the moment.

"Where did you get that from, you pig!"

"It was a fair play, you-who-were-not-born-but produced-by-farting!"

"And your father was a pig, and your mother was a pig! . . ."

More voices filtered through from the next section beyond the partition. They sounded like Siberian dialects from Soviet Central Asia. The gambling had begun immediately after the evening meal, the squabbling soon thereafter, and the aroma of strange substances being smoked was wafting around the partition. Rashazzi had warned McCain that this went on all the time, but not to worry about it. From others who had crossed through on their way between the rear of the billet and the mess area outside, McCain had caught snatches of Czechoslovakian and recognized several Russians. The bunk above creaked as Mungabo shifted his weight. McCain stared up at it. Escape was surely out of the question. Finding something purposeful to focus on in this place could get to be a problem, he decided.

A figure came along the center aisle from the far end of the billet and stopped near the bottom of the bunk. "No, we don't want none today," Mungabo's voice said from above. The figure ignored him. McCain looked out when he realized that the figure was staring at him. He was tall and lean, thirtyish, perhaps, with waves of blond hair flowing to the base of his neck, a yellow mustache, and clear, penetrating eyes set in a hawkish face. The addition of a beard would have made him a natural for the lead role in any Bible movie. "Hello," he said. "I guess we should get acquainted." He spoke in even, measured tones, with what sounded like a Midwest accent. McCain swung his legs off the bunk and sat up. The other stretched out a hand. "Paul Nolan, Springfield, Illinois."

"Lew Earnshaw, just about everywhere, but Iowa originally."

Nolan sat down on the edge of Scanlon's vacant bunk opposite. "So, how did you manage to get yourself in here?" he asked lightly. When McCain didn't reply immediately, he went on, "I heard a rumor going around that a couple of American journalists were arrested a while back, during the May Day tour. Were you one of those?"

McCain's eyes narrowed. "I'm not sure I want to start answering questions like that," he said.

Nolan smiled condescendingly, as if he had been expecting as much. McCain didn't like people who smiled too easily. "That's wise. I started out training to be a lawyer, you know. It's not all the way people think. It's vicious and competitive, like going back to the jungle. There's no sense of decency or ethics left anymore. Just money. They all sell their souls to the corporations. So I got out. Ended up in government, with the IPA in Washington—on their legal staff."

"The Industrial Policy Agency was scrapped years ago," McCain said.

"Yes, well, that was a while ago . . ." Nolan seemed to be about to say something further, then changed his mind. "Anyway, what I came to tell you was that Luchenko wants to talk to you. He's down at the other end."

McCain raised his eyebrows, wondering momentarily what the American was doing running errands for the Russian foreman. Then he dismissed the thought with a shrug and stood up. "Okay. Let's go."

They walked past the torrent of varied suidian insults still flying prolifically from the game in progress on one side, and through into the section beyond that. A bearded man at the center table was making tea from a hot-water pot that seemed to have a permanent place there, while another talked as he watched: "She never believed anything anyone said. She'd call on the phone and ask if her daughter was there. I'd tell her, 'No, she's out.' And then five minutes later the woman would call again and ask the same thing. She'd try to disguise her voice, but I could tell it was her because . . ." The next section contained more Asiatics on one side and empty bunks on the other, except one in which a pink-faced man with a high forehead was lying reading.

Passing through the next section, McCain caught snatches of a man who sounded Polish talking to a group. "They stopped short of Warsaw and sat there for two months to let the Germans wipe out the Polish Resistance for them. It was deliberate."

"That's a lot of rubbish," someone replied. "They couldn't go any farther. Look how far they'd advanced all through July."

The first voice dropped to a murmur. "Hey, Smovak, who's he?"

"New arrival today—in the front section."

An older man sitting with them threw in, "My father was there, you know—with Konev's army. . . ."

"An American," Smovak said.

There was a man lying on a bunk, staring morosely at a photograph of a woman on the locker beside him. . . . Finally they arrived at the end section. Five sections, eight men per section. Space for forty in the whole billet.

Two men were waiting at the last table. The one at the end was roundly built and on the heavyish side, with thinning hair combed straight back from the forehead in typical Russian style, and a fleshy moon-face amply provided with chins. McCain's first thought was that he'd have looked more in place in crumpled clothes at the front of a schoolroom, or fussing with rosebushes outside a house in the suburbs. The younger man sitting across the corner from him was his opposite: solidly muscled, with a mat of short, curly black hair, a chin of blue-shadowed battleship armor, and scowling eyes that were already weighing McCain as a potential adversary. The moon-face motioned for McCain to sit down. McCain did so, across the bouncer. Neither of them proffered a handshake, and McCain didn't volunteer. Nolan, whom McCain had mentally dubbed "Creeping Jesus," sat down two chairs away on the same side.

The moon-face had a buff-colored cardboard folder open on the table in front of him, containing papers. A clipboard with a chart of some kind lay next to it. "You are the new American, Mr. Earnshaw, two-seven-one-zero-six," he said, glancing down. "From Pacific News, California."

"That's right."

"It says here you are a journalist."

"Uh-huh."

"My name is Luchenko. I am the foreman of this billet. This is Josip Maiskevik." McCain gave a curt nod. Maiskevik continued staring at him without moving. "You know how things work here?"

"They told me a little about it at the front desk when I checked in."

"Do not think of Zamork as a punishment institution. Its purpose is to encourage socially desirable attitudes and behavior. It operates by incentives and privileges, not by coercion. But the privileges have to be earned. I am responsible for seeing that the rules are followed in this billet. If you wish to initiate any communication with the authorities or lodge any complaint, you do so through me. Also, I pass out the work allocations. You will be working in one of the machine shops in the Core, commencing tomorrow morning."

Luchenko went on to explain about working hours, rules, and procedures. Next in line beyond him was a "block supervisor," who was also an inmate. The supervisor was the means of access to the commandant in charge of the block, whom the captain had mentioned when McCain was admitted. In the case of Block B, the commandant was a Colonel Bachayvin. Then there was the governor, Fedorov, who reigned above the block commandants. But it appeared that he dwelt on a higher existential plane, from which he seldom descended to deal with prisoners in person. Incorrigibles who were unimpressed by the incentive process could expect a harsher time and solitary detention. The penalty system was more or less standardized, and everyone soon got to know how much time various infractions could be expected to bring. Failing to be back in one's block an hour before lights-out was good for three days, and being insolent to a guard who was in a bad mood that day, a week. Fighting with other prisoners or sabotaging the work output put you in the month-plus class. Attacking a guard was worth three days at most— "Before they shoot you," Nolan interjected, smiling.

"I believe in being reasonable," Luchenko concluded. "You will find I deal fairly with those who deal fairly with me. Nolan can fill you in on other details. Do you have any questions for now?"

There was something about Luchenko's manner that didn't quite fit, McCain had been thinking as he listened. The Russian was trying to affect an air of brusqueness, but it wasn't him. He was like a salesman trying to put into practice what he'd read on assertiveness, but without the force of character to pull it off. The appeal to reasonableness was for his own protection more than anyone else's, McCain guessed. And what was the reason for Maiskevik's brooding, silent presence at the table? A hint, maybe, of how the power structure really worked for anyone who didn't buy the reasonableness line? That added up. Luchenko's style would require a strong-arm man behind the throne.

"One thing," McCain said. "When I was arrested, I was with a colleague, also from PNS. Her name is Paula Shelmer. I haven't been told anything of her whereabouts or her condition. I want to talk to the block commandant or whoever I need to talk to for some news."

Luchenko pursed his lips for a second, then leaned forward to scribble a note on one of the papers in his folder. "I can't promise anything," he said. "The request will be passed on."

"I'd appreciate it."

"Anything else?"

"I guess that's it."

"Very well. As I said, follow the rules, and you will find that life can improve rapidly. Play fair with me, and I will play fair with you. That is all I have to say for now."

McCain walked back to the front section of the billet and sat down at the far end of the table from Rashazzi and Haber, who were still in the throes of their animated mathematical discussion. Nolan, who McCain hadn't realized had followed him, pulled up the next chair. "It'll be a change to have another American in here," Nolan said.

"Are there many around?"

"Only a couple, in other billets. I don't have a lot to do with them—too brash and loudmouthed." Nolan had a habit of smiling all the time, as if he were anxious to avoid being annoying. McCain found it overplacating and as annoying as hell. But this was only McCain's first day, after all. The onus was on him to show some willingness to fit in.

"Illinois, eh?" McCain said. "I knew girl from Chicago once . . ."

"Women know nothing about politics."

"She wasn't into politics."

"All they're interested in is clothes, painting themselves up, and other people's money. They're not intellectual."

"This one happened to be a doctor of recombinant engineering. She ran a company that remodeled plant DNA."

"Mutating nature for profits."

"It sounds like you disapprove. Have you got something against feeding people?"

"No, against greed and criminal corporate vandalism."

McCain nodded. Suddenly he was losing interest in trying to be accommodating. "Now I'm beginning to see what kind of government lawyer you were. Or did you flunk that, too?" he said.

"I told you, I got out of the whole rotten system. I emigrated—to the Soviet Union."

McCain regarded him distastefully. "You mean you defected."

Nolan sighed, conveying the understanding tolerance of one who had heard this a thousand times, but whose eyes see farther. "I betrayed none of my principles," he said calmly. "Americans are forever preaching about freedom and the right to choose. Well, I exercised my right and chose. Why is the choice wrong just because you happen to disagree with it?" He leaned closer. "None of you understand. It's because of the brainwashing that you—all of us—went through. The USSR is a rich, strong nation. The people are happy with their leaders, and together they are building the world of tomorrow—a world based on equality and justice for everyone. Oppression and exploitation will end. It will be what mankind has been struggling toward for thousands of years."

"And you're calling *me* brainwashed?"

"I simply know what's true."

McCain waved a hand to indicate the billet around them, and by implication the rest of Zamork outside it. "Well, your faith's been rewarded. Why did they put you in here? Was it what you wanted, too? Okay, good. Have fun." He made to rise to go back to his bunk, but Nolan caught his sleeve.

"That was another story. I thought I understood the philosophy of socialism, but it wasn't true. I was brought to realize that *I*, too, had flaws which I'd never suspected. But they are curable. Being here is part of the process, you see. As Luchenko said, it's not a punishment. I don't think of it as imprisonment at all."

"What, then—a vacation resort?"

"A process of guided enlightenment, as in a monastery, I guess. Purification."

"So why the gulag and the KGB? Why do you need land mines and barbed wire to keep the workers in Paradise?"

"That's only temporary. When world revolution is achieved, it will change."

"Bullshit."

Nolan nodded as if he had been expecting it. "It's possible that you may come to change your outlook while you are here," he said, rising from the chair. "I just wanted you to know that I'd be happy to talk, whenever you feel like it."

McCain watched as Nolan returned to the far end of the billet. Then he got up and went back to his bunk. Mungabo was beaming at him from the top tier. "I knew all Americans couldn't be like him. It looks like maybe you and me might get along." He thrust out a pink-palmed hand. "Name's Abel."

"Lew."

"From Iowa—I heard you earlier."

"That's right."

"D'you ever see the New York Bears play?"

"It's the Chicago Bears. Or do you mean the New York Yankees?"

"Just testin'. You passed."

"That doesn't prove anything, Abel. A KGB plant would know things like that."

Mungabo grinned. "True, but that wasn't the test. You'd never imagine the horseshit those people believe. A real Russian, trying to pretend he's American, wouldn't have shaken hands."

McCain grinned back. Actually, a real KGB man would have known that the horseshit was horseshit. The popular view of American racism expounded by Tass was purely for Russian domestic consumption. That told him that Mungabo was probably straight, too.

CHAPTER TWELVE

Metal shrieked on metal as whirling sawteeth bit into toughened aluminum alloy. The note dropped while the motor labored under the load, and then soared again as the blade broke through and the end of the length of L-section girder dropped onto the pile in the scrap bin. McCain released the vise and transferred the piece to the stack waiting behind him for Scanlon to drill and deburr. Then he lifted another uncut length from the rack and laid it on the bench to be marked and center-punched against the standard jib. If he ever got out of Zamork and back to normality, he decided, he'd buy himself a waterbed. He'd never want to see another metal bedframe. What the powers that ran *Tereshkova* thought they were going to do with so many bedframes, he couldn't imagine. Did they plan on turning the whole place into a prison?

Kevin Scanlon was the Irishman who occupied the single bunk opposite McCain and Mungabo in B-3, enjoying a measure of extra space that afforded one of the minor but worthwhile comforts of life. He had become mixed up with espionage and the GRU—the Soviet military-intelligence organization, which in many ways paralleled the KGB—in the course of his former IRA activities and connections through them to the Cubans and Palestinians, until one day he found himself on the wrong side of one of Moscow's eternal comradely vendettas. He had sparse hair, with a lean build and gaunt, hollowed face that made his eyes seem protrusive, especially when he was in one of his intense moods, which usually produced either passionate discourses on Irish history or invective harangues about the "Brits." McCain had worked with the British when he was with NATO in Europe, and he'd found them likable enough despite their occasional stuffiness. But he kept his opinions to himself, and on the whole he and Scanlon got along, which was as well since Luchenko had assigned them as regular working partners.

"What I'd give to be able to walk out and down the

street for a pint o' the porter now," Scanlon called across from the drilling table, lifting a gloved hand and wiping his brow with his sleeve.

"Something else to think about for when you get back, I guess."

"Or the Guinness. Pure Liffey water the Guinness is made from in Dublin. Nowhere else in the world does it have the same taste."

"If anyone ever gets back."

"Cream. The head on it is as smooth as tasting pure cream."

A horn somewhere overhead gave two raucous blasts to indicate the midday break for lunch. McCain thumbed a red button, and the saw freewheeled to a stop. The din in the rest of the workshop subsided as other machines were turned off and the figures attending them stripped off their greasy coveralls before joining the general movement toward the main door. Scanlon came round the bench, wiping his hands with a piece of rag. "Now, isn't it nice to think of all the Ivans and Vladimirs who'll sleep comfortable in their beds for the charitable work we're doing here today? And wouldn't Father O'Halloran from Ballingarry be proud of me for that?"

McCain hung his coverall on the end of a storage rack. "Is that where you're from?"

"Ah, many years ago now, it was. That was when I met my first Americans. There was a development estate set up not three miles from the village—light industry, they said, electronics and the like. An American company came first and built a computer factory there. Then the Germans and the Japanese came, I recall. We weren't exactly wild about being invaded by all the foreigners, but the money they paid was good."

They came out of the workshops and began walking along a wide corridor of grimy, battle-scarred, lime-green walls. Meals were brought to each block and eaten in the common mess area. "How did the Americans fit in?" McCain asked.

"They were always chasing around after the girls, which didn't please the local lads at all. There were fights sometimes. The Germans preferred their beer, but they liked ordering people around too much. Me, I had more time for the Japanese than any of them. Very polite people—always bow and smile sort of apologetically before they knock anyone's teeth in."

"I thought it was the Irish who were supposed to be famous for all those things."

"Is that a fact, now?"

"Great lovers, drinkers, and always good for a fight, isn't that what they say?"

"You don't strike me as the sort of man who pays much attention to what people say. How about yourself? Are you blessed with any Irish in the family?"

"I'm not sure," McCain replied, with deliberate vagueness.

"Surprising. I thought all Americans were obsessed with genealogy."

"I guess what I'm trying to say is that Earnshaw sounds more English to me, if anything."

"Hmm, yes, now. Kind o' what I was thinkin' meself. . . . But you're not so bad a fella for that."

They came out of the Core and turned south onto Gorky Street.

Compass directions in *Tereshkova* were the same as on Earth. The spin axis through the hub defined north-south, with the direction that the hub docking ports faced being arbitrarily taken as north. Following the convention of a normal, spherical, inside-in and outside-out planet, the equatorial plane was perpendicular to the axis and midway between its poles, dividing the entire wheel of *Tereshkova* into a north zone and a south zone—like a tire cut in two along a line running around the middle of the tread. The equator itself was the circle where this plane intersected "ground" level in the ring—i.e., the midline of the central valley floor. It followed that a person walking along the equator—or parallel to it at any level from the rim to the hub—would be moving east or west.

Once more the familiar convention applied: when facing north, east was to the right and west was to the left. Which way the colony happened to be rotating had nothing to do with it.

Zamork lay off-center against the colony's south wall, on the eastern side of Novyi Kazan. The front, which consisted of administrative offices and guard quarters, faced the roadway and monorail tracks, with the road running above the monorail at that part of the ring and entering Zamork on a higher level. The rear of the administrative section opened onto the main thoroughfare known as Gorky Street, which closed on itself to form a square dividing the inner Core complex from the surrounding blocks that formed the rest of the facility. The Core, which was also on two levels, contained the kitchens, laundry, stores, a library, and workshops for such activities as machining, tailoring, and shoemaking. Outside the Core were six prisoner blocks, two on each of Gorky Street's remaining three sides. A walled exercise compound open to the "sky" lay on the east side, behind A and B Blocks. Blocks C and D were segregated for women prisoners, who wore light blue tunics instead of gray and had their own, fenced-off portion of the east compound. Segregation was not total, and the male and female inmates sometimes found themselves working alongside each other in the Core and on some of the outside labor details. This made communication between them routine, and for a moderate outlay in ingenuity afforded ample opportunities for amorous diversions. None of the women whom McCain got a chance to exchange a few words with knew of an American fitting Paula's description, however.

As Luchenko had said on McCain's first day, a high emphasis was placed on incentives. Prisoners could earn "points" for above-quota job performance, and there was a store at which points could be converted into additional comforts such as tobacco, candy, games, and materials for hobbies. Accrued points could also be traded for bonus time off work. So, when a prisoner spent his savings on the basics for a new pastime, he then found that he needed to behave himself for the extra time that he now needed to enjoy it. Prisoners could even debit and credit points among themselves by voucher, using individual accounts maintained in the administrative computer system and known collectively as "the Exchange." This could be useful for things like buying illicitly distilled vodka—for which a thriving underground market existed, acquiring goods to barter on the colony's black market when on outside work details, and settling gambling debts. None of it fitted with what McCain knew of the way the Russians ran their prisons. Why, in fact, would the Russians bring prisoners this far at all? He found it difficult to believe that it was just to provide cheap labor for the mundane work. There had to be more to it.

As McCain and Scanlon entered B Block from Gorky Street, Oskar Smovak and Leo Vorghas, who were also from B-3 billet, caught up with them. "Two points, I'll lay you two points!" Oskar Smovak exclaimed to Vorghas as they joined the line inside the mess area and began shuffling forward with their metal messtins. At the table in front, a kitchen orderly in a smock that looked greasier than the machine-shop coveralls was ladling stew out of a hatch in a rubber-tired, stainless-steel trolley, covered in flaps and lids, that looked like a scaled-down armored car. "No trotter ever timed a mile in under a minute fifty. Three points!" Smovak was Czechoslovakian, a stocky, solidly built cannonball of a man, with black hair, a ruddy face, and dark eyes looking out over a Fidel Castro beard. He had a voice that was loud and cutting, but most of the time it was because he was being jovial rather than pugnacious, McCain had learned. He claimed to have been arrested because of a relative of his who was caught photographing missiles being loaded into a Russian submarine at Murmansk.

Leo Vorghas was a Lithuanian, in his early forties, perhaps, with an open, high-browed face, thin, sandy hair, light-colored rounded eyes, and a pinkish complexion. The breast pocket of his jacket always bulged with spectacle case, ruler, and an assortment of more pens than anyone could ever know what to do with. His claim to notoriety was that as a government statistician he had made extra money on the side by selling details of the Soviet economic disasters to Western journalists: they'd paid better money than Western intelligence agencies had offered.

"One forty-eight point something." Vorghas insisted. "I remember reading it. No, wait a minute, the Ukrainian over in F-ten—he showed it to me in a book. You ask him. He'll tell you."

"Ah!" Smovak roared. "That was a *pacer*, not a trotter. No trotter has ever beaten one fifty. Check it out, Leo. You lose."

"Bah. Well, it's the same thing."

"It most certainly is *not*. Trotters move the diagonally opposite legs together. Pacers move the ones on the same side."

"But the carriages are the same, aren't they? I say that makes it the same thing. Nobody wins."

"Oh, nonsense."

They each collected two ladles of a tolerable concoction containing potatoes, cabbage, and a few scraps of mutton, a plate with two pieces of dark bread smeared with margarine, a slice of sausage, an apple, and a mug of black tea, and carried them over to one of the tables.

"What do you say, Mr. American?" Smovak asked, giving McCain an unusually keen look. "Know anything about racing?"

"Not really. . . . It's not my scene," McCain answered.

"That's surprising," Smovak said. "I thought it was popular there. Russia and America have had a common interest in trotting since long before the Revolution."

"I didn't know that."

"Oh yes. They're both large countries, you see—with bad roads that couldn't take heavy stagecoaches, before there were any trains. So they both bred horses for pulling light carriages over long distances. You mean you didn't know?" McCain shrugged and carried on eating. "Does the name Sam Caton mean anything?" Smovak asked him.

"Never heard of it," McCain said.

"Oh, why don't you come straight out with it, Oskar? Tell him you're wondering if he's really an American at all," Vorghas said irritably.

"Well, I've never heard of the fella either," Scanlon threw in. "Oskar, will ye lay off giving Lew a hard time. The man's only after hanging up his hat, for heaven's sake. What kind of Czechoslovakian welcome do you call that?"

"Kevin is right," Vorghas agreed. "This place breeds mistrust. Prudence is all very well, but it can go too far."

"And how will you ever become a priv if you don't trust people?" Scanlon asked. Vorghas laughed.

McCain had heard the expression before. It was a saying of Luchenko's and seemed to be a joke of some kind among the inmates. "What's a priv?" he asked, looking at the others.

"Hasn't anyone told you about them yet?" Vorghas asked. McCain shook his head.

"Privileged-category prisoners," Smovak said. "You're only regular category, see."

"They live up on surface level," Vorghas said.

Clearly that hadn't conveyed much to McCain, either. Scanlon explained, "There's an upper level to Zamork, out on the surface, above the part that we're in down here. They live in huts with grass around them, and trees—not packed into smelly billets as is good for the likes of us. There's less work for them to do, of course, and more frills—just like in the real world. *And,*" he added with a wink, "the women and the men are mixed together. Now, there's a carrot for you if ever there was one. Mungabo, the poor fella, drives himself wild thinking about it."

"They've even got a beach up there," Vorghas said.

"A beach!" Smovak repeated, as if daring McCain to challenge it. McCain stared at them in astonishment.

"You see, there's a high-level reservoir next to this place, between Zamork and the town," Vorghas said. "It feeds the water system that drains down through the recreation area between Novyi Kazan and the ag zone. Well, the privs have got a beach on it up there."

"What kind of people are these privs?" McCain asked, growing more curious.

"The professional class of the classless society," Smovak told him.

Vorghas nodded. "Scientists, teachers, and such— dissidents that the Party wants to keep out of the way for a while, but without upsetting them too much. They're worried about the risk of bad publicity later."

"Frightened of changes in the winds that swirl through the Kremlin's blustery halls," Scanlon recited lyrically.

McCain smiled faintly as he chewed his bread. It was heavy and grainy in texture. "And people from down here can get promoted?" he said.

"It happens," Scanlon replied. "But 'tis a rare thing when it does. Many a Luchenko lives in hope, but few are chosen."

McCain nodded distantly. So the foremen and the block supervisors had their incentives, too. It fitted with the general scheme of things, but that still didn't shed any light on the reasons why. "So what's it all for?" he asked the others. "Why is this place here, and why is it the way it is?" There was a quick exchange of glances among the others, and a pause of a second or two. McCain obviously wasn't the first to have wondered about such questions.

"Progressive psychology," Vorghas declared. "I think it's an experiment that the KGB psychologists dreamed up— a new approach to behavior modification." He leaned forward and let his voice fall a fraction. "Look around. You haven't got any of your ordinary criminals and riffraff here. These are all potentially useful people. Think of the advantages if you can find out how to rehabilitate people like these and save their skills for the state." He gestured vaguely around and overhead with the spoon he was holding. "It's the isolation. Everything is supposed to take on a new perspective from this oasis of humanity out in space—the vastness of the universe and the puniness of Man, and that kind of thing. We're supposed to come to see that we're all alike underneath and have to work together. . . ." He shrugged and resumed eating. "That's what I think, anyway." McCain listened but wasn't convinced. That might have explained the privs with their huts and beach upstairs, but what about the rest? That was a fat lot of vastness of the universe to be seen from a bottom bunk in the lower level of B-3.

"Why make a complicated issue out of it?" Smovak asked. "The Russians are a century behind the times. They're only just finding out about methods the rest of the world has been using for years, and they don't want to admit it. So they've set their experiment up nice and quietly, away from where it would get attention, so they can fold it all up and forget it without any embarrassment if they make a mess of it. That's Russians all over."

"Ah, is that so, now?" Scanlon challenged. "That's every bit as involved as what Leo said, I'm sitting here thinkin'. Why couldn't they simply be doing the same as the rest, and shipping the troublemakers as far away as they can from where they might do damage? Didn't the Brits have to send half o' themselves all over the world because there wasn't a decent one of them? I can't agree with what either of ye is saying, now. Jet planes and telephones have moved Siberia a lot closer to Moscow than it used to be, and that's all there is to it."

McCain looked down and carried on eating his stew in silence. He'd listened to the answers, and he didn't believe any of them. The curious thing was that he'd watched the people giving the answers, and he didn't think they believed them any more than he did. But they were safe answers. The simple fact was that nobody in the place trusted anybody.

Maybe that was the whole idea.

CHAPTER THIRTEEN

McCain sat at one end of the center-aisle table in the front section of the billet, contemplating the diagram that he had been sketching. On the top bunk behind him, Mungabo was admiring a new addition to his collection of lascivious pinups. Mungabo's passion for Americana—an attitude that had done little to improve his credibility with the KGB at his court-martial—it turned out, derived from his dream of the kind of life he'd seen blacks living in American porno movies, which he took to be representative of the typical New England suburban social scene.

"Hey, Lew, waddya say to this for a piece of pink-shot?" he called down dreamily. "Isn't that the horniest thing you've ever seen in your life? Did you ever make it with a chick like that back in the States?"

"All the time," McCain drawled over his shoulder. "They come as extras with the hotel rooms. Hell, I did better'n that while I was at college." Mungabo sighed and stared agonizedly at the picture. He'd never understood why the Russians wanted to take over the West if they got the chance. Now it was all starting to make much more sense.

McCain's sketch was of the system of mirrors by which sunlight illuminated the interior of the colony. It had begun with an idea that Scanlon had mentioned first in the machine shop. Scanlon had tried drawing it but didn't have enough knowledge of the details, whereas McCain had the benefit of the information he'd memorized for the mission.

The first component of the system was a large, annular, primary mirror that hung detached in space a mile away along the colony's axis, looking like an enormous version of an ophthalmoscope, which old-time eye doctors wore on their foreheads. It produced a ring-section beam of reflected sunlight—a tube, like a hollow tree-trunk—and according to the relative motions of the Earth-Moon-Sun system could be steered by thrusters to keep the beam trained down on the axis, onto the hub. Here the beam encountered a ring of plane secondary mirrors around the hub, which relayed the light radially outward to the roof of the outer torus, where an arrangement of louvered reflecting slats admitted visible light and heat, but blocked cosmic rays. The secondary mirrors could be tilted independently to illuminate or darken different parts of the torus as required.

The path that a ray of light followed was thus from the Sun to the primary mirror, from there down the axis to a secondary mirror, and after a couple more reflections in the chevron-section roof slats, down to a point somewhere on the "ground" inside. Scanlon's thought was that if a laser were aimed at the roof from the ground inside, its beam ought to trace the same optical path, but in the opposite direction. In other words, it might offer a means of communicating information out. The problem, of course, was that whoever the information was intended for would have to be looking for it, which presupposed that some other way of talking to them existed in the first place. Besides, Scanlon wasn't even sure if the idea was feasible, and McCain didn't know either. This would be more in Paula's line.

He sat back, chewing his pencil while he watched Haber and Rashazzi over by the bunk on the far side, fiddling with an improvised contraption of lenses and mirrors. They seemed to have access to an inexhaustible number of sources of components and materials for the Rube Goldberg gadgets that they made to demonstrate the incomprehensible things they talked about. Those two would know if the idea was feasible, McCain thought. But how was he to broach the subject? His instincts told him that they, if any in the billet, were clean; the problem would be convincing them that he was.

He was certain now in his own mind that Rashazzi was no biologist, although the Israeli kept cages of mice in the washroom at the back of the billet, which he told Luchenko were for breeding experiments. But on one or two occasions he had used figures of speech that were straight from the specialist jargon that McCain was used to hearing around the Pentagon—such as "eggbuster," for an X-ray battle laser tuned to vaporize the hardened shells of warhead reentry vehicles. He was pretty sure that Razz was a defense scientist of some kind.

He hadn't formed any clear impression of what Haber was. All Haber had told him was that he'd been apprehended in Moscow and accused of receiving Soviet military secrets during an exchange visit. From his varied topics of conversation, he seemed to be one of those all-rounders from the grand old classical school of scientists.

The problem was the universal mistrust. Fostering mutual suspicion among enemies and subjects was the traditional Russian way of making organized opposition all but impossible. And it was also part of the traditional Russian character to submit, which was one reason why totalitarianism had survived there for a century. But McCain was not a Russian, and it wasn't in his nature to conform to other people's ideas of how he should behave. He *needed* some way—even if just a token—of defying the system. But how? Escape, the usual outlet for such urges in this kind of situation, was surely impossible. Blind rage and destruction was hardly his style. What else was there? Whatever he came up with, he'd have to start finding out pretty soon who his friends were.

"If Americans designed a space colony, it wouldn't be like this one, would it, Lew?" Mungabo said from the bunk behind. "It wouldn't be all antiseptic."

The question caught McCain far away in his reverie. "What? . . . I don't know. What do you mean, antiseptic?"

"Look around at the towns and places. Everybody lives in nice, clean, respectable boxes, and does nice, clean, respectable jobs, and they play healthy games in the parks, and the kids sit in lines in nice schools. . . . You see, it's all the perfect picture of an academic professor's or some social-work counselor's idea of how other people oughta live. Except nobody asked the people. It's like living in a museum. . . . How can anyone have fun being a respectable social statistic?"

McCain half-turned and rested an elbow on the back of the chair. "How would you change it if it were up to you?"

"Hell, I'd add a bit of nightlife to them squeaky-clean towns they've got out there—a few bars, maybe some strip joints, the things that make *real cities* cities. Give people a chance to be honest-to-God, flesh-and-blood people, know what I mean? That's how Americans would have done it, right?"

"Maybe," McCain said. "It goes to extremes both ways, I guess."

"I remember when I was a kid growing up in Ziganda, we had this preacher came all the way from Boston to save us from hell," Mungabo said. "He told us that America was God's second chosen nation. And do you know how he figured that?"

"How?"

"He said it was a revelation because 'USA' was right there inside 'Jer*usa*lem.' Ain't that something?"

McCain blinked, looked back over his shoulder, and thought for a moment. "Was that the same God that put the ass in Massachusetts?"

Mungabo threw back his head and laughed. "Can't say I know about that. But you know, Lew, that whole business that guys like him talk about—it always struck me as the neatest con operation that anyone ever dreamed up. I mean, they're selling eternity, and your payoff in some hereafter, right? Well, that keeps 'em all pretty safe from complaints by dissatisfied customers, don't it—or from being sued because they didn't deliver? When did the last person come back and tell everyone it ain't the way they were told it is?"

"Well, I guess it's not my problem," McCain said. "It's not something I ever did buy any stock in."

Razz, Haber, Mungabo, and Scanlon were probably okay, McCain had decided. What about Koh? . . . He still wasn't sure. As proverbially impenetrable as the Chinese side of him, Koh was a philosophical observer of life—and hence of everybody and everything—with innumerable ancestors, and living relatives seemingly everywhere on Earth. Nobody knew how he had come to be in Zamork. McCain had heard some say he was an obvious plant; and others that no plant would be that obvious.

What about the rest? McCain turned in his chair and surveyed the billet. Nolan was too transparent. He had to be the decoy. So who was the real one? Luchenko, of course, was excluded from the list of potential allies. Along with Luchenko, McCain eliminated the rest of the group that seemed to form a constellation around him at the far end, which apart from Nolan and the Bulgarian Maiskevik, included Borowski, a Pole, and a morose Frenchman called Taugin.

And yet, for all that watching and listening was part of the foremen's job, McCain was discovering that they could, usually for a price, be surprisingly ready to turn a blind eye to some of the things that went on. The underground distillery trade and black market with the towns, for example, couldn't have existed without their knowing; and he'd heard of one instance where the foreman of another billet had cooperated in covering a prisoner's absence from work. Why would a foreman put his own privileges at risk when there was nothing to gain? It wouldn't make sense. So in reality it had to be a covert part of their job. If that were true, then the security precautions and detention-style discipline were to a large degree a superficiality carried out for effect—a charade to satisfy expectations. What did that mean?

"Uh-uh. Shouldn't have taken the name in vain," Mungabo's voice murmured behind him. Nolan was approaching through the next section, where Smovak and Vorghas were engrossed over a game of chess. He sat down at the end of the table a couple of places from McCain. McCain folded the papers he had been drawing on and tucked them into his jacket pocket.

"How are you finding things?" Nolan inquired casually.

"I've seen better."

"The place isn't so bad?"

"On the whole, I'll take Manhattan. You never give up, do you?"

Smovak looked up from the next table and groaned. "Oh God, you two aren't starting all that again, are you? Look, I'll tell you what the difference between capitalism and communism is. With capitalism, man exploits man; with communism it's the other way round. See? Ha-ha-ha!"

"I just want you to see that it isn't all black and white," Nolan said.

"I never said it was," McCain answered. "But I do know that where I come from, you live how you want, you go where you want, and you say what you want, without needing a permit from any commissar. And US soldiers don't shoot US citizens in the back for trying to leave the country. That mightn't be black and white to you, but it's getting pretty close for me."

"But what about the inequities, the injustice . . ."

"Unlike in the classless society? Oh sure. Everyone in Moscow drives a Cadillac?"

"Crass materialism. The cravings of greed. Can't you see that it's competition and rivalry that lead to conflict? Such things can't be permitted in today's world. We must impose harmony, which can only come through serving the collective good. Peace must be objective, at any price. If we fail in that, then everything else is lost anyway. You must agree with that."

"No objective is worth *any* price," McCain said.

"Not even preventing a global nuclear war?"

McCain shook his head. "No."

Nolan stared disbelievingly. "What price could conceivably be too high to pay for that?"

"Submitting to the kinds of things that some people have had inflicted on them in recent times," McCain said. "If it meant seeing kids being put into gas chambers by thugs, I'd rather fight and risk the consequences. If it meant having innocent people dragged from their homes to be worked to death as slave labor, I'd rather fight. If it meant giving up the right to be me, I'd rather fight." He sat back in his chair and regarded Nolan oddly for a couple of seconds. "I don't understand what it is with people like you. You come from the best-fed, best-educated, healthiest country, that gives you more opportunity than anywhere, anytime in history, and you want to tear it down. . . . Where d'you come from, out of curiosity? Want me to guess? Pretty-well-off family, was it? Was that the problem—you felt guilty because you were rich in a world where not everyone was rich?" McCain saw a flicker of discomfort cross Nolan's countenance. He nodded. "Well, you could always have made yourself feel better by giving it away. But that wasn't good enough, was it? Everybody else had to be made to give theirs away, too, so *you* could be equal." Smovak and Vorghas were watching from the next table; Rashazzi and Haber were listening, also. At that moment the door opened and Scanlon came in. He stopped when he saw them all watching McCain. McCain went on, "It was rage and envy against a world that didn't *need* people like you. You didn't have anything to offer that people wanted freely, by choice. So get rid of freedom, eh? We'll *make* them take notice of us. Pull down the system, paint everybody gray, and we can all be happy nobodies together." He got up and turned away to go back to his bunk. "Fuck you, Nolan. We'll keep our bombs. If you think you can take what we've built, come on and try. But don't try selling me a guilt trip that says it's my duty to give it away."

Nolan stood up flushed and tight-lipped, and marched toward the door without saying anything. The light above came on, the beeper beeped, and he was gone. The two scientists stared for a moment longer and returned to what they had been doing.

"Hear, hear," Smovak murmured barely above his breath, and looked back at the chess game. Mungabo was cackling delightedly in the top bunk by McCain. Scanlon moved over to his own bunk opposite and sat down. "I see ye've been getting a piece o' the indoctrination," he said to McCain.

"Doesn't he ever quit?" McCain asked.

"He's worse with the new fellas," Scanlon said. "Either he makes a friend, or he shuts up . . ." he nodded at McCain, "and sometimes somebody shuts him up. It's a little peace we'll all be having for a while now, I'm thinkin'." Scanlon watched until McCain turned his head toward him, then pulled the top of his jacket aside to reveal the top of a metal flask. He winked, and his voice fell to a whisper. "From a little still that somebody's got running in a place I won't mention. As good as poteen, but I can't vouch for how well it compares to your own mountain dew. Maybe a drop or two later, eh?"

"Sure. Is there a price?"

"Oh, let's say it's on credit. When I need a favor, I'll let you know." Scanlon scratched the side of his nose pensively. "But then again, from the tail end of what I just heard, I'd say you've already earned it."

"Well, I never argue with a guy who's buying."

Scanlon gave McCain a long, curious look, as if weighing him up. "And it's not as if that system of theirs is anything for himself to be getting so excited about."

McCain looked uncertain. "What system? You mean Nolan? The Russian system?"

"Ah, sure, and what else would I be talking about?" McCain frowned, wondering what this had to do with anything. Scanlon rolled his eyes pointedly, indicating that walls had ears.

"They don't trust anyone, either," McCain replied, nodding to show that he understood. "It's kind of a conditioned reflex. Did you know that Tolstoy's serfs didn't want him to free them when he tried? They thought it was a trick. They wouldn't have a school either. They said the only reason he wanted to educate the kids was to sell them to the czar as foot soldiers."

Scanlon shook his head solemnly. "That's terrible, now."

"I wonder what does it."

"Centuries of living under rapacious rulers," Scanlon said. "A system that did nothing to discourage exploitation."

"You mean like the Brits?"

Scanlon stared back fixedly for a moment. "Let's go for a walk outside," he suggested.

"It seems to me that you're already well on your way to understanding the way things are in Zamork, Lew," Scanlon said. "I've a feeling you're from some kind of background that hasn't exactly made you a newcomer to such things, but what it might be I'll leave as your business." They had come out through the door at the rear of the B-Block mess area into the general compound, which contained its usual evening crowd of gray-clad figures standing, walking, talking, watching. "What do you make of the place so far?"

"Strange kind of a prison," McCain answered.

"It is that. And have ye had any thoughts as to why that might be?"

McCain could see nothing to lose by being frank. "It's an information mine," he said.

"Now there's an interesting thought," Scanlon answered.

"Mines have miners in them. Also, there has to be something to dig. But in this mine it's hard to tell the difference."

For McCain's conclusion was that the whole place was set up for the gathering of sensitive information—the practice of which had always been a Russian passion. From foreign intelligence operatives like himself to Russian domestic dissidents, Zamork was full of people who knew a lot about the enemies of the regime at home and abroad, and their intentions—a priceless trove of information to be gathered. It followed that the place would also be full of others put there to do the gathering. He was unlikely to be the first to have arrived at such a conclusion, and no doubt that was why nobody trusted anybody. The theory fitted, too, with the laxness in discipline beneath the superficial pretense: the authorities *wanted* the inmates to mix, talk, and go through the motions of defying the system—and the looser their tongues became in the process, the better.

They passed a group practicing gymnastics on homemade equipment, and Scanlon steered McCain toward a gathering in the center, where an improvised choir a dozen or so strong was delivering a hearty rendering of a Romanian folk song. "Well, Mr. Earnshaw or whoever you really are, I've decided to take a chance on ye." He had to lean close to McCain and shout into his ear to be heard. McCain noticed that most of the others around them were behaving similarly and taking no notice of the singing whatever. He smiled faintly as the meaning of the choir dawned on him.

He turned his head toward Scanlon. "Why?"

"Three things ye did that stoolies don't do."

"Such as what?"

"It doesn't matter," Scanlon said. McCain thought he already knew, anyway. He hadn't posed as a transfer from elsewhere in Zamork, which would have provided a reason for being familiar with anything a new arrival wouldn't know about; he hadn't denied that he spoke Russian; and he hadn't shown any eagerness to tell a cover story and get it accepted. Scanlon went on, "And besides, I pride meself on being a sound judge of people."

"Okay, Kev, I'm glad to hear it. So what do you want?"

"To buy your soul. What else would you expect from the devil himself?"

"Who said it was for sale? In all the stories I've read, it never turns out to be a good deal."

Scanlon clapped him on the back. "Aha, always the cautious one, eh! That's good. Now, I'm thinking that there's some of us as might be able to be of a little help to ye."

"I'm interested. Go on."

"My understanding is that you've been trying to obtain certain information through the official channels via Luchenko."

"I asked him for an interview with the commandant," McCain agreed. "I brought it up the day I arrived, and again three days after that."

"And what was the result?" Scanlon asked.

"Nothing. I think they're jerking me around."

"What was it that ye wanted to know—in general, if you take my meaning? You don't have to be specific."

"I was with a colleague when I was arrested. I just want to get some news."

Scanlon nodded and watched the singers for a while, who had switched to a song that McCain recognized as the melody of part of a Brahms violin concerto. Then, as if abandoning that line of conversation suddenly, Scanlon said, "It's not that Russians are incapable, you understand. But their system doesn't give them sensible goals to aim at. They're not rewarded for being efficient. They're rewarded for achieving the Plan, even if the Plan makes no sense." He paused, and added absently, "It leads to a lot of corruption—endemic to the society, you might say. . . . A man will get nothing done without paying the right price to the right person. And then again, if you look at it the other way round, there isn't anything that can't be done, provided you know who to ask."

"If Luchenko needs greasing, he should find a way to say so," McCain said. "I don't read minds."

"Ah well, it's his way to let people stew until they get anxious. It raises the price. But then, on the other hand, maybe it isn't Luchenko that ye need to be dealing with at all." Scanlon paused, giving McCain a sidelong glance, and moved his head closer as he came to the point. "Some of us have a little understanding with one of the guard officers, who has access to central record information. I can put you in contact with him. He'll be able to find out if there's any news of your friend."

"And what will he want out of it?" McCain asked.

"What does anyone want out of anything? Money, drink, sex, a good time. A new coat for the wife, if he has one, or bikes for the kids. Asian and Western goods still fetch fabulous prices on the Soviet black market."

"Look, this may come as a surprise, but I didn't come here stocked up for a long stay. And I don't think of myself as all that pretty."

Scanlon went off on one of his apparent tangents again. "Tell me something, Lew, is it a fact that ye've been something of a Russian scholar in your time? You seem to know a lot about them."

"I majored in modern history and languages. That's not uncommon for a journalist," McCain said. Both statements were true. It was best if cover identities drew as much from reality as was practicable.

"Did you ever read Dostoyevsky?"

"Sure."

"Then ye'll have heard of the secret society of thieves who as good as ran the Russian criminal underworld back in the times of the czars. They penetrated the prison system, too, got themselves special treatment, and sometimes intimidated the authorities. Also, they had a communications network that bordered on being uncanny." McCain nodded. And as Solzhenitsyn had described a century later, they were still around and doing a thriving business long after the Revolution. Scanlon drew on McCain's sleeve and they began walking slowly across the compound, keeping their distance from the walls. "It works like this," he said. "Today it's turned into a sophisticated operation called 'the Cooperative,' and survives through having connections into all the state bureaucracies, even the KGB. And it exists here, too."

"In Zamork, you mean?"

Scanlon waved a hand vaguely. "Around *Tereshkova,* generally."

"Do we know who?"

"Not unless they want you to. But there are account numbers in the Exchange that you can voucher points to, which through processes that we needn't concern ourselves with will end up as rubles in a Moscow bank.

Through a code system, you authorize your creditor—in this case the guard officer that I mentioned—to draw it out. So whether he wants a blonde for himself or a bike for the kids, he'll find the wherewithal waiting for him when he goes back on his next Earthside leave. Then, when you finally get out, you settle your accumulated account with the Cooperative in US dollars, yuan, or yen—plus interest, naturally."

"In other words they're offering a loan service for bribing the guards."

"Exactly."

"How much does this cost?"

"Well, it's not cheap, I'll admit. But then again, we're not talking about the world's most secure line of investment either."

"Suppose a guy doesn't get out."

"Bad debts are factored into every business. So you can see why it wouldn't be cheap—the losses have to be recovered somehow."

"Suppose somebody forgets to settle up when he does get out?"

"I'd advise strongly against it."

McCain fell silent as they turned at the tripwire five feet inside the wall and began retracing their steps. With the ability to put guards, officers, and possibly even some of the senior officials in their pocket, a termite operation like that could undermine the whole system. The fact that it extended into Zamork suggested that somebody influential somewhere had been persuaded that he'd serve his own interests better by not interfering. If this typified what was going on beneath the surface everywhere, then maybe the whole Soviet Potemkin illusion was on the verge of caving in.

He thrust his hands into his pockets and considered the implications and risks. If the officer failed to deliver, all McCain would have lost would be a few points of Monopoly money, and the Cooperative would have forsaken any opportunity of doing repeat business. If he got what he wanted but rubles failed to materialize in the Moscow bank, that would be the officer's problem, not McCain's. What was Scanlon's angle on it? he wondered. The Irishman made no secret of having worked with terrorist groups, and McCain had already categorized him, beneath his superficial bonhomie and calculated loquaciousness, as capable of acting with utter ruthlessness if a situation called for it: a killer. Not somebody who was disposed to handing out favors just to be nice to people.

They came back to the group standing in front of the choir, and stopped. "So, what's in it for you?" McCain asked. "Are you on a percent of the take or something?"

Scanlon continued staring ahead impassively and shrugged. "A man has to make a living," he said. It was as much of a concession as anyone could have asked for.

McCain drew a long breath and sighed. "Okay, deal me in," he agreed. "Where do I sign?"

"Leave it with me," Scanlon told him. "You'll be hearing."

CHAPTER FOURTEEN

The next morning, four of the Siberians in the central part of the billet went on strike. Although from different nations and sects, they shared a religious taboo about pigs, and were protesting at being assigned to a work detail that involved cleaning out animal pens in one of the agricultural sectors. It was McCain's turn for cleaning the billet that day, which meant that somebody from one of the other billets would be working the shift in the machine shop with Scanlon.

Some of the cleaning materials kept in a closet in the washroom area at the rear of the billet were getting low. McCain made a list of the items he needed and picked up an empty cardboard box to take to the OI store to collect them. When he came out into the billet, the Siberians were still sitting impassively on their bunks, as they had been when he passed through. Luchenko was standing in the center space, remonstrating with them. "Let us discuss this reasonably. You be fair with me, and I'll be fair with you . . ." He directed his words mainly at a tall, clear-skinned Uzbek called Irzan, who seemed to be the strike organizer. Maiskevik, as always, was standing a few paces back, arms folded across his chest, scowling and silent.

News of the strike had spread, and when McCain emerged into the mess area he found a crowd of inmates from B-3 and other billets gathering outside the door to demonstrate their solidarity with the Siberians. A guard officer was facing them with several guards, urging them to disperse and leave the matter with the authorities. McCain left the mess area and went out onto Gorky Street. He crossed to the other side and began walking in the direction of the next corridor leading into the Core.

"Settling in?" a voice called from behind him. McCain turned and saw he was being followed by Peter Sargent, an Englishman from B-12, one of the upper-level billets. He was in his late thirties, with light hair and somewhat boyish features which he attempted to disguise, McCain suspected, with his ragged, sandy-colored mustache. McCain found him cheerful and amiable, reminiscent of some of the British he had worked with in Europe.

McCain waited for Sargent to catch up, and they resumed walking together. "I'll get used to it, I guess— even all these crazy Asian gambling games. Why doesn't someone teach 'em to play decent football or something?"

"Do you mean soccer?"

"No, our kind, you know . . . NFL, super Bowl?"

"Oh, *that!*" Sargent sniffed. "I can't imagine why you call it 'football' at all."

"How come?"

"Well, for one thing it's not a *ball*, is it? If you're going to be logical, it ought to be foot-prolate-spheroid. And then, why 'foot,' when they spend most of their time running around throwing it?"

"What part of England are you from?"

"Cheltenham, over towards the west. Ever been there?"

"Not to that part. I was in England a couple of times, though. I like the cities that you can still walk around in. Too many of ours got turned into airports with streets on them."

"You have to walk," Sargent said. "It's the only bloody way to move."

Just then, they heard the sound of feet crashing in unison and growing louder, and a moment later a squad of guards led by a captain and moving at the double appeared from around the corner and passed, heading in the opposite direction. McCain turned his head and stared after them uneasily. "Something's up somewhere," Sargent said. Obviously he had been elsewhere and wasn't aware of the latest developments in B Block. McCain spent a few minutes updating him, then left Sargent at the intersection and followed the corridor from Gorky Street into the Core.

He made his way past several workshops and the laundry to the OI store, where he passed his box over the issue counter along with the list he'd compiled. Two women were there also. McCain realized that they were watching him intently while he waited. After a while he turned his head and acknowledged them with a quick upturn of his mouth. "Hi."

The taller of the two, who had black hair tied high, looked him up and down with shameless approval. Her face wasn't bad looking, but it had a hardened edge to it. "I haven't seen you around."

"Do you know everybody?"

"No, but I remember faces."

"What accent is that?" the other one asked. She was dumpy, with a rounded face, snub nose, and reddish hair. They both sounded Russian.

"American."

"An American!" The tall one looked impressed. "That's a rarity. We don't see many of them. You are new here, yes?"

"Fairly."

She pouted and stretched out a finger to toy suggestively with the top button of McCain's shirt. "Are you making many friends—I mean *close* friends? There are ways, you know. Interested?"

"Who knows? How do I call? They haven't installed my phone yet," he said. The small, dumpy woman giggled.

The taller one gestured across the counter as a mountain of a woman dumped McCain's box down on the counter. "Just leave a message with Hannah anytime. Only fifty points on the Exchange. For eighty you can have two girls and a really good time."

"I'll think about it."

"What do we call you?"

"Lew. But for now, I gotta go."

"Lew. I'll remember. I'm Zena."

McCain walked away carrying his box and wondering what the West imagined it could teach the Russians about the profit motive.

When he got back, it was obvious that there had been trouble. The prisoners in the mess area were standing back behind a cordon of guards with weapons at ready, and in the cleared area around the door of B-3 more guards were hauling out three of the Siberians. Luchenko was to one side of the door, gesticulating to the guard captain and Major Bachayvin, the block commandant. As McCain drew nearer, Maiskevik appeared in the billet doorway. He paused to send a strangely challenging look out across the faces of the prisoners watching from a distance, then moved over to Luchenko. Seconds later, four more guards came out, supporting the sagging form of Irzan between them. His mouth was puffed and swollen on one side, his face bruised, and there was blood on his chin and down the front of his shirt and jacket. It seemed the strike was over.

A squad of guards formed around the four Siberians. The captain rejoined them, and the group began moving toward the exit out onto Gorky Street. Major Bachayvin remained behind with two aides and the rest of the guards.

"Well, what are you all staring at?" he said to the watching prisoners. "The mess area of this block is to be cleared, and movement outside restricted for the rest of today. Everyone will return to their billets immediately." Murmuring angrily among themselves, the prisoners dispersed under the threatening muzzles of the guards' weapons, after which the guards closed the barred gate onto Gorky Street that McCain had just returned through.

McCain went into B-3 and found Smovak, Borowski, and another Asiatic Siberian, whose name was unpronounceable and whom everyone referred to as Charlie Chan, straightening out the furniture in the center section of the billet. Evidently McCain's first cleaning day wasn't going to bring him much of the solitude and contemplation that Koh valued so highly. He went on through to the washroom at the back and found a pool of blood on the floor, with stains on the back of the door and down one wall. Rashazzi's mice scrabbled about in their cage indifferent to it all. He stood looking at the pattern and could almost reconstruct the events. Had the guards delayed coming into the billet until Maiskevik had finished with Irzan, or had they left the two of them alone for a few minutes after they took the other three Siberians out? McCain wondered. He was still staring at the scene when the door opened wider and Luchenko looked in and gazed around casually with no show of surprise. Then he looked at McCain curiously with his expressionless moon-face. "You'd better get busy," he suggested.

Scanlon came back with the rest when it was time for the midday meal. With the Gorky Street gate closed, guards posted there to admit only B-Block inmates, and the mess area cleared except for those eating, he didn't have to be told what had happened. "So that's how the system works, eh?" McCain said. "I see now where Maiskevik fits in."

"He's a nasty piece of work, right enough," Scanlon agreed He looked at McCain curiously. "Do you think you can handle him?"

"Why should I think about that?"

"Because you're going to have to, if you're to do what you're wanting to," Scanlon said. McCain forced a questioning frown, but Scanlon's insight was so close to the mark that he didn't reply. There was nobody else nearby and Scanlon went on, "I don't know exactly what kind of mischief it is ye've in mind, but there's something. And you're fly enough to know that there isn't a lot that a man can do on his own. The rest o' the fellas in here are all waiting for the right man, and the man they'll follow will be the first who can take the Bulgarian. It might not be exactly what you'd call sensible, but it's the way the world is, and the way that everyone kings to scoundrels has always had to deal with it—as if there was any difference."

McCain reflected on the prospect. He was fairly sure he'd never take Maiskevik in an even fight if it came to that. . . . But on the other hand, he wasn't from a school that had placed too much stress on fair play and giving the other guy an even break, either.

The next day, back in the machine shop, Scanlon told McCain to go to the library on the upper level in the Core later that evening, and to open an interactive file at one of the reference computer terminals under the label ARCHITECTURE, BYZANTINE. Scanlon also conveyed the hardly illuminating, and high questionable observation that "Cabbages dance in Kamchatka."

"What the hell's that supposed to mean?" McCain asked him.

"Just remember it."

McCain did as instructed, and at 19:10 hours that evening was seated before one of the reference screens in the library, when without warning the text he had been reading vanished, and in its place there appeared the question, *Where do cabbages dance?*

McCain entered in reply, *Kamchatka.*

The screen cleared, and then presented, *Understand you are in need of certain information. Can possibly assist. Require details.*

McCain composed a brief message explaining about Paula Shelmer and asking for news. The screen cleared once more, and the invisible correspondent stated a price. McCain rejected it. *Must appreciate market realities,* the screen advised, and repeated its offer. Again McCain refused. They haggled, and eventually struck a deal. McCain was told he would hear more in the next day or two, and then he was staring at his original material again, with no trace that the conversation had ever taken place.

He calculated on the basis of the going conversion rates of points into rubles and rubles into dollars that the exercise had cost him almost a quarter of a day's worth of his Washington salary. He dreaded to think what the total might be by the time he got out if much more of this went on. If UDIA's Accounts Section didn't accept it as legitimate, reimbursable business expense, he reflected, he'd be in real trouble.

CHAPTER FIFTEEN

The road surface was loose and gravelly because of the repairs in progress, and there was a break in the line of traffic going the other way. A short distance behind, the black KGB Chevrolet had been stopped by a delivery van pulling out ahead of it. And there were no police cars around.

"Watch this," Bernard Foleda said. He accelerated suddenly when the oncoming gap was just ahead, then braked and spun the wheel to send the car slewing round in a one-hundred-eighty-degree turn to point back the way it had come. He throttled off for a moment to regain grip, then accelerated again and slipped smoothly into the stream, heedless of the indignant toots and blares from the startled drivers behind, and sending a cheerful wave at the faces staring helplessly from the stranded Chevrolet.

"Bernard, what in God's name are you doing?" Barbara asked in amazement from the seat next to him.

"Keeping my hand in. It's nice to know you can still do it." Foleda lifted a hand from the wheel to make a throwing-away gesture. "Anyhow, every once in a while I get tired of it. It can get to you—having those creeps behind you everywhere you go."

"Do you do this kind of thing when Myra's with you, too?"

"Would you believe me if I told you that she showed me how to do it?"

Barbara gave him a curious look. "You know, I would. Why, is it true?"

"Yes. Her brother used to do stunts for movies when she was a kid."

"Didn't they cover it when you took field training?"

"Oh sure, but Myra's way is better."

They left the road to cut across the parking lot of a shopping mall, and exited into a lane at the back. "Are we still going to make it on time?" Barbara asked, glancing at the clock in the dashboard.

"Probably sooner than we would have it we'd gone the other way, from the look of how they had that road dug up," Foleda said. "This leads to another route to Langley. It's worth knowing." They were in route for the CIA's headquarters. A man by the name of Robert Litherland had called from there to say that the CIA had picked up something that would be of interest to Foleda's department, but didn't elect to go into further detail. However, since Gerald Kehrn from Defense was also going to be there, Foleda guessed it had something to do with *Tereshkova*.

"Anyhow," Barbara prompted, "before this sudden urge seized you to recapture lost youth, you were saying . . ."

"Oh yes, about Lew McCain and the Air Force woman. The impression I got when Uncle Phil and I talked to Volst was that State and the Soviets are playing a cat-and-mouse game over the whole thing. It took us long enough to even come clean and admit we're missing two people. We want communications contact, and until the Soviets give it to us, our people will only refer to the cover identities.

But the Soviets are rejecting that as ludicrous. They want the real names and positions, and an admission that it was all official and we goofed."

"But they're not going public?"

"Not so far, anyway. That's something they can afford to keep in reserve. Meanwhile, we don't know what's happening with our two people. We don't even know for sure where they are."

Barbara sighed and stared out at the procession of well-kept, older-style clapboard homes with screened porches, bright-painted shutters, and glimpses of lawns sheltered in privacy behind barricades of flowering shrubbery. "Lew can take care of himself, I don't doubt," she said distantly after a while. "I feel more for that Air Force woman, Bryce. It's a sorry way to wind up when all she wanted was a little adventure." Foleda grunted—either noncommittally or in sympathy; it was difficult to tell. Barbara looked across at him. "What kind of a person is she? Did you find out much when you talked to Colonel Raymond up at Hanscom?"

"Some. She's from a family with something of a military tradition, mainly Navy. Born over in Tacoma, Washington State. Her father was an engineering officer on nuclear subs, and her mother was a Navy brat, too—raised around bases from Scotland to Japan even before she married Bryce's father. So the mother was used to getting along without a man around. Raymond figures that was what gave Bryce her stubborn streak."

"Stubborn, eh? That might not be too bad a thing in this situation."

"Maybe so, maybe not," Foleda said. "Raymond and I couldn't make our minds up. Apparently she's good as a scientist, but defensive about it to the verge of fanaticism—you know, the ethical purity of science, objectivity, honesty, that kind of stuff."

"Uh-huh. So?"

"It makes her more than a little disdainful toward things like politics and the reasons why this kind of job needs

to be done. Raymond says it can make her difficult enough
to work with sometimes, even when she's on the same
side. In other words, she won't take easily to the idea of
knuckling under to people she feels inwardly are her
intellectual inferiors. That sounds like good news. But
if she came up against an interrogator from the same
mold, and it turned into a battle of will, it could backfire.
Let's just hope it isn't getting her a harder time than is
necessary."

The story at the CIA was that a prominent Russian
scientist, director of a major research and communications
establishment, wanted to defect. He had approached an
American called Melvin Bowers at a scientific conference
in Japan, and Bowers had initially contacted the embassy
in Tokyo. Now Bowers was back in the US.

Foleda sat back and tapped absently at his tooth with
a thumbnail while he stared at the map of the Soviet Union
being presented on a wallscreen. His brow creased beneath
his wiry, short-cropped hair. "Where's this place, again?"
he asked after a thoughtful silence.

Gerald Kehrn operated a control on a panel inset below
the edge of the table. For once, to Foleda's relief, he was
managing to keep reasonably still this morning. On the
map, a light-cursor moved to seek out a point located in
the Vilyuisk Mountain region, in a desolate part of Siberia
between the Olenek and Lena rivers. A moment later,
one of the auxiliary screens beside the main one showed
an enlarged satellite picture of a fenced-in cluster of
buildings and other constructions scattered among a forest
of communications antennas. A pattern of rectangular
buildings arrayed in monotonous, barrack-like lines was
partly visible outside the fence on one side, while an open
expanse of wet-looking terrain broken by patches of scrub
and an occasional tree rose toward a ridge of hills on the
other.

"It's called Sokhotsk," Kehrn said. "Located on the Central
Siberian Plateau about two hundred miles southwest of a

city called Zhigansk. We know it's a major node in the Soviet military- and emergency-communications network; also, it's one of their primary space-operations groundlink stations."

Litherland, a solidly built CIA man in his late thirties, with collar-length blond hair and broad, linebacker shoulders, was sprawled casually in his chair in the center in a way that contrasted with Kehrn's tense, upright posture. He tossed up a hand loosely to interject, "There's more going on at that place than we've figured—something very big and very classified. That's why Cabman could be extremely useful." In the eternal double-talk that pervaded the intelligence world, "Cabman" was the code name that had been given to Professor Dyashkin.

"Is that the nearest town—the one two hundred miles away?" Foleda asked, still studying the display.

"There's a small industrial town called Nizhni Zaliski about ten miles north," Kehrn replied. "About five thousand people. But it doesn't have much connection with Sokhotsk. It was built for the workers of a new mining and construction project over the mountains from Sokhotsk."

"How far from Sokhotsk is this project?"

"Aw, six to ten miles, I'd guess." Kehrn glanced at Litherland. Litherland confirmed with a nod.

"Over the mountains," Foleda said.

"Yes." Kehrn looked puzzled. "Is it important?"

Foleda shrugged. "Who knows? Just trying to get the picture." He looked at Barbara. "Did you have any other points, Barb?"

She glanced at her notes. "Is Bowers okay?"

"Yes, how about this Professor Bowers from California?" Foleda asked. "Are we happy he's clean?"

Litherland nodded. "First-rate record. He's had top clearance for government work for six years. Stable, married, no personal problems, and a history of everything okay in the family. We're running a check on anything that may have changed since his last review."

"Is he available if we need to talk to him?" Foleda asked.

"He's staying in the area, for the time being," Litherland confirmed. "Fifteen minutes from here."

Foleda nodded, satisfied. He glanced first at Kehrn, then at Barbara for possible further questions or comments, then looked back at Litherland. "Okay. So, Robert, what can you tell us about Comrade Professor Igor Lukich Dyashkin, alias Cabman?"

Litherland called a databank record onto the tabletop screenpad that everyone had before them. A heading CABMAN: SUMMARY PERSONAL PROFILE appeared at the top, and below the name. Underneath, a picture appeared in the upper left corner of a man in his late forties, fresh-faced with a straight mouth, candid stare, and boyishly cut hair parted conventionally on the left. Beside the picture was a summary of height, weight, and other personal statistics. After a couple of seconds, a synthetic voice began reciting details of Dyashkin's history, which appeared as text in the space below, line by lie, as each was narrated.

Born April 6, 1964, Tula, USSR.

Father: Anton Konstantinovitch, b. Leningrad, 1935, production engineer.

Mother: Natasha Pavlovich, nee Sepirov, b. Odessa, 1939, civil servant.

1973 Moved with family to Orel.

1979 Joined Komsomol, Young Communist League, @ high school.

1982 Admitted Kharkov University. Graduated 1987, electrical/electronic engineering.

1987-1994 Soviet Navy. Two years postgraduate studies, Naval Technical Institute, Leningrad. One year posting to satellite tracking station, Archangel. Two years Pacific Fleet communications, based Vladivostok. Discharged with honor, second lieutenant.

1994 Naval Underwater Research laboratory, Sevastopol, work on submarine communications.

> *Awarded doctorate in communications systems, 1996.*
>
> 2003 *Married Anita Leonidovich Penkev, administrator with Aeroflot. Marriage subsequently dissolved, 2011.*
>
> 2005 *Professor of Communications Engineering, Moscow State University. Also, permanent consultant to Ministry of Space Sciences on strategic military command networks. Admitted to Soviet Academy of Sciences, 2010.*
>
> 2015 *to present, Director of Operations at Sokhotsk facility.*

Foleda continued studying the text for a while after the voice had stopped speaking. Then he looked up and gazed at the far wall. "Seems pretty solid," he murmured. "Do we have any leads on why he might want to come over?"

"We're not sure," Litherland said frankly. "He does have something of a reputation as a ladies' man—it seems that screwing around too much was what got him divorced. He could have upset some of the prudes among the high-ups—but that hardly sufficient. Obviously it's something to go into when we start talking to him."

"Yes, exactly," Barbara said, as if she had been waiting for them to get to that. "How are we going to do that? Where is he now?"

"Back in Siberia, as far as we know," Litherland said.

"So, how do we talk to him?" Foleda asked.

Kehrn answered. "That was part of what was inside the folder that he slipped to Melvin Bowers in Japan. It contained a number code that he's proposing to use to communicate to us directly, via the NSA system."

"You mean straight into our communications net?" Barbara checked. "None of the usual things like drops for our embassy in Moscow?"

"He's three thousand miles away from Moscow," Kehrn reminded her. "And besides, what does he need melodrama methods for? He's got a billion rubles' worth of some of the most sophisticated communications equipment in the world sitting right there."

"Okay . . . so how is he proposing to use it?" Foleda was beginning to look uncomfortable.

"He's in a position to initiate all kinds of transmissions worldwide that NSA listens in on all the time," Kehrn said, shrugging. "Now that we know what code he's proposing to use, we just wait for anything that comes in addressed to us."

"And can we reply the same way?" Barbara asked.

"Sure, why not?"

"How hard is this code of his?" Foleda asked.

"Grade-school," Kehrn admitted. "He's a professor, not a spy."

"So we know their codebreakers will read it."

"So, they fish it out of the air," Kehrn agreed. "But even if they know what we say, it doesn't follow that they understand what it means. And on top of that, they won't have any way of knowing who we're saying it to."

Foleda looked more uncomfortable. "It's another technical gimmick," he said. "We've seen enough already. First we had a 'foolproof' way of getting the Tangerine file down from Mermaid. But we never got any file, and Magician wound up in Lubyanka prison. Then we sent two people up after it with another gizmo that was the wonder of the age. We still don't have the file, they never came back, and this time we don't even know where they are. Now you want me to buy into this."

Kehrn tugged at his mustache, then leaped to his feet and paced across the floor. He turned in front of the large screen still showing the map. "But this time, believe me, Bernard, it really is different," he insisted. "I've been through the details personally, and I'm satisfied. This time we don't have to send anyone anywhere. All the guy wants to do is talk. We just listen. And when we want to say something back, all we have to do is squirt it out through one of the computers at Fort Meade on a regular beam that we transmit all the time, anyway. All the risks are on the other side this time."

"It sounds like too many things I've listened to before," Foleda answered.

"But Cabman's out where the reindeer are, in the middle of Siberia," Kehrn said. "What else are we supposed do?"

"Hmph." Foleda began tapping his tooth again, and stared moodily at the pad in front of him, studying the face of Dyashkin once more and then shifting his gaze back to the satellite picture of the Sokhotsk groundstation. Finally he looked away again and asked Litherland, "Why are you people involving UDIA, anyway? This kind of thing is routine for the CIA. You must figure we have some stake in it."

Kehrn moved forward from the screen and rubbed his palms together agitatedly. "You're right. Where it involves UDIA, Bernard, is that Sokhotsk is the groundstation that handles the main communications beam up to Mermaid, where our two people might still be."

Litherland added, "And if Cabman is looking for favors, he'll be expecting us to ask for some evidence that he's genuine. Maybe we can persuade him to try and find out something about what happened to your people. It seems worth a shot."

Foleda was looking more interested already. "So what's this?" he said. "The CIA handing out freebies?"

Litherland returned a faint grin. "I guess we've decided that maybe we're on the same side after all," he said.

Foleda looked at Barbara. She inclined her head in a way that said she couldn't find any snags. "Okay," he announced resignedly. "Let's suppose I'm sold. But it's obvious that Cabman can only serve our purpose for as long as he stays at Sokhotsk. Therefore we should react encouragingly, but keep stalling him."

"That's what we were hoping you'd say." Kehrn came back to his chair and sat down.

Litherland nodded. "Fine."

"Callous, calculated exploitation of another human being," Barbara remarked.

"It's that kind of business, Barb," Foleda agreed with a sigh.

CHAPTER SIXTEEN

Back in the days when she was an engineering student, Paula Bryce had had a poster among the pictures, astronomical charts, and assorted samples of encapsulated philosophy cluttering the wall of her apartment, which read:

He who knows not, and knows not that he knows
  not, is a fool. Avoid him.
He who knows not, and knows that he knows not,
  is ignorant. Teach him.
He who knows, and knows not that he knows, is
  asleep. Waken him.
But he who knows, and knows that he knows, is
  a wise man. Follow him.

At the bottom, in a fit of exasperation one day, she had scrawled, *He who knows not whether he knows or knows not anything at all is a politician. Get rid of him!* Paula had never been exactly enamored with politics.

After growing up in a Navy family with an independent-minded mother whom she admired, she had found most of the girls she met in her teenage years silly and boring, and the boys either crude and immature or despairingly wimpish, rarely somewhere in between. So she tended to spend her time in solitary occupations, usually at a computer keyboard or behind a book. She read Ayn Rand, Kant, and Nietzsche when she was in a serious mood, hard science-fiction to relax, and books that debunked UFO's, psychic powers, quack medical fads, ancient astronauts, and the like, for amusement. She experimented with drugs, which she didn't like, alcohol, which was okay, and sex, which was great. In her studies she found the challenge and rigor of the sciences stimulating, but kept liberal arts and the humanities to a minimum; they struck her as wishy-washy, too subjective in their conventional wisdoms, and they invariably attracted in droves precisely the kinds of people she couldn't stand.

On one occasion during the campus period of her life, she found herself representing the opposition to a group of sociology students who claimed to have obtained positive results in a series of ESP card-guessing tests, which they challenged the science fraternity to debate. Paula showed how a comparable score could be derived by matching the results to a selected portion of a random-number string, thus proving once again to the world that sometimes people have lucky streaks, sometimes unlucky, and most of the time they muddle along somewhere in between. The revelation would not have surprised any experienced gambler, but her efforts made little impression on the judges and the editors of the college magazine, who awarded the verdict to the paranormalists on the grounds that "the influence of ESP has not been disproved." And neither had the existence of Santa Claus ever been disproved, Paula pointed out in disgust, but to no avail.

Deciding on a career in science or engineering but unable to face the prospect of more years in academia, she followed the family tradition by opting for the services, and joined the Air Force in 2000 at age eighteen. After basic training she entered the USAF electronics school at Keesler AFB, Missouri, qualified there for a grant scholarship, transferred to Communications Command, and went on to complete her doctorate under Air Force sponsorship at the University of Chicago. After that she moved to the Pentagon to work on the performance evaluation of special-purpose military hardware, which involved stints at NASA, Goddard, and the USAF research center at Langley. Life settled down to a fairly humdrum routine in these years, and she relieved the boredom through a protracted affair that she rather enjoyed with a married officer twenty years her senior, called Mike.

He was the kind of nonconformist who attracted her, and had earned his promotions through competence rather than the kind of social image-building that was typical in any nation's peacetime officer corps. But after two years Mike was posted to the Mediterranean, and for a change of scene Paula applied for a posting to Systems Command. She was accepted, and eventually became a specialist in analyzing purloined Russian and East European hardware.

In all this time her disdain for politics and economics persisted. In her view, for anybody with the brains to see it, breeder reactors and fusion, spaceflight, computers, and genetic engineering had laid Thomas Malthus firmly to rest. There was no longer any necessary reason for people anywhere to starve, or anything logical for them to continue fighting each other over. In fact, wars squandered the resources that could have solved the problems that the wars were supposed to be about. Scientists had been saying for over fifty years that there was plenty of energy and everything else, that the planet wasn't overcrowded and would never come close, and that modern-day lifestyles were incomparably healthier, safer, more prosperous, and more varied in opportunities than "natural" living had ever been. But nobody told the public. It wasn't news, and what the media didn't talk about didn't exist. Politicians couldn't see it, or perhaps they pretended not to because it wasn't the kind of talk that generated fears and attracted funding, and in the course of it all they had created the cultural pessimism that was handing the twenty-first century to Asia. That labeled them in Paula's book as just about the worst class of people to be running the world.

And ineptitude seemed to be just as much a mark of whoever was responsible for running the place she was in now, she thought wearily as she sat with her back to the wall on the thinly padded cot and surveyed the austere cell that she'd been cooped up in for she didn't know how long. The single unshaded bulb in the ceiling was turned down sometimes but was never out, the intervals varying erratically so that she had lost all track of time.

They had moved her here from a double cell, where the series of cellmates who had come and gone had been so transparently planted that, on the one occasion since her capture, she had actually laughed out loud. If that was an example of the Russian fiendishness that had kept the West paralyzed for a century, then the West deserved to be eclipsed by Asia, she concluded.

First there had been Hilda, the East German, with her smile, blond fringe, and baby-doll blue eyes. "I am your friend. It is a mistake that I am here in this place. I know some important people outside, and I can help you after I am released. But first I must know more about you. What is your name? Where are you from? . . ."

Then there had been Luba, supposedly arrested for spreading subversive propaganda among students in Rostov. Her line had been scare tactics: "They tell the world that they've changed their ways, but they haven't. Nothing has changed. They're still as bad. They will keep you from sleeping for a week or more, leave you for days in a cell below freezing, and starve you until you can't stand up. By the time you meet your own people again there will be no marks. But you'll tell them what they want to know eventually. I like you. I don't like to think of you doing something like that to yourself. Why not make it easy?"

But the effect had been the opposite of that intended. Paula's initial fear had given way to a resolve that stemmed from a growing feeling of contempt. As the interminable interrogations went on without change of tune, and the facade had peeled away from Protbornov and his troupe to reveal them as played-out actors in roles that had become mechanical and stylized. The monotony was not, after all, a deliberate ploy to wear her down, as she'd first thought. In fact it wasn't anything clever at all. She had vague, incoherent recollections of her interrogators rambling on about religion, social sciences, things that had nothing to do with the present situation—anything to take up time, it seemed. The simple fact was that they had nothing else to say, nowhere left to go, and they were waiting for somebody else to figure out what to do.

She leaned forward on the cot to pull the blanket up around her shoulders and tuck the edges under her knees. That was another thing: the room was always either too chilly or too hot, but never comfortable. She snorted beneath her breath. Was this really a measure of the opposition she was up against? If so, it wasn't just mediocre, but infantile. People could do themselves a disservice by overestimating their opponents, she reflected. Maybe the West had been doing just that for a hundred years.

During the days, weeks, months—however long she'd been shut up—she had occupied herself by going through old debates again in her head. She remembered reading tales of calculating prodigies, and tried devising methods for performing calculations rapidly in her head. There had been a woman in India who could mentally multiply two thirteen-digit numbers in the astounding time of twenty-eight seconds. Paula found the best way was to work from left to right, adding the part sums progressively, rather than from right to left as taught in schools. She wondered if schools taught it that way because it used less paper. She had passed the time playing word games in her head (how many palindromes could she think of?), compiling lists of useless facts (how many place-names start with G?), playing with scientific speculations (what would the world look like if Planck's constant were a millions times larger?), and reminiscing over events in her life.

From the time she had spent in Massachusetts, she remembered warm summer Saturday evenings in the waterfront marketplace of downtown Boston, where she went with her occasional dates to walk among the crowds and the sidewalk restaurants, maybe visiting a bar or two before deciding where to have dinner. The hearty locker-room types who made opening gambits by cracking off-color jokes had never lasted long. The ones with something worthwhile to say, and an interest in what she thought, did better. Earnshaw had refused to oblige by fitting into any of her categories. She often wondered what had happened to him since the first of May. Perhaps he was no longer even on *Tereshkova*.

The sound of the door being unlocked interrupted her thoughts. It swung inward, and a blank-faced guard with Oriental features stepped through while a second waited outside. "You come now." Paula sighed, pulled the blanket aside, and stood up. She did her best to smooth her crumpled shirt and slacks, and instinctively brushed the ever-recalcitrant curl of hair from her forehead. The guard moved a step nearer and reached out as if to jostle her elbow to hurry her. She moved her arm out of the way and glared. The guard hesitated, then stood aside. Paula walked by him, out into the familiar corridor of gray walls and numbered doors.

They went up a flight of stairs, around a corner, and along another corridor to a narrow hallway with benches by the walls on either side. The doorway into the room that General Protbornov used was open, and Paula could see him already seated behind the desk inside, smoking a cigarette. The guard who had been leading motioned her forward, but before she had moved more than a step a telephone rang inside the room, and another officer appeared in the doorway with his hand raised for her to wait. He closed the door, and Paula drew back. The two guards had reverted to zombie mode and were standing a few yards away, one in each direction along the hall, apparently without much idea of what was supposed to happen next. She sat down on one of the benches to see what they would do. They didn't do anything.

Then she became aware of a commotion of raised voices coming from behind one of the other doors. She looked up curiously, and as she did so the door opened partly and a Russian lieutenant started to come out. A woman's voice called from behind him, unmistakably sarcastic in tone, but Paula could catch only a few of the phrases since her Russian was not fluent. "That's right, run and call a guard . . . afraid I'll bite? . . . and *we* expect *you* to protect us!"

"Please sit down," another man's voice pleaded from inside.

The lieutenant turned to talk back into the room. "Look, you said you wanted to talk to somebody with the appropriate qualifications. Well, I'm going to fetch somebody now, all right? As you say, we do not have the qualifications."

"You don't have the sense, you mean," the woman's voice retorted. "What do you take me for, a common criminal or something—a pickpocket or a whore? Look, I am a senior scientist from Novosibirsk." Paula raised her eyebrows. Novosibirsk was one of the major Soviet scientific centers, especially for advanced physics. "Does that mean anything to either of you? I have been brought here because of political protest, which I claim is my right, and I object to the way this is being dealt with. I demand to speak to whoever is in charge of this entire establishment. Don't you realize this could get you shipped back to Earth and ten years in a camp?"

"Be patient, if you are capable. I will seek instructions." The lieutenant turned back from the doorway into the hall. The two guards straightened themselves up. "It's all right, at ease," the lieutenant muttered. "See that the bitch in there doesn't leave." He saw Paula sitting on the bench. "Oh God, another one." She watched him walk away along the corridor, shaking his head.

The lieutenant had left the door open, and through it Paula could hear the voice of the other man who had spoken earlier. "Yes, this is Colonel Tulenshev. I want to know if Sergei Gennadevitch is there. Have you seen him recently? . . . We have a small problem here. See if you can find him and put him on the line, would you? . . . No, it's not serious, but I would like . . ."

Then Paula realized that the woman who had been doing the shouting was standing in the doorway. She looked at Paula for a moment, and then, tossing an indifferent glance at the two guards, came out and sat down next to her on the bench. The guards had been told not to let her leave.

She wasn't leaving. So they remained where they were and didn't intervene.

The woman was somewhere in her mid-forties, Paula guessed. She had fiery hair, almost orange, tumbling to her shoulders in waves, a firm face with high cheeks, a sharply defined brown, an outthrust determined chin, and clear, unwavering eyes. Her body was full and rounded beneath a tan sweater and brown skirt, and her breasts heaved visibly as she recovered her breath. She studied Paula's face for a few seconds, then muttered something quickly in Russian. Although Paula didn't catch the words, the tone was sympathetic and curious. A wave of eagerness surged up involuntarily inside Paula, something from deep down, reaching instinctively for the promise of a first true contact with another human being since the day she and Earnshaw were captured. She shook her head and explained that she was a foreigner and hadn't understood.

The woman stared at her. "*Anglicanka?*"

Paula shook her head again. "*Nyet. Amerikanka.*"

"Ah." The woman nodded slowly and spoke in English, keeping her voice to little more than a whisper. "I heard a rumor of two American spies being arrested a while ago. You were one of them?" Paula shrugged and said nothing. The woman smiled faintly. She leaned closer and rested a hand lightly but reassuringly on Paula's arm. "Listen to someone who knows them. They will try to frighten you. Don't let them—it's just bluff. Stalin has been gone a long time. The fossils in charge of things today are not made of the same stuff. Their whole rotten system is about to fall apart, and they know it. Face up to them. Admit nothing. When they see they can get nowhere, they will give up."

Before Paula could reply, the colonel who had been speaking on the telephone inside came out. "What is this?" he thundered at the two guards. "The American woman is under solitary detention. She is not permitted to talk with anyone! Anyone!—Is that clear!" He looked at the Russian woman. "And you, high and mighty as you may think you are, you have not been dismissed to go walking about the building. The general is on his way here now." He held open the door. The Russian woman rose and went back in, carrying herself proudly and without haste. Just before she disappeared, she turned her head and sent Paula a faint nod of reassurance, as if to stress her words. It had been just a matter of seconds, but, maybe because she needed to so desperately, when Protbornov finally called her into the other room, Paula felt as if some part of the indomitable strength that the Russian woman seemed to radiate had rubbed off on her. She admitted nothing. They threatened; she defied them. It was the same the next time, and the next.

And finally, as the Russian woman had predicted, the interrogators gave up. They informed Paula one day that she would be going elsewhere, pending further directions from Moscow. She was to be moved, they told her, to a place called Zamork.

CHAPTER SEVENTEEN

With smoke billowing around them from a German tank burning in the street below, two Red Army infantrymen with tommy guns slung across their backs clambered to the rooftop of the shell-scarred Reichstag building in Berlin and unfurled a Soviet flag. The theme music rose to a triumphant crescendo, and the camera closed in on the hammer-and-sickle emblem flying proudly on red against a background of three Stormoviks crossing the sky in formation.

Applause spattered from the more appreciative among the audience as the lights brightened. The Saturday night movie in B-Block mess area was over. It had been about a Russian James Bond figure from the days of the "Great Patriotic War," called Stirlitz, who infiltrated the Nazi SS and sabotaged an attempt by Heinrich Himmler and Allen Dulles, then the head of American intelligence in

Europe, to make a separate peace in the West in early 1945. Such an arrangement would have allowed the Nazis to concentrate their remaining forces against the Soviet Union—and after Hitler was removed, the film implied, would have prepared the way for the Americans, British, and Germans to join forces against Russia in a typically treacherous bid to protect their capitalist interests.

The rows in front of the screen dissolved into groups of prisoners dispersing to carry their chairs back to their various billets, and the guards who had been watching from the back returned to their duties. McCain was walking alongside Peter Sargent, when Oskar Smovak caught up with them. "So, there you are," Smovak told them. "Now you've seen it for yourselves—how Stirlitz saved us from you scheming Americans and British. We don't know how much we have to thank our leaders and the Party for, eh?" McCain never knew whether or not to take Smovak seriously. Stirlitz was obviously fictitious, and the story as depicted bore only a remote connection to the events that had actually taken place.

"You don't really believe all that, do you?" Sargent said incredulously. From their conversations, McCain had come to suspect that he was connected with Western intelligence, too.

"Stirlitz has become legendary among the Russians," Smovak said. "A lot of them accept him as real, without any question."

"Yes, and everything else that it said, by association," Sargent replied.

"How do you know it wasn't so?" Smovak challenged. "The Russians get their brand of bullshit. You get your own bullshit. How do you know which is right. How do you know any of it is?"

"When the Moscow Film Studio can make a movie that doesn't have to be passed by Party censors before you can see it, then come and talk about it," Sargent said. He upended the chair he was carrying and turned toward the stairway leading to the upper level. The others continued walking to the door of B-3 and entered the billet to a frenzied accompaniment of red flashes and beeps. In the mess area behind them, a deeper note sounded from a klaxon to signal five minutes to go before in-billets—the time for the mess area to be cleared and everyone inside. Lights-out would be one hour later. There was little of the roll-calling that had characterized earlier prison environments. Counting and checking that people were in the right places was performed automatically by remote computers monitoring the electronic bracelets that everyone wore.

Inside the billet, Koh, propped upright at the end of his bunk with an open book, watched silently as the moviegoers trooped in. Rashazzi and Haber were taking turns to scribble on symbol-packed papers littering the front table. "Now we need a way of relating v-prime to theta, and eliminating x-bar," Rashazzi was saying.

"Use the expression for the work integral," Haber suggested, rummaging. "Where was it? . . . Yes, here."

"Why don't you two learn a language that other people can understand?" Smovak grumbled as he passed behind them.

"Perhaps we like it better if they can't," Haber said pointedly. Smovak raised his eyebrows and moved on.

Mungabo climbed up onto his bunk above McCain's and clasped his hands behind his head as he lay back to stare at the ceiling. "There's never any ass in them Russian movies," he complained. "Nobody cares about all that political shit, and some of the action was okay . . . but there's never any ass." Luchenko moved past the bunk, heading toward the far end of the billet, with Maiskevik and Nolan close behind. "Never any ass," Mungabo repeated in a louder voice for his benefit.

"Imperialist decadence," Luchenko tossed back. "That's all they have to offer."

"I'll take it, I'll take it," Mungabo murmured, eyeing his pinups.

McCain grinned to himself as he folded his jacket and

stowed it in the flat drawer beneath his bunk. Yevgenni Andreyov, who was following, stopped by the end of their bunk. Andreyov was probably around sixty, with patches of white hair on either side of a balding dome, and a white beard, but twinkling gray eyes that could have belonged to somebody thirty years younger. McCain always found him genial, and trusted him more than he did the others at the far end of the billet.

"They brought it upon themselves, you know—the Germans," Andreyov said. "In 1917 they sent Lenin back so that he would take Russia out of the war. But the state that Lenin created was the one that finally destroyed Germany. That's irony for you."

"You seem to know a lot about all that," McCain commented.

"Yes, well, my father was there, you know—with Konev's army in 1945."

Scanlon came in just as McCain turned to head for the washrooms at the far end of the billet. He was carrying a string bag containing grapefruits, which he deposited on his bunk. McCain indicated them with a questioning motion of his head. "A fella who has a friend who works in one of the ag zones," Scanlon said. "I got them during the movie. It's legal. You can get your bonus in kind instead of in points if there's a surplus."

"I haven't seen one of those since I left the States. How much?"

"A point . . ." Scanlon caught the look on McCain's face, "for two."

"Capitalist!" McCain snorted.

"Sure, a man has to live."

McCain picked up the bag containing his toilet gear and began walking through to the far end of the billet. At the middle table of the next section, Smovak and Vorghas were sitting down to a card game with Charlie Chan, the Amurskayan whose name nobody else could pronounce. Chan was slenderly built and studious-looking, with olive skin, slit-eyes, and a pencil-line mustache. He was notorious for his appalling jokes, which the other Siberians seemed to find as hilarious as he did. Behind them the Hungarian, Gonares, was already asleep in his bunk. Gonares was currently on outside work assignment, shifting freight in the cargo bays at the hub. Farther along, a Yakut called Nunghan and an Afghan were experimenting with the latest gambling creation—a pinball game that involved shooting glass marbles up an inclined wooden board to roll down again through an obstacle course of holes and nails. The idea had been Rashazzi's, who had charmed "the Dragoness" —the stern-faced woman-mountain who ran the OI store—into getting a box of marbles from a children's toyshop in Novyi Kazan specially for the purpose.

McCain now hardly noticed the strange smell that had greeted him the day he first entered the billet. It was due, he had since discovered, to a kind of wild garlic that certain Siberians, Yakuts in particular, once ate traditionally during the long winters when no other vegetables were available, and now chewed through habit. The scent reeked on the breath and exuded from the pores. "Yes, I know what you mean—we've got it, too," Peter Sargent had said when McCain tried to describe it. "An extraordinary olfaction—fermenting birdseed in a crappy petshop," which at least conveyed the intensity, if not the precise quality. McCain wondered if they'd bribed somebody in the ag zones to grow a patch of the awful stuff for them specially. He couldn't imagine it being included in the production lists drawn up by the omniscient planners in Moscow.

On the far side, Taugin, the Frenchman, was stretched out with his head propped on one hand, staring mournfully at a woman's picture framed on the locker next to him, as he seemed to do for most of his free time. The rest of it he spent prowling morosely about the compound or along Gorky Street. From time to time he would murmur things like, "Mimi, where are you now?" or "Oh, Mimi, where did we go wrong?" but the name was different on different days, and the pictures changed.

Luchenko, Maiskevik, and Nolan were together in the

rear section. On the other side of the table from them, Borowski, the Pole, was getting up from his bunk. In contrast to his Gallic neighbor, Borowski was pragmatic, cheerful, and always willing to help. But how much did that mean? He was still one of the group at the far end, which McCain looked upon as Luchenko's personal circle. Russia was notorious for nothing being what it seemed. Zamork was a good microcosm of it.

"Profits before people," Nolan fired at McCain as he passed. "That's capitalism. It destroys life. There used to be beavers on Manhattan Island. Did you know that? And what about the passenger pigeon?"

"Ask the Siberian mammoth," McCain said, and went through into the washroom. A moment later he stuck his head out again. "And there's plenty of beaver in Manhattan. Ask Mungabo." He disappeared back inside to relieve himself.

The door opened again a second later, and Borowski came in. They stood side by side, staring at the wall. Abominable noises and odors came from the cubicles behind, where two of the Siberians were entrenched. The damn garlic affected everything. "It's a miracle that Razz's mice survive in here," Borowski commented. A flurry of scampering in the cage behind the door acknowledged the remark. McCain didn't answer. He'd caught the expressions on Luchenko's and Maiskevik's faces when he poked his head back out to retort at Nolan. The back of his neck was prickling.

"What did you think of the movie?" Borowski asked.

"Hmm? . . . Aw, standard stuff."

"You know, in Russia they teach that it was their entry into the Japanese war that brought victory there, too. But that was only a week before it ended, wasn't it? Hadn't America already dropped the first atomic bomb by then?" Borowski saw that McCain wasn't listening. As he zipped himself up he leaned closer and murmured, "Watch yourself out there." Then he left.

The sound of flushing came from one of the cubicles

behind. McCain recreated in his mind every detail that he could recall of the situation in the end section just beyond the door when he had passed through. Luchenko had been sitting to the right of the end table, about midway along, with Maiskevik standing behind him and Nolan farther back by his bunk. Taugin was on his bunk to the left, and Borowski would probably have gone that way, too, after leaving the washroom. On the table in front of Luchenko there had been a pack of cigarettes, a book, a tin lid used as an ashtray, and at the near end a couple of magazines. Near the far end there had been a large enamel mug almost full of steaming tea, perhaps left there by Borowski. McCain thought carefully; then he opened the door of one of Rashazzi's cages of mice and scooped a large fistful of feed grain into his left hand.

When McCain came out, Luchenko was still at the table, and Nolan had sat down on his bunk. But Maiskevik had moved to stand in the center aisle at the far end of the table, covering the way through to the rest of the billet. To the left, Taugin hadn't moved, and Borowski was getting something from his locker. The mug of tea was still standing where it had been. McCain moved to the left to pass by the table.

"Earnshaw." Luchenko's voice was unusually clipped. "I may have some information on your colleague." McCain stopped and looked inquiringly. "But first, of course, there is a price."

"You never mentioned anything about that," McCain said.

"I must have forgotten. Nothing is free here. I'm sure that being American, you will understand."

"You expect me to pay you for doing your job?"

"It is the custom here."

"No, thanks."

McCain turned in the direction he had been heading, but Maiskevik moved to block the way. "If you choose not to avail yourself of the service, that's up to you," Luchenko said. "But I have done my part. It must still be paid for."

Maiskevik shoved McCain roughly in the chest with the flat of his hand to stop him, and stood stroking the knuckles of his clenched fist. "Everybody in here pays their taxes," he growled. It was one of the few occasions on which McCain had heard Maiskevik speak. The message was clear enough. On the fringe of his awareness, McCain registered that the rest of the billet had suddenly gone quiet. He heard somebody come out from the washroom behind him and stop.

McCain looked quizzically at Luchenko. "I thought you said we could always discuss these things reasonab—" His left hand shot the grain into Maiskevik's face, and as the Bulgarian blinked reflexively McCain's other hand swept the mug up off the table to follow with the tea. Maiskevik bellowed and staggered back, clawing at his scalded face. McCain kicked hard into his crotch, then seized the lapels of his jacket with both hands to pull the Bulgarian forward onto a murderous head-butt full in the face. Maiskevik fell back against the end of Borowski and Taugin's bunk, his eyes glazed and blood gushing from his ruined nose. McCain kicked his feet away, and he crashed into a sitting position on the floor. Incredibly, he was trying to get up again. McCain grabbed a fistful of hair to jerk Maiskevik's head back and delivered a straight-fingered jab to the exposed throat. Maiskevik gagged and crumpled to sit with his head lolling to one side, with rivulets of blood from his nose running down the front of his clothes.

It had been too fast and violent for anyone else to react. Luchenko was gaping from his chair across the table, Nolan was staring ashen-faced from behind, while a few feet from McCain, Borowski was still frozen in the act of turning from his locker. Forcing himself to be calm externally despite the adrenaline charge pulsing through his body. McCain replaced the mug on the table. "I've just filed for an exemption," he told Luchenko. Then he stepped over Maiskevik's legs to continue on his way. The others who had come forward from the other sections of the billet parted to let him through. He stopped halfway to pour himself a cup of tea at the center table, and carried it back to his bunk.

Slowly the billet came back to life behind him. At the far end, Luchenko was still sitting, stunned, while Nolan, Borowski, and a couple of others hauled Maiskevik to his feet and steered him into the washroom.

Scanlon was leaning forward on the edge of his bunk when McCain sat down opposite him. "Here," he said, holding out his flask. "A little drop o' the hard stuff will do you more good than that."

McCain took a long swig and nodded. "Thanks." He handed back the flask and sipped his tea.

Scanlon regarded him curiously for a while. Then he took a sip from the flask himself and looked across at McCain again. "So, Mr. Earnshaw," he said at last, "what kind of a school of journalism was it, I'm wondering, that they sent you to, now?"

Inside the Government Building at Turgenev, General Protbornov and the three other men with him watched a replay of the incident as it had been recorded through a wide-angle lens built into one of the ceiling lights in billet B-3. The title on the thick, red-bound folder laying in front of Protbornov read, MC CAIN, LEWIS H., U.S. UNIFIED DEFENSE INTELLIGENCE AGENCY. ABSOLUTE TOP SECRET.

Sergei Kirilikhov, from the Party's Central Committee, nodded tight-lipped and pivoted his chair to face away from the screen. "You were right after all, General," he said to Protbornov. "He reacted just as your people predicted he would. My compliments."

Protbornov patted the folder on the table affectionately. "When he was a teenager in California, there was a gang of bullies at the school he attended who liked to terrorize other students, especially Hispanics. Well, one day they made the mistake of picking on a new batch of students who turned out to be the children of Nicaraguan mountain guerilla fighters recently arrived in the country, and almost got themselves killed. The affair made a deep impression on McCain. Later, when he was with NATO, he hospitalized a would-be mugger in Berlin. What we have just seen was fully in character."

Maxim Sepelyan, from the Ministry of Defense, stroked his chin dubiously. "You, ah . . . you don't think that this man could be too headstrong—too impulsive, perhaps?"

Protbornov shook his head. "We have studied his motivational psychology intensely. Despite what you just saw, he is not a person primarily disposed toward violence. He only resorts to force when compelled to in self-defense. His ideological convictions reflect the same principle. When given a choice, he bases his relationships on reason, persuasion, and patience. But he is defiant, and he has a strong sense of loyalty to his beliefs. Those are exactly the qualities we want."

The other man present, General Andrei Tolomachuk, from the KGB's Ninth Directorate, gestured toward the screen from Protbornov's other side. "I presume that what we saw there was genuine. The Bulgarian wasn't acting under instructions?"

"Definitely not," Protbornov said. "That was all quite genuine, I assure you. Part of the objective was to test that McCain's ability and determination are as we have assessed them."

The four exchanged inquiring looks. "Very well, I am satisfied," Kirilikhov pronounced. Tolomachuk agreed. Sepelyan thought for a moment longer, then nodded. "When I get back to Moscow, I will advise that the next phase of the operation proceed as planned," Kirilikhov said.

Protbornov looked pleased. "So the countdown remains on schedule. We're still talking about a November seventh D-day." Kirilikhov nodded.

"Four months from now," Sepelyan mused. "The waiting will make it seem like a long time."

"It's the centenary," General Tolomachuk said. "We've been waiting a hundred years. What are four more months compared to a hundred years?"

"What are they compared to owning the world?" Protbornov asked.

CHAPTER EIGHTEEN

Maiskevik was taken to the infirmary the next morning for treatment following an "accident," and Luchenko was summoned to a talk with Major Bachayvin, the block commandant. An hour later two guards appeared at the billet to collect Maiskevik's things, and by lunchtime the prevailing opinion was that he wouldn't be coming back. No official reason was given. Luchenko reappeared later and had nothing to say on the matter except that two replacements would be coming to B-3 in Maiskevik's place. McCain carried on in the metalworking shop through the afternoon, expecting to be hauled away at any time, but by the end of the shift nothing had happened. He could only conclude that the management, for reasons best known to themselves, were going along with the accident story officially. Maybe Luchenko was on the take to a greater degree than he cared to make known to his bosses, McCain reflected. Or maybe they were all part of it, too. Either way, it could add up to possible opportunities to be exploited.

When McCain arrived back at the billet, Nolan brought him a note from the mail pouch that a messenger delivered every day to Luchenko. It advised that the book McCain had reserved was being held in the library. McCain hadn't reserved any book. He went to the library and was handed a gaudy paperback entitled *A Hero's Sacrifice*. It was one of the standard pulp inspirational pieces churned out for the masses by Party hacks, and carried a cover picture of a standard Soviet workaholic hero, muscles taut beneath bronzed skin, steely-eyed, and complete with hard hat and jackhammer, shown against a background of cranes, bulldozers, and an oil refinery under construction.

McCain took the book to the general compound and

shielded himself among a group of prisoners placing bets on a Siberian variation of the shell game before he ruffled through the pages. The slip of paper that dropped into his hand read:

SUBJECT OF QUERY WAS DETAINED IN SOLITARY AT SECURITY HQ TURGENEV UP TO FOUR DAYS AGO FOR CONTINUING INTERROGATION. CONDITION GOOD. NO GROUNDS FOR CONCERN. HAS RECENTLY BEEN MOVED TO ZAMORK, RESTRICTED SECTION, BLOCK D.

The message also included instructions for McCain to follow to reestablish contact, should he need further information on anything. McCain wasn't sure whether he felt reassured or not, although, according to Scanlon, the source had proved consistently reliable in the past. Reputation was everything in any good business, Scanlon had reminded him.

He saw Andreyov approaching as he was about to begin walking back across the compound, and stopped to wait for the older man to join him. "Have you met the two new arrivals yet?" Andreyov asked. He had a thick woolen cardigan beneath his jacket and swung his arms across his body as he spoke, as if it were cold. McCain could picture him in a black overcoat and fur hat in a Moscow street scene.

"No, I've been in the library," McCain said. "So they're here already, eh?"

"And straight out of training, if I ever saw KGB before. You've stirred things up properly, you know. They don't trust you an inch now. A bodyguard for Luchenko, that's what they are. Mungabo has christened them King and Kong."

"It seems strange," McCain commented, mainly to see what Andreyov would say. "I've have thought they'd have shipped *me* out."

"Oh, they couldn't leave Maiskevik there, could they? Not any longer—after what happened. He's lost face. . . . Wouldn't be able to carry the same weight any more, in the billet. Not after what happened."

"And I don't get put away for a while to cool down?"

"No, they couldn't do that, could they? Not if they want to pretend it was an accident."

"That's my point. Why would they pretend that?"

"Who knows why they do things?"

McCain gestured at the compound in general. "So, is it likely to be everybody's gossip for the evening?"

"No, it won't be spread around."

"How come?"

"It's best."

They began walking slowly toward the door into the throughway between A and B Blocks. Andreyov turned his head to peer at McCain, as if weighing something in his mind. Finally he said, "You seem to be a man of strong opinions—strong impressions of things."

McCain thrust his hands into his pockets. "Some things, maybe. I don't know. . . . What did you have in mind?"

"The things you argue with Nolan about. You have strong ideals."

"I never really thought of myself as an idealist."

"Principles, then?"

"A few, maybe."

Andreyov hesitated, then said, "I admire that. Everybody who is anything worthwhile has to admire that. But, you know, it troubles me that you should think so badly of Russia." Before McCain could reply, he went on, "It isn't everything you think. We are proud of our country, as you are of yours. Like you, we worked hard and we suffered to make it what it is. And we have transformed our Motherland from backwardness to one of the world's strongest nations, and extended its influence everywhere— out into space, too. There are many positive things that you should remember, things we have achieved. Creative things. Our history, our arts . . . Russia has produced men of words and ideas that have swept through the civilized world as have few others. Russians have brought glory to music and ballet, and at one time to painting and architecture.... And hospitality and friendship! Do you know what the educated Russian values more than anything else? Good friends and stimulating conversation. There is nothing anywhere else in the world to match the loyalty of Russians who are close friends. You have to spend an evening at home with an apartment full of them, when the talking goes on over food and vodka until long into the night. Or I am on my own and the telephone rings at three in the morning, and it's my friend Viktor who I have known for forty years and he tells me, 'Yevgenni, I have problems and I need somebody to talk to. I am coming over.' Or it is Oleg, who says, 'I have been thinking about what you said last week. We must discuss it.' So what do I do? I put the water on to boil for some tea. Where would you find that in New York? Oh, no, there I must get up and go to work because I have to be 'successful' all the time, or make money, money, or please the boss whose ass I want to kick, but then he fires me from my job and I sleep in the street. Is it not so?"

They emerged into Gorky Street and turned to follow it for a short distance to reenter the B Block area through its front entrance.

"No, you misunderstand," McCain said. "I don't have any quarrel with the Russian people. I respect everything the Russian tradition stands for—all the things you said. But the present political system is something alien to all that. That's not the real Russia."

"Yes, we've made our share of mistakes, it's true," Andreyov agreed. "Especially in Stalin's time. And I admit we are still too bureaucratic and paranoid about foreigners. Russians worry a lot what people think of them, you see. They can't stand the thought of being compared unfavorably, or of being seen in a bad light. They're like a wife who is too fussy about her house and won't let anyone in when she thinks it's untidy. And we still tend to feel embarrassed by some things, so we hide ourselves from the world. But it's changing. Someday we will show the world. Not in my lifetime, maybe . . . but it will happen."

"Well, when it does, then I'll feel a lot easier," McCain said.

They walked on in silence for a short while. Then Andreyov said, "That movie last night, my father was there, you know—he was with Konev's army that linked up with the Americans in Germany. Within months there was talk that now they were going to start fighting the Americans. He told me some of the soldiers wept when they heard it. They couldn't understand why."

"Life can be crazy," McCain agreed.

"You don't understand it either?"

"I gave up trying to. I just believe that you pay what you owe, you collect what you're due, you protect what you have, and you help if you can. Otherwise mind your own business and leave people alone."

"You don't want to destroy the Soviet Union?"

"Not unless it tries to destroy me."

"What about if you thought it was about to? Would you attack it preemptively?"

McCain nodded as he saw the point. "Like Maiskevik, for instance?"

"We are taught that the capitalists will start a desperate, last-ditch war to try and save themselves rather than submit to the inevitable triumph of world socialism," Andreyov said. "Doesn't what you've just said confirm it?"

"Look at Japan, China, and the rest of Asia and tell me again about the triumph of world socialism. I'd say it's the other way round: it's not us that's in the ditch. Maybe we feel the same way about you."

Andreyov shook his head sadly. "No trust, no trust," he sighed. "Why does it always have to be that way? You know, I heard a story once about two men from a ship that had sunk, and they were floating on top of a chest full of food and water in a sea full of sharks. But to make enough room to open the door, one of them would have to jump in the water. Now, they had an oar also, which meant that the other one could beat away the sharks. But if he didn't beat away the sharks and allowed the other one to be gobbled up, then he would be left with all the food. They both knew that they would maybe survive if they cooperated with each other, and that they would both die if they didn't; but if one was left with all the food, then he would certainly survive. So neither of them would jump, because neither trusted the other. And they both starved to death, on top of a chest full of food." Andreyov looked at McCain. "It's the same problem, isn't it. What's the solution?"

McCain thought for a while. "I guess first we have to decide who the sharks are," he said. They stopped inside the B Block mess area. McCain took in the usual evening scene, then his eyes came back to Andreyov. He wondered how a seemingly harmless old man came to be shut up in a place like this. "What did you do to get in here?" he asked.

"Oh, it's a funny story. . . . I don't really have any family left now, you see, so I volunteered for the experimental population that they were bringing up to inhabit the colony. But they didn't like some of the things I said, so they put me in here rather than send me all the way back again. Subversive, they said I was."

"Not many guys your age get to go into space," McCain commented.

"Hah! I might as well not have bothered, for all I can remember," Andreyov replied. "Very peculiar, it was. I don't have any clear recollection at all of that trip. A lot of others I was with said the same thing. All like part of a dream, it was . . ." He paused and rubbed his temples. "In fact, even thinking about it makes me tried. And it's past my time to rest, anyway. Not as young as you people. . . . If you'll excuse me, I think I'll turn in."

"Sure. Thanks for the talk. 'Night."

Andreyov went on into the billet. McCain spotted Scanlon and Koh at one of the tables and went over to sit with them. It could have been his imagination, but despite what Andreyov had said about gossip not spreading, McCain got the distinct feeling that many eyes were following him; too many heads seemed to look away suddenly as he let his gaze wander over the mess area. He looked back at the other two.

"How's Andreyov tonight?" Scanlon asked.

"He always strikes me as a lonely kind of person. That's why he talks a lot, and I listen. He only came up here because he doesn't have any family down there." McCain shrugged and gestured at the figures in the mess area. "Maybe this is his family now. I don't think the idea of going home even crosses his mind."

"Ah well . . ." Scanlon looked curiously at Koh. "Don't you ever think about going home?"

"Not a lot." Koh was packing his long, straight-stemmed pipe with the mixture of tobacco and herbs that he smoked. "There is really no point. And besides, not everyone back where I come from agrees that what I did was an honorable thing." Koh never pinpointed exactly where he considered himself to be from. "And that's very important, of course. It's conceivable that I'd have a harder time back there than up here."

"Don't you want to contribute something to what a lot of people are saying is Asia's century?" McCain said.

Koh chuckled as he lit his pipe. "Maybe I already have." He sucked several times, and was rewarded with a cloud of aromatic smoke that he puffed into the air.

"What did you do?" McCain asked.

"Maybe I'll tell you one day," Koh answered mysteriously. He went on, "In any case, whatever is destined to evolve will do so in the long run, with or without me. With all their glorification, I don't believe that even the Christs, Napoleons, Hitlers, and Genghis Khans really influence history that much. All they do is slightly accelerate or slightly retard what would have happened anyway."

"So Asia was due to take the twenty-first century anyway?" McCain said.

"Yes, eventually," Koh replied. "You had Malthus, and thought you were running out of resources; we had Confucius. But people are the only resource that matters, because human ingenuity creates all the rest—and we have thirty percent of the world's supply. When you think of it that way, the outcome was inevitable sooner or later."

Scanlon was staring with his head cocked to one side, as if this put a lot of things in a perspective that he hadn't seen before. "Go on, Koh," he said. "That's a thought, now. So it was all inevitable, you're telling us?"

Koh shrugged. "Eventually. But the West itself speeded up the process."

"How come?" McCain asked.

"You made the Third World into colonies and held it back for centuries. But in doing that you were compressing a spring. And when the spring was released after the Second World War, nothing could contain the energy and the urgency to make up for lost time. In half a century Asia went through social changes that had taken the West a thousand years. America lost confidence in itself—the very thing we had admired most. You made the same mistake that the British had a hundred years before."

"Trust the Brits to be at the bottom of it," Scanlon muttered.

Koh went on, "The power and wealth of their ruling class was tied to industries that were becoming obsolete. Instead of adapting and moving with the times, they tried to entrench themselves around technology that was being superseded. It can't work. Neither the lion nor the zebra can stop evolving and hope to survive. One would starve; the other would be eaten." It was true, McCain thought to himself. While the two powers that represented the culmination of the Old World remained deadlocked in their military stalemate, the forerunners of the New were racing ahead with developing the energy-dense, nuclear-based industries that would power the twenty-first century and carry mankind across the Solar System.

"Different dogs have their days," Scanlon said.

"Quite," Koh said. "Likewise, human culture as a whole is all the time evolving, but it doesn't evolve evenly, everywhere at once. It's like an amoeba, where first one part moves, than another. The center of action shifts from place to place, and so civilizations rise and fall: the East and Middle East long ago, Greece, Rome, and the classical civilizations of the Mediterranean, the power struggles of Europe, and the rise of America. But there was no law of nature which said that once the focus shifted to America, it had to remain there forever. What we're seeing is simply the next step in the process. The era of Western civilization that sprang from the European Renaissance a thousand years ago is over. . . . Actually, the term is a misnomer. What happened back at that time was not the *rebirth* of anything. It was the *birth* of a completely new culture. Oh, true, a new civilization might pick up a few stones that suit it needs from the rubble of an old one, but that's not the same thing as rebuilding it. . . ." Koh sat back and smiled through the cloud that was beginning to engulf him. He held out an upturned hand in a gesture that could have meant anything, and an ecstatic light crept into his eyes. "They must free their souls to soar . . ." He paused, looking at the other two for a moment as if they had suddenly materialized there from nowhere. Then he carried on, his voice rising and falling in cadences of lyrical rapture: ". . . unfettered essence of distilled turpentine."

McCain and Scanlon glanced at each other. They knew they wouldn't get anything more that was coherent out of Koh for the rest of the evening. And then, which was just as well, the lights blinked to signal that it was time to move into the billets. They each took one of Koh's arms and helped him to his feet.

"You never struck me as a student of cultural evolution, Kev," McCain said as they steered Koh toward the B-3 door.

"Well, aren't the Irish students of life itself, and isn't that everything?" Scanlon replied. He looked across at McCain for a moment. "Anyhow, it's the evolution of what's going on in this place that ye should be thinkin' more about, yourself."

"How d'you mean?"

"Whatever it is you have in mind to do, you've got it off to a fine beginning. But, Mr. Earnshaw, journalist, as the bishop said to the parlor maid, 'Where do we go next from here?'"

CHAPTER NINETEEN

From its position two hundred thousand miles away from Earth and some distance above Earth's equatorial plane, *Valentina Tereshkova* had permanent lines for its communications lasers to at least two of the Soviet synchronous satellites, which redistributed message traffic among surface locations and other satellites, depending on the signals' final destinations. The West's military establishment also maintained a system of "Auriga" surveillance satellites, which between them were able to keep a constant watch on both the Soviet satellites and *Tereshkova*. The Aurigas were equipped with telescopes designed for operation in the infrared range, which could pick up the stray reflections from both ends of the Soviet communications beams; thus they were able to eavesdrop on the message-flow to and from *Tereshkova* as it took place. From space, the intercepted stream of Soviet communications code was routed down through a complicated chain of links and relays, eventually becoming grist for the computer batteries of the National Security Agency's code-cracking mill at Fort Meade, Maryland.

For as long as *Tereshkova* had been operational, a portion of its signal traffic had used virtually impregnable top-security coding algorithms—which had done little to alleviate the West's suspicions over what was supposed to be an innocuous social experiment in space-living. By summer of 2017, however, the hungry NSA cryptoanalysts in the section that handled "Teepee," as the intercept traffic to and from *Tereshkova* was code-named, had received a windfall of a different kind.

The standard procedure followed by both sides for sending encrypted messages over communications links was to transmit the code as a stream of five-digit number groups. That way, anyone intercepting the transmission with the intention of decoding its content would receive none of the clues that a structure reflecting the varying word-lengths would have supplied. To complicate the task further, the transmitting computers then obscured where the different messages in a stream began and ended, by filling the gaps between them with random five-digit number groups so that the channel simply transmitted continuously twenty-four hours a day. A message buried in the stream carried a special number sequence that the computers at the receiving end were programmed to watch for.

For some time the pattern-searching routines that the NSA computers subjected incoming material to as a first pass had been detecting irregularities in the filler groups used to pack the gaps in Teepee transmissions from *Tereshkova* to Earth: the random numbers weren't as random as they should have been. Further analysis revealed a concealed coding system. It suggested that the West had unwittingly tapped into illicit traffic between personnel at two of the Soviet Union's own establishments—an intriguing notion. The "Blueprint" code, as this traffic buried inside Earthbound Teepee was designated, turned out to be comparatively unsophisticated, and clearly not a creation of professional Soviet cryptographers; furthermore, its sender was too chatty, providing the Fort Meade veterans with sufficient material to break it fairly quickly. In late June the names "Earnshaw" and "Shelmer" appeared in the plaintext translation of one of these signals, which, from the lists that the NSA kept of who was likely to be interested in what, caused copies to be routed, via Litherland at CIA, Langley, to Bernard Foleda.

Three weeks previously, the CIA had arranged for a message to be beamed into the Soviet communications net in accordance with the protocols that Dyashkin had passed to Dr. Bowers in Japan, indicating interest and a willingness to "talk" further. Dyashkin had acknowledged, and in the ensuing unusual dialogue—phrased very obliquely to keep the Soviet counterpart of NSA off the scent of who was talking to whom—the Americans had requested Dyashkin, implicitly as a test of good faith, to try to find out if the two visitors who had disappeared on *Tereshkova* at the beginning of May were still being held there. A week later, a response from Dyashkin had stated that they were.

What was interesting about the Blueprint intercept that contained the references to Earnshaw and Shelmer was that it occurred a day before Dyashkin's reply. In other words, a message from the mysterious correspondent up in *Tereshkova* was known to have contained the answer a day before Dyashkin sent it to the CIA. Here, then, was evidence that Dyashkin was the hitherto-unknown recipient at the Earth end of the Blueprint line; also, it corroborated that his information was in fact coming from where he said it was coming from.

Bernard Foleda looked at the report that Barbara had brought in and studied the figures on the appended sheet. It was an estimate of the amount of political indoctrination included in the Soviet school curriculum for various grades. "They always go for the children," he murmured as he read.

"Who do?" Barbara asked.

"Fanatics, extremists, every kind of nut with a cause. The way to their utopia is by getting at the minds of the children, so they try to control the schools. Instead of getting educated, the kids end up as political putty. Maybe the Chinese are right: governments should stay out of the whole business."

"Is that what they're saying?"

"It was something that Myra and I talked about a while back." Foleda sat back and tossed the report down on his desk. "Did I ever tell you?—that might have had something to do with how I got into this kind of work."

Barbara sat down on one of the chairs at the meeting table and looked at him curiously. "I don't think so."

Foleda stared at the window. "There was something that happened when I was a teenager—not really so sensational, but it's always stuck in my mind, so I suppose it must have made some kind of impression. Two people came to have dinner with us one night—a Jewish couple that my parents had been friends with for a long time. They talked about the past year that they'd spent traveling around overseas. All their lives they'd been busy with their own affairs, until one day they looked at each other and realized they hadn't seen anything of the world, and if they didn't do something about it soon, they never would."

"Too wrapped up with family and business, you mean?" Barbara said.

"Yes, exactly. Anyhow, I can remember Ben—that was his name—saying to my father, 'You've known us for a long time, Chuck. I've never had any time for politics. But, do you know, after what we saw in other places, I *never* want to set foot outside this country again. I don't want to see our grandchildren growing up the way we saw others made to. And I'll tell you something else: I would give thousands of dollars, no, *tens* of thousands, to any political party—Republicans, Democrats, I don't care; they're all the same to me—just so long as they're committed to defending this country.'"

"That was how you got into intelligence?"

"Oh, I wouldn't exactly say that. But I think it played a part. I'd been looking for a way to express what I felt about the world, and that just about summed it up."

Barbara was used to Foleda's inclination to ramble off like this for no obvious reason. It usually happened when he was preoccupied with something that he hadn't said much about. Some people claimed that they did their hardest thinking while asleep. She had come to see this as his way of distracting his consciousness while a deeper part of his mind tussled with something else. "Do you think everyone in this business needs an ideology like that?" she asked.

Foleda shook his head. "I don't know of any rule that says they have to. Take Lew McCain for instance. Totally pragmatic. He's not interested in keeping the world free for democracy. He just likes challenges with some risk thrown in, and believes in being free to be himself. In fact, the way he operates, an ideology would probably be more of a hindrance. Maybe that's why he's a good field man and I fit in better behind a desk. And yet in another way . . ." Foleda looked away from the window. "How do you feel about this whole Dyashkin business?" he asked Barbara suddenly.

She had worked with him long enough not to have to ask pointless questions. "What bothers you about it?"

Foleda stared down at the papers strewn across his desk. "It's coming together too easily. . . . Look at it. First, two of our people get stuck up on Mermaid. A month later this professor shows up in Japan with a story that he wants to defect, and he just happens to run the primary groundstation that Mermaid talks to. And while all that's going on, the hackers at Meade find a code that turns out to be easier to break than it ought to be, and they discover that somebody up there has their own private line down to him." He tilted his chin questioningly.

"Even if NSA hasn't found it yet, he has to have some way of talking back," Barbara said.

"Right. What does that make you think?"

Barbara shrugged. "Maybe we can get the use of his line to make contact with our two people up there somehow."

"Why would you need to do that?"

"Because the Soviets are coming up with any excuse not to let us talk to them officially . . ." Barbara's eyes narrowed as she began to see what Foleda was driving at.

"Nine out of ten. And what else does it make you think?"

She frowned for a few seconds, then said, "Is that what somebody somewhere wants me to think?"

Foleda nodded. "Ten out of ten." He got up and moved over to the window, where he stood staring out silently for a while. "Anything that involves Mermaid is serious. There are questions we need answers to before we can let this go farther. Who is this line to Dyashkin from? What was it set up for? Why does he want to defect? And most important, is he genuine? We can't go walking blind into something like this."

Barbara waited. She understood the situation, but at the same time could see no immediate pointer to a way of getting the answers that were needed. It would be another exercise in the long, uphill grind that was ninety percent of intelligence work: sifting through uninteresting-looking scraps, looking for patterns and connections, and hoping something useful might emerge. Where, then, would they begin accumulating more background information on somebody like Dyashkin?—personal things, glimpses of his character and loyalties, things that might help fill in the blanks. Barbara looked over the desk for possible clues to the way that Foleda's mind had been working. One of the reference screens was displaying a summary of notes he had extracted from various databank records. At the top was the heading, *Dorkas, Anita Leonidovich. Codename "Cellist."*

Foleda had turned away from the window and was watching her. "The Aeroflot administrator," he commented. "Dyashkin's former wife."

"Yes, I know," Barbara said.

"Except she's not with Aeroflot anymore." Foleda moved to where he could see the screen. "In 2014, three years after she and Dyashkin went separate ways, she remarried, this time to a character by the name of Enriko Dorkas, who's listed as a foreign correspondent with *Novoye Vremya.*"

Barbara pursed her lips silently. *New Times* was a

magazine of news and current affairs that had been founded in 1943 for the specific purpose of providing cover for Soviet intelligence officers abroad. "Which presumably means he's KGB," she said. "Where are they posted?"

"He's a colonel," Foleda confirmed. "They're both in London, with the Soviet Residency in Kensington. Officially she's a clerk at the embassy. But it gets more interesting. You see, according to a report that we have on file from SIS, Anita Dorkas—Penkev before she married Enriko—is connected with an underground Soviet intellectual dissident organization known as the Friday Club. As is often the case with senior officers, she and her husband don't live in the embassy quarters, but have an apartment in Bayswater. A double advantage for somebody mixed up in dissident activities: one, opportunities to travel abroad; and two, a lot of freedom to meet with outside groups and sources of foreign aid. The SIS desk that's been dealing with her says she's being extremely cooperative."

"You mean the British have recruited her?"

"So they claim."

Barbara nodded and was about to reply, but then she checked herself and sat back to stare at the screen again thoughtfully. "Unless, of course . . . she's really with the KGB too. The dissident story could be a cover for tracking down the dissidents' overseas connections."

Foleda gave a satisfied nod. "And that's the key question: Did she maneuver her way into marrying an upward-bound KGB man to gain a unique base for her dissident activities? Or is she a loyal Party agent-wife posing as a dissident? Which way round is it?"

"How confident do the British sound about her?" Barbara asked.

Foleda shrugged. "She's provided personnel lists of embassy staff that they requested, organization charts, the names of some contacts over there who are passing information to the Soviets. It was material that we already had from other sources, so we could tell if what she was producing was authentic. But on the other hand, if the

Soviets already figured we had it, they wouldn't be losing anything by letting her give it to us again. So it doesn't really prove anything."

"Hmm . . ." Barbara sat back in her chair. "How long ago did you say she married this Enriko?"

"Three years—since 2014," Foleda replied.

"If she's a genuine dissident, she must have set herself up with him that far back. What do our people in Moscow have on her?"

"A lot that corroborates her claim. But then, the Soviets have been known to plant agents with covers long before they're activated. However, there is evidence that she's been mixed up with the Friday Club for at least eight years." Foleda looked at Barbara curiously as he said this, as if inviting her to read the implication.

"Eight years," she repeated. "That would take us back to 2009 . . . while she was still married to Dyashkin."

"Ye-es."

Now Barbara saw the point. "If Anita is genuinely a dissident, and was that long ago, then possibly Dyashkin is too."

"Right." Foleda moved around the desk and sat down in his chair again. "Wouldn't that be a worthwhile thing to find out about him?" And finding out shouldn't prove too difficult, for Anita was not only accessible outside the Eastern bloc, but was already talking to British intelligence.

"Okay, I get it," Barbara said. "So what now? Do you want me to start getting questions together for the London people to work on?"

Foleda shook his head. "No, not them."

"Who, then?"

"When was the last time you had a trip to England?"

Barbara's eyes snapped wide in surprise. "Me? I haven't done anything like that for years."

"Then, let's get rid of some cobwebs. Don't you have a pet ideology to save the world or bring in the millennium?"

"Me? No. Didn't Thoreau say that as soon as something starts ailing people, even constipation, they're off trying to change the world? I'm happy minding my own business."

Foleda's craggy, dark-chinned face split into a grin. "Then, that makes you a natural for the field, like Lew. Maybe we should have left you there in the first place. Let's just say that I'd like to keep this business in the family for the time being."

CHAPTER TWENTY

The woman the others called Nasha brought to mind a vision of an obscenely fat toad. Stiff black hairs bristled from the warts on her multiple chins, her arms creased at the joints like columns of boneless brawn, and her piglike eyes darted constantly this way and that in their fleshy slits, pouring disapproval on everything they surveyed. "They're not even half done yet," she scolded as she waddled up to deposit another wire basket full of dirty crockery and cutlery on top of the one that Paula hadn't had a chance to empty yet. An odor of stale perspiration accompanied her. "There's more to come, and after that the floor needs doing. What's the matter—haven't you ever worked before in your life? I suppose you always had oppressed blacks to take care of you in America, eh? Well, here it's different. Everyone works to eat." She bustled away with a final remark in Russian that Paula didn't catch.

Paula lifted a stack of plates from the basket into the sink full of hot, greasy water and poured in more detergent. The scum coated her arms, and her hair clung to her forehead in the clammy air. Her hands were sore, because the gloves they'd given her had holes in them. "There are no others available." Couldn't we get some? "That is impossible"—the eternal Russian answer to everything. They could build an artificial world in space with materials mined from the Moon, but they couldn't make a dishwasher that worked. Why couldn't the dishwasher be fixed? "That is impossible." Why? "It is impossible."

They had brought her to a place on the edge of the

urban zone called Novyi Kazan—the women's section of what was apparently a sizable detention facility located below the surface. After a degrading physical examination and search during the admission process, she had been issued a two-piece tunic of light gray and a few personal effects, and brought to a barred cell that held seven other women in addition to herself. They ate and slept there, and the few amenities they enjoyed were brought there. Life alternated between the cell and the workplace, which in Paula's case meant the same hot, noisy kitchens for ten hours a day, and the drab-paneled corridors that she walked through from one to the other. She longed to be back in solitary. At least on her own she'd had time to think.

"What do you call this? Do you call this clean?" The toad was back again. "You have to press harder to wipe off the grease. Are people expected to eat off this? What's the matter—are you worried your arms might ache?"

"The detergent is almost gone. It needs more detergent."

"There is no more detergent."

"Why can't we get some more?"

"That is impossible."

"Why?"

"It is impossible."

She ate alone at one end of the cell's single table, doing her best to ignore the taunts that the novelty of having an American among them provoked from the rest of the company.

"What is the matter with her this evening, do you think?"

"Her hands are chapped. Can't you see her hands? Obviously she's not used to working."

"Why not? Doesn't anyone work in America?"

"Well, of course somebody has to work. The blacks work, and the oppressed classes work, for their capitalist masters."

"Then, she must be a capitalist."

"A capitalist's princess daughter—much better than the likes of us."

"Sophisticated, you see."

"Very noble and haughty."

"It won't do her much good here, though, will it?" Giggling.

"Hey, is that right, Princess? Is your father a capitalist? Did you grow up in a big mansion with silk sheets and servants to wipe your nose for you?"

"And her behind!" Shrieks of laughter.

"Now you know how much fun it was for your servants."

"In Russia, everyone wipes their own nose."

A small washroom containing two basins and a single, unscreened toilet bowl opened off the rear of the cell. Paula was attempting to clean off the day's grease with lukewarm water and the gritty, seemingly unlatherable soap provided, with Katherine, a thinly built Byelorussian with long black hair and pale skin, came in. Katherine had a comparatively reserved disposition bordering on aloofness, and said little; but her eyes had a studied look as they took in the surroundings, and her words when she did speak were those of a person with a different background from most of the others. She hung her towel on one of the hooks behind the door and set down a plastic bag that she had been carrying. From it she took a piece of soap, a toothbrush, a tin of tooth powder, and a comb, and then turned on the faucet without saying anything. The faucet shuddered violently, hissed with the release of trapped air, and then began emitting a trickle of yellowish water. Water in the colony was supposed to be recycled through a closed ecological system. Sometimes Paula wondered.

The soap Katherine had laid out was whiter and creamier looking than the gray cake that Paula was holding. Paula looked at it, then she shifted her eyes to catch Katherine's in the metal mirror and inclined her head. "Where did you get that?"

"It was issued."

"I got this. Why is it different?"

"Oh . . . sometimes it varies. If the storewoman has preferences . . ."

"Some people are favored, you mean."

"You have to be accepted."

"And I take it I'm not."

"She maybe has something against Americans."

"But not just her."

Katherine shrugged and hung her shirt and pants next to the towel. Paula carried on scrubbing her arms in silence for a while. Then she said, "Can I talk to you, Katherine?"

"I cannot prevent you from talking."

"There's something I don't understand. Look, *why* do Russians believe all that propaganda? I mean, they've got eyes, haven't they? They've got brains—they can think. Surely you people don't believe everything they tell you about us. I mean . . ." Paula made a helpless gesture in the air. "After a hundred years of it, you *must* know . . . Our politicians tell us stupid things about Russians, too, but we know that's just the way they are. We might not like everything the Soviet system stands for, but we don't confuse that with the *people*. We don't have anything against you as individuals."

"You talk about having eyes and brains, and about people, but it is you who serve the system that crushes people."

"But that's not true. The things they tell you aren't true. People are free under our system. It's—"

"Then, that makes it even worse. If you had no choice because you were forced to be slaves, that would be oppression. But if you are free and choose to be slaves . . . And it is us who you say are propagandized?"

Paula shook her head wearily. "You really believe that every American is hostile to all Russians?"

"America is the heart of capitalism. It is inevitable that the capitalists must try to destroy progressive socialism before they themselves are swept away. Our priority has always been to defend ourselves against this. It had to be. Look how many times you have attacked us. . . . And you accuse *us* of hostility!"

Paula stared at her bemusedly. "We attacked? . . . I don't understand. What are you talking about? No Western nation has ever attacked you—except Hitler, and then we were all on the same side. No Western democracy ever attacked Russia."

"You see, they lie to you," Katherine said. "In the very first year of the nation, in the summer of 1918, the capitalists sent their armies into Russia in an attempt to help treacherous counterrevolutionary forces destroy the new Soviet state. Is that not attacking us?"

History had never been one of Paula's consuming passions. She shook her head. "I don't know. . . .I guess I never really looked into that particular period."

Katherine nodded. "There, you see. Yes, American, British, French, Japanese, they all came. You didn't know? And even after Russia had been weakened by four years of war in Europe and then torn apart by the Revolution, still the people's Red Army was invincible. And then you say Hitler was not one of you, because you are the democracies. But it was the so-called democracies that rearmed Germany and allowed Hitler to rise, so they could send him against Russia to fight the war for them that they were too cowardly to fight themselves. They tried to start a war that they would wriggle their way out of like worms, but they underestimated Stalin."

"I'm not so sure about that. I—"

"Pah! What do you know? You know nothing. And then, when the tiger they had tried to ride about-turned, it was Russia that killed it and saved them. And then it was Russia that drove the Japanese invaders out of China and ended the war. Russia has always defended countries that were invaded. After the war, you Americans and your puppets tried to invade Korea. And you tried to invade the Middle East, you tried to invade Cuba, you tried to invade Vietnam."

Paula stared. "You mean that's what they teach?"

Katherine shook her head uncomprehendingly. "And you say we have never been attacked, that we are being

paranoid. You think you are victimized, and wonder why.
It is we who have *always* been attacked."

Paula sighed. "I don't know, your propaganda, our
propaganda . . . Who's to say what's right? But neither one
of us is responsible for whatever really goes on. Why should
any of it affect us here, personally? In here of all places,
I'd have thought we had enough in common to outweigh
all that, whatever the real story is."

Katherine looked at her coldly. "The reason I'm in here
is that my loyalty is in question," she said. "I used to have
a husband. He went to London with a Soviet trade mission,
and while he was there he met a reporter from a New
York art magazine, and she seduced him. The Americans
let him return with her, and now they are living down
there somewhere with a family. So, you see, Princess, I
do not exactly have strong reason to be fond of Americans,
American women in particular, and especially American
women journalists. Does that answer your question?"

Paula lay in the dark, clutching the coarse blanket around
her and staring up into the black shadow of the bunk above.
She was picturing teenage days of sailing among the islands
in Puget Sound, the shining towers of downtown Seattle
across the water, and the Olympic Mountains, green in the
sunlight, rich with recent rain. As she thought back, she
wondered what had become of the self-assurance and single-
mindedness that she thought she had learned from her
mother, Stephanie. With Paula's father being so long away
at sea, and having come from a naval family before that,
Stephanie had always been in control of herself and her
life. She'd socialized a lot and thrown lots of parties. There
was always a stream of visitors calling at the house. Hence,
for Paula, learning to assert herself with people around
had been simply another part of growing up. One thing
that had made an impression on her, she remembered, was
her mother's adroitness in handling the advances—usually
tactful, but sometimes crude—that an attractive woman
left on her own for long periods of time was subjected to

by the men who came to the house. Ever since then she'd tended to regard men as polarizing into two groups: either they were strong, or they were weak; they were either smart, or stupid; worth getting to know, or not worth wasting time on. She could respect the ones who met her standards . . . but there weren't many of them. When she was about fifteen, by which time they had moved to the East Coast, she remembered one of those intimate mother-daughter conversations, in which Stephanie had confided that, yes, sometimes she had gone along with those propositions when Paula was younger—with discretion, naturally. Intrigued, Paula had wanted to know which ones. Stephanie mentioned a couple of names, and Paula had found that she approved the choices. Instead of feeling indignation as she had half expected, she had found her mother to be a suddenly far more human and exciting person.

"Hello, American Princess," a voice whispered from nearby. "Are you awake?"

Paula turned her head and made out a figure crouched by the bunk in the darkness. "Who is it?"

"It is I, Dagmar." Dagmar was an East German girl, about the same age as Paula, auburn-haired, not unattractive, with a firm, shapely body and freckled face.

"What do you want?"

"To say hello—to be friends. Is not right they all mean to you like this. I think is not Princess's fault if world can't get along, yes? So I come, make good. We can be friends together, yes?"

Paula blinked sleepily—she had been farther gone than she'd realized. "Why not? . . . Maybe."

She sensed the face coming closer in the darkness. There was alcohol on the other woman's breath. "Yes, Dagmar and Princess can be good friends. No sense to fight . . ."

Paula felt the blanket being lifted and the hand sliding softly over her breast. "Fuck off!" She knocked the hand away sharply, pulled the blanket back around her neck, and turned away.

"Stuck-up bitch!" Dagmar's voice hissed.

Paula heard her straighten up and stamp away to the far end of the cell. Peals of female laughter came through the darkness a moment later. "What, Dagmar, no luck? What did we tell you?"

"*Der Seicherin!* That's it. She can rot for all I care now."

"How much did we say you owe me, Dagmar? Or would you rather climb in here instead and call it quits?"

Paula pulled the blanket around her face and put everything out of her mind but sleep.

CHAPTER TWENTY-ONE

"I remember an American couple I met last year, when I was on vacation with a girlfriend over in Connemara on the Irish Atlantic coast. Nice looker, too: used to model flimsy knickers and things—you know, the kind you see on the posters in the tube stations. . . . Anyway this couple— a carpenter of some kind and his wife, they were, from Michigan—had bought a porcelain figurine, you see, that they'd found in some little antique shop in a fishing village they'd driven through. It was rather attractive, I must say— two leprechauns with long pipes and evil grins, hatching mischief over jugs of grog. It could easily have been a hundred years old or more. . . ."

"Jeremy," from the British Special Intelligence Service, paused to smile at the recollection as he sat between the two women in the rear seat of the London taxicab. He was suave, urbane, smooth-shaven, wavy-haired, and nattily dressed in a dark three-piece suit with a buttonhole carnation. His speech and manner evoked something of an image that Barbara thought had gone out of style with tailcoats and dreadnoughts.

He continued, "Well, this figurine had an inscription round the base in Gaelic which had been intriguing them for days, but nobody they'd met had been able to translate it for them. But Gaelic poetry was something I used to dabble in, back at university. Would you have believed

I'd decided to try and become a playwright, years ago? I actually got a couple of things staged, too—the usual provincial kind of thing, you know."

"So what did it say?" Sylvia asked from his other side. She was also from SIS, and had been carefully picked for the job because of her tall, lean build, tapering face, and black, shoulder-length hair. She was wearing a navy two-piece costume with polka-dot scarf and trim, white shoes and matching purse, a floppy white hat, and carrying a lightweight pastel-blue shoulder wrap over her arm.

"That was the funny part," Jeremy said. "You see, it said, ha-ha . . . it said, 'Made in Taiwan.' "

Barbara smiled and looked away at the crowd thronging the sidewalk on Oxford Street, a few hundred yards east from Marble Arch. It was well into July, and the summer sun and blue skies had brought out the colors on the London streets: the shirts and dresses of the tourists and late-morning shoppers, the seasonal offerings in the windows of the fashion houses, and riotous displays of orchids, roses, and lilies on the carts of streetcorner flower vendors. There were couples old and young, some arm in arm, some with children; businessmen strolling to lunch, jackets slung over their shoulders, women in colored slacks and bright summer dresses; two Arabs studying a painting in one of the shop windows; an Indian in a turban, munching an ice-cream cone. Just ordinary people, wanting nothing more than to be left alone.

Barbara liked watching people minding their own business. It summed up her outlook on life, as she'd said to Foleda. She thought it a pity that so many people were incapable of doing likewise. And always the wrong people. For invariably, it seemed, it was those of mediocre talents but inflated ambitions, with no affairs of their own worth minding, who meddled the most in other people's. So the people most likely to end up making decisions about other people's lives were usually the last ones anyone would want doing the job. Although she worked for a government, privately she thought they were not unlike germs: the only thing anyone really needed them for was to protect themselves from other people's.

The cab crossed the end of Baker Street, and Jeremy glanced at his watch. They were exactly on time. The driver slowed down and cruised for a block. A woman was waiting on the corner of Duke Street. She was tall and lean, with a tapering face, black shoulder-length hair, and wearing a navy two-piece costume with polka-dot scarf and trim, white shoes and purse, a floppy hat, and carrying a light-weight pastel-blue shoulder wrap. "That's her, Freddie," Jeremy said, pointing. The woman was looking at the taxi-cabs in the oncoming traffic. She saw the yellow-bound notebook wedged on top of the dashboard inside the windshield and raised her arm. The cab pulled over, and she climbed in, seating herself next to Sylvia, who was on the curb side. Because of the tinted rear windows and the high upright back with just a tiny window in the center that London taxis had, it would not be apparent to anyone watching that it was already occupied. The woman would seem to have simply hailed a cab and climbed in.

"Gawd, it's 'er twin sister!" Freddie chirped.

"Just drive, there's a good fellow," Jeremy said. He closed the driver's partition, and they pulled back out into the traffic.

"This is Anita Dorkas," Jeremy said to Barbara. "Anita, this is the American who wants to talk to you. Don't worry about this other person. She's you, as you've probably gathered already, so there's nothing I can tell you about her. So how are things? Do you still have the afternoon free?"

Anita nodded. "I need to be back at the embassy by five, though." She spoke English competently, though her Russian accent was distinctive. "I'm pleased to meet you," she said to Barbara.

"Me, also."

"Did you arrive in England this morning?" Anita asked.

"Nobody said I'd just come here from anywhere," Barbara pointed out. "Only that I'm American."

"Incurably Russian and suspicious," Jeremy said breezily. "She fishes compulsively."

Sylvia was scrutinizing Anita carefully, from her hat down to her shoes. "Tch, tch. You're not wearing lipstick," she said reproachfully.

Anita raised a hand to her mouth involuntarily. "I forgot. I'm sorry—I hardly ever use it."

"Terrible capitalist muck, anyway," Jeremy remarked.

Sylvia produced a handkerchief and mirror from her purse, moistened the handkerchief with her tongue, and wiped her own lips clean. "How's that?"

Jeremy looked her up and down, then Anita, and nodded. "Splendid. Two peas in a pod."

They made a right into New Bond Street, followed it down to Picadilly, and there turned left to head toward the Circus. Jeremy slid the partition open again. "Here'll do, Freddie." The cab pulled over and stopped. Sylvia squeezed by in front of Anita's knees to open the door and climb out. She paid Freddie the fare and added a tip, then strolled along the sidewalk for a few yards before stopping to admire a diorama of the South Seas in a travel agent's window. A half block back along the street, the thickset man in the felt hat and baggy blue suit, who had gotten out of another cab following a few cars behind, stopped in a doorway and studied his newspaper. After a few seconds Sylvia began moving again, and so did he. By that time the cab carrying Barbara, Anita, and Jeremy was already lost in the traffic and on its way to a hotel near Regent's Park, where a suite had been reserved. Meanwhile Sylvia had a slow, solitary but relaxing afternoon ahead of her, leading her tail, whom she had already spotted, around the circuit that Anita had memorized: window shopping along Picadilly and Regent Street, lunch in Leicester Square, a visit to the National Gallery, and then a walk across St. James's Park and coffee over a magazine in a boulevard cafe near Victoria Station before the rendezvous in Buckingham Palace Road to work the switch back again. And she was getting paid for it. There could be worse ways of making a living, she supposed.

Barbara stuck her head through into the bedroom of the hotel suite. "Don't hang up. Anita wants milk, not cream, for the coffee," she told Jeremy, who was sitting propped on the bed with his back against a stack of pillows and his legs stretched out in front of him. His jacket and shoulder strap with holster containing a .38 were draped over the back of a chair, and he was holding a book lying open on his lap.

He addressed the viphone by the bed, which was switched to voice only and at that moment connected to room service. "Oh, one moment. Could we have some milk as well as cream for the coffee, please?" He glanced at Barbara. "Is that it?" She nodded. "That will be all, thank you."

"Thank you, sir," a dignified voice acknowledged from a grille in the unit. "It will be about fifteen minutes." The voice signed itself off with a click.

"Everything going all right?" Jeremy asked.

"Better than we hoped," Barbara said.

"Good-o. The firm likes to please, you know." Jeremy settled himself back more comfortably and returned his attention to his book.

Barbara turned from the doorway and walked back across the lounge to where Anita was sitting in one of the two easy chairs at the table by the window. The view outside was a rolling green sea of Regent's Park treetops, with the buildings of the zoological gardens visible above like white cliffs in the distance. Anita resumed talking as Barbara sat down.

"It was a difficult decision in many ways, but I came to the conclusion that there are basic human values that have to come before patriotism. Certainly that's true if one defines loyalty to the present Soviet regime as patriotism. But that isn't how we see it. Before 1917, Russia was socially and politically backward compared to Western Europe,

I admit, but when you allow for the effect of a czar who was living in a different age and an emotionally unbalanced empress, it was making tremendous strides to catch up. Russia was starting to assert itself as a modern state. The charade of archaic pomp, royal courts, and fairy-tale palaces was played out. Nothing could stop the tides of industry and trade that were sweeping Russia into the twentieth century. The uprising in March was the voice of the real Russia. That was the direction that it should have kept going in. What happened in November was all wrong, an aberration. That is what has to be undone. At the time of the Revolution, Maxim Gorky—and he was no lover of czarism—warned the people not to destroy the palaces and treasures of the old order, because those things represented a cultural heritage that would continue to grow in the new Russia. But instead, it was stunted. What we have seen in the last hundred years is a cancer of barren political dogma and mindless slogans that has suppressed culture. That is what we are committed to ending. Our loyalty is to the Russia that should have been, and which will be one day."

Anita sat on the edge of her chair, polite, but at the same time tense and unsmiling. Her face, though at first sight attractive in proportion and line, revealed an undertone of pallor and tiredness in the daylight by the window which seemed to accentuate the spareness of her frame. Barbara's impression was of someone very serious and very dedicated, for whom one ideal had come to dominate all other considerations in life. Her instinct was to accept Anita as being what she claimed to be—but, of course, something more substantial than that would be needed eventually.

"What I wanted to ask you about was something else," Barbara said. "It goes back a number of years, now. Your former husband, Igor. What can you tell me about him?" She watched Anita's face but was unable to detect an immediate reaction that hinted either of aversion, lingering affection, or any other emotion.

"A lot of things," Anita replied. "What would you like to know?"

"You don't seem surprised or curious about why we should be interested in him."

"Nothing surprises me anymore. I'm sure you have your reasons."

"You were a member of the Friday Club as long as eight years ago," Barbara said, making it a matter-of-fact statement rather than a question.

"Yes."

"And other affiliated groups before that." That was a guess, but worth a stab.

"Yes," Anita answered.

"What kinds of activities were you involved in back then?"

"Is this really necessary? I've been through this over and over with the British. Don't you people talk to each other? I'm sure I don't have to remind you that we have limited time. My understanding was that you considered this meeting to be very important. I would like to make it as useful as possible."

Barbara conceded the point with a nod. "Tell me, then, was your husband also involved in the dissident movement? Did you work together? How close were his views to the ones you expressed a few minutes ago?"

"We were in Sevastopol then. He was working on submarine communications," Anita said distantly. "Then we moved to Moscow. He was made a professor at the university."

"Yes, I have seen his chronological record."

A pigeon alighted on the sill outside the window. It strutted a few steps with its chest pouting and its head extending and retracting like that of a comical clockwork toy, then stopped and cocked an eye to peer in through a pane for a couple of seconds. Then it flew away. "He was one of us," Anita said. "He lived for the same cause. But he was never as passionate about it as some of them were. Maybe it had something to do with his being a scientist. Or maybe he became a scientist because he was that way to begin with. . . . But he was always more unexcitable and analytical. And very patient. He could have waited a hundred years for the system to change."

"Does that mean he might still be actively involved?" Barbara asked.

"Oh, I don't doubt it," Anita said without hesitation. "He's not the kind to be easily changed."

"Do you know where he is now?"

"The last I heard was that he'd moved to Siberia, some kind of scientific establishment somewhere—but that was several years ago now."

"You haven't kept in touch since you separated?"

"No."

Barbara looked surprised. "I'd have thought you work would have required it."

Anita hesitated, then said, "My marriage to Enriko—my present husband—was a very fortunate occurrence for our group. As you can see, it provides opportunities for extending our contacts and gaining overseas support. It seemed better, in order not to risk jeopardizing such a stroke of good luck, to cut my connections with the past." The explanation didn't stand up. If Dyashkin were ever exposed by the KGB, his ex-wife would automatically be on the suspect list regardless of whether she stayed in touch with him or not. That Anita's marriage to a KGB officer had been allowed to go through said, as clearly as anything could, that so far Dyashkin had managed to stay clean. Barbara stared back and said nothing.

Anita became agitated and reached for her purse, which she had set down by the window. She rummaged inside and took out a box of pills. Barbara picked up the jug of fruit juice from the tray standing on the table by the recorder taping the conversation, filled one of the glasses, and held it out. Anita took one of the pills and recomposed herself. "There was more to it than that," she said. "Igor always had an eye for women—maybe you already know that. They responded to him, too, even though he never said very much. He had a way of radiating an aura of . . .

well, call it mystery, or dominance, if you will. You know the kind of thing."

Barbara smiled and tried to look encouraging. "Sure. Who hasn't met a few like that?"

Anita went on, "Perhaps our getting married was a mistake. Igor was a brilliant man. Sometimes I felt I couldn't provide the amount of intellectual stimulation he needed. He was in the Navy when we met, and for a time things seemed to go all right. But after he got his doctorate and we began meeting more academic kinds of people . . ." Anita drained the rest of the glass of juice. "One of his affairs became serious. Of course, the woman was also a scientist—a nuclear expert of some kind. I met her a few times. A very spirited woman. Her hair was the most noticeable thing. Like fire. Yellowy red, almost orange."

"Can you tell me her name?" Barbara asked.

"Oshkadov. Olga Oshkadov."

"Where was she from?"

"I don't know. But she worked at the science city, Novosibirsk."

"I see. Go on."

Anita shrugged. "There isn't really a lot more to tell. He was adamant that he wanted to separate. Because of our underground activities, however, we both saw that it was in our interests not to quarrel or get emotional about the situation. He agreed to a generous settlement financially to smooth things over. I have no complaints, really."

"Was Olga also a dissident?"

"I don't know. If she was, I was never told. But then, you'll appreciate that we were hardly in the habit of publicizing such matters."

Barbara nodded. "And your present marriage to Enriko. Would you say it was, well . . ."

"How far does affection enter into it?" Anita shook her head and smiled humorlessly. "Oh, there's no need to worry about that. I've had my share of those kinds of delusions. Now only the cause matters to me. Enriko means nothing.

This time it's purely a matter of expedience—an opportunity that was too good not to seize."

There was a tap on the door. Jeremy ambled out of the bedroom and opened it to admit a waiter with a cart loaded with plates, silver dishes, and pots. "Oh, jolly good. Just leave it there, would you? Here, buy yourself a drink on us."

"Thank you very much, sir." The waiter left.

"Just one last thing," Barbara said.

Anita looked at her. "Yes?"

"Were you or your husband ever involved with a group known as the Committee for Freedom and Dignity?"

Anita looked puzzled. "No."

"You didn't deal with a person who went by the name of 'Tortoise'?"

"No."

"You're sure?"

Anita shook her head. "I've never heard of either of them. Who are they?"

"You really don't know?"

"No. . . . Can't you tell me who they are?"

Barbara finished the notes she had been making and closed her book. "It doesn't matter," she said. "It's time for lunch."

It was hardly surprising that Anita had never heard of either the Committee or the Tortoise, for neither of them existed. The terms had been invented purely for introduction into the conversation as "tracers." If they turned up in the official Soviet communications traffic intercepted by the Western intelligence in the weeks ahead, it would be a give-away that Anita's loyalties were not as she claimed.

CHAPTER TWENTY-TWO

It hit Paula first when she was on her way to the kitchens, a half hour after the cell's cheerless breakfast of watery oatmeal, black bread with margarine and jam, and tea. A hot flush came over her suddenly. She found herself fighting for breath, and her legs became lead. She tottered against the corridor wall and put a hand out to steady herself.

The female guard who was leading stopped and looked back, while the other three prisoners in the detail waited with no show of concern. "What's the matter with you? Come on."

"You by the wall, move!" the second guard snapped from the rear. She poked Paula sharply in the back with the baton she was carrying.

Paula lurched a couple of paces along the wall, tried to stand, and fell back against it once more. Her chest was pounding, and she could feel perspiration trickling down her body inside her shirt. Nausea welled in her throat. "Can't . . ." she gasped.

"Oh, you don't feel like working today? Is that it? What do you take us for, fools? You don't get away with that kind of thing here. You and you, take her arms. We'll take her to work if she won't walk."

Paula felt two of the other women hold her on either side, and then she was on her way along the corridor again. She had a fleeting impression of somebody going the other way stopping to look curiously, two prisoners in work smocks wheeling a cart into an elevator on one side, and all the time the back of the guard striding ahead . . . wide hips swinging beneath the plain brown military skirt; massive calves encased in thick tan stockings; heavy, flat-heeled shoes. Now they were at the doors leading into the kitchens.

Her first breath inside was like an intake of hot, fetid gas from a furnace, and sent her reeling against one of the aluminum worktables. The Toad was there suddenly, saying something, but all Paula could hear was incoherent snatches of her voice mixed with the guard's.

". . . matter with her? Doesn't she . . ."

"I think it's . . . on the way here . . . malingering?"

"Yes, *you!* I'm talking to you! What do you *babble-babble, cluck-cluck-cluck-cluck-cluck* . . ."

Paula was distantly aware of her knees buckling. Her arm pushed out against something as she slid down the side of the table to the floor. There was a crash and the sounds of breaking glass. The faces of the Toad and the guard were peering down at her with their mouths moving, but both the sight and the sounds were out of focus. After the effort of trying to stand, the relief of sitting was like an escape to nirvana. She let her head fall back against the metal door behind her and closed her eyes, not minding if she stayed there forever. She couldn't get up again, didn't want to get up. Nothing could make her. That was all there was to it.

. . . Then she was being stretched out along the floor. A coat or something was being tucked around her. She drifted. . . .

"Hey, can you hear me?" Someone was slapping her cheek lightly. She was still lying on a hard floor, feeling cold and shivery now. A hand was feeling her pulse . . . then her eyelid was being lifted. A bright light . . . Collar being opened, dermal diffusion capsule taped to the side of her neck. She opened her eyes briefly and saw a woman in a white cap and a medical smock lowering a red blanket. Warmth, blessed warmth . . .

Voices echoed from far away. "Oh no, she's got something all right . . . Couldn't guess at this stage . . . will be notified in due course . . ."

Hands were lifting her. . . .

She was watching Mike showering. Mike had been the oldest of the lovers she'd had. She liked his body the most. He had big shoulders and a barrel chest, and even the thickening around his midriff had excited her as a sign of maturity. He reminded her of Robert Mitchum, one of her favorites from the old-time movies, before they'd been taken over by health-faddist adolescents. She and Mike used to shower together after they made love. The best times had been late in the evening, before going out to dinner, or maybe to a party somewhere in Washington.

He grinned and gestured for her to join him. But as she moved he began changing into the Toad. The closer she approached, the more he transformed. She recoiled, and it was Mike again. There was no way to get to him.

The dream dissolved, leaving her tense and agitated. She turned her head to the side and felt it resting on a pillow that felt soft and smelt clean. The remnant of the image in her mind died away, and her tension with it. Her toes were rubbing on the luxury of smooth linen. The sounds of a woman's footsteps on a hard floor, lasting for a few seconds, stopping, then starting again, and a man's voice talking in Russian, filtered through into her awareness.

She opened her eyes and saw a room with beds and lockers, pastel-yellow walls, and some kind of wheeled apparatus consisting of metal flasks, rubber tubes, and a panel with lights and switches standing at the far end. Raising her head, she saw she was in a small medical ward. A blond orderly was collecting dishes from the other beds and taking them to a cart standing in the center aisle, and a woman on the far side was watching something on a flatscreen mounted on a hinged arm extending across the bed. Another woman was reading, others were sleeping. Paula tried to sit up, but she was too weak and her head swam from the attempt. She followed the orderly with her eyes, licked her lips as she summoned up the effort, and finally managed to croak, *"Pozalsta . . ."*

The orderly looked round, put down the plate she was holding, and came over. She had blue eyes and a pretty face. "So, you are awake now," she said in Russian. "How do you feel?"

"Could I get something to drink?"

"Water, yes? I don't know if anything else would be good." She half-filled a glass from a pitcher on the locker by the bed and helped Paula to lift her head. Nothing had ever tasted so good.

"Better? I'll get the nurse to come and look at you. Sleep some more, now."

"Spasiba, spasiba." Paula lay back and closed her eyes. Simply to be talked to like a human being again . . . She put out of her mind any thought about how long it was likely to last.

They told her it was food poisoning. She told them she wasn't surprised. It would soon pass, they said. One more day of rest, and then there would be no reason for her not to return to work. No, she protested, surely not so soon. She didn't feel up to walking, let alone laboring for ten hours. One more day—they were adamant.

Paula found herself dreading the thought of going back. Several of the other women with her in the ward were also Russians, but they exhibited nothing comparable to the hostility she had been subjected to back in the cell. It seemed she'd managed to get herself confined with just about the worst mix of personalities that she could have run up against.

The woman across the aisle was called Tanya and came originally from Volgograd. It used to be Stalingrad before the Party went through one of its periodic interchangings of black and white and deglorified the great dictator's memory. Tanya was a teacher, and had been arrested for promoting among her pupils ideas that conflicted with the official ideological doctrines. "I couldn't care less about their stupid doctrines," she told Paula. "And that's one of the worst crimes for a teacher. I couldn't make the bureaucrats understand that objective reality *is* what it is, and that it doesn't care what any Party tries to say it should be. We can only discover. Children should be taught *how* to think, not *what* to think. That was all I cared about— children's minds."

"And that can be a crime?"

"A potential threat to the regime—the ultimate crime. But surely it's the same everywhere. Isn't religion used in America for the same purpose—to instill obedience and stifle questions?"

Paula shook her head. "No—it's just there if people

want it. In fact, you can't mix it with education, by law."

Tanya looked at her curiously. "Really? That's interesting. I didn't know that. I haven't met many Americans. They don't give you permission to travel to other countries very easily over there, do they?"

"You don't need any permission. Anybody can just get on a plane and go where they want."

"I hadn't heard that before. . . . You *are* being serious, I suppose?"

In the next bed was Anastasia, from Khabarovsk on the Pacific side of Siberia, who said her brother had been convicted of passing secrets to the Chinese. "I hope it doesn't affect my son's career," she told Paula. "He's such a bright boy. At school they're teaching him to program computers. Do American boys ever get to see a computer when they're only fifteen?"

Paula was told she would be moving back to her cell after the evening meal. As the afternoon wore on, she grew quieter, and became inwardly nervous to the borderline of being fearful. She tried to read and rest to recover her strength as best she could, but the emotional strain was draining energy out of her faster than it was recharging. She even toyed with the thought of staging an accident—anything to put off the moment of having to return to the kitchens and the cell.

And then, when there was less than an hour to go before the evening meal was brought in, she heard a voice that she recognized remonstrating loudly in the corridor beyond the ward door, which was open. "I don't care if you are a doctor. It isn't doing her any good, I tell you. It isn't of medical knowledge, it's a matter of common sense." Paula looked up sharply. The Russian woman with fiery, shoulder-length hair had stopped just outside. She was wearing a light-green two-piece tunic and talking to a gray-bearded man in a knee-length white coat. Paula caught a glimpse of her firmly defined, high-cheeked features and determined chin as she half-turned and raised a hand to make her point. The man said something in a lower voice that Paula couldn't catch, and then they moved on. "Then, I'll make sure that somebody in higher authority is informed. If you won't sign a simple . . ." The orange-haired woman's voice faded away.

Suddenly Paula was seized by uncontrollable desperation. "Anna!" she called out.

The blond orderly came out of the instrument room at the far end of the ward. "You wanted something?"

"Yes, look, somebody I know just went past, out there in the corridor. She went that way, with a doctor. Please catch her and tell her I have to talk to her, would you? It's very important. She has red hair, and she was wearing a green suit."

Anna nodded and hurried out into the corridor. Paula lay back against her pillow and found that she was trembling. But she couldn't let the chance pass by. Slowly she calmed down. Chance? . . . Chance of what? Now she didn't even know what she was going to say.

Footsteps sounded outside, and a moment later Anna came back in. "I found the lady," she announced, looking at Paula oddly. "She doesn't know an American woman called Paula Shelmer. But she will come and see what you want. She'll be here in a minute or two, she says." Anna disappeared back into the room at the rear.

Paula looked around. Tanya was sleeping, and Anastasia was sitting at the table at the far end of the ward, writing something. Of the other three from the nearby beds, two were away undergoing therapy, and the other was at the table with Anastasia. So it would be possible to speak with some privacy at least. She lay back, trying to force herself to breathe normally and relax.

The orange-haired woman reappeared in the corridor outside, entered, saw Paula without showing a flicker of recognition, and continued looking around. Eventually her eyes wandered back. Paula nodded and mustered a smile. The Russian woman came over to the bed and stood looking down with a puzzled expression on her face. "You are the American?" she said in excellent English. "Do I know you? . . . But yes, your face does seem familiar."

"Turgenev six weeks ago—the Security Headquarters. You were giving two officers a tough time. I was outside. You came out and spoke to me."

Comprehension flowed into the Russian woman's face. It was an amazingly expressive face. "Yes, of course! The nervous girl in the corridor. I was trying to place you somewhere here, not back there. So, we both wound up in Zamork." She waved a hand briefly. "But why are you in here?"

"Food poisoning, they said. A bug or something. . . . I don't know."

"You are an American, so. And your name is Paula. I am called Olga. But the girl said there was something important. What is it?"

Paula looked over her shoulder and then back. "It's not really something I'd want to make public knowledge . . ."

Olga moved closer and sat down on the edge of the bed. She looked at Paula questioningly. "Well?"

"You said not to be intimidated."

"That's right. They will try, but you mustn't let them. Once they find a crack, they have you. Then they keep hammering in wedges. But strength, they respect. It's all they respect. If only America had understood that sixty years ago."

"The place they've put me in is dreadful. And the people there . . . It's not so much intimidation as degradation."

"Yes, that is another of their nasty tricks. I sympathize. Make a fuss until they change it. You Americans are like the British and try to compromise to please everybody. It can't be done. You just end up pleasing nobody. That's not the way to deal with Russians. They all shout, and whoever shouts the loudest and longest gets his way." Olga patted Paula's arm affectionately and started to rise. Paula caught her by the sleeve.

"I heard you telling those officers that you are a scientist."

Olga hesitated, then sat down again. "So, what of it?"

"And that's how you come to speak English so well?"

Olga nodded but didn't reply. Paula went on, "What does a scientist do in a place like this? I mean, are there opportunities to use your mind, to think? Are there others you can communicate with?"

"Naturally there are. This is a space habitat. Resources are limited. They don't ship people this far to open doors and count heads."

Paula took a long breath. "I am a scientist, too," she said. She'd decided before Olga came in that she could hardly do any damage by revealing no more than Protbornov and his interrogators had already established.

"Well, that's very good, and I respect you as a fellow professional. But I still don't see what—"

"You have influence. You can persuade people. Look, I scrape grease off dishes in a stinking kitchen and scrub floors, day after day. Can you talk to someone who might get me moved out? I can do more good somewhere else— better for me, and better for the colony."

Olga frowned. "Are you saying you want to work for them?" Paula noticed she said "them" and not "us."

"I'm not talking about changing sides," Paula said. "I just want to work as a person—on something that has no military value. There must be such things here. You just said yourself that resources are valuable here. Why waste any? There are children in the colony—I could teach science, maybe; or there might be something connected with medicine, agriculture . . . anything."

Olga looked dubious. "Well, I really don't know what I can do. . . ." She caught the imploring look in Paula's eyes, but that only seemed to make her more defensive. She got up and began turning. "My own problems are one thing—I can shout at them about things like that. But interfering in policy on something like is different. I am sorry, but I'm sure it will all straighten itself out in good—" she stopped as if a new thought had just struck her, and turned back. "What kind of scientist are you?"

"Communications electronics. Computers . . ."

"Where did you learn that?"

"I'd rather not say."

"Hmm . . ." Olga regarded her with what seemed like a new interest. "You know something about communications-system protocols and operating software? Encryption routines and hardware microcode?"

"Some," Paula replied cautiously.

"What about Russian systems?"

"I've dealt with them."

"I see." Olga brought a hand up to her chin and stared at Paula for what seemed a long time. Then, abruptly, she seemed to make up her mind. "I can't make promises, and I don't do miracles," she said. "So don't hope for too much. But we'll see." With that she turned away again and left the room.

The women who were attending therapy returned a short while later, and Paula did her best to match their chatter through the evening meal. When it was over, the same two guards who had escorted the work detail arrived to collect her. Anastasia and Tanya gave her a bag of candies to take back, which they had put together between them. "To show how Russians and Americans ought to be," Anastasia told her. Tanya smiled and patted Paula's arm. Paula kissed both of them and found that her eyes were watery.

"They would be, if only they were left alone," she said. Then, with a sickening feeling of dread rising in her stomach, she went back to her bed and picked up the bag into which she had already put her things, while the guards waited stone-faced just inside the door.

At that moment hurried footsteps sounded in the corridor outside, and Dr. Rubakov, the senior physician, came in, waving some papers. "Ah, good, she's still here." Rubakov turned to the two guards. "The order has been rescinded. The American woman is to remain here for a further three days' rest and recuperation. Here is the countermanding order and papers, all signed and approved. You may go." He showed the papers to the senior of the two guards. The guard took them, scrutinized the top sheet carefully, turned it over, and nodded finally to her companion with a shrug. They left, closing the door behind them.

The reprieve had been so sudden and so overwhelming that for a moment Paula thought she was going to collapse again. She sat down shakily on the end of her bed. Rubakov looked pleased. "I'm glad they changed their minds," he said. "You need more time to get over it." He moved closer and studied Paula for a few seconds, at the same time stroking his mustache with the knuckle of his forefinger. "So perhaps we can do a deal, eh?" he murmured in a lower voice. "I can get good cosmetics—French brands, no less. Make you feel and look a new person. Interested, maybe?"

Paula closed her eyes and sighed. "What kind of deal?"

Rubakov looked suddenly alarmed and embarrassed. "Oh no! You misunderstand." He shook his head and spread his hands. "I just want lessons to improve my English!"

CHAPTER TWENTY-THREE

It was like a reprieve from a death sentence. Paula couldn't be sure that the last-minute change of plan had anything to do with Olga's intervening somewhere, but for the moment she was content to make the best of the opportunity to regain her strength, and leave the question to answer itself in due course. But secretly the hope was there, though she tried not to admit it to herself consciously because of the risk of a greater disappointment later. She became brighter and more cheerful toward everyone around her.

Dr. Rubakov appeared the next day with the ultimate luxury in the form of a box of milk bath salts, with some lotion and even nail polish for her hands, and a lipstick to add some color for her face—tawny pink, just right for her complexion. After a breakfast of poached eggs and ham with a spiced potato-onion hash, buttered toast, and real coffee, she kept her side of the bargain by giving an impromptu one-hour English lesson before he went on duty. He came back for another hour during his midday break, and again in the evening.

"I never realize is so, so . . . *uzasno?*"

"Terrible."

"*Da*, terrible!" Rubakov threw up his hands and shook his head despairingly at the pieces of paper that he and Paula had accumulated between them on the table. "Here words are spelt the same but sound different; those ones have same sounds, all written different. Where is sense? How can anyone know ever what to write? But children, they learn this?"

"I didn't invent it. I'm just telling you how it is," Paula said. "Maybe that's why your guys and our guys have had such a hard time getting along." They both laughed.

"It's all a result of ancient vernaculars, you know," Tanya, who had been listening, said in Russian from her bed behind them.

"What do you mean?" Rubakov asked, turning.

"Ever since long ago, back to the time of the Greeks and Romans, people had the problem of trying to talk to the slaves that were brought back from conquered nations," Tanya explained. "So 'vernaculars' emerged between household members and servants—simplified mixtures of languages which combined all the oddities from the originals. Over the centuries that followed, waves of successive migrants from religious and political persecutions, and so on, came to Britain, all bringing their own languages with them. They landed at different places, and by the time they all met in the middle, all the conventions were firmly established and nobody was going to change. So, you see, English came out of it as *the* vernacular of all the vernaculars of Europe."

"And now America has continued the process by mixing in Yiddish, Negro, Hispanic, Amerind, and heaven knows what else," Paula said. "It's a superset of English."

"Russians have never had the problem," Anastasia

commented from the far side. "Nobody is clamoring to get in. They all want to get out."

The next morning, Rubakov told Paula that General Protbornov would be arriving later to talk to her. The announcement jolted her back to reality, and for the next couple of hours she became subdued, viewing her prospects with a mixture of excitement, which she didn't dare let herself dwell upon, and trepidation. Protbornov appeared shortly before lunch, accompanied by Major Uskayev. They collected Paula and went into the duty nurse's office, just inside the ward door. Protbornov took the chair behind the desk and motioned Paula to sit opposite. Uskayev sat by the wall to one side.

Protbornov emitted a heavy sigh that made Paula think of a lumbering bear. He rested an elbow on the arm of his chair and stroked the sides of his craggy face with thumb and fingers for a few seconds. "I gather you have met Comrade Oshkadov," he said at last.

"Oshkadov? Is that Olga, the scientist from Novosibirsk?"

"A spirited woman, even if misguided in some ways. A kindred spirit of yours, I would imagine. In fact, you told her that you are also a scientist."

Paula shrugged. "It's not as if it were something you didn't already know."

"You value science highly, don't you, Lieutenant Bryce," Protbornov said. The fact that he knew her identity was no reason for her to make it public knowledge. If Earnshaw, wherever he was, found a way to contact her, he would seek her by her cover name. "You show a total dedication to its ideals."

"I value worthwhile knowledge and methods for acquiring it that have been shown to work," Paula agreed. "Things that matter."

"But ideas, laws, how societies should be structured and governed—such things do not matter?"

"Politics, you mean?"

"Politics, religion, ideology—call it what you will."

Paula wrestled with the question. Obviously the

proposition couldn't be denied outright. "Of course things like that make a difference to the lives of people—a big difference," she said finally. "But the things that interest me are the ones that were true long before there were any people, and which will remain true if people disappear."

"You just want to get to the stars. It doesn't matter who with, under what flag?"

"I didn't say that. The stars can wait a bit longer. They're good at it."

Protbornov's mouth twitched in what could almost have been a smile to acknowledge the rebuffed gambit. "You say these things. Yet you are with the United States Air Force, engaged in espionage. A strange career to pick, for a woman of such a political disposition, wouldn't you think?"

Paula sighed and brushed a curl of hair away from her brow. "It was personal. I joined the service for the independence . . . to be away from home, and for the education. Understanding science was important to me. This other business . . . it was something I got talked into. It's not what I do."

"What do you do?"

"We've been through all that. I won't answer."

"So you say you were talked into espionage work. You were forced to spy for the American military? Would you be willing to make a statement to that effect?"

"No, I wouldn't."

"You know, for someone asking favors, you could be more cooperative."

"I didn't ask for favors. I offered a trade."

Protbornov glanced at Major Uskayev, at the same time raising his eyebrows and straightening his fingers momentarily from his chin. The gesture seemed to say, well, it had been worth a try. He paused, giving the subject a moment to fade into the background, then came to the main point. "I understand that you indicated to Comrade Oshkadov that you are willing to be more useful to us."

"Within limits."

"Why should you wish to benefit us?"

"I don't. I wish to benefit myself."

"Frankness is something I respect. So, what are the limits?"

"I have no desire to defect. I wouldn't work on anything of military significance, or act against the interests of my country. But outside that, I'd be willing to explore possibilities for mutual accommodation."

"Why should we be interested in coming to any accommodation?" Protbornov asked.

"Because your resources are limited up here," Paula replied. "You can't afford people who are dead weight." Protbornov grunted and shifted his eyes inquiring to Uskayev.

"We are told that you have expertise in the field of communications," the major said, leaning forward.

"Some."

"Would you be prepared to do work involving communications?"

"Such as what?" Paula asked guardedly.

Uskayev pouted his lips. "Oh, development and improvement of facilities for communicating to Earth and other space stations, perhaps."

"No. I said I won't get involved in anything military."

"But *Valentina Tereshkova* is not a military facility. It is purely an experiment in sociology."

"Oh, come on. You know that anything developed here would have potential everywhere else."

"How about high-speed data-compression and -protection techniques?"

"No. Look, why don't we forget about my specializations altogether. They're not for sale. But apart from that, I'm familiar with basic scientific principles that apply to any field—teaching, maybe, or medicine. There has to be room for some kind of deal that we can come away from and both be better off than we would have been without any deal at all. That's all I'm saying."

Uskayev studied his hands, paring one thumbnail against the other. Finally he looked up and shook his head dubiously. "I don't think she can be of very much use to us," he said to Protbornov.

Protbornov, however, didn't seem satisfied. He started to reply, then changed his mind and looked at Paula. "I'd like to speak to Major Uskayev privately for a few minutes. Please wait outside."

Paula sat at the table in the ward aisle, turning the pages of a magazine but not seeing them. Wrong, wrong, wrong, she told herself. She'd blown it. She had been too stubborn. As Protbornov had said, a person in her position could hardly expect to get away without making a few concessions. She could see the two officers arguing and gesticulating through the observation window of the nurse's office. She should have indicated a tentative compliance for the time being—to get herself transferred out of those dreadful kitchens—and worried about the specifics later, when it would have been more trouble for them to move her back. Why did she always try doing things all at once, instead of taking them a step at a time? Olga had told her how the Russians achieved their ends slowly, by working wedges into cracks. Here had been her chance to delicately insert a wedge of her own. Instead she'd swung a sledgehammer.

At last they called her back in. "We have agreed on a compromise offer," Protbornov said. "We will assign you to work with Comrade Oshkadov for a probationary period. She will be able to give you a better idea of the possibilities available. During that time you must consider what you would be prepared to contribute that might justify a more permanent arrangement. The situation will be reviewed in one month. In the meantime, we accept your claim of being a scientist and not a professional spy. Your status will be adjusted accordingly if you accept. Well?"

"I'll take it," Paula said at once. By this time, she had no stomach left for being obstinate.

❖   ❖   ❖

They gave her a light-green tunic like the one Olga had been wearing in the infirmary, and moved her upstairs to an above-surface part of Zamork that she hadn't known existed. The terrain sloped upward to the containing wall in keeping with the general layout of the central valley, and westward toward Novyi Kazan a high-level reservoir bounded the detention facility and separated it from the urban center.

Within this area, the privileged category of prisoners, which Paula learned she had now joined, lived in four-person huts beneath *Tereshkova*'s ribbon-suns and peculiar, curving sky. Although the surroundings of coarse grass, leathery scrub plants, and some uncertain-looking trees holding their own in the cindery soil formed a setting that would have fitted a refugee camp more than a Florida country club, after the cells and the kitchens below it was idyllic. Some of the huts boasted patches of flowers. There was even a beach fringing the reservoir, with a bathing area enclosed by a wire fence twenty yards or so out—admittedly not in use currently because of oil leaks from somewhere and a problem with algal blooms—but the feeling of wind blowing across open water after seeing nothing but bare cell interiors and drab, riveted walls for more weeks than she had been able to keep track of was exhilarating.

And on her first evening there, when she walked down through the rows of huts to the reservoir, along by the water, and back following the outer hull wall via the hill at the rear, it rained.

CHAPTER TWENTY-FOUR

At the end of July, the Russians privately released to a number of selected Western and Asian governments a recording of what they claimed was a voluntary confession by Magician. In it, Magician appeared at ease, composed, and in good health. In their consensus, the doctors, psychologists, and experienced interrogators who viewed the recording found no evidence of coercion.

Magician claimed that for many years he had been obsessed with concern over the international situation. He abhorred the distrust the Communist world and the West, and the prospect of its leading to a global calamity horrified him. So, when what seemed like a unique opportunity presented itself, he had attempted to make his own single-handed contribution to easing world tensions. The file of information he had compiled to substantiate the claims of advanced weapons systems being concealed on *Valentina Tereshkova* was a fake. He had invented the data and misled Western intelligence deliberately, in order to provoke public accusations and denials. He had believed at the time that this would force the Soviet government into a more open policy and lead eventually to full international inspection. Thus a major source of potential misunderstanding would have been defused. His intentions had been for the best, as he saw it. However, since then he had come to realize that he had acted naively, and in fact had aggravated the situation instead. He hoped that in setting the record straight he would undo some of the damage he had caused. He regretted his actions, asked the West to understand, and expressed thanks to the Soviet counselors and doctors who had helped him see everything more clearly.

"What do you make of it?" Philip Borden, the UDIA's director, asked Foleda after they had viewed the recording with others in a conference room inside the Pentagon.

Foleda shrugged. "How can anyone know what to make of it? You know as well as I do, Phil, that with the things they've got these days, they could have turned the pope into an atheist since Magician was grabbed. I'd be closer to being convinced if they let some of our people talk to him freely, face-to-face. If he's genuine, what would they have to lose?"

Foleda wasn't the only person to feel that way. After consultation, the US ambassador in Moscow, on behalf of a number of interested nations, challenged the Soviet government to make Magician available for unsupervised interviews by experts freely selected by the West. To the surprise of everyone involved, the Soviets readily agreed.

CHAPTER TWENTY-FIVE

". . . in the formation of a class with *radical chains*, a class of civil society which is not a class of civil society, an estate which is the dissolution of all estates, a sphere which has a universal character by its universal suffering and claims no *particular right* because no *particular wrong* but *wrong generally* is perpetrated against it; which can invoke no *historical* but only its *human* title, which does not stand in any one-sided opposition to the consequences but in all-round opposition to the presuppositions of . . ." The tall, bearded Estonian standing on the box in the general compound delivered his reading from the works of Marx in an untiring, strident monotone that sounded like the long-playing version of a Moslem call to prayer from the top of a minaret. The audience before him continued murmuring among themselves with total inattention, reasonably confident that even the most diligent KGB eavesdropper who might still be glued to a directional microphone capable of distinguishing anything intelligible would long since have been put to sleep.

"We could pool some points and try getting approval to start glassblowing as a hobby, for ornaments or something," Rashazzi suggested. "That would get us some basic equipment and materials. For the optical cavity we'd need, oh . . . say, a meter or two of Pyrex tube. Then for—"

"Sealing it would require a gas-oxygen torch," Haber said. "Soda lime glass could be worked with a propane torch, which would be easier to get hold of."

"Okay, soda-lime glass. Then we'd need some optical-quality glass to make Brewster windows, an abrasive powder for sawing and grinding, and components for the end-mirror cells. . . ."

Haber was still shaking his head. "It's formidable. You still need a vacuum pump and manometer . . ."

"We use the glassblowing setup," Rashazzi said.

"And then the electronics."

"I know where I can get neon-sign electrodes from somebody in the town. A plain, double-sided, epoxy-glass PCB could be made into a twenty-kilovolt capacitor. We've already got some rectifiers."

McCain kept quiet. There wasn't much he could have contributed, anyway. He'd asked them if it would be feasible to home-build a suitable laser device for the method that Scanlon had first speculated about to communicate messages out of *Tereshkova*.

"Gas-dynamic would be simpler to construct," Haber said. "Although there would still be the problem of procuring suitable nozzles and fuel supplies."

After more than two months of observing, listening, and getting to know how the system at Zamork worked, McCain had come to the conclusion that there might still be a chance of carrying out the mission he'd come here to accomplish. True, there was scant likelihood of obtaining the Tangerine file now; but that had been only a means to the end of ascertaining *Tereshkova's* true nature. His unique situation compared to the rest of the interested section of the West's intelligence community put him in an ideal position to do just that. It couldn't be a one-man operation, however, and that raised the eternal Zamork problem of trying to decide who was reliable. He'd already recruited Scanlon and Mungabo, and now he was putting out feelers to Rashazzi and Haber. It was difficult to imagine anyone with their kind of knowledge earning a living as jailhouse stool pigeons.

"Perhaps you're right," Rashazzi said resignedly to Haber at last. "It's complicated. Maybe the answer isn't to try making our own laser at all. Suppose we just get enough pieces to make what looks like a broken Russian one. Then we find some way to switch it with a working one—there must be some in the labs in Landausk, for example. Or what about alignment lasers? There's still construction going on in some areas."

Haber admired the young Israeli's enthusiasm, but remained pessimistic. "It's no good," he told McCain. "There simply aren't enough places to hide all the parts we'd need, never mind to assemble and test the finished device. Such a task could never be concealed from surveillance."

In the background, the Marxian chant continued with no sign of abatement. "What we need is somewhere permanent to do it, free from surveillance," Rashazzi muttered, staring down at the floor.

"Something like a workshop," McCain said.

"Yes, that's it exactly. We need a workshop."

If Andreyov was a plant, it was the best piece of acting McCain had ever come across. But that in itself didn't make him potentially useful—he was getting old, and he had a loose tongue. All the same, McCain tried making a few indirect references to subverting the system to see if he would catch the gist. Andreyov missed the point and responded typically.

"The system wasn't always like that. The czars, oh yes, they were authoritarian all right, but then Russia has always been authoritarian. It wasn't the same kind of thing. The arts flourished then, because artists were allowed to express what they felt. It wasn't all political. There were Tolstoy and Tchaikovsky, Borodin . . . And there were some executions, yes—a few, mainly criminals—but nothing compared to what came later. Political prisoners weren't treated badly under the czars, you know. The jailers got reprimanded if they didn't address them respectfully. Most of them were cultured, you see. Gentlemen. Not like the rubbish that took over later—murderers and thieves, the lot of them, no better than Hitler. Worse than Hitler.

"Do you know what lost Hitler the war? It was the

Nazi racial lunacies. When the Germans invaded Russia in 1941, whole nations of people that the Bolsheviks had taken over wanted to help throw the Communists out—Estonians, Latvians, Lithuanians, Ukrainians. Eager to fight they were. But Hitler thought they were subhumans and wouldn't use them. He wanted Russia to be defeated by Germans. But it wasn't, of course."

"I heard a joke about Russians," Charlie Chan said, who was listening. "Ivan and Boris meet in the square outside a railroad station in Moscow, you see. Ivan says to Boris, 'Where are you going?' and Boris says, 'I'm catching the train to Minsk, to get bread.' 'But you can get bread right here, in Moscow.' Boris says, 'I know, but the line starts in Minsk.' "

Antonos Gonares, the Hungarian who shared a partitioned bay with Smovak and Vorghas, interested McCain because he often went on work details to the hub. The official plans of *Tereshkova* showed the zone behind the docking ports as housing the nuclear reactors that powered the main generating plant and provided process heat for some of the manufacturing operations. Other reports, however, held that the manufacturing was less extensive than claimed, and that most of the space in those compartments held other installations.

"What kind of work do you do in the hub?" McCain asked Gonares casually one day.

"It varies. Sometimes we move freight around in the cargo bays. Sometimes it's cleaning out tanks or scraping down metal for repainting."

"In the cargo bays? You mean behind the docking ports, back near the nuclear area?"

"Yes, sometimes. Why?"

"Oh, you know journalists—always curious. I was just trying to get a clear picture in my mind of the layout. Who knows?—I might end up writing about it someday. I, ah, I'm sure I could persuade my editors to cash a few points for more details . . . if they proved useful."

"Ah, I see. . . . What kind of details?"

"Oh, nothing very demanding. What's inside which compartment. The positions and directions of the bulkheads. What kind of security they operate there. Maybe a sketch or two?"

"How much might we be talking about?"

"What are the risks, and what would make them worthwhile?"

"Well, maybe. . . . Let me think about it."

Oskar Smovak rubbed his bushy, Fidel Castro beard as he stood watching McCain, who was staring out across the B Block mess area. "What do you see?" he asked after a while. For once, his usually cutting voice was low and measured.

McCain turned his head. "How to you mean?"

"You watch people, and you think. You say little. What are you looking for?"

"I'm just a compulsive people-watcher."

"Is that a common habit among journalists?"

"Probably. How can you report what you don't see?"

"Come on, you're no journalist, Lew. I just wanted to say that if I can, I'd like to help. Okay?"

"Help? What with?"

"Whatever you're planning."

"If I find myself planning something, I'll bear it in mind."

Smovak sighed. "Yes, I know, it's difficult knowing who to trust, isn't it. But for what it's worth, I've managed to get some information for about the American woman that you came here with." McCain looked round at him sharply. Smovak went on, "She was in a close-confinement cell in D Block up to about a week ago, but she got sick and was taken to the infirmary. She hasn't come back since."

"Who told you that?"

"A nameless friend in another billet who screws an East German wench from the cell she was in. It sounded as if the others gave her a hard time."

"I see. . . . Okay, thanks, Oskar. And I'll let you know if I need a hand."

Borowski, the Pole, had warned McCain minutes before the incident with Maiskevik. "How did you know?" McCain asked him one day as they talked in the compound.

"I just had the feeling they were setting somebody up that night. I figured it had to be you."

"So how come I was left alone afterward?" McCain asked.

"You would have exposed Luchenko's sidelines. He probably bribed someone higher up not to pursue the matter."

"Wouldn't that someone have guessed already?"

"Probably. But why go looking under shitty stones when you can be paid not to?"

Which was pretty much what Andreyov had said. But McCain had never been fully satisfied with that explanation. If the authorities already knew about the graft systems that were operating around the place, Luchenko wouldn't have stood to lose much from exposure. So he could have continued with his taxation racket *and* have kept face by having McCain put through the mill. Something didn't add up—but McCain wasn't about to get to the bottom of it just then, and there would be no point in pursuing the matter. "Why'd you do it?" he asked instead. "Did you have something personal against Maiskevik?"

"We all had something personal against Maiskevik. But on top of that, I'm Polish. I've heard you talk; you know our history—how Stalin carved Poland up with Hitler and stabbed us in the back in 1939, and Katyn, and what happened to the Warsaw resistance army. The Russians have always dreaded the thought of a strong Poland. We've never had any reason to feel exactly charitable toward the Russians."

" 'Tis very sociable you're becoming all of a sudden, I can't help noticing," Scanlon said over lunch. "Little tête-a-têtes going on all the time wherever I turn my head. I take it you're recruiting."

"As you said, just being sociable."

"Oh, come on now, I thought we were supposed to be partners. Don't I even get to know who it is I'm likely to find meself working with?"

"If there's a need."

"Aha, always the cautious one, eh?"

"You know the rules. It avoids risking embarrassing complications."

"You went to a good school, I see. Purely out of curiosity, what part of Western intelligence were you with?"

"SIS—the Brits. They infiltrated me in here specially to keep an eye on you. You got yourself such a reputation in London."

"Oh, it's like that, is it? Very well, Mr. Earnshaw, journalist, then here's me with a little tip for ye that'll make your life a whole lot easier. Talk to Koh. He'll put you in touch with the escape committee. They're the people with information of the kind ye could be using."

McCain stared incredulously. "Escape committee? You're joking!"

Scanlon gave a satisfied nod of his gaunt, hollow-cheeked face. "Yes indeed, now, that's put a different tune in your fiddle, hasn't it? I hope ye've a conscience in you, Earnshaw, because it's shame ye should be feelin'."

"Who's on this committee?"

"Ah, come on, now. You know the rules. I've given you my tip. It's Koh that you need to be talking to."

CHAPTER TWENTY-SIX

The Soviet embassy in Kensington was an eleven-story gray stone building of solid, uncluttered lines, built in the last ten years, standing in a walled enclosure of well-tended lawns and shrubbery behind a thick screen of trees. Inside the same compound, an adjacent apartment building of similar size housed most of the Soviet diplomatic personnel stationed in London. Despite such comforts as the swimming pool, sauna, gymnasium, and tennis courts that life within the compound offered, Anita Dorkas was more than grateful to live outside, a privilege that a *Novoye Vermya* correspondent enjoyed.

For one thing it meant she and Enriko could usually manage to skip the dreary weekly Party meetings that were obligatory for everyone else, and live their private lives away from the stultifying cloistered existence led by those within—most of whom knew no more about the world outside than they were permitted to see on supervised tours made in groups. But more important, it enabled them to escape the omnipresent web of informants competing to discover anything derogatory. The wives were notorious for courting mutual confidences in order to curry favor with the chiefs by disclosing what they had learned, while two men would spend the night drinking together and then race to file reports on each other the next morning. The privilege existed to allow Enriko, in his capacity as a KGB case officer responsible for recruiting sources among British nationals and foreign residents, to operate more freely, since the embassy itself was under constant surveillance by the British; the irony of it was that the same convenience made it easier for Anita to conduct her own extramural dissident activities, too.

As was her habit on days when she was on duty, she took the tube to Holland Park station and walked from there. Enriko was using the car that day, anyway, to go to Hatfield for a luncheon interview with the chairman of a British industrial association. The Englishman prided himself on his political astuteness and was flattered at the suggestion of being quoted in a restricted-circulation newsletter that Enriko had assured him was read daily by the top Soviet leaders. Enriko would insist on making a small payment, of course, because ". . . our accounting procedures require it." In time, as what had ostensibly begun as a friendship based on common business interests deepened, Enriko would ask for gradually more demanding favors and the payments would get bigger, until one day the victim would wake up to find himself way out of his depth. Then the high-pressure business would begin. There were four basic vulnerabilities that led people into being recruited, Enriko sometimes said, quoting an American acronym that the CIA taught their people. "MICE"—Money, Ideology, Compromise, Ego. In the case of the soon-to-be-recruited British industrialist, clearly it was Ego.

The gate attendant waved her on through, and she entered the marble foyer of the embassy building through the main entrance. An elevator took her up past nine floors of regular embassy rooms and offices to the tenth, where she emerged into the windowless anteroom of the London Residency of the KGB's First Chief Directorate, which handled all operations abroad. As with its counterparts in Washington, Paris, Bonn, Rome, Brasila, Bangkok, New Delhi, and elsewhere, it existed solely for the purpose of subversion and information gathering. Anita's special key opened the outer steel door. The security officer on duty checked her ID via a remote viewpanel and opened the second door, three feet beyond the first, from inside. She entered, nodding a good morning to him in his guardpost as she passed, and went through into the central corridor of the lower level.

The thing that most people noticed immediately upon entering the Residency for the first time was the sepulchral quiet pervading the place. It was because the outer walls, floors, and ceilings of the building's entire top two floors were all double to ensure soundproofing, with electronic noise beamed through the spaces between to frustrate listening devices. The few windows were formed from a one-way opaque glass that was also soundproof and impervious to all known types of eavesdropping equipment. A whole social order based on treachery, deceit, mistrust, and paranoia, Anita thought to herself. How was it possible to avoid becoming embroiled in it along with everyone else?

She passed the large General Programs room, with twenty-odd work booths at which a number of case officers were already busy drafting reports, translating documents, and formulating operational plans. The important work of the case officers was considered to be not the obtaining of restricted information and documents—although this was valuable enough—but the discovering, cultivating, and eventual recruiting of "agents of influence": politicians, government officials, journalists, academicians, and the like—persons able to influence policy-making and public opinion. For the mission of the KGB was still what it had always been: to preserve and expand the power of the Soviet Communist Party oligarchy throughout the world by essentially clandestine means.

Across the corridor, on the far side of a wood-paneled outer room furnished with antique cabinets, a sofa, leather-backed chairs, and a conference table, was the office of the Resident, Major General Dimitri Turenov. Beyond that were two more offices. The first was shared by two of the line chiefs: the chief of Line X—the KGB field term for Directorate T, which collected foreign scientific and technological data—and the chief of Line N (Directorate S), which was responsible for supporting "illegals"—Soviet-bloc nationals infiltrated into other countries under various identities. The next office belonged to both the chief of Line KR (Directorate K), whose task was countering British counterintelligence, and the internal-security officer, who looked after the embassy's protection, the guarding of important Soviet visitors to the country, and recapturing defectors. Opposite these was the larger office shared by the chief of the American Group, who compiled dossiers on resident American businesspeople, scientists, technicians, servicemen, and others who had come to their attention as potentially useful; the chief of a similar group that watched West Europeans; and the active-measures officer, who handled covert operations and orchestrated disinformation and propaganda campaigns among the British news media.

Halfway along the corridor she came to the stairway

and elevator connecting the tenth and eleventh floors. Halfway up the stairs she met Ivan, one of the case officers, and Anatoli on their way down. Anatoli was one of the technicians who monitored local British police and counterintelligence-service radio frequencies. If, for example, a sudden increase in British surveillance communications activity occurred just before an agent from the Residency was due to meet with one of his contacts, the agent would be signaled by radio to abort the appointment.

"Good morning," Anita said to them.

"Did Enriko come in with you?" Ivan asked.

"I'm afraid not. He'll be out until the afternoon. Is it important?"

"Popovechny wanted to talk to him. He asked me to mention it if I saw him, that's all." General Vadim Popovechny was the Residency's second-in-command and also the head of Line PR, specializing in political intelligence. He was dedicated, ambitious, and injected the ideal measure of toughness into the place to complement Turenov's more intellectual and sophisticated management style.

"Any idea what it's about?" Anita asked.

"Sorry, no."

"Where's he gone?" Anatoli inquired.

"Hatfield, I think he said."

"Oh well, see you later, anyhow," Ivan said.

"Yes. Maybe at lunch."

"See you later," Anatoli said.

The eleventh floor contained the electronics-surveillance officer's domain, which included an enormous room packed with radio and microwave receivers, recorders, computers, terminals, and equipment that communicated with satellites via antennas on the roof. Next to that were the Technical Operations and Photography labs, and then the Translation Office, which Anita entered. Grigori and Eva were already there. Anastasia had a dental appointment and wouldn't be in until later, she remembered, and it was Viktor's day off. "Good morning," she said.

"Hello, Anita," Grigori answered. He was in his late twenties, and had come out from Moscow fairly recently to spend a couple of years familiarizing himself with overseas routine before becoming active in the field.

Eva, cheerful and freckle-faced, was both physicist and linguist, and had taught English at the Foreign Intelligence School of Moscow University's Institute for International Relations. She looked around from the screen that she was working at and grinned. "Hi. Say, I like the coat. Is it new?"

Anita took her coat off, held it up for Eva to see, then hung it on the rack inside the door. "I got it a couple of days ago in Queensway. On sale, too."

"I love the color. And that collar has such a stylish look."

"Oh, Viktor worked late and finished the Chalmers article, so you don't have to worry about it," Grigori informed her. "It's all filed and logged."

"Good," Anita said. "I don't like dealing with that heavy technical material, anyway." She sat down at her own terminal, activated it, and entered a call to the classified section of the computer records for the file she had saved yesterday. "It's going to be a hot day."

"I was thinking of going for a swim in the compound at lunchtime," Eva said.

"Sounds like a good idea. Maybe I'll join you." Anita produced her magnetic key and inserted it in her desk to open the drawer containing the original documents that she had been working from. She was about to say something further, then stopped and frowned down at the drawer as the lock failed to disengage. Either it was faulty, or her key had been invalidated—all the electronic locks in the building could be reprogrammed remotely from the Security Office downstairs. An instant later a message on her screen announced: ILLEGAL ACCESS CODE. REQUEST DENIED.

Anita stared perplexedly at the screen. Then she realized that Maria Chorenkov, the section's supervisor, was standing in the doorway of her office adjoining the Translation room.

"Comrade Dorkas, would you step this way, please," she said. She was a tall, straight-bodied woman with a sharp face, thin-rimmed spectacles, and graying hair tied in a bun, who always wore thick, utilitarian stockings and drab tweedy clothes. Her voice just at this moment fitted the image. Confused, Anita followed her into the office. Behind her, Eva and Grigori exchanged apprehensive glances.

"You won't be needing access to the records, since you will no longer be working with this section," Chorenkov told her without preliminaries when the door was closed. "You are being transferred downstairs to the Secretariat, effective immediately. Collect your personal belongings, please. And thank you for your help during the time you have been with us."

Anita was flummoxed. "But this is so sudden. I don't understand . . ."

"All I know is that I have direct instructions from General Popovechny."

"He gave no reason?"

"Not to me. And I didn't ask."

"But . . . Could I speak with him, please?"

"That is impossible. He will be out until tomorrow."

Anita collected her personal belongings, mumbled a bewildered farewell to Grigori and Eva, and went back downstairs to report to the Secretariat, which provided the Residency's clerical services. She was given the job of searching through British newspapers, magazines, specialist journals, and the public dataservice for references to certain listed topics. All the information was freely available in the public domain; it gave her the uneasy feeling that her security clearance had been suspended.

But by lunchtime she was telling herself that she had overreacted. The mundane work had to be done, after all, and somebody had to do it. Maria Chorenkov's brusqueness and insensitivity had been typical. Tomorrow there would be a simple explanation. By midafternoon she had just about recovered from the shock, when Colonel Felyakin, the internal-security officer, called her into his office.

"You are scheduled for leave tomorrow, I see," he said.

"Yes," Anita replied.

"I hope you haven't made any important plans, because it will be necessary to change your arrangements," he told her. "A couple of people from Moscow will be here, and one of the things they want to look into involves you and your husband. Apparently there has been an administrative mix-up over the dates and durations of some of the postings, and we'd like to get it straightened out. Can you manage that all right?"

"Why, yes . . . I suppose so."

"Thank you. Shall we say ten o'clock? Oh, and your husband also. I've checked, and he is due in tomorrow, anyway."

"I'll tell him."

"And make sure you have your passports. We'll need to check the dates and visas in them."

"Yes. Ten o'clock tomorrow," Anita repeated mechanically.

"Excellent."

By evening Anita's imagination had turned her fears into certainly. Somehow they were on to her. Enriko called to say he had been detained during the afternoon and would be going straight back to the embassy for an evening appointment with the Line KR chief, Colonel Shepanov. The solitude aggravated Anita's nervousness. She paced restlessly about the apartment, smoking more cigarettes than she was accustomed to and fussing with knickknacks and ornaments that didn't need rearranging. She poured herself a drink and sat staring unseeingly at the television for an hour, searching back in her mind over the events of the past few weeks for a hint of anything that might have gone wrong or something indiscreet that she might have said. She could find nothing, but that didn't really amount to much. The biggest danger in this kind of business was having to depend on other people.

Every time she looked at the clock, another slice of time had been shaved off the interval that remained until ten tomorrow morning. She found herself dreading the thought of reentering the embassy. If a KGB officer's wife had come under suspicion, it would be automatic for his reliability to be questioned too. Who were these people from Moscow who wanted to talk to them? Why the need for passports? She didn't believe the explanation that Felyakin had given.

It was around midnight when Enriko finally appeared, having left the car at the embassy and taken a taxi. He and Shepanov had been drinking together, and although he wasn't sufficiently far gone to be called drunk, it showed. This happened from time to time. Anita saw it as a safety valve against the stresses that made ulcers, high blood pressure, and nervous problems routine occupational hazards of a KGB officer's life—and Enriko always had enough sense not to let it get out of hand. But whereas he usually came home bright-eyed and talkative after an evening of drinking with friends, on this occasion he returned morose and distracted. Obviously there was something heavy weighing on his mind.

"What is it?" Anita asked him.

"Nothing."

"Look, I can see something's wrong. But I can't read minds. How can I help if you won't say what's the matter?" He just looked at her strangely for a while and wouldn't answer.

Finally, after he had poured himself another drink and was sitting opposite her on the couch in the lounge, he said, "Shepanov is heading for trouble, you know. He has problems with his marriage, and that is leading him into a problem with drink. It's a familiar story."

"I've heard gossip around the compound about his wife and one or two names," Anita replied. "Yes, it happens."

"And he's lonely away from Russia and his friends. He likes having someone to talk to. But sometimes he opens up too much and says things that he shouldn't." Enriko seemed to be working up to something. Anita waited. Then he took a gulp from his glass and asked suddenly, "How much do you know about that woman scientist from Novosibirsk that your former husband took up with?"

Instantly anita stiffened. Normally her reaction would have been to remind him that they had agreed not to talk about such matters, but it was too close to the things that had been preying on her mind all evening. Instead she asked, "What do you mean? What about her?"

"Oh, I'm not interested in your personal affairs or anything like that. But what about her . . . politically?" Enriko took another drink, and for the first time Anita wondered if he really had gone past the limit. "Was her loyalty ever in question?"

Anita stared at him for a few seconds, trying to fit what he was saying in with the other things that had happened that day. "Why?" she asked. Her voice was strangely dry and hollow. "What's happened?"

Enriko looked up to meet her eyes directly. "Shepanov told me tonight that she was arrested three months ago on charges involving illegal dissident activity. That, of course, would put Dyashkin under suspicion straight away." Enriko didn't have to spell out the rest. All of Dyashkin's close associates and relatives would also be subject to investigation, and especially Anita as his ex-wife. That was something that Enriko could have done without as far as his own career prospects were concerned. "Were you ever mixed up in anything like that?" he demanded.

"Of course not. I went through enough screening before we were married. You know yourself how rigorous they are."

"They have made mistakes, nevertheless."

Anita felt herself grow cold and start to shake. She needed to escape for a moment to compose herself. "Let me get you a coffee," she said.

"Anita, look at me. I ask you again—Were you ever involved in anything like that?"

She forced herself to react angrily. "I told you, no! Sober up, you're being ridiculous. Would you like a coffee?"

Enriko slumped back on the couch. "Yes, maybe I should. . . ."

Anita got up and hurried through to the kitchen. Her mind was too agitated to think while she opened a cabinet and took out the coffee and two mugs. Then, as she stood staring at the jar in her hands, the realization came over her that if she went back to the embassy tomorrow morning, the only way she would ever leave it again would be under escort, heading for the airport to board a Moscow-bound plane. Enriko would no doubt weather through eventually. She wouldn't last a day. Very likely she was finished already.

She stood there, gnawing at her lip, dismissing from her mind preposterous thoughts of what she could do. Then she slowly raised the jar of coffee in both hands, hesitated for a moment, and smashed it on the floor. By the time Enriko appeared in the lounge doorway, she was already past him in the hall, slipping on her coat. He looked at her uncertainly. "What was that? Are you all right? Where are you going?"

"The coffee jar—it slipped. I'm just going to get some more at the shop on the corner. Be a dear and clean it up while I'm gone, would you?" And before Enriko could reply, she had let herself out the hall door and was heading for the stairs. The apartment was only one floor up, and instead of using the front entrance, she went on down another level and left the building via a side door from the parking basement.

Anita walked several blocks, then took a cab to Knightsbridge on the south side of Hyde Park. She went into a hotel that she knew there and sat for a while, steadying herself with a drink in the upstairs bar and thinking what to do next. Then, reaching the conclusion that she had no other choice, she went to a phone booth in the lobby and called the special number she had been given by her contact at SIS.

In an operations room of the British Special Intelligence Service located in a labyrinth that had existed beneath Whitehall since the days of World War II, the duty officer who took the call consulted a supervisor, and then sent out a radio signal coded for emergency priority. Two miles away in Chelsea, the signal activated an ordinary-looking communicator in the pocket of a jacket that had been thrown over the back of a chair, underneath a pile of clothes. The unit had been set to reject incoming calls. However, it contained special-purpose circuitry that caused the standard setting to be bypassed.

Jeremy had been waiting months for this. The chateaubriand for two had been splendid, the wine impeccable, and the atmosphere enchanting. Now, with the soft strains of violins and the scent of roses pervading her bedroom, the evening was almost complete.

Daphne kissed him on the mouth and lay back, smiling seductively as she opened her robe to uncover her perfect body. Jeremy allowed his eyes to feast on the sight. "I say," he murmured. "I've always had a thing about flimsy little knickers like those. Is what's underneath as pretty as the rest?"

"Why don't you find out?" she whispered.

His hand stole down from her cheek, lingered at her breast to excite her nipple, then stroked downward, over her stomach, as the muscles tensed in eager anticipation.

Beep! Beep! Beep! Beep! . . .

"*Bloody Christ, not now!* . . . Blast! Blast! Damn and blast the buggering sods! They can't—"

"What is it?" Daphne shrieked, sitting up.

"I have to call in."

"You said you were off all night."

"I am. I mean . . . Oh, it's too complicated to explain now."

"Can't you turn the bloody thing off?"

"It's somewhere under all this stuff . . ."

"Be careful with that dress, darling."

"There. Oh, God! . . ."

Daphne pulled her robe back around her and reached for a cigarette. She sighed resignedly. "The phone's there. Better luck next time?"

"Oh, there will be a next time, then?"

"But of course. In fact, I think you did it on purpose, just to heighten the suspense."

"You really are insane. But I'll still take the rain check."

"Rain check?"

"Oh, it's what the Americans say."

"What does it mean?"

Jeremy stopped as he was about to punch in the number. "Do you know," he said, suddenly bemused, "I have absolutely no idea."

Jeremy collected Anita in a cab from a rendezvous at Hyde Park Corner and took her to an address south of the river, in Lambeth. When they arrived, Sylvia was already there with another woman from SIS. Two agents would be there twenty-four hours a day until Anita was moved, and the police would be keeping a watch on the outside discreetly.

"What do you think will happen next?" Anita asked them.

"That's not up to us," Sylvia answered.

"Since the Americans have been showing so much interest in you, it wouldn't surprise me if you ended up being whisked off over there," Jeremy said.

"I do hope I haven't been a nuisance," Anita told them.

Sylvia laughed. "Of course not. It's our job. What a silly thing to say!"

"Never let it be said that we allowed anything to come before King and Country," Jeremy recited staunchly. Sylvia gave him a curious look. He sniffed disdainfully. "I rather think I'll go and put on some tea." With that he marched out of the room and across the hallway outside—stopping to deliver a hefty kick at the umbrella stand on the way.

CHAPTER TWENTY-SEVEN

Getting anything organized in Zamork on the systematic basis that McCain had in mind would require ways of evading the informers and electronic surveillance devices—

and if McCain's theory of the whole operation having been set up as an "information mine" was correct, the Russians were unlikely to have settled for half-measures.

Rashazzi and Haber had developed several techniques for locating and disabling concealed microphones, and were experimenting with ways of neutralizing the bracelet monitors. To mask these activities and at the same time provide some amusement for himself, Rashazzi had been training his mice to eat the polyvinyl insulating coatings of Russian electrical wiring, and then releasing the mice into the spaces behind the floors and walls. When Russian technicians arrived to trace the faults that the two scientists' tamperings sometimes caused in the security system, they invariably found short-circuited wiring that looked for the world as if it had been nibbled by busy rodent teeth, usually with mouse droppings nearby. The ruse didn't last long, however, and instructions came down through Luchenko for Rashazzi to get rid of the mice. Then they mysteriously escaped from their cages and presumably disappeared into the hole that just as mysteriously appeared in the wall underneath the tank in one of the B-3 toilet cubicles. Their mobility must have been extraordinary, for within days repair crews were rushing frantically all over Zamork in response to a plague of electrical failures and burned-out lighting circuits. Luchenko was in trouble with the block supervisor, and Rashazzi lost a stack of accumulated privileges, but the reactions went no further than that.

The exercise provided a smoke screen for finding out more about the security system, but it really didn't solve the overall problem. The Russians had long been adepts at deception, and it was never possible to be sure that the surveillance measures uncovered at one level were not decoys intended to divert the prisoners' attention while a more cunningly hidden level continued operating unimpaired. Long after Rashazzi and Haber had become experts at ferreting out wired microphones, for example, they discovered another kind embedded in the walls, which operated without any telltale leads at all: they were connected by strips of conducting paint, which were then concealed by a layer of ordinary paint. Rashazzi made a probe tipped by a pair of fine needles that could detect the strips, but it was tedious work.

It was possible to play various games to try and deduce if a particular location was being monitored, such as deliberately staging a provocative-sounding dialogue there and watching for any Russian response. The trouble was that Russians could play games like that too, by weaving their net with a wide mesh and purposely allowing the small fry through in order to catch the bigger fish later. How many were willing to be fall guys to find out?

McCain concluded there could be no safe way of communicating inside Zamork's regular environment. The outside work details offered better prospects, but he had no control over who was assigned to them—and he himself was confined to working inside Zamork, anyway. But then, he asked himself, was it so essential to get out of Zamork itself, after all? Surveillance devices would be in the places where people went: in the billets, corridors, mess areas, and so on. But in addition to places like those, the structure included spaces behind the walls, machinery compartments between decks, and shafts carrying cables and ducting off in all directions. If there were some way of getting into places like that . . .

McCain put the question to Rashazzi one morning as they were walking along Gorky Street, staying close to a tractor hauling a trailer loaded with trays of rattling pipe fittings.

"Albrecht and I have been looking into that for some time," Rashazzi said. "The problem is that the wall- and floor-panels everywhere carry a system of conductive strips on the back that will cause open circuits and set off alarms if they're moved."

"Couldn't you jumper the connections or something before the panels were lifted, so the circuit wasn't broken?" McCain asked.

"You could, if you knew the circuit layout. But you can't

trace the layout until you lift the panels. So it's a vicious circle. A lot of people around Zamork have gotten themselves stretches in solitary through fooling with it. It's a tricky business."

McCain fell silent and stared moodily at the floor as they walked.

Without some way of being able to talk and exchange information freely, he wasn't going to get anywhere.

The outer torus of *Valentina Tereshkova* was a little over three miles around, which meant that the total length of the colony's road system was not large. Therefore the Russians hadn't bothered shipping up heavy road-maintenance machinery to stand idle most of the time; they made use of the labor force already available there instead. When centralized planning failed to produce enough bolts to match the number of holes that Scanlon was drilling, bedframe production ceased while the planners brooded over their schedules, and McCain was sent on an outside assignment with the road-resurfacing gang that Koh was with, working near the edge of one of the agricultural zones. He hoped this would give him the chance he'd been waiting for to talk with Koh in less restrictive surroundings.

The road that the gang was working on ran between rows of corn, at the base of a series of terraced plantations of vines, fruit trees, soybeans, and tomatoes. Above, through the transparent roof section by the nearby agricultural station, one of the minor spokes soared upward to merge into the clutter of the hub structure a half mile overhead. A mild breeze was blowing from the west, and the environment provided a welcome change from Zamork for the guards as well as for the prisoners, which meant that nobody was in any hurry to get the job done, so supervision was minimal. Two of the guards were playing cards across the hood of one of the trucks and another was sitting reading in the driver's seat, while the rest sauntered about casually, sometimes exchanging words with the prisoners. McCain was working with Koh a short distance away from the others, using rakes to spread a sticky gray concoction of lunar-rock furnace slag and binding compound processed from industrial leftovers.

"So, what did you do?" McCain asked.

"How do you mean?" Koh replied. McCain had the feeling that Koh knew quite well what he meant.

"You said once that you'd tell me sometime about what you did to wind up in here."

Koh worked on in silence for a while. McCain thought he was ignoring the question, when suddenly Koh chuckled. "Do you remember the incident at the Asian Industrial Fair in Chungking a couple of years ago?"

"Seems to ring a kind of a bell. . . . There was a fire, wasn't there? Something to do with the KGB."

"A Chinese traditionalist movement called White Moon was making a nuisance of itself, campaigning against industrialization and modernization," Koh said. "They staged a demonstration at the Chinese pavilion . . . or at least, that was the way it was supposed to look."

McCain nodded. "Now I remember. Except they weren't White Moon people at all. They were imposters. It was a stunt set up by the Chinese intelligence service to discredit them and justify imposing tighter restrictions. But later, the guy who authorized it admitted he was working for the KGB. So all the time, it was a deception orchestrated by Mosc . . ." McCain's voice trailed away. He stopped what he was doing and looked up suddenly. "Wait a minute. Nakajima-Lin Kohmei-Tso-Liang—it was *you!* You were the KGB's inside man, the head of Chinese intelligence."

"Deputy head," Koh said.

"Whatever. So what went wrong? How'd you wind up in here?"

Koh chuckled again. "Yes, it was my idea—a bit unfair, I suppose, but you've no idea how difficult White Moon was becoming. It was just intended to be a demonstration. The people we hired weren't supposed to burn the whole pavilion down. That was entirely due to an overzealous subordinate. But it was my responsibility, and we do have a strong sense of honor . . ." Koh shook his head from side to side, and his breath came in quick, shaking gasps, as if what was amusing him was too much to bear. "But, you see, the KGB had nothing to do with it, hee-hee-hee. . . . I only made that confession after everything was blown anyway."

"You mean you never worked for the KGB?"

"No. It was probably the first piece of international mischief in which they were genuinely innocent, ha-ha-ha . . . and nobody believed them!"

McCain smiled and turned back to his raking. "And so?"

"So, the KGB kidnapped me to make sure I wouldn't do anything like that again, and here I am."

The dump truck arrived to deposit another load of material and then went to collect a fresh charge from the mixer at the far end of the workings. One of the guards came close to inspect what they were doing, then moved away. They worked on in silence for a while. Finally McCain said, "Scanlon told me I should talk to you."

"Oh yes?"

"Have you ever heard of an escape committee, back at Zamork?"

"One hears all kind of things in Zamork."

"Do you think it's possible at all—escaping from here?"

"They say all things are possible."

It seemed McCain was going to have to work for it. He tried a more oblique approach. "If there were an escape committee, and if it were up to you, who would you trust to recruit into it?" he asked.

"I get the impression that you are already doing an excellent job of working that out for yourself," Koh said.

"Who are the dangerous ones? Who would you leave out?" Koh didn't answer at once, and McCain prompted, "I'd assume not Luchenko and that bunch at the far end, for a start—Nolan and the rest."

Koh frowned. "I'm not so convinced Nolan is one of

them," he said at last. "I don't doubt he's a true believer, but that doesn't mean they'd trust him enough to be a plant. Their leaders tend to be contemptuous of true Marxists, you know. Stalin wasn't at all happy when Beria proposed recruiting upward-bound idealists from English universities back in the nineteen-thirties. He didn't think people who believed such twaddle could make reliable spies."

At least Koh was talking more out here than he usually did. McCain sought to keep it going. "What motivates people like Nolan?" he asked.

"Fear of freedom."

"That sounds like a strange thing to say."

"Not if you think about it. In the long term, humanity is evolving toward the emergence of individualism. Merging the Western philosophy of individual freedom and the political and economic principles that go with that into its own culture is probably the greatest single thing that has happened to Asia. It's the force that is shaping the twenty-first century."

"The good old American system."

"Yes. But nobody ever said it had to stay in America. In any case, it originated in Europe."

"Okay."

Koh went on, "But sometimes social changes are too fast for people to adapt to. When that happens, people are left feeling insecure, threatened by forces they don't understand and can't cope with. So they try to escape by turning the clock back. Early social orders like the feudal systems suppressed individuality, but in return they provided security and certainty. You knew who you were, where you belonged, and what was expected of you—as in childhood, where the authority of the family constrains, but at the same time protects."

"Children have to grow up eventually."

"Yes, and so do people. But when the change is too fast and leaves them feeling isolated, people turn to authoritarianism for the certainty and security they have lost. Hence the rise of Reformation religions of Luther and Calvin when European feudalism collapsed. The middle classes flocked to prostrate themselves before an all-powerful God whose strength would protect them."

"That's just about what happened with Nazi Germany, too," McCain said as he worked.

"Precisely. They weren't ready to become a liberal democracy when the Allies tried to impose it on them after 1918. They, too, yearned for the kind of authority they were used to, and for a strong leader who would take responsibility and make the decisions." Koh shrugged. "And they found one." He lifted a hand from his rake to gesture vaguely at the colony around them. "And the same thing is true of this Soviet political monstrosity. Progressive? Pah! Nothing of the kind. It's the last relic of an order that's on its way out."

"You and Scanlon seem to talk about that kind of thing a lot," McCain said.

"Aren't all the Irish supposed to be philosophers of life, 'which means everything'?" Koh replied.

McCain straightened up and drew a handkerchief from his pants pocket to wipe the sheen of perspiration from his forehead. "Getting back to Scanlon," he said. "About four days ago he told me—"

Koh cut him off with a wave of his hand. "You can save yourself the lengthy explanation." He nodded toward the truck a hundred yards back along the road, which carried the tools, lunch bags, and other oddments. "When you pick up your jacket, look in the inside pocket. You will find something there that should answer your questions. Think of it as a gesture of good faith by the escape committee. They feel there might be grounds for you and them to get together. I get the impression that you feel the same way."

"Then it does really exist?"

"Certainly."

"But how? . . ."

Koh smiled and shook his head. "Never mind how I

know the things I know. Let's just say, Mr. Earnshaw, that both of us know something about the intelligence business."

CHAPTER TWENTY-EIGHT

When the gas pedal of an automobile is pressed harder, the vehicle goes faster. Within the throttle's operating range, the output of the process changes smoothly with input. The mathematical relationship connecting the two is an example of a "linear" function. When pressure is steadily increased on the trigger of a gun, on the other hand, the operation is markedly nonlinear: nothing much happens until the mechanism is on the point of tripping, after which an infinitesimally small further increase of input brings about an abrupt and spectacular change in system output—the gun fires.

Most mathematical representations of nature take the form of functions that change smoothly. The real-world processes that they model, however, invariably lead to discontinuities when taken far enough, and the models turn out to be merely approximations that are close enough to be useful over limited ranges. Thus, solids eventually melt, liquids boil, a star condenses, or a new species emerges: suddenly a phase change occurs in which the former behavior breaks down, new laws supplant the old, and all the previous limits and projections cease to mean anything. These boundaries are the places where the really interesting things in nature happen. Crossing them is what is called Evolution.

Paula had received her first insight into the astonishing complexities that can arise from nonlinear systems when she was studying complex-number theory at college. A "complex" number consists of two independent parts, like the latitude and longitude components of a map reference. And like the points on a map, the total field of all complex numbers can be represented by the infinity of points on a plane—unlike ordinary, one-part numbers, all of which can be represented by the points on an endless line. Now, infinitely many points exist between any two points on a plane, however close to each other they might be; and an infinity of numbers exists between any two of the numbers in the complex-number plane. Therefore, if an arbitrary path is traced across the plane, the value of the numbers that the path passes over will change smoothly with the distance moved: an infinitesimally small change of position will yield an infinitesimally small change in number value. There are no sudden jumps.

The function that particularly excited Paula is called the "Mandelbrot Set," and has been described as the most complicated object known to mathematics. Yet the method of generating it is amazingly uncomplicated. A point is taken on the complex plane, and the number that it corresponds to is used as the input to a simple equation. The equation is then evaluated to produce a result. Depending on the range that the result falls in, a color is assigned to the corresponding point on a display screen. Repeating the procedure for all the other points generates a color map of how the result obtained changes from place to place for the originally smooth-changing number field. The outcome is not a mixture of formless patches as might be supposed, which would denote lumplike properties varying steadily from region to region. Instead, what emerges is highly organized, infinitely detailed *structure!* Totally unexpected discontinuities and instabilities appear, in which the minutest variations of input send the results fleeing away to infinity; and yet a curious connectedness remains, producing spirals, snowflakes, filaments, and strangely beautiful compound forms, ever-varying in an unending regress of successive levels of detail down to whatever resolution might be explored.

Reflecting on how a simple mathematical relationship could create such astounding richness of form out of nothing more than a smoothly graded number field, Paula had suddenly made the connection to the generation of form and structure in the natural world—for the shapes and whirls and connecting threads revealed in the graphics imagery *were* compellingly evocative of the structures found in nature. And was not the entire physical universe the product of physical "processors" operating analogously upon steadily varying gradients of electric and magnetic fields, chemical concentrations, pressures, temperatures, velocities, and densities, from the molecular fields that guide the differentiation of growing embryos to the ridges and chasms of space-time that mold galaxies? That was when she had experienced her first true excitement at the world of physical sciences, from which had grown the compulsion to comprehend more of its workings that she had known ever since.

She was reminded of those natural hairspring mechanisms now, as she sat staring at a display screen in a computer-graphics lab in the Government Center at Turgenev. One of the things the *Valentina Tereshkova* experiment was revealing already was that there was still much to be learned about maintaining complex closed ecologies. With Olga's help, Paula had ended up working in a section of the Environmental Department, creating computer models of plant and microorganism interaction cycles. The hope was eventually to integrate such models into a comprehensive simulation of the colony's entire biology—although that goal could easily be still many years away. She traveled with an escorted party of others to Turgenev every day through a five-day week, and back to Zamork in the evening. She spent most of her time there in the graphics lab of the central computer facility. The lab was located in a less restricted part of the same general computing complex in which Magician had met his downfall.

On the screen, an intricate, constantly changing network of colored symbols interconnected by flow lines and feedback loops modeled dynamically the collective metabolism of one of the closed aquatic ecosystems being tested in the biolab area at Landausk. Currently the ecology inside *Valentina Tereshkova* was sustained by using industrial engineering processes to produce atmospheric gases, recycle water, and remove wastes. The longer-term intention was to develop a self-regulating biological system to perform these functions—an Earth-type ecology in miniature. But the subtleties and complexities of the interactions involved, even in a small, isolated aquatic system simpler than any farmyard pond, were endless and fascinating. She had thought for a long time at the back of her mind about quitting the Air Force and defense work for a field to which she could devote herself with total absorption. But for some reason she had always put it off for just one more year. . . .

The door of the room opened and Olga came in. She had tied her orange hair high and was carrying some books and a sheaf of papers, which she set down on the desk behind Paula's chair. "Still busy, I see," she said. "I talked to Stefan and got the things you said you wanted to read. Here they are."

Paula turned her chair away from the screen. "Thanks."

"How are things going?"

"Oh . . . more complicated than we expected, but interesting. How much longer before the Zamork bus leaves?"

"About an hour. Why? Do you want to take the later one again? I'm sure it can be arranged."

"Yes."

Olga smiled. "A prisoner applying for overtime. Whoever heard of anything like it?"

"I feel like a person again."

"I was only teasing. I understand." She nodded at the screen. "Are you on the track of what went wrong in test tank three?"

"I think so. The green algae blooms support the fish as food and produce oxygen. Also, they detoxify some of the harmful gases, such as ammonia. The problem with the way it's set up is that the system won't produce a dense algae population, no matter what you do. So it pollutes itself through oxygen starvation."

"Any idea why?"

"The macrophytic plants that they put in as purifiers upstream to oxygenate the shell-bacterial filters also produce an antibiotic that interferes with the reproduction cycle of the algae," Paula said. "But it would be difficult to eliminate them, since they supply feed for the White Chinese Amur fish. So we need some way to break down the antibiotic. Bigheaded carp cause blue-green algae to predominate, whereas Silver Chinese carp, which are phytoplankton eaters, produce a shift toward diaton algae." She sighed. "The whole ecology changes completely with even a slight shift in fish-species composition. In other words, the way they're trying to do it doesn't have enough resilience against change. It's too sensitive. It needs more negative feedback."

Olga looked impressed. "Did you work all this out?"

"No I picked it up from the biologists. I'm just helping out with the software."

Olga moved round the desk and sat down in the chair on the far side. "This kid of thing really interests you, doesn't it," she said.

"Biology?"

"Not that, so much. I know you're a physicist."

Paula leaned her chair back and stretched out a leg to rest her foot on the edge of the console. "Evolution interests me—not in the biological sense especially, but the way order and complexity emerge out of chaos, generally."

"That's what I mean: the underlying processes common to all of science." Olga seemed to be trying to say that science, the common search for truth, was something that united people of all races and nationalities. They adhered to the same standards of ethics and intellectual honesty, and spoke the same language. Deception—especially self-deception—was the only enemy, and it was the enemy of all of them.

Paula looked across the desk and met the Russian woman's questioning look. "Yes, exactly," she said. In other words, they were both on the same side of something that had nothing to do with flags or frontiers. She looked around the room and up at the ceiling, shrugged, and sighed. Olga nodded her head, acknowledging that there was nothing more they could safely say just there and then. But Paula sensed that Olga had accomplished what she'd come in for.

The met again later that evening back at Zamork, on the gray beach fringing the reservoir. The strip-suns overhead were fading in simulated dusk, and other figures were out, making the best of the brief evening that would persist until the perimeter lights were switched on. A cool breeze was coming across the water. Olga turned up the collar of the coat she was wearing over her tunic, and they began walking slowly along the water's edge toward where the beach ended at the hull wall.

"Would it come as any great surprise to you to learn that I might have had my own reasons for agreeing to help you that day back in the infirmary?" Olga asked.

At the time, Paula had been too overwrought with her own circumstances, and later too relieved to know she would be escaping from them, to think about it. But since settling in to her new status, she had wondered. "No it wouldn't," she answered honestly.

"I have no interest in political ideologies," Olga went on. "They are nothing but medieval religion and superstition, hiding behind different slogans. Their purpose is the same: to control the minds of people through dogmatism and manipulation. Neither system respects truth, freedom, or any form of independent thinking, or tolerates opposing opinions. The inquisitors of Galileo were no more interested in the way the Earth moves than American creationists care about the true origins of life on this planet. The real issue in both cases is that of traditional, unquestioned authority being challenged."

"But with science it's different," Paula completed. "Okay, we see eye to eye on all that. So, where is this leading?"

"Along with others, I came to the conclusion that the ethic and rationality of the scientific approach to understanding reality could help form the basis of a saner world," Olga replied. "But Neanderthal political systems stood in the way—particularly the ones like ours that suppress free expression, which is essential if anything better is to evolve. So I became politically active as a dissident, and upset a lot of people in the process. To cut a long story short, I ended up losing my academic titles, being arrested, and eventually getting shipped up here."

Paula nodded. "So?"

"The dissidents that I worked with are still active back there," Olga said. "Most of them are the kind of people that we have talked about—*our* kind of people: scientists, intellectuals, and thinkers who believe in the possibility of a safer, more civilized world based on reason and honesty." They had neared the point where the wall of the outer hull rose sheer at the water's edge. Behind them, the ground above the beach rose steeply to become the hill forming the valley side, lined with the huts of the special VIP's. They stopped, and Olga turned to face Paula directly. "Many others were arrested over the years. We could never find out what had happened to them. But when I came to Zamork, I found many of them up here, alive and well."

"Go on," Paula said, still not seeing any connection with herself.

Olga's voice dropped instinctively, even though they were alone. "I managed to establish a way of communicating with somebody down there."

"To Earth?"

"Yes. I was able to send information about the people who were up here—there were colleagues down there who could make good use of such information, besides friends and relatives who needed to be told. And more than that. With early notification of the new arrivals up here, our people down in Russia knew who else was at risk—the KGB works in predictable patterns. Many were smuggled out of the country in good time. The KGB was going insane trying to discover where the information was coming from."

"Well, that great, but why are you telling me all this?" Paula said.

"The channel was cut, due to an accident. I need a communications specialist to restore it. Now I'm asking you to help me."

So *that* was what had caught Olga's interest in the infirmary. Now it all fitted together. They turned and began retracing their steps slowly along the beach. Lights were coming on around the perimeter and along the wire barrier twenty yards out in the water. "How did it work?" Paula asked.

"Does that mean you will help?"

"I don't know at this stage if I can. You'll have to tell me more about it."

"I once had a lover who was a university professor," Olga replied. "Let's call him Ivan. Oh, it wasn't so terribly serious—he was formerly a Navy man, and quite active with the ladies from Archangel to Vladivostok, I suspect. But whatever, we found that we shared certain values, and we remained good friends even after the passionate stage wore off."

"What kind of professor is he?"

"Was—communications engineering. But now he's at a research establishment in Siberia. It also happens to be the groundstation that handles the main communications link from *Valentina Tereshkova*." Olga turned her head to glance at Paula as they walked. "Now do you see?"

Paula stopped walking, and her eyes narrowed. Olga waited. "The place you've got me into at Turgenev . . . that's no coincidence either, is it?" Paula said slowly. "It's practically next door to the Communications Center."

"You catch on fast" Olga murmured. They resumed walking. Olga continued, "I assume you're familiar with the random-number streams that are used as fillers between messages on secure channels as routine procedure."

Paula saw the implication immediately. "You piggy-backed on the beam, using the gaps."

"Right."

"How?"

"Ivan smuggled a specially programmed electronic chip up to me via a flight-deck officer on one of the transporters. It was designed to replace the random-number generator in the encoding processor of the primary Earthside commlink, inside the Communications Center. The way it worked was, first I'd plug the chip into a BV-Fifteen and preload it with the message text that I wanted to send— I could do that myself anywhere. Then a certain insider whose name doesn't matter would switch the chip inside the Communications Center for me, and the message was transmitted automatically."

"Okay, I get it." Paula nodded. The BV-15 was a standard Soviet general-purpose computer, used as a net terminal or stand-alone system and found all over *Tereshkova*. There were two of them in the graphics lab where Paula worked. "So what went wrong?"

"There was an equipment fault that caused a power surge and blew up the chip," Olga replied simply. "I still have my contact inside the Communications Center. The procedure should still work. But we no longer have the hardware."

"And you want me to program a new chip," Paula concluded.

"Exactly. I have specifications of the BV-Fifteen program for loading the chip, and I can get documentation for the transmission encoders. You already have access to the equipment you need in the graphics lab. There would be no need for you to physically enter the Communications Center itself, or any other secure area."

"What about the messages coming in from Earth?" Paula asked. "How do you handle them?"

"I can take care of that myself," Olga answered.

"If we do it, is there any guarantee Ivan will still be listening after all this time?"

"No. Let's just hope that he is."

They stood looking in silence at the lights and the water

for a while. "When do you want an answer?" Paula asked
at last.

"I was hoping for one now."

"I have to think about it."

"Tomorrow, then?"

"Okay, tomorrow."

When they met the next day, Paula had been having
some ideas of her own about how a private communications
link to Earth might prove useful, too—except that the
people she had in mind to communicate with had nothing
to do with Soviet intellectual dissidents or with spiriting
fugitives out of Russia. How she might be able to extend
the link from the groundstation in Siberia to the West's
military-communications network, she at present hadn't
the faintest idea. But in the meantime, the opportunity
for setting up the first phase was too good to miss. Her
fingertips were already itching impatiently at the prospect.

"All right," she told Olga. "You've got yourself a deal.
Let's hope Ivan's still listening—I'll give it a try."

CHAPTER TWENTY-NINE

McCain rinsed off the suds and dried his face briskly
with his towel in front of the mirror. Gonares was working
at the hub again that week, and had been bringing back
descriptions and sketches as McCain had asked. From
his initial perusals of them, they seemed to McCain to
bear out the officially published construction plans. Maybe
Foleda had allowed himself to get carried away for once.

The door opened as if a grizzly bear had swiped at it,
and Oskar Smovak came in. He threw down a plastic box
containing his soap and shaving gear, and began peeling
off his shirt. "Sounds as if we're going to be getting the
place spruced up before very much longer, eh, Lew?" he
said, leaning forward to examine his beard in the mirror.

"How come?"

"This place is going to be the big attraction."

"Zamork?"

"No, the whole of *Tereshkova*. Haven't you heard?"

"Heard what?"

"Big celebrations for the centenary. All the Russian bigwigs will be coming here—First Secretary Petrokhov, Chairman of the Council of Ministers, Kavansky, the whole Politburo, most of the Central Committee . . . *Tereshkova* will be the showpiece of the Communist world." November 7 was the day the Soviets traditionally celebrated the Revolution. This year would be extra special, since it was the centenary.

"Well, don't forget to write down all your complaints and suggestions," McCain grunted.

When McCain came out of the washroom, he found Luchenko sitting with Nolan at the end table. Andreyov was reading something to Borowski nearby, and Taugin was lying morosely on his bunk. King and Kong, as usual, were hovering not especially inconspicuously in the background. Luchenko caught McCain's eyes and tilted his head to beckon him over. McCain stopped.

"You have been getting good reports from your work detail," Luchenko said. "I'm glad to see it."

"I like to think I earn my keep," McCain answered.

"You seem to be behaving yourself more these days."

"People are leaving me alone more these days."

Luchenko let the remark pass. "Just to show that such things do not go unrecognized, I will be assigning you to more outside duties around the colony," he said. "I trust you will find that agreeable."

McCain raised his eyebrows in genuine surprise. It fitted in with his own aims perfectly. "Sure," he replied. "I like to be out and about."

"Of course. Well, just so you know what to expect." Luchenko stared up with an expression that said he had made a concession and would be expecting some reciprocation. McCain returned a look that said maybe, and moved on. He guessed that Luchenko had had no choice, so was making it look like a favor. In other words, Luchenko had been notified that there was going to be need for a lot of outside work around the colony. It fitted with what Smovak had just said.

Charlie Chan was with Irzan and Nunghan, who were dealing cards over a bunk in one of the middle sections. "I know a funny joke," he said, catching McCain by the sleeve as he passed.

"Oh?"

Charlie Chan shook, barely able to contain himself. "A Russian from Moscow goes into a Yakut's hut on the tundra and sees a glove hanging from the ceiling. He says, 'What's that?' And the Yakut replies, 'A cow's udder.' "

"Go on."

"That's it. A cow's udder!"

Chan collapsed onto his bunk, where he lay shrieking and writhing with mirth. McCain walked on, shaking his head. He still hadn't managed to fathom Charlie Chan's weird humor. Maybe it was a glimpse of how it had all begun, he mused—the first dazzling insight to metaphor, back in the winter gloom of some Neanderthal cave, which had evolved down through the ages from those beginnings through the court jester and the music hall, to Buster Keaton, Laurel and Hardy, the banana peel and the custard pie.

"I know another one just as good," Charlie Chan's voice offered behind him as he reached the front section.

"Tomorrow," McCain called back. "I couldn't stand it."

Mungabo was sitting on the top bunk, sewing a tear in his pants, and Rashazzi and Haber were debating something abstruse at the center table. Scanlon and Koh were sitting on opposite bunks in the bay on the far side, and seemed to be talking about the evolution of cultures again. McCain wandered around the table behind the two scientists and sat down next to Koh. "Smovak tells me we're going to be getting some visitors," McCain said.

Koh nodded. "So it appears. I've also heard a rumor of amnesties being granted—part of the public-relations spectaculars. They plan on making this a big event."

"Does that mean we're all going home?"

"I wouldn't hold my breath. If there's anything to it at all, it probably only applies to the privs."

The talking and the activity among the occupants of the billet's front section were to cover their underlying tension in the time left before lights-out. For tonight was when they would make their first attempt at breaking through into the underfloor space.

"Koh was just saying some fascinating things about history," Scanlon told McCain. "And isn't that something you're always talking about yourself?"

"It was one of my majors, sure," McCain replied.

Koh nodded. "We were discussing the European Renaissance."

"Except that the man's saying it wasn't a Renaissance at all," Scanlon said.

"The term is a misnomer." Koh settled himself more comfortably on the bunk. "It was the *birth* of a new culture, not a rebirth of anything." McCain remembered hearing this before. But on the last occasion, Koh had been smoking his herbal mixture and had become incoherent before he could get any further. Koh went on, "Teachers and professors like to think that their subjects are part of a glorious legacy that spans down through the ages in an unbroken succession from the distant past. It gives them a feeling of noble pedigree. So they present architecture, or art, or mathematics, or whatever as a continuum and divide it into periods that they call Classical, Medieval, Modern, and so on. But the continuity they see is an illusion. Each culture possesses its own unique way of conceptualizing reality— a collective mindset that determines how the world is perceived. And everything which a culture creates—its art, its technology, its political and economic system— is unavoidably part of an expression of its unique worldview. Oh, it's true that a culture might adopt some things it finds useful from others that went before, but that doesn't constitute a lineage. The splendor of Rome was the voice of the Roman worldview; the New York skyline spoke of America. They were products of different minds and perceptions. There was no line of descent from one to the other."

The ceiling lights blinked three times to signal five minutes to lights-out. Haber and Rashazzi got up from the table and came over. McCain moved his legs to make room for Haber to sit down. Rashazzi stepped up to the top bunk and turned to sit with his legs dangling over the side.

Koh continued, "Rome was an expression of Classical Man who never mastered the concept of infinity, but shrank from it at every encounter. Look at his pictures and vase paintings. They show only foregrounds, never any background. You see—they avoid the challenges of distance and limitless extent. His temples were dominated by frontages that denied and suppressed inner space. He shunned the open ocean and seldom sailed out of sight of land. His world was timeless: its past lay hidden in an obscure, unchanging realm of gods, and he made no plans or provision for any future. . . . In other words, everything that Classical Man created expressed the same thing: perception of a world that was finite and bounded. Even his mathematics confined itself to the study of finite, static objects: geometric figures bounded by lines; solids bounded by planes. Time was never recognized as a dynamic variable—that was what confounded Zeno and led to insoluble paradoxes. And Classical Man's number system contained no negatives and no irrationals—not because he was intellectually incapable of dealing with them, but simply because his worldview encompassed nothing that such entities were needed to describe. In a finite, tangible world, numbers merely enumerate finite, tangible objects. And it was perfectly natural that the form of art that dominated his culture should be sculptures: static, finite objects bounded by surfaces."

Rashazzi seemed about to say something, then rubbed

his chin thoughtfully and nodded, evidently deciding not to interrupt. The sound of Smovak bellowing about something came from farther along the billet.

"But Classical Man died, and Europe stagnated through the centuries of its Dark Ages before Western Man appeared. That's the way every new culture arises: nothing significant happens for thousands of years, and then, suddenly, a new breed of Man with a new worldview bursts forth in a frenzy of creativity that sweeps the old order away. Western Man appeared out of the wreckage when European feudalism collapsed—not as a reincarnation of Classical Man, who was gone forever, but born in his own right, from his own beginnings.

"Western Man not only comprehended change and infinity, he delighted in them—with a restless, thrusting energy, the like of which the world had never seen. After the stagnation of the Dark Ages, everything that spoke for him was an exultation of the newfound freedoms that they symbolized. The calculus of Newton and Leibnitz was the language of a universe no longer static and bounded, but dynamic and unlimited, to be explored through the scientific passion for discovery and the voyages of the global navigators. His mastery of perspective and soaring Gothic arches rejoiced in the experience of boundless, endless space. And what was his dominant form of art, which reached its zenith of expression along with the high point of his culture in the eighteenth century? Music, of course. For what else is the music of Mozart and Beethoven than flute and strings exploring vast, orchestra-created voids—the flourishes of baroque porticoes and the curves of the infinitesimal calculus, the commitment to reason and the power of intellect—set to sound?"

Koh paused and stared solemnly into the space opposite him. His voice took on an edge of regret. "But, like Classical Man before him—in fact, any organism that is born lives out its span and dies—he was not immortal. And like Classical Man he balked before realities that his nature was unable to assimilate. The problems that have plagued him since are the consequences."

"You mean the problems we're in right now, today?" Rashazzi said.

"Yes. Whereas Classical Man couldn't come to terms with infinities of space and time, what confounded Western Man was the confrontation with physical infinities: the infinity of potential growth and achievement that is implicit in the evolutionary process itself and in the creative power of the intelligent mind. For although free of the tyranny of feudalism, Western Man is essentially Malthusian in his worldview: always bounded by the currently perceived limits and possibilities. He extended his vision to the horizon, but not beyond it. As the continuous functions of his mathematics aptly symbolize, his is a world that changes smoothly, an orderly, civilized world, unable to accommodate to sudden leaps. Was it mere coincidence, then, that the world of Western Man fell apart at the end of the nineteenth century, when it came face-to-face with the discontinuities of relativity, quantum mechanics, evolution, and the implications of industrialized economic growth? He couldn't cope with phase changes. Oh, some individuals played with the concepts academically in the same way that Zeno played with mathematical infinities; but the collective mind-set of Western Man was unable to *feel* what the concepts *meant*. And so, he has foundered into his own, cultureless, Dark Age."

The lights-out warning flashed. "Time to break it up, you lot at the end," Smovak's voice called out. "Let's have some quiet."

"Oskar, you make more noise than all of those guys put together," Mungabo shot back from the far side of the table. The group dispersed back to their own bunks.

" 'Tis a small part we are of everything, when ye think about it, and that's the truth," Scanlon said from across the aisle as McCain climbed into bed.

"What makes you so interested in all that stuff of Koh's?" McCain asked.

"I'm not sure. It's a new way of looking at things." Scanlon paused. "I suppose a man likes to think that what he is and what he does will add a little to something that matters. Like them stones that Koh talks about . . . Wouldn't anyone rather think that what he did would be built into something worthwhile than be left in the rubble?" McCain turned his head and looked across at him. Scanlon was staring up at the ceiling, deep in thought. Then the lights went out.

A half hour later, McCain was lying in the dark, waiting for his senses to register the pattern of stillness that would tell him that the billet had settled down for the night. It was possible that the surveillance might include infrared sensors capable of tracking body movements in the darkness or other devices that Rashazzi had failed to detect—but there had to be some risks.

"Okay?" he breathed into the darkness when he judged the time to be right.

"Okay," Scanlon's voice whispered back.

"On your way," Mungabo muttered above.

McCain raised his head and whistled quietly through his teeth. A similar signal acknowledged from the far side, which meant Rashazzi agreed. McCain lifted his blanket aside and rolled noiselessly onto the floor. He slid the drawer out from underneath his bunk and placed it on top, then turned and removed Scanlon's drawer also, lifting it up on top of his own. Then he moved out between his and Scanlon's bunks toward the center space of the billet. The black-clad shape of Rashazzi was already wriggling along the floor on the far side of the table to meet him. McCain reached under the table and grasped the ends of the wires that Rashazzi pushed through for him. Then he crawled back between the bunks, passed one wire to Scanlon, and drew the other into the space underneath his own bunk, where the drawer had been.

The "gesture of good faith" that Koh had brought for McCain from the escape committee had turned out to be a set of wiring diagrams showing the layout of heating, lighting, and security circuits, which were standardized and the same for every billet. In particular, they showed the locations of the conducting strips on the backs of the structural panels, and their connection points to the alarm wiring. The information would make it possible to bore holes in just the right places to attach jumper leads for bypassing the breaks, *without* having to disturb any panels beforehand. Then, with luck, they would be able to lift the bypassed floorpanel and explore the recesses beneath without triggering the alarm system. That was the purpose of the night's experiment.

Apparently the escape committee had obtained the diagrams through bribery followed by blackmail from a Russian electrician. Exactly who the committee were, or at least which of them were responsible for this particular venture, Koh hadn't said. Their problem was that they were in a billet on the upper level, and going down from there would simply have brought them through the ceiling of the billets below. Hence they needed the cooperation of people who were already on the lower level.

McCain and Scanlon had spent much of the previous night taking turns to lie in the narrow space between the bunks, laboriously cutting two saucer-size holes through the soft-alloy floorplates in the positions indicated on the diagrams. McCain removed the disk on his side, which had been resealed with a compound of aluminum dust and a nonsetting goo that Rashazzi had concocted, and felt beneath the floorplate for the low-voltage cable running beneath the hole. He scraped an inch of the cable bare and attached the wire that Rashazzi had passed from across the room, securing it with adhesive tape. Meanwhile Scanlon had done the same on his side, hanging his arm around the edge of his bunk. There was nothing more for them to do now until Rashazzi completed the more complicated connections on the far side of the room. When that was done, they would have constructed a bridge circuit across the end of the billet, bypassing the pattern of contact strips beneath the floor. While Rashazzi worked on the wiring, Haber and Koh, working from the bunks on either side, should already have taken the heads off the remaining rivets holding down the panel.

"How are we doing?" Scanlon's voice whispered from the darkness close to McCain's ear.

"It's attached. I'm waiting for Razz." Rashazzi would be measuring resistances and voltages before he risked breaking the circuit.

"Any bets on what's downstairs?"

"Probably bilgewater." Only McCain and Rashazzi would actually be going. There was no need for a circus.

At last, the wire in McCain's fingers jerked three times. He acknowledged. "That's it," he told Scanlon. "They've got the plate up. I guess this is it."

"Good luck, Lew."

McCain crawled back to the center space and stopped to listen, but could detect nothing abnormal. Moving slowly and soundlessly, he crossed the center between the end of the table and the door, and then moved toward the space between the two opposite bunks.

He found the edge of the hole with his fingers. Rashazzi had already gone down. Haber reached out in the darkness and handed him a purloined flashlight and a cloth bag containing tools, some nylon rope, and other items that might come in useful. McCain patted the German's arm, and then lowered himself full-length down into the opening between the bunks. He felt hard protrusions and structural beams around him, all the more constricting and entombing in the total darkness now pressing in from every side. Then he heard the floorplate being replaced above him.

Light appeared ahead, silhouetting Rashazzi's form against a clutter of supporting members, pipework, and cabling. There was little clearance, and McCain's first thought was to wonder if the expedition might have ended already, right there. They began examining the surroundings methodically inch by inch, shifting their flashlights to opposite hands and rolling over to study first one side, then the other. Rashazzi spent some time on his back, examining the conduction strips from the underside. One of the tasks for tonight would be to install a second bypass circuit below the floor, so that in future they'd be able to lift the plate up again without repeating the whole procedure every time. They found no sign of surveillance devices in the below-floor space. Then Rashazzi began worming his way forward. McCain could see nothing of what lay ahead, since Rashazzi's body was between him and the light.

After he had progressed eight feet or so, Rashazzi stopped and began moving the light around to reconnoiter. McCain moved up behind him. It was a tight squeeze. Than, as Rashazzi continued angling his lamp this way and that, a glint of light caught McCain's eye for an instant, reflecting off something *below*. He pointed his own lamp down between two of the metal ribs he was lying on, and brought his face close to peer along the beam. There was a much roomier space down there, with glimpses of machinery. Suddenly McCain realized that he and Rashazzi were not truly in the below-floor space at all. They were lying in a shallow frame carrying pipes and cables immediately beneath the flooring; the true interdeck compartment was still beneath them. He tapped Rashazzi's leg, and light blinded him as Rashazzi aimed his lamp back to look over his shoulder. McCain pointed at the metal work beneath them and jabbed his finger up and down several times. Rashazzi understood and probed the darkness beneath with his beam, but from where they were, there was no way down. Rashazzi continued wriggling forward, stopping after another ten feet or so to let McCain catch up.

By now they were well under the next billet, if not beyond, with a steady background of humming and throbbing coming from the darkness beneath. Rashazzi shone his lamp ahead to check the next stretch. Then he emitted a soft "Ahah!" and resumed crawling. McCain followed and saw that a large pipe that had been walling them in on the right made a sudden turn away, leaving a gap in the side of the frame large enough to squeeze through. Rashazzi was already lowering himself down. Then he provided the light while McCain joined him.

They were in a space barely high enough to stoop in, standing on a metal floor. Around them were runs of ducting, blowers and other machinery, pillars and braces supporting the deck above, and a maze of pipework. Shining their lights upward, they could see the frame they'd been crawling inside. They spent some time checking again for surveillance devices, but could find nothing. "It looks clean," Rashazzi whispered, finally. "You know, I think we might just have done it—a place where we can avoid surveillance, without having to get out of Zamork."

"Maybe," McCain replied. "Let's check out some more of it."

They had already agreed that to get as far from the known parts of Zamork as they could, they would continue exploring downward rather than laterally if they did get below the billet, and accordingly they set to work examining the floor. It consisted of reinforced metal plates secured by spotwelds. Rashazzi had made a hand-operated trepan-like device for cutting sheet metal away around such welds, but it would be tedious and time-consuming. Rather than commit themselves to such a task, they moved along to the next panel, but found the same thing. And with the next; and the next. But the one after that was different: it was secured not by welds, but by snap fasteners.

"Considerate," McCain grunted. "Must be removable for maintenance or something."

Rashazzi shrugged in the torchlight. Without further ado, he loosened the panel and lifted it aside. Below was a shallow space containing a lighting fixture in what was apparently the ceiling of yet another level below. The Israeli felt in one of his pockets for an electrician's screwdriver tipped with a neon indicator and squatted down to probe around the connections. The neon failed to light. "It's not live, anyway," Rashazzi said.

They turned their lamps off while McCain tested the ceiling panel. It lifted freely and showed no trace of light from below. Rashazzi switched his lamp on again, while McCain swung the panel upward on its cables and lodged it to one side. They peered down through the gap and made out more machinery, with portions of metal flooring some distance below; but it was difficult to judge how far. McCain unraveled the rope from his bag and lowered one end down while Rashazzi tied the other end to a pillar. McCain checked that his bag was securely tied at his waist, then swung his legs into the hole and lowered himself down hand over hand until his feet found the floor below. Rashazzi followed.

They were in a narrow walkway that could have been intended for maintenance. It led between pumps, transformers, and large, squat cylinders wreathed in pipes, that seemed to be storage tanks. Or perhaps it could have been used during construction of *Valentina Tereshkova*, for the absence of power in the ceiling light suggested that the place was visited infrequently. "I wonder where this leads," McCain said. "We might have an open gateway here, right out of Zamork, anytime." The floorplates this time, however, were solidly seam-welded, precluding any possibility of penetrating further in the downward direction without enormous effort. They began exploring the surroundings.

Farther on, another walkway went off to one side. They followed it between the last of the storage tanks and girderwork abutting a bulkhead to a series of bays containing power-distribution equipment and banks of enormous batteries—a backup supply system for emergency power. An intermediate deck split the space beyond into two levels. The upper level was cluttered with more piping and structural work. But the lower space, the floor of which was actually sunken a few feet to make it considerably deeper and roomier than it appeared from even a short distance away, was comparatively empty. Conceivably it had been left as expansion space in which to install more equipment at some later date. McCain and Rashazzi glanced at each other in the torchlight, then moved closer and lowered themselves down into the space.

It went back perhaps twenty feet, ending at a solid bulkhead wall, which Rashazzi estimated could well be the near side of Gorky Street, extending down to the lower levels. That fitted with the mental map that McCain had been constructing, too. A wall of cable guides running between roof supports closed in one of the sides, while the other was semi-open to a forest of supports and tiebars that disappeared into the blackness behind the storage tanks.

Rashazzi stroked his chin and looked around. "I don't know where we might be able to get to from here," he said. "It will take some time to check. But you know something, Lew? Think of it—here we are in a pretty secluded place, with another whole level above full of machinery making nice background music to screen out noise. If we could run some power into here from somewhere, this would make the perfect workshop that Albrecht and I were looking for." He nodded and looked around again with evident satisfaction. "Yes I'd say that tonight's expedition has already been well worth the effort."

CHAPTER THIRTY

The warm, dry summer had done wonders for Myra's health, and by the middle of August her face had regained its color and filled out again. "Yeah, I figure you'll last a few more years yet, at least," Foleda told her approvingly as they sat sipping iced orange juice at a sunshaded table on the veranda at the back of the house.

"Doesn't she look so much better," Ella said from where she was sitting with her legs dangling in the pool, watching Johnny and two other boys of about his age from along the street playing in the water on the far side. "You look like a brand-new woman, Mother."

"I feel like one," Myra replied.

"See," Foleda said. He always managed to look outrageous on his days off, and on this occasion was wearing Bermuda shorts of a deafening tartan, sunglasses, and a straw hat. It reminded Ella of pictures she had seen of Churchill in some of his wartime outfits. "That's what having an attentive husband does for you."

"Are you going to let him get away with that, Mother?" Ella asked Myra.

"Sure, if it works both ways," Myra said. "Because I score higher. I mean, look at the state of him. He hasn't had a day sick for years."

"And people always think that kind of work is so stressful. You're a fraud, Dad—and living off us taxpayers, too."

"Nonsense. I work hard all the time. It's the best deal you people ever got—worth every penny."

"How come no heart attacks, then?"

"The light heart and inner tranquility that come from being honest."

Myra laughed delightedly. "How can you possibly mean it, Bernard? What about the fuss you had last week with the attorney general over that Argentinean minister's hotel suite your people bugged?"

"Hell," Foleda grunted. "I said honest, not legal."

A call-tone came from the screenpad lying by the tray on the table. Myra picked it up and acknowledged. It was Randal, Ella's husband, from inside the house. "Is Bernard there?" he asked. Myra passed the pad over.

"What?" Foleda said.

"There's a news item just coming in about that Russian space colony you're always interested in," Randal told him.

"*Tereshkova?*"

"Yes. I thought maybe you'd like to see it right away. . . . Or I could store it for later."

"No, I'd like to see it now," Foleda said. He started to get up.

"Want me to put it through on the pad out there?"

"No, I'll come inside. Why spoil the party?"

A bright-red beach ball bounced on the surface of the water and bobbed against the poolside, with Johnny splashing after it. "Where are you going, Grandpa?" he called up.

"Just inside for a minute."

"Ask them, they'll know," one of Johnny's friends said, coming across behind him.

"We'll know what?" Ella asked them.

"Which *did* come first, the chicken or the egg?"

"Ask your grandma," Ella answered. Johnny looked at Myra.

"Ask your grandfather," Myra said.

"Didn't they teach you at school that birds evolved from reptiles?" Foleda said as he made to leave.

"Sure."

"Well, there's your answer: dinosaurs were laying eggs before there were any chickens."

Foleda found Randal sprawled along a couch in the window-lounge a half level below the kitchen and dining area, a handpad resting on his knee. "What have we got?" Foleda said, perching himself on an arm of one of the chairs facing the wallscreen across the room.

Randal touched a button and the screen came to life with a view of Moscow's Red Square, showing the Kremlin wall and St. Basil's Cathedral. After a few seconds it switched to columns of parading tanks and missile carriers, and then a line of heavily muffled Soviet leaders saluting from the reviewing stand atop the red-marble mausoleum of Lenin's Tomb. "It came in live a few minutes ago," Randal said.

The commentator's voice-over narrated: "News from Moscow today of a big break with tradition. The customary military parade held every November seventh to celebrate the uprising that brought the Communist Party to power, which has long seemed an inviolable national institution, will not take place in this, the Revolution's centenary year. A spokesman for Tass, the Soviet news agency, announced this morning that this year the occasion will be commemorated out in space. Instead of reviewing the traditional military parade in Red Square—which tends to be a cold business around November in Moscow—the Soviet leaders will be traveling en masse to the experimental space colony *Valentina Tereshkova*, two hundred thousand miles from Earth" —a view had appeared of *Tereshkova* hanging in space, followed by standard shots of a transporter docking at the hub, a view of the Turgenev urban zone, and a harvesting machine at work in one of the agricultural sectors, while the voice continued— "to see not marching soldiers and rockets, but scientists, engineers, farmers, and spaceborne factories. So, what does it mean? Are they sending us one of those famous 'signals' we're always being told about? Some of the experts will be giving us their interpretations later. Frank Peterson talked in Moscow with Mr. Gorlienko, the Soviet foreign minister."

"What do you think?" Randal said to Foleda. "Doesn't that look like a change? Come on, Bernard, give them some credit when it's due. This is, exactly the kind of initiative we need more of. We have to reciprocate."

"We'll see." Foleda sounded skeptical.

"Dammit, anyone would think you people wanted a war," Randal said, shaking his head in exasperation.

It was a subject they often argued about. Randal was a psychiatrist. He considered all nuclear weapons immoral and had pronounced the world leadership collectively insane. Foleda, on the other hand, contended that the nuclear-tipped ICBM was the most moral weapon to have been invented since the days when kings led their soldiers into battle. It put the wealthy and powerful of all nations right up in the front line, where the risks were no longer exclusively other people's. "With true democracy," Foleda maintained, "everybody is in the trenches."

On the screen the Soviet foreign minister was telling an interviewer, "Yes, you could describe it as a gesture. We see it as symbolizing the direction of the Soviet Union's commitment to the twenty-first century. Coming in the one hundredth year of our existence as a modern nation, the completion of *Valentina Tereshkova* is a model to the world of what can be accomplished under a communist system. Your economists and experts said it couldn't be done—that our system was too inefficient to achieve any significant nonmilitary goals. They discouraged the emerging nations of the world from trying to emulate us. But we have shown them! Tell us now what we are or are not capable of achieving. That is the direction in which we will continue to grow—stronger and more prosperous. And is it not appropriate that on our centenary, when this policy becomes demonstrable reality, that is where our leaders should be?"

"It's an honest, straightforward, goodwill gesture," Randal said across at Foleda. "Somebody has to start trusting somebody."

Foleda didn't reply, but stared hard at the screen, trying in his mind to reconcile what he had just heard with the most recent trends to be distilled from the various intelligence sources that his people tapped. Deliveries of fuel and supplies to Soviet naval bases had been increasing significantly. The Warsaw Pact nations had announced plans in the weeks ahead for military exercises to be held in Eastern Europe and Siberia that would involve large-scale troop and armor movements. Soviet aircraft had been doing a lot of practice flying lately. Fourteen hospitals near major cities had installed emergency generating equipment in the last three months alone. A KGB general had taken charge of the Soviet civil-defense organization. No single item stood out as grounds for anything conclusive, but taken together they added up to precisely the kind of situation that made intelligence analysts nervous.

But the signs didn't seem to anticipate the same level of activity extending into the longer term. The Soviet military units undergoing mobilization, for example, were not being issued with winter clothing and equipment; the quantities of spare parts being ordered from factories were not consistent with demand requirements extending far into the future. It seemed that whatever they were hatching would happen soon, and was expected to be over with quickly. At a time of acute first-strike apprehensiveness everywhere, such a thought was blood-chilling. And now here was a specific date, less than ten weeks away, slap in the middle of the time frame that seemed to be indicated. Suddenly Foleda felt the sickening certainty that he could already look at a calendar and put his finger on doomsday.

". . . you'd think that some people wanted a war." He realized that Randal had been saying something.

"What are you saying we should do, disarm unilaterally?" he asked, snapping himself back to the present.

"Why not? If we did, they would. Then the problem would have gone away. That's simple enough, surely."

"But suppose you were wrong, and they didn't," Foleda said, his voice still numb. "Would you be willing to run *that* risk? Which would you see as greater?"

Before the exchange could proceed any further, a flashing symbol appeared in the bottom corner of the screen to indicate an incoming call. Randal touched a button on the handpad. "Foledas'. This is Randal."

"Hello, Randal, this is Barbara Haynes, calling Bernard," a woman's voice said from the unit. "Is he around?"

"Hi, Barb. Sure—one moment."

"I'll take it up in the kitchen," Foleda said, relieved at the chance to extricate himself. Randal redirected the call, erased the stored bulletin that they had just watched, and settled back to see what else had come in on the news.

Barbara was calling from a house that the CIA owned on some tree-covered acres in Maryland. "We collected Mrs. Jones and took her to the farm. Everything's fine. Shall I confirm that you'll be coming out tomorrow to talk to her? It meant that Anita Dorkas had arrived from London, been smuggled through the airport despite attempts by Soviet officials to intervene, and was now installed at the safe house.

"Good work," Foleda said. "You bet I'll be there."

The room had a large marble fireplace, a molded plaster ceiling, and high windows with rich, heavy drapes, looking out over lawns and a rose garden. It was furnished traditionally with a slender-legged Georgian sideboard, davenport, side tables, and several settees and wing-backed chairs. A grand piano stood at the far end, inside the arched entranceway from the hall. Anita Dorkas was sitting at one end of the long central table, with Foleda across the corner from her on one side and Barbara on the other. Harry Meech, also from the department, sat at the other end with a portable screenpad, surrounded by files and notes. Gerald Kehrn from the Defense Department was pacing around agitatedly, first studying the pictures on the walls, now picking up a vase, then stooping to examine the china in one of the glass-fronted cabinets.

"And that was enough to make you so certain you'd been discovered?" Foleda said again.

"It wasn't just that. It was a combination of several things," Anita replied. She sounded tired, but not resentful. This kind of thing was necessary and not unexpected. "The behavior of my superior at the embassy that day. The fact that they chose a time when Enriko was away. And when he told me what Shepanov had said—about the woman that my ex-husband had taken up with being arrested—the implications were obvious. Igor—my ex-husband, Professor Dyashkin—would have come under suspicion immediately. We had both been involved in underground dissident activities, and for all I knew he might have been arrested, too, by then. Either way, it was only a matter of time before they got onto me. I was afraid that if I went in to work the next morning, I would only come out again under arrest, en route for Russia."

"You just walked out," Foleda said. "Not a word to your husband? You didn't say anything? You've never seen him since. Isn't that a little odd?"

"I've already explained: I used him. He was head-to-toe KGB. There was never anything between us as far as I was concerned. I had no qualms in that respect."

"How did he feel about it?"

"As far as I could tell, he saw ours as a normal marriage."

"How would you describe his attitude to your relationship?"

Anita hesitated and searched for words. "He was . . . well, considerate enough in our dealings, I suppose . . . not ungenerous. We had ups and downs occasionally, but on the whole we got along all right. You could have described it as a friendly accommodation, not exactly romantic . . ."

"Was it successful sexually?"

Anita nodded. "Yes, I'd say so."

"But you've just said he was pure KGB," Foleda pointed out. "Earlier, you painted a pretty clear picture for us of your ideological convictions. They're very strong. Wasn't there any basic emotional conflict here? A paradox, maybe?"

"I'm not sure I follow you," Anita said.

"Didn't it bother you to go to bed with a dedicated officer of the KGB?" Barbara asked her.

Anita looked at her squarely, then at Foleda. "No. He was quite good, if you must know. And it is fun. Why not make the best of it?"

"Did he have other women, too?"

"If he did now and then, it wouldn't have surprised me."

"Would the thought have troubled you?"

"No."

"How about yourself?"

"Never among the embassy staff. I couldn't afford to risk compromising my own work."

"But elsewhere? Your illegal contacts in London?"

"There was one, yes."

"You didn't contact him the night you decided to get away—before you called the SIS number?"

"No."

"Why not?"

"It simply wasn't that strong a thing. I needed help, not friendship."

Foleda nodded, satisfied, while Meech scribbled furiously at the far end of the table and tapped buttons on his screenpad. It would have been easy for Anita to have tried harder to justify her action by depicting herself as having had a rougher time from her husband, and putting more blame on him for the problem. What she had said didn't have the ring of a cover story about it.

There was a short pause. Anita refilled her water glass from the pitcher on the table, took a sip, and lit a cigarette.

"Getting back to Professor Dyashkin," Kehrn said over his shoulder from across the room. "You and he were married when, did you say?"

"August third, 2003," Anita replied.

"And divorced? . . ."

"2011. I forget the precise date."

"In Moscow."

"Yes."

"Which was after he'd begun his affair with Olga . . ."

"Olga Oshkadov. Yes."

"But before he moved to Sokhotsk."

"Where?" Anita frowned. "I've never heard of that place.

Kehrn made a pretense of forgetfulness. "Oh, that's right, I'm sorry. You didn't keep in touch, did you?" Meech nodded to himself unconsciously as he recalled earlier answers onto the screen for comparison. Kehrn came back to the table and rummaged through some papers. "Presumably you have heard of *Valentina Tereshkova*, though," he said.

Anita shrugged lightly. "The space colony? Why, of course. In fact, wasn't it in the news yesterday?"

"Does it hold any special significance for you?"

"No, none. Should it?"

"Does it hold any significance for Professor Dyashkin? Do you connect him with it in any way? Did he ever talk about it?"

Anita could only shake her head. "If he was connected with it somehow, I was never aware. He never mentioned it in any special sense—only the casual references that anyone might make concerning things that appear in the news."

"And you said that you didn't know he'd moved to Siberia?"

"No, I didn't say that. I knew he'd moved to Siberia. I didn't know exactly where. Was it to the place you mentioned a moment ago?"

The interview went on in a similar vein until it was time for lunch. Kehrn went through with Anita to the table that the house orderlies had set in the dining room, where two CIA officers who would be questioning Anita further in the afternoon were due to meet them. Foleda announced that he would go for a stroll around the pond at the rear of the house to feed the ducks and get some air before joining the party. Barbara accompanied him.

"What do you make of it?" he asked her.

"I still think she's genuine. In fact, I'm more convinced than I was in London."

"Uh-huh. What else?"

"Well, if Professor Dyashkin is also mixed up with the Friday Club, and his ladyfriend Olga has been arrested, that maybe answers one of the big questions we've been asking: Why does he want to defect? He can feel the heat closing in on him, and wants an option for an out."

"It's obvious, isn't it." There was a note to Foleda's voice that said perhaps it was too obvious. He stopped as a flotilla of ducks arrived from across the pond and waited a few feet out from the bank for pieces of breadrolls he'd picked up from the plates that had come in with the coffee earlier. "Then, how's this for a long shot?" he said. "Let's suppose that Olga was moved up to *Tereshkova* for some reason, and that she's inside the prison camp there. We already know that Dyashkin is at the receiving end of the Blueprint transmissions. See my point?"

Barbara nodded. "It's a good bet that Olga's the person at the other."

"That's the way it looks to me." Foleda broke another roll and tossed the pieces into the water.

"How can we find out for sure?"

"Easily—by asking Dyashkin. He must know who is it he's talking to."

"Would he tell us?"

"Why shouldn't he? He confirmed that Lew McCain and the Bryce girl are up there. And besides, he's sweating and he might want us to get him out, so he's not of a mind to refuse favors." Foleda turned back from the pond. "Now let's string all those facts together. We've never been able to discover how he works his end of the Blueprint line, but we know he's got some way of sending messages up to Mermaid. Now we're pretty certain his contact up there is Olga, and Olga was arrested for anti-Soviet activities. Now let's assume that Olga's inside the same place that Lew McCain and Bryce are in . . . and bearing in mind that we already possess a link between us and Dyashkin . . . See the possibilities?"

Barbara shook her head and blinked at the audacity of what Foleda was suggesting. "Then, maybe we could use his line to get through to our own people up there," she completed.

"A neat idea, eh? Who knows what kind of use we might find for a connection like that?" Foleda threw the last of the bread. "Well, the ducks look happy. Let's go back and get some lunch ourselves."

CHAPTER THIRTY-ONE

The secret belowdecks workshop became known as "the Crypt." By the time McCain, Rashazzi, and Haber got there, Haber was breathing heavily from the exertions of the journey, which was still strenuous, even with the rope ladder that Rashazzi and McCain had attached at the light-fixture panel. The worst part was getting down from the pipe-supporting frame underneath the billet floor. Now that they could examine and neutralize the security circuits from the rear, what they needed was an easier way in. They had identified several out-of-the-way places in the

Core where entry might be possible, which would have the added advantage of making the Crypt available during the day. Besides giving them more productive time, this would provide relief from the exhausting loss of sleep that was beginning to affect all of them.

By now the Crypt was powered and lit from a junction box that Rashazzi had tapped into, and had acquired a spacious workbench, boxes, storage racks, and a staggering assortment of tools, test equipment, instruments, electronic components, and jars of chemicals, gadgets, and parts, which the two scientist-thieves had materialized from a score of hiding holes that McCain had never suspected, and the whereabouts of which he still hadn't the foggiest notion. The laser was at one end of the bench. Scanlon had managed to purloin a broken research model from the scrap heap at the university in Landausk, where he'd been working since bedframe production was suspended. It needed some replacement parts, which the two scientists said they could hand-make, and a new electronic control unit. In addition, a number of other contraptions and devices were at various stages of construction.

"Come this way, Lew," Rashazzi said. "This is what we wanted to show you." He beckoned McCain through into the space behind the bench. Haber followed, after collecting a notebook and some other items from the bench. Supported between two boxes was a shallow cylinder cut from one end of a drum about three feet across, containing six inches or so of water. The hole in the center was plugged, and a loop of stiff wire sticking up through the water from the plug formed a handle to pull it out. On the floor between the two boxes and underneath the cylinder was a bowl for the water to drain into. It seemed a very simple arrangement, and McCain could attach no significance to it. He waited curiously.

Haber had placed a meter rule across the dish with its edge above the center of the plug, and was waiting with a pencil and notebook. "Ready when you are," he told Rashazzi.

Rashazzi picked up a dropper and used it to deposit spots of a purple dye at intervals across the liquid. Then he grasped the wire handle and, taking care not to disturb the water, slowly drew the plug out. The water began falling through into the bowl beneath. "The liquid has had over twenty-four hours to settle," Rashazzi said, watching. "That's to allow any swirling introduced during filling it to dissipate completely. Did you know that when water in a bathtub back on Earth forms a vortex, the direction of rotation usually doesn't have anything to do with the way the Earth spins, as most people think? It's an accidental consequence of the motion left over from when it flowed in and how it was sloshed about. To see the true effect of the Earth's rotation, you have to eliminate such residual currents."

"No, I didn't," McCain answered tonelessly, staring at the falling surface of the water and trying hard not to let his feelings show at that particular moment. If they were going to preoccupy themselves with this kind of academic fussing, the whole effort was a waste of time already. What good could come out of it?

As the water level in the dish fell, the drops of dye elongated into threads along the flow lines and traced out the counterclockwise swirl that was beginning to appear, slow on the outside and getting faster nearer the hole. Rashazzi leaned over the dish to read the measuring scale, and used a stopwatch to time the rotation speed at increasing distances from the center. "One, one point three; two, one point nine; three, two point four . . ." he recited to Haber, who scribbled the numbers down. McCain watched the process without interrupting.

When the dish was empty and the experiment over, Rashazzi straightened up and remarked, "Conservation of angular momentum, you know. That's what makes vortexes form."

McCain grunted noncommittally. The principle was the same as with twirling ice skaters, where pulling in the arms causes them to spin faster.

Rashazzi went on, "If an element of the fluid possesses

momentum about the center, its rotational rate must increase as the radius it's at decreases. The same thing causes tornadoes and hurricanes. You can see how the water in a tub at Earth's north pole, for example, would be rotating."

"Sure," McCain said.

"And what about at the equator? Would you agree that the water in that case is not rotating?" Rashazzi asked. McCain looked uncertain. "It's not rotating around the hole—in the plane perpendicular to the hole's axis," Rashazzi said.

McCain nodded. "Okay. So?"

Rashazzi looked across at Haber. "The situation on a rotating cylinder, such as a floor inside the ring of *Valentina Tereshkova*, is identical to that at the Earth's equator," the German explained to McCain. "There should be no vortex induced by rotation."

It took a second for the point to register. Then McCain stared bemusedly at the bottom of the empty dish, looked up again, gestured vaguely with his hand. "But? . . ."

"Exactly." Rashazzi nodded. "There's something odd about the mechanics of this place. Since the colony rotates a lot faster than Earth does, the effect is much stronger here. It can overwhelm the residual currents I mentioned earlier. We'd have noticed it long ago if all the sinks and showers here didn't have suction drains—not one good old-fashioned plughole anywhere."

McCain shook his head as if to clear it. This was all completely unexpected. "Have you got any idea what it means?" he asked.

"Not really," Rashazzi admitted. "But the motion of the colony must be more complicated than we've supposed. It wasn't something we wanted to even talk about upstairs. I'm not sure what it might mean."

"That game that Nunghan and his friends play out in the mess area was what first made us curious," Haber said. "If you look very carefully, marbles don't roll straight over long distances. There's a slight curve. That's something else you shouldn't get in a rotating cylinder. We established that it wasn't due to any slope in the floor, but it wasn't possible to measure anything accurately without being conspicuous. That was why we needed a place like this."

"And also the laser," Rashazzi said. "If we can get it up to the surface level somehow, there are some other things we'd like to try with it. For example, if we can—"

At that moment a rasping sound came from a buzzer fastened to one of the supporting pillars. It meant that something had broken one of the infrared beams that Rashazzi had installed to cover approaches to the Crypt. Instantly Haber flipped a switch to put out the light. They moved back against the wall and waited. After a minute or so, lights flickered in the direction of the walkway through the pump and storage-tank area, accompanied by the sounds of people approaching. They came to the side branch that led to the Crypt and followed it. There were three lights, and a muttering of voices. McCain and the others tensed. The approaching figures were moving purposefully, not in the manner of people searching, but of ones who knew where they were going. They reached the edge of the sunken level and shone their beams down into the space below to pick out the three men crouching in the darkness. McCain, Rashazzi, and Haber moved out from the wall resignedly, holding their hands high and empty in front of them.

Then, from out of the darkness beyond the lights that were blinding them, an English voice said cheerfully, "Sorry, didn't mean to startle you chaps. It's just what you might call a good-neighbor visit." It was Peter Sargent, from upstairs in B-12.

Rashazzi turned on the light again and Haber sat down weakly on a nearby box. McCain glared up as the three newcomers switched off their flashlights and clambered down into the Crypt. "What the fuck are you doing here?" he growled.

One of the two men with Sargent was swarthy-faced, with a short beard and dark eyes that were constantly darting suspiciously this way and that. He looked Indian. McCain knew his face from around the compound but had never talked to him. The other, McCain hadn't seen before. Heavily built, with reddish curls fringing an immense brow, and a face that somehow managed to combine decisive, sharply lined features with a rounded, babyish shape, he was wearing a priv-category green tunic. He moved a pace forward into the light and took in the surroundings with a cool, dispassionate stare that could have signified ownership.

"We thought it was time to introduce ourselves personally," Sargent said. He gestured toward the big man first. "Eban Istamel, who is Turkish. . . . And this is Jangit Chakattar, originally from Delhi." He looked pleasantly at McCain. "We were delighted to hear that the information from the escape committee turned out to be so useful. But we also heard from Koh that you had doubts if the committee exists at all. I can assure you that it does." He gestured toward himself and at his two companions once again. "You see, it was *our* present. We run the escape committee."

McCain looked from one to another for what seemed a long time, in silence, but from the expression on his face his mind was working furiously. Finally he asked Sargent, "Which one is in charge?"

"Eban." Sargent indicated the big Turk. "He is the chairman."

"Very pleased to meet you," McCain said. The Turk extended a perfunctory hand. . . . And McCain hit him squarely on the jaw.

The big Turk sat on a box with his back propped against one of the roof supports, dabbing a folded handkerchief at the swelling on one side of his mouth. McCain, Haber, and Sargent were also sitting in a loose circle, while Rashazzi leaned against the bench and Chakattar stood looking on from behind. "It's all right," Istamel had mumbled to his two astonished companions when McCain punched him. "He had the right. We used them."

For what McCain had realized in the moments following the appearance of Sargent and his two friends was that he and his group in B-3 had been set up. The fact that they had come through without mishap was beside the point. They had been the ones at risk. Supposedly this had been necessary because the committee people occupied an upper-level billet, and penetration belowdecks required access from the lower level. But clearly the new arrivals had not come via the route that McCain's group had been using, through the floor of B-3. That meant they had another way of getting into the belowdecks region. Moreover, Istamel's presence showed that it connected with the privs' level up on the surface, somehow. Very likely they'd had such an alternative all along, but had played safe by getting the B-3 group to try out the method first. McCain had guessed their appearance now represented a bid to take over the operation, and the disdainful manner that the Turk had exhibited did nothing to dispel the suspicion. But McCain's action, in accordance with the rough-and-ready unspoken code by which such things were asserted, had symbolically redressed the imbalance of status which the advantage the escape committee had gained for itself implied. The meeting could now proceed as a discussion between equals.

"You people are really serious?" McCain sounded mildly incredulous. "This escape committee business. You think there's a hope of getting away from a place like this?"

"Probably slim," Sargent admitted. "But studying the possibilities does help keep the mind busy, all the same. It wouldn't do to allow oneself to vegetate, would it?"

"What kinds of possibilities have you identified?" Rashazzi asked curiously.

"Really you can't expect us to divulge details of such things freely," Chakattar protested from where he was standing. "Much effort was involved—all kinds of confidential things. We don't know anything about you three."

"True," Haber sighed. "Nor do we know you."

The eternal Zamork impasse. The position was ridiculous. McCain saw from his expression that the Turk was thinking the same thing. Somebody was going to have to make a first move. "Look," he said, addressing the company in general. "We all know the problem. But we've all put a lot into finding a place like this, specifically to get away from the environment upstairs. You got the information to make it possible; we did the work. Now, if we're not going to pool what we know, what's the point of all this?"

Istamel glanced at his handkerchief and put it back in his pocket. "The problem isn't so much of knowing who's trustworthy, but the risk that if someone were caught, the more he knew, the more would be compromised," he said. "So we are reluctant to give away anything without a good reason. I'm sure the same applies to you, also."

"How are we supposed to help each other achieve our respective goals if we don't share information?" Rashazzi asked.

There was a short silence. "Very well," Chakattar said at last. "You talk about goals. Ours is very simple: to find ways of escaping. What is your goal?" Rashazzi and Haber looked at McCain.

It was McCain who had proposed that somebody had to start trusting somebody, and he accepted that the onus of making the first concession was his. Besides, he could see nothing to lose from appearing to be forthright by revealing to the present company what the Russians would already have concluded for themselves, anyway. "All right, I'll be straight," he said. "I was sent here on a mission by a branch of Western intelligence. That mission involves establishing the nature of equipment believed to exist in locations around *Valentina Tereshkova*. I intend if I can to carry out that mission, and to find a way of communicating the findings back to Earth. In other words, my immediate goal is to conduct a reconnaissance of the entire colony and a detailed examination of certain parts of it. One piece of information that might help a lot would be knowing how you got in here." He looked from the Turk to the Englishman to the Indian and spread his hands. "We have a common need here. You're looking for ways to get out—a detailed knowledge of the place is essential for any specific plan. So, for the time being at least, our goals are identical. When the time comes to revise that, then hopefully we'll all have gotten to know each other better."

Istamel looked at Sargent and Chakattar, in a way that said it was good enough for him. Sargent gave a shrug and nodded. Chakattar, however, was still unhappy. "You want us to give you concrete information," he pointed out. "But all you are offering in return is a promise of good intentions. That doesn't seem like a good trade to me. What do you have that would be of tangible benefit to us right now?"

Rashazzi caught McCain's eye for an instant, and indicated the drum at the rear with a slight questioning motion of his head. He was asking if they should mention the vortex experiment that McCain had just witnessed. McCain returned a barely perceptible shake of his head. They needed to know more about what it meant themselves, first. Instead, he looked back at Istamel. "It's clear that your way in involves access to the surface level."

"Maybe so." Istamel shrugged. The expression on his babyishly round yet shrewd face remained neutral.

"But any serious plans about escaping would require freer movement around *Tereshkova*. You'd need ways of getting out of Zamork entirely. Do you have ways of accomplishing that?"

"There are the outside work details."

"Yes, but they're guarded," McCain said.

"Guards can be bribed."

"Sure," McCain agreed. In fact, some of the things he'd been asking people like Gonares in B-3 to do involved just such arrangements. "But what I'm talking about is freedom of movement anywhere around the colony, without any hassle from guards or limits on time," he said. "Interested?"

Istamel looked very interested. "You can provide this?" he said, sitting forward.

"If we can find a way to get out through the perimeter of Zamork itself," McCain said. "And it sounds as if what you've done could already represent half the job. You see, this is the kind of way I'm saying we can work together."

Sargent held out an arm and pulled back his jacket sleeve to display his wrist bracelet. "But even if you did get out of Zamork, you've still got a problem with these," he said. "You'd trigger an alarm the first time you came within range of an interrogating sensor. And they're all over the place."

"Then, let us show you something we've discovered," McCain said. "Razz?" He got up and walked over to the bench, while Rashazzi went to fetch a flat box from one of the racks before joining him. The others came over and gathered round. McCain took off his jacket and rested his forearm on the bench with the electronic unit of his own bracelet facing upward. As with all of them, it consisted of a square metal frame with rounded corners to which the bracelet attached and, fitted in the frame's recess, a plain black rectangular insert that contained the electronics. Rashazzi took a scalpel and cut along one side of the joint between the edge of the insert and the frame, at the same time swabbing a solvent fluid into the crack. Then he began working along the second edge.

"My unit has been tampered with," McCain said. "The insert is only held by a soluble adhesive that Razz cooked up. You see, whoever designed these devices was careless. The insert in the center contains the ID electronics, but the power cell and the detector for a break in the wristband are housed in the frame. So, the two can be separated without triggering an alarm. What's more, the chip was only secured by cement around the edges, which Albrecht found a way of breaking." As McCain said this, Rashazzi tested the bond by prying an edge of the wafer with the blade, and finding it sufficiently softened, lifted it clear for Haber to remove with a pair of tweezers.

"Well, I'll be damned!" Sargent exclaimed.

McCain held out his arm to show the bracelet with its empty frame. "One way you could use this is to switch ID's," he said. "Suppose you" —he looked at Sargent— "needed to go to Turgenev or somewhere, but I had a work assignment there. We could switch the inserts. Much more flexibility."

Haber pointed at the insert, which he had placed on a glass plate. "But even better, the inserts in the badge ID's that outside civilians wear are identical. If we could get hold of a general-clearance badge somehow, we could substitute its insert for the one in your bracelet, and you'd be able to go anywhere you wanted."

McCain looked at Chakattar. "Is that tangible enough?"

"Would it work, though?" Sargent asked doubtfully. "Wouldn't the ID coding in the security computers be changed as soon as the badge was missed?"

Rashazzi shook his head. "It doesn't work that way. You only get that degree of security here, inside Zamork. Outside, individuals aren't tracked place to place. A general-clearance insert is just like a key that will get you in anywhere. That's all it does. They all transmit the same code."

Istamel and his two colleagues exchanged glances. "And you think you might be able to obtain such a device?" he said.

Haber smiled, and gestured at the workshop around them. "We do appear to have something of a flair for, shall we say, larcenous inventiveness."

"Very good. I am satisfied," Istamel pronounced.

McCain turned from the bench to face him directly. The Turk stared him in the eye and nodded. "You have a deal, Mr. Earnshaw. We have too much in common to waste our energies on rivalry. We work cooperatively, yes? . . ." He bunched a fist and brought it up close to the side of McCain's chin. McCain looked back at him unblinkingly. Istamel thumped the side of his jaw, not hard enough to hurt, but solidly enough to be more than playful.

"As partners, eh?" A flicker of a grin crossed his face. McCain grinned back at him. They shook hands.

CHAPTER THIRTY-TWO

Two guards escorted Paula from the interview room in the Surface Level Administration Building to the security post at the door opening out into the general area where the huts were situated. She made her own way back to Hut 19 from there. The climate-control engineers had been experimenting again that day and had created strange conditions around Novyi Kazan, in which evaporation from the reservoir and other nearby bodies of water formed a mist below the roof that reduced the ribbon-suns to indistinct, watery blurs. A month previously they had managed to produce a miniature cyclone that wrapped itself around the town's central tower and sucked all its windows out. Half of them still hadn't been replaced.

She walked past the Recreation Building, where the gymnasium and hobby rooms were located, and turned right onto the path running between Huts 10 and 17. Several of the green-clad figures who were out nodded or called a greeting as she passed. The session with Protbornov and Major Uskayev had followed the course that had long ago become usual. Why couldn't she communicate with her government? she had demanded to know yet again—they must be pressing for information. She could, the Russians replied, if she would only agree to be more cooperative. How did she like her new work? It was fine. She did realize, of course, that they could always send her back to the lower levels? That was up to them. Unnerving as she found the thought inwardly, she was keeping to the tactic that Olga had urged. And although as yet she hadn't won her battle, the contest was beginning to feel more equal.

She shared Hut 19 with three Russian women. Elena came from Minsk and was a sociologist, a field of study traditionally frowned upon by the authorities, since from the time of the state's inception "hard" science and engineering had been viewed as more relevant to its industrialization goals. Elena had been a little too zealous in compiling and supplying to foreign publishers statistics on health and wealth in the people's utopia that the people's leaders had found embarrassing, and found herself consigned to Zamork as the only place sufficiently safe and far away to keep her out of mischief. Svetlana was a deactivated agent of the KGB. After undergoing years of tutoring and training, she had been infiltrated into Austria posing as a German immigrant, and had been granted Austrian naturalization. But then she had gone on to develop a taste for Western living and an open disdain for Marxist orthodoxy that had made her superiors nervous, and Zamork became her destination after recall to Moscow. Lastly, Agniya was a former Moscow art and literature critic. She had persisted in criticizing the censors instead of the artists, and dismissed the officially promoted idols as mediocrities. After Paula's experiences on the lower level, their company and intellectual stimulation was like a release from the grave.

Svetlana, the former KGB agent, was in when Paula got back to the hut, trying a new picture in different positions on the walls. It was a scene in a city of tall buildings. The city was inhabited by a mixture of all the monsters that had ever crashed, roared, terrorized, and demolished their way across the world's movie screens—Godzillas, mutant spiders, giant ants, barrel-chested gorillas, creaking Frankensteins, and shapeless blobs. But these monsters were panicking, fleeing in wide-eyed terror through the streets and pulling their baby monsters after them, while others shrieked from windows. It was also, evidently, a city of monsters-in-miniature . . . for looming above the buildings in the background, silhouetted against the sky as it lumbered closer, was a spacesuited human figure. Paula studied it and managed a smile despite her weariness after the past few hours. "Cute," she pronounced. "Where'd it come from?"

"You met Maurice, the Frenchman who paints," Svetlana replied. "It's one of his."

"I thought he was going back. Wasn't there an exchange deal that the Russians worked out with the French and the West Germans, or something?"

"Yes, that's right. He went a couple of days ago. This picture is a parting gift that he left for me, but I only got it this morning. . . . I was thinking, maybe here, by Elena's baskets. How does it look?"

"Perhaps a little more to the right . . . there, that's good. Want me to hold it?"

Paula watched while Svetlana fixed the corners of the picture with pieces of adhesive tape. Svetlana had dark hair with a reddish tint, brushed into long waves that curled forward beneath her ears, and a trim figure whose curves not even the standard baggy green priv's tunic could hide. People got along well with her, and it seemed natural that the Frenchman should have left her a farewell present. It was strange, Paula thought. She had been arrested while on a professional espionage assignment for the United States government, Svetlana was a former KGB agent, and yet here they were living together and acting naturally like affectionate sisters. It said how people everywhere could be if only those who aspired to power would leave them alone. Or was it the people's own fault for taking any notice in the first place of those who presumed to command them?

Svetlana finished fixing the picture and stepped back. "Yes, I think that looks fine. We'll leave it there." She put the tape back on a shelf. "I've just made some tea. Would you like some?"

"I could use something," Paula said.

"How was it today?"

"The usual. They want me to take a guided tour around the colony and send a vigram home saying there are no nasty things hidden up here." Since the West had never concealed its suspicions about weapons on *Valentina Tereshkova,* Paula wasn't revealing anything that Svetlana didn't already know about.

Svetlana poured strong tea into two cups and topped them up with hot water. She handed one to Paula, added sugar and a drop of lemon juice to her own, and sat down on one of the hut's two double-height bunks. Paula sat down at the table and sipped her tea, savoring the taste and the feeling of the hot, refreshing liquid moistening her dried mouth. The Russian woman lit a cigarette. "Well, why don't you do it?" she asked Paula. "Surely it can't do any harm. I mean, if what they say is true, it could only be for the best if the West were told about it."

"I don't know," Paula said after considering the question. "I guess I don't like the thought of being used as a political mouthpiece. It's not my kind of business. I'm a scientist."

"Then, what are you doing here?" Svetlana asked.

"That's what I mean—I've gotten mixed up in more than enough of what I should have stayed out of, already." Paula seemed dissatisfied with her own answer and frowned while she drank from her cup again. "Anyway, it shouldn't be up to me. If the Russians want to convince the Americans that this place is legitimate, all they have to do is bring them here and let them walk around. Why should it need to be my problem?"

Svetlana sighed. "You know how it is with stubborn old men who worry about what history books might say about them." She fell silent for a while, contemplating the smoke from her cigarette. "We got to be quite friendly, Maurice and I," she said at last in a distant voice that seemed to change the subject.

Paula smiled. "I can't say I'm surprised. You are quite attractive, after all, and he was, well . . . very French."

"No, I didn't mean that way. I meant just as friends. We used to talk a lot. He was very intellectual as well as artistic."

"Oh, I thought—"

"That's all right. He seemed to know a lot about science—to me he did, anyway, which doesn't say all that much. You'd have liked him. It's a pity he's gone." Svetlana hoisted her legs up onto the bunk and shifted back to prop herself against the end wall. She looked at Paula quizzically. "Were you really a spy?" she asked matter-of-factly.

"Come on. You know better than that."

Svetlana didn't seem to have expected a straight answer. "You know, I think Maurice might well have been. He never said so, but when you've worked as I have, you develop an instinct for these things."

"With the French intelligence people, you mean?"

"Yes. You know it's funny, the different reasons why people get involved in espionage. With me it was virtually automatic. My father was a KGB colonel, and I went into the academy at Bykovo straight from university. It was just a job that the family expected me to go into, and quite an exciting one, too—almost a game, in fact. But some people do it for very deep, premeditated reasons, such as ideological beliefs. Maurice was like that. He was one of those serious minded people, always worried about humanity and where it was heading for a thousand years from now."

Paula thought instinctively about Earnshaw, but couldn't place him in that category. For him it came closer to soldiering—a job that had to be done that obviously everyone couldn't leave to everyone else. His motivation reflected short-term realities more than distant ideals.

Svetlana went on, "Maurice worried that the stubborn old men might get the world into a war. They were all just as paranoid, he thought—yours as well as ours—all equally responsible for the lunacy that things have come to. 'Impotent dinosaurs, stuck in a swamp with nothing but umbrellas,' he used to say. And finding out the truth about the weapons that some people say are hidden up here concerned him a lot."

"What bothered him so much about that?" Paula asked.

"The thought that all the suspicions might be nothing more than the products of fantasies and preconoeptions. If that turned out to be so, then how many more crucial judgments are being based on equally wrong perceptions?"

Paula was staring at the far wall. Suddenly she glimpsed

the entire situation and her own relationship to it from a new perspective. What she saw didn't make her feel entirely comfortable. "It would be insane," she agreed in a faraway voice.

"Yes. And the really insane part is that we could end up blowing everything for no other reason than wrong information. Maurice's big obsession was to make sure that the right people got the right facts. You see, intelligence work was almost a religion with him. That was why the Russians were always moving him around the colony so much. Probably that was why they let him go."

"How do you mean?" Paula asked.

"They offered him the same kind of deal as they did you: a tour around, if he would agree to relay back what he saw. And he went along with it."

"Did he ever say what he found?"

"Not in so many words—not to me, anyway," Svetlana said. "But think about it. If he discovered anything that shouldn't have been there, would he be on his way home right now? That must say something." Paula cast an eye around at the walls and ceiling and gave Svetlana a cautioning look, querying if they ought to be talking aloud like this about somebody who was quite possibly not out of the Russians' hands yet. Svetlana laughed. "What does it matter if they are listening to us?" she said. "He would only be confirming what they themselves have been telling the world for years." She lifted her head and called out in a louder voice, "Can you hear me, former comrades? Am I right? Are we saying anything you don't agree with?"

Paula fell quiet as she sipped the rest of her tea. Suddenly she saw the role that she had been slipping into as one of mere academic detachment—an irrelevancy. The thought made her feel, in a way . . . irresponsible. It was the first time that the job she'd come to *Tereshkova* to do had felt like something that really mattered.

CHAPTER THIRTY-THREE

The big news in the second week of September was that the Russians had yielded suddenly and unexpectedly to the international pressure that had been building up for several years. In a surprise announcement from Moscow, the Soviet foreign minister stated that *Valentina Tereshkova* would be opened to unrestricted international inspection immediately following the November 7 celebrations. This was also the colony's official completion date. The Russians pointed out that it was not normal to permit outsiders into any site while construction was still in progress. It had always been their intention to declare an open policy, they claimed; but the persistent Western harassment would have been an affront to anyone's dignity. As a further gesture toward reconciliation, and to mark the departure from precedent, they invited the nations of the West to send delegates to join the Soviet leaders for the centenary, to symbolize their common commitment to a harmonious and prosperous future.

The banner headline of *The New York Times* read: DRAMATIC CONCESSIONS IN SURPRISE SOVIET INITIATIVE. Philip Borden, director of the UDIA, tossed a copy of the morning's San Francisco *Chronicle* down on top of it. MOSCOW SAYS "DA"!

"The news grid and networks are full of it. Peacenik lobbyists have been hounding congresspeople around Washington all morning," he told Foleda across his desk. "I've got to present our assessment to the Security Council at three this afternoon. Half the country's clamoring for a big gesture of reciprocation, and some of the European governments are already indicating a willingness to accept. The secretary of state says he agrees, and we expect the other intelligence agencies to be cautiously in favor. But you're not happy, and you think we should sit tight."

"It was also the Europeans who went rushing off to Munich, don't forget," Foleda reminded him. "I don't like the passive position it puts us in. I don't like a precedent where they call the tune and we jump. I don't like the thought of our making a spectacle of falling over ourselves with gratitude just because they've said they'll act reasonably for once—as if that represented some kind of favor. Hell, when did they ever make a big show of being grateful all the times we acted reasonably?"

Borden stared for a moment. "There's more, though, isn't there?"

Foleda thought for a second, then looked up to return Borden's look directly and nodded. "I think this whole business about November is a cover for something else—something a lot bigger. I still think it could be a strike. We're talking about eight weeks to go, Phil."

Borden sighed. They had been through all this with the Security Council and the defense chiefs, and the consensus had been that the fears were exaggerated. "Hell, I can't go back with that again. Don't you think that just maybe, this time you're being a little too suspicious?"

"We're paid to be suspicious. We're good at it, too. That's why we've worked together for a long time."

Borden drew a long breath and looked dubious. He gestured at the headlines lying on his desk. "It would mean making myself about as popular as smallpox this afternoon. I mean, do we have anything new to go on? Everything the Dorkas woman says checks out. NSA's tracer scans didn't turn up anything, and some of the information she's come up with is too valuable to have been a gift pack. What else can we say about her?" The tracer scans referred to the Committee for Freedom and Dignity and the Tortoise that Barbara had mentioned during her meeting with Anita in London. The National Security Agency had reported no occurrence of these terms in the Soviet communications traffic that they listened in on. Although it constituted negative evidence, it did support Anita's story.

"No, that's not it. They can run all the checks they like. I'm satisfied that she's okay," Foleda said.

There was other evidence supporting the Soviets' proclaimed position, too. A confidential report recently received from the French Deuxieme Bureau concerned a French agent by the name of Maurice Descarde, who had been released in an exchange deal from internment in *Valentina Tereshkova*. Apparently Descarde had returned to Earth a week previously and was now back in Paris. During interrogation he had stated that on numerous occasions he had worked in parts of the colony where weapons systems and ancillary equipment were supposed to exist, but had never seen any signs of them. Physiological and psychiatric tests indicated that he was in good health, functioning normally, and in complete command of his faculties.

"Okay, Bern, I'll try stalling things for a bit longer and push for using Cabman," Borden said finally after more wrangling. "We've all done our evaluations of Anita Dorkas— us, CIA, the British—and as far as it's ever possible to be sure, we all think she's clean. So we'll assume that Cabman's straight and play your hunch that he's got some way of getting messages up to Oshkadov that NSA hasn't uncovered, and that Oshkadov is inside the same place that Sexton and Pangolin are in." The names were McCain and Paula's code designations. "Let's stop pussyfooting around and tell Cabman now that we know who he's talking to, and that we want a through-channel to our people up there. I'll stall at the meeting on the grounds that we're trying to get independent confirmation."

Foleda sat back and massaged his eyebrows uneasily for a few seconds. He started to reply, but then stopped, sighed, and then nodded his head in a way that said he was as satisfied as he could expect to be. "Okay."

"We can't do a lot more." Borden waited, looking at Foleda curiously. "What is it that's really bothering you about this whole thing?"

Foleda took a moment to choose his words. "Go right back to the beginning and work through everything that's happened since. Now ask yourself, What would the implications be if Magician had been a double agent all along?" he replied.

CHAPTER THIRTY-FOUR

The escape committee's route led out through the ceiling of B-12 billet, which had the advantage of an unusually cooperative foreman, and from there climbed to the surface through an intermediate level of pipework and plumbing. It emerged in the basements of the Services Block, a building at the east end of the surface level that contained the canteen and other amenities that privs enjoyed, and the back of which screened a drop down to the general compound used by the prisoners on the lower levels. From the Services Block it connected across the surface to Hut 8, which Eban Istamel occupied with three others. The hut was situated roughly in the center of the surface residential area, which put it above the Core zone of the lower levels. Istamel and the others had tunneled down through the floor of Hut 8 and penetrated the upper subsurface machinery galleries, and from there gained access to one of the elevator shafts running down through the Core and continuing on down past the lowest billet level. A maintenance cover in the side of the shaft opened through to the machinery deck where the Crypt was located.

The ways of escape that the committee had been looking into all involved gaining access to the hub—as was inevitable, since that was where the Soviet transporter ships, the only means for leaving the colony, docked. The possibilities that Sargent outlined included stowing away in the consignments of materials and equipment shipped up the spoke elevators to the hub, impersonating Russian personnel going there on official duties, getting there concealed illicitly among the work details assigned to the hub, and making the half-mile climb through the systems of ducting, conduits, and structural supports outside the elevator shafts.

The big problem with all of these proposals was the stringent security measures that the Soviets enforced to protect every conceivable way to entry to the spokes.

Every car destined for the hub was combed inside and out three times before departure. The ID checks of Soviet personal were impregnable. The structure surrounding the elevator ports was a jungle of alarms and detectors. As the inmates who knew the tricks for vanishing from work details had found out, the security that applied to movement among the various places around *Tereshkova*'s outer ring could be surprisingly lax. But getting into the spokes, as most of the escape committee's guinea pigs had discovered to their cost, was a different matter. But since the spokes represented the only way out of the colony, and at this distance from Earth guards came at a premium, it probably made sense that things should be so.

After thinking the matter over, however, McCain wasn't so sure that the only way to the hub was indeed through the spokes. "Why," he asked Rashazzi and Haber when they were alone in the Crypt one day, "can't we go *outside* them?"

"Sure, why not?" Rashazzi shrugged. The proposition was too absurd to argue about.

"No, think about it," McCain urged. "It would exploit the very weakness that the Soviets have built into their own system. Apart from in Zamork, security around the ring isn't very tight—in fact, in most places it's nonexistent. They only bother seriously guarding the access routes into the spokes. Why? Obviously because there isn't anyplace else to go. It never occurred to them that anybody might ever want to break through to the outside!"

Rashazzi was staring at Haber with an expression that said his initial reaction was already giving way to second thoughts. Haber blinked back at him. Clearly there were problems to be solved, but the idea was starting to make a crazy kind of sense. McCain waited. "Do you think it's feasible, Razz?" Haber asked.

"I'm not sure. . . . Maybe."

"Obviously such a scheme would require protection and life support," Haber said. "The Russians must keep regular

EVA suits at maintenance and emergency posts around the ring. . . . What do you think?"

"Mmm . . ." Rashazzi looked dubious. "They'd be difficult places to get into. And I can't think of anywhere they're likely to be here, in Zamork."

"Do you need them?" McCain asked. "What about improvising something? Is that such a crazy idea?"

"Homemade spacesuits?" Haber evidently thought it was.

This time Rashazzi wasn't so sure. "No . . . perhaps we don't need regular suits," he said slowly. "You know, Lew might be onto something. There are places we can get into that contain firefighting and rescue equipment that includes various kinds of breathing gear. That would take care of the hardest part." He paused, thinking rapidly. "The other part would be maintaining a pressured environment for the body. Actually that's not as much of a problem as most people think—not for what we need, anyway. In fact, you can stand up to about ten seconds in a hard vacuum without any protection at all."

"Very well, now tell us how we climb a kilometer up to the hub in ten seconds," Haber said.

"Obviously we'd need longer," Rashazzi agreed.

"But maybe only enough to get past the high-security zone at the base of the spoke," McCain pointed out. "An hour or even less, say. Then you get back inside again."

Rashazzi nodded. "Breathing pure oxygen would require a pressure of about two psi," he said to Haber. "That's not such a big difference over the outside. It should be possible to seal a mask over the face and eyes so that it doesn't blow off. It might leak a bit. But as long as the supply's enough to hold out, so what?"

"Would your eyes and ears be okay?" McCain said. "How about the rest of your body?"

"Not too big a problem," Rashazzi answered. "People in space vehicles and simulators work in low pressures all the time. The biggest thing to watch is gases in the body expanding or coming out of solution in fluids to form bubbles. So, you don't eat the wrong food before you go out, and you breathe pure oxygen for an hour to denitrogenate the blood. There isn't any gas in the eye structure to expand, and because of the way ears are made, they get uncomfortable from ambient overpressure, not underpressure."

Haber's attitude seemed to warm as he listened. He began nodding. "It would be necessary to prevent fluids from migrating, and evaporation from the skin. Some kind of elastic wrapping garment to maintain a pressure around the body would probably be sufficient, but not so tight as to restrict breathing and movement. A material that expanded up to a point and then went rigid would be ideal."

"Stretchy stuff with some kind of slack fiber woven into it, maybe," Rashazzi agreed. "What can we get hold of that's like that?"

"Getting an outside view of the place would answer a lot of questions," Haber mused thoughtfully.

McCain thrust his hands in his pockets and paced a few yards to the bench. He stared down at the laser for a moment, then turned back to face them. "Okay, supposing it works and we get to the hub. The next thing we need to know more about is Sargent's ideas for getting into one of the transporters . . ." He realized suddenly that Haber's remark had had nothing to do with escape bids, but had gone off on a different tangent that meant something to the two scientists but not to him. "What's wrong?" McCain asked. "Have I missed something?"

"We were going to mention it anyway," Haber said to Rashazzi.

"You're talking in riddles," McCain said to both of them. "Mention what?"

"We've found something else that's odd," Rashazzi said. "Come and look at this." They led McCain to the rear of the work area. Suspended from a support quite high up in the girders overhead was a line with a metal ball at the end. A pointer attached to the ball extended downward, almost scraping a large sheet of card marked with a circular scale graduated in degrees, which was lying flat on the floor. Rashazzi reached out and set the line swinging.

"From the length and period of a pendulum, a simple formula gives the local acceleration due to gravity," he said. "That in turn determines the force with which an object presses down on the floor—in other words, what you weigh." He looked up at McCain. "Do you remember feeling a little heavy when you first came here? But after a couple of days it had gone away? Most of us did. You thought it was due to fatigue, maybe? Well, it wasn't so. The rotationally induced 'gravity' in *Valentina Tereshkova* is approximately ten percent greater than Earth-normal."

"Seems strange," McCain commented.

"It's very strange," Rashazzi agreed. "If anything, you'd expect a space colony to be designed for a level somewhat *lower* than Earth's—to reduce the stresses upon the structure, and hence permit lighter and cheaper construction. But why would any designer go the other way?"

"I don't know. Do you?"

"No. But that's not all." Rashazzi motioned toward the pendulum as it passed over the centerpoint of the circle, slowed to a halt a couple of inches outside the scale, and began its swing back again. "This is what's called a Foucault pendulum. That means it's free to swing in any direction."

"Unlike the kind in a grandfather clock, which is constrained to move in a plane parallel to the back wall of the cabinet," Haber interjected.

McCain nodded. Rashazzi went on, "Like a gyroscope, a pendulum tries to conserve momentum by continuing to swing in the same direction in space. Imagine one set up at the north pole on Earth. Pick an arbitrary direction—that of the constellation Aries, for example. Pull the pendulum back in that direction, and release it. Now imagine it continuing to swing in the same plane, away from Aries and then back toward it again for a whole day. The Earth will have turned a full three hundred sixty degrees beneath it. Or, if you were standing on the ground next to the pendulum, you would have observed the Earth as staying still and the plane of the pendulum's swing rotating through a circle—in fact, as Aries moves in its circle around the pole" —Rashazzi pointed at the card on the floor— "you could measure its rotation rate on a scale."

McCain remembered seeing this in science museums when he was younger. "Okay," he agreed. "Now what?"

"Now let's repeat the procedure at the equator," Rashazzi said. "Aries no longer moves in a circle around the center of the sky overhead, but rises and sets. We start the pendulum moving just as Aries peeps over the eastern horizon, and it continues to swing east-west. But six hours later, Aries will be overhead. Now, is the pendulum still moving toward and away from Aries as it was before? Hardly. It would have to be yo-yoing up and down, which would be a miracle. No, instead it's still moving east-west with respect to Earth. In other words, an observer there would see no rotation of the plane it swings in. Between the pole and the equator both effects combine, and the plane will rotate not through a full circle, but through a certain angle and back again, which depends on latitude."

McCain had been on *Tereshkova* long enough to know of the rim's equivalence to Earth's equator. "So a pendulum here should keep going in the same direction," he concluded.

Rashazzi nodded. "Quite. But it doesn't. The plane of the swing rotates. We've measured and timed. Its oscillation period is eighty-eight seconds."

"As the colony spins," McCain said.

"Except that with the official dimensions as given by the Russians, and allowing for ten percent above Earth-normal weight, it ought to be about a minute," Haber said.

Rashazzi looked at McCain quizzically for a second, as if challenging him for an explanation. "One answer that would give a slower rotation rate would be if the diameter of *Tereshkova* were considerably larger than it's supposed to be." He showed his palms briefly. "But that's impossible, of course. Ever since the Russians started building it, *Valentina Tereshkova* has been studied by enough groundbased and spacebased telescopes and other instruments for us to be under no doubt that it is the size they say it is."

McCain could only look at them in bafflement. "So what do you make of it?" he asked them. "Anything?"

Haber shook his head.

"There's something very strange about the geometry of this whole place," Rashazzi said. "Never mind Eban's escape projects. Even without them, we need to get out and conduct more tests all over *Tereshkova*. One look at if from the outside would tell us a lot. That's one attraction of the idea you had. But right now, I can't tell you what this business means."

"Should we tell the escape committee about this?" Haber asked.

McCain shook his head. "Not until we know what's behind it. Right now they don't have any inkling of this. So it's not something that could reach the wrong ears if any of them were careless. Let's keep things that way for the time being."

CHAPTER THIRTY-FIVE

The amenities for privileged-category inmates at Zamork included a library that was larger and more diverse than the one available in the subsurface Core. In particular it possessed a more comprehensive reference section. Now, reference books tend to weigh a lot, and payloads hauled up out of Earth's gravity well at considerable expense could be better devoted to other things. So the bulk of the reference material in the Zamork library resided in electronic form, and was updated by periodic transmissions from Earth. In fact, it was a subset of the main public library maintained in Turgenev.

Since Communists are supposed to exhibit a passionate zeal for setting constantly new records of production, this material included vast tables of industrial-output statistics, construction figures, agricultural yields, and five-year forecasts of everything from zip fasteners on Aeroflot flight attendants' uniforms to millions of barrels of oil from the drilling platforms in the Caspian Sea. In reality, few people were even remotely interested, and none of those who were believed the official numbers anyway. Hence, for all of the technological ingenuity and organizational skills that beaming these tables from Earth to *Valentina Tereshkova* and having them instantly accessible on library screens represented, they were hardly ever read by anyone, let alone checked. Hence, anyone who wanted to, and who had access to the necessary facilities down on Earth, could encode messages into those data with little risk of being discovered. Of course, the intended recipient would have to know what numbers to watch and how to interpret them. This was the method that "Ivan" had used to communicate from Earth into *Tereshkova*—the other half of the Blueprint dialogue, which had persistently eluded the NSA.

After the accident that lost Olga the special chip which Ivan had provided, the transmissions from *Tereshkova* had ceased. Coded messages from the Earth end had continued to appear, embedded in the statistical updates beamed into the library, but Olga had had no way of responding until she acquired the electronic chip that she had asked Paula to program for her. Three days after Paula gave her back the finished chip, Olga was waiting in the hut when Paula returned from her day at the Environmental Department. They chatted about local matters with Svetlana and Elena for a while, and then Olga suggested a walk on the hill above the reservoir.

"I was in the library today," Olga said when they were alone. "A reply from Ivan has come in. He received our message. The link is working again!"

Paula was pleased. "So, there were no hitches. You're in business again. I'm glad I was able to help."

"I'm sure Ivan is feeling relieved now," Olga said. "He must have been getting quite worried."

They walked on for a while. Paula became thoughtful as some of the things that she had been brooding over during the past few days came back to her. "What kind of a person is he—Ivan?" she asked at last. "How well did you know him?"

A surprised look flashed across Olga's face, but she shrugged and replied, "Well, I told you we were lovers once. He's . . . well, quite sophisticated in many ways, I suppose you'd say, cultured—"

"No, I meant politically. You said he belonged to that dissident organization that you were part of back on Earth. Does that mean he's opposed to the Soviet system? Is he . . . well, how loyal does that make him?"

Olga frowned. "That depends. Obviously he's less than completely happy with the present regime and what it represents. But he's a strong nationalist. He loves everything Russian."

"What about the international situation—all the tensions?" Paula asked.

"It's something that concerns him deeply," Olga answered. She slowed her pace and studied Paula's face searchingly. "Very deeply, in fact. His main reason for being active in the dissident movement is to promote greater understanding worldwide. Why do you ask?"

Paula struggled for the right way to put the question. "How far would he go to achieve that, do you think?"

"I'm sorry. You'll have to explain what you mean."

"Well, take this channel that we've got now, down to Siberia. He's in a communications station, with access to all kinds of equipment. From the way he's able to read our signals and inject his own into the upbound beam, I'd assume his position there must be a fairly senior one."

Olga nodded slowly, still looking puzzled. "Yes."

"Do you think he might be willing to extend the link farther if we had a good reason to ask him—beyond the borders of the Soviet Union, for example?"

Olga stopped and turned to face Paula fully. "What strange questions you're asking all of a sudden. Extend the link farther to *where* beyond the borders of the Soviet Union?"

Paula hesitated, then drew in a long breath. "Do you think he might relay a message from us here, into the Western military-communications system?" Before Olga could reply, she plunged on to explain. "You knew Maurice, the Frenchman who was exchanged. Svetlana told me he'd seen for himself that at least some of the weapons that are supposed to be up here don't exist. He'll have told his people as much of course, but it'll only be one man's word. Would he be believed? It's information that could be crucial to policy decisions at a time like this. Through Ivan we could be in a position to corroborate it. Or even to find out more . . . I don't know . . ." But then, suddenly, a feeling of futility at even thinking about it overwhelmed her. She shook her head with a sigh and resumed walking. "Oh, forget it, Olga. It was a stupid idea. Why should a senior scientist want to risk his neck transmitting messages to the West? It just seemed—"

"Now wait a minute. I'm not sure it is such a stupid idea." Olga was staring at her keenly. "Ivan is already risking his neck—I told you, he is very concerned about the present tensions. And look at it this way: if all we were asking him to do was relay confirmation to the West from a source it might trust—one of its own agents—of what the Soviets have been saying publicly anyway, they could hardly accuse him of betraying secrets or being disloyal, could they? I wouldn't write it off so quickly as a lost cause. It might be worth a try."

Paula frowned uncertainly. Olga continued to shoot questioning looks at her as they walked, but she kept quiet. Finally Paula asked, "Have you managed to get any news on Lew Earnshaw yet? If I could talk to him about it somehow, it would help a lot."

"I'm still trying. As soon as I hear anything, of course I'll let you know."

"I see."

"I could include a feeler to Ivan in my next message," Olga offered.

"Don't rush me. I need to think about it some more," Paula said.

"As you wish."

But inwardly Paula had already as good as conceded that in the end the decision was probably going to have to be hers. She didn't even know if Earnshaw was anywhere within two hundred thousand miles.

Less than a hundred feet below the hill in an entirely different environment, McCain, Scanlon, Istamel, and Sargent were sitting, like a conspiratorial circle in some smugglers' cave of old, in a pool of yellow light surrounded by darkness around a makeshift table of aluminum drums and wall paneling. McCain unwrapped the package that Rashazzi had left for them, revealing two pieces of charred, twisted plastic about the size of a credit card but thicker, which had obviously been severely burned. Istamel picked one of them up and examined it.

For the frame, Rashazzi had welded together plastic pieces cut from a razor-blade dispenser of an acceptably close shade of blue, which he had found in the general store. He had fashioned the securing clip from the clip of a ballpoint pen, using as a guide for its shape and dimensions the imprints of a genuine clip that Peter Sargent had somehow obtained in a bar of soap; and for the plastic-encapsulated electronics insert in the center, he cut a square out of a slice sawn from the base of a black chess king. Then he had incinerated his handiwork in a bowl of shredded rags soaked in alcohol. To a casual inspection, the result looked impressively like a standard Russian general-clearance badge that had been in a fire.

Istamel gave a satisfied grunt and placed the fragile object down again carefully. "It's good," he pronounced. He picked up the other and looked at it briefly. "I see no problem. These are fine."

"Well, I'm pleased to hear it," Scanlon said, sitting forward. "And now maybe ye can tell us what it is ye have in mind that we'll be needing them for."

The Turk drew his hands back to the edge of the table and ran his eyes quickly around the group. "I know of a situation that would suit our purpose," he told them. "I am a doctor by profession—of physiology. In particular I specialize in the regulatory mechanisms of the circulatory system. I have privileged status here in Zamork because I agreed to work cooperatively in the Space Environment Laboratory at the hub. They develop different kinds of spacesuits, do research into conditions and effects of working outside—things like that." He shrugged and thrust out his lower lip as if acknowledging that some kind of explanation was called for. "It enables me to pursue my own work and keep my knowledge up to date. So if helping their interests to a degree also serves my interests, why not? We're all traders at heart, yes?"

McCain nodded curtly. "Sure, we hear what you're saying. And?"

"The technical people there are Russian civilians—doctors and technicians from around the colony. Most of them carry general-clearance badges—which will give access to anywhere within the colony's regular environment outside a few restricted zones, such as parts of Landausk and the Government Center, which require various grades of special-clearance badges." McCain and Scanlon glanced at each other and looked more interested. Istamel went on, "I've noticed that when they change into their lab coats and working clothes, they tend to leave the badges on their regular coats, which they hang in a closet by the lab entrance. Now here's the interesting part. Heavy-current cabling to an air compressor and some welding equipment passes through the bottom of that closet. Also, the space below the hanging rail is always piled with bags and boxes that contain who-knows-what. Now you see my point: if a fault developed that caused those cables to heat up and ignite something that happened to be in one of those boxes . . ."

"You mean you'd put a package in there of your own to make sure that a couple of the coats at least were destroyed," Scanlon said, nodding.

"Exactly," Sargent threw in.

"But could you guarantee that the cable would set fire to the package?" McCain queried.

"We don't have to," Istamel replied. "We make the package a self-igniting incendiary device—something that Razz and Haber can put together. We fake some kind of fault in the electrical system and cover the cables in the closet with something that will burn, simply to make it look like an accidental fire. So the way it works is, first we switch these" —he indicated the burned dummies lying on the table— "for two of the badges, and at the same time plant the materials to start the fire. Then, just when it's due to go up, we put a short-circuit somewhere in the electrical system. Afterward, the Russians recover the two dummies, write them off officially as destroyed, and supply replacements to whoever they were issued to. Meanwhile, we have the real ones in working order."

McCain thought for a while but couldn't fault it. "Can you manage it all on your own?" he asked.

"Given the materials, then everything in the closet, yes," Istamel replied. "But the electrics, I'm not so strong on."

"Now, that would be my department if there was a way of getting me there," Scanlon said. "The IRA gives a good apprenticeship in things like that."

"But there isn't," McCain said.

"I'm not so sure," Istamel murmured thoughtfully. "We do have regular-category prisoners on work assignments around the hub. They deliver materials to the lab sometimes, cart away the trash, and so on. If we could get you on something like that . . ."

"But Luchenko isn't in the habit of handing out favors on request, and my bracelet isn't programmed for the hub," Scanlon said.

They debated various possibilities at some length, but got nowhere. Then Sargent returned to their first thought by asking, "What about this scheme that Razz came up with for swapping the inserts between two bracelets? Maybe we could find somebody assigned to the hub who'd appreciate an extra holiday in exchange for letting us borrow his insert for a day. Maybe we could get Kev to the hub that way—with the insert that's programmed for the hub mounted in his bracelet."

"Wouldn't the guards notice his face was different?" Istamel asked.

"Possible, but unlikely," Sargent said. "They're not exactly the most diligent or the brightest in the place. So, fair enough—it's a risk."

McCain looked inquiringly at Scanlon. "What do you think, Kev?"

"Ah, and why not? I've done riskier things in me time. Sure, I'll go with it."

"We seem to have settled it, then," McCain said. "So let's get it moving as quickly as possible. The sooner we have the badges, the sooner we can be mobile. There's a lot I want to find out about this place." He turned again toward Istamel. "Changing the subject back, you said you're a doctor of physiology?"

"Yes," Istamel replied.

"And you're helping develop designs for spacesuits?"

"In the Space Environment Laboratory. That's right."

"That's interesting," McCain said. "Let us tell you about something else we're working on that maybe you can help us with. . . ."

CHAPTER THIRTY-SIX

Russians, Paula decided, simply weren't happy unless they were suffering. From what she had read of their poets, dramatists, novelists, and historians, their compulsion expressed itself in the sense of tragedy and glorification of sacrifice that permeated their national spirit. Another manifestation, she thought, could be the innate genius they displayed for creating agricultural disasters. Peasant revolts had been a standard part of the czarist background scenery. Stalin's forced collectivization of the farms had produced starvations on a scale that even now could only be guessed at; Lysenko had risen to become head kook in charge of biology with state backing; successive disastrous postwar harvests had been offset only by exports from the evil West; and now, three quarters of the farming experiments in the sector known as Ukraine—between Turgenev and Landausk—were turning out to be dismal failures.

The reason, as the Soviets had now admitted publicly, was clear to Paula from the dynamics of the simulation she was running to test a program modification before finishing for the day. The notion that lunar dust could be force-fed into becoming living, tillable soil by introducing a few selected bacteria strains and saturating it with bulk nutrients might have been attractive to quota-obsessed bureaucrats, but the problem was that it didn't work. The process wasn't amenable to brute force. The Western and Asian space programs had opted for an approach based on self-evolved biosystems, where all the ecological subtleties were allowed to develop in their own time, even though nobody could say for sure why all of them were needed. It was a far slower method, and helped explain why the non-Soviet programs had not gone for large-scale colony construction yet. But it was showing positive results. Now, goaded by we-told-you-so jeers from the rest of the world's biological community, the Soviets had commenced a crash program to ship thousands of tons of terrestrial soil up to *Valentina Tereshkova* for enriching certain areas, then dressing those areas with huge quantities of transplanted crops and plants to provide an acceptable setting for the Soviet leaders to make speeches about progress in when they came up for the November 7 celebrations.

Dr. Brusikov, the Russian section-head whom Paula worked under, came in from the corridor. In his dealings with her he always confined himself to business, never alluding to personal or political matters. "I wanted to catch you before you went," he said. "How does it look?"

"It's running and seems to be okay. I've added the defaults."

"Excellent." Brusikov rubbed his palms together and moved over to the screen. "Well, I'll carry on playing with it for a while this evening. Same time tomorrow, is it? You're not off, are you?"

"No." At that instant a double beep sounded from the unit on Paula's wrist. It meant that the computers monitoring the security and access system had noted the time, and she was now free to move beyond her working vicinity.

"There's your signal," Brusikov said. "Very well, we'll see you tomorrow. Good night."

"Good night." Paula went out into the corridor and turned in the direction of the elevator. Two more figures, one of them dressed in the familiar green priv tunic of Zamork, emerged from another door and headed the same way.

The Zamork inmate's name was Josip. He was a statistician from Yugoslavia, who was also working on ecological models. "I see they're going ahead with this idea of sending tons of dirt up to us," he said. "Have you ever heard of anything so crazy? All to avoid embarrassing their illustrious leaders. It's Potemkin villages all over again."

The civilian was called Gennadi. He was a Russian, younger than Josip, with fine, handsomely lined features, blond hair, and blue eyes that shone with devotion to the Party and the system. In an earlier period, allowing for the turnabout of ideology—which wouldn't have made a lot of difference, since all fanatical ideologies are interchangeable, anyway—he would have qualified as the Nazis' Nordic ideal. He detested everything Western, and anything American in particular. Whenever possible Paula avoided him.

"Well, aren't you going to tell us how incompetent we

are?" he asked her as they stopped to wait at the elevator. Paula sighed and said nothing while she continued staring at the doors.

"Oh, lay off, Gennadi," Josip said. "We've all had a hard day. Your great Russian bosses blew it. There's no getting away from the fact, so why not shut up?"

Gennadi took no notice. "You see, it's not really the soil we need. It's the bacteria and things that come with it. But then, *we* are only fallible mortals. We don't have supernatural beings to help us." His tone was sarcastic. Ridiculing religion was one of Gennadi's favorite lines.

"What's that got to do with it?" Josip asked.

"Didn't you know? Why do you think their God told Noah to build the ark? You didn't imagine it was to save all those animals, did you, Josip? Oh, my word, no! The animals were simply the vehicles to carry God's most precious creations, you see: the flea, the hookworm, the body louse, the intestinal parasite, the polio virus, and the dysentery bacterium. Aren't malaria, cholera, yellow fever, and bubonic plague the punishments that this infinitely wise, compassionate, and forgiving Father preserved to inflict upon His children? The victims that He hounds the most gleefully are always the poor, the hungry, the defenseless. What kind of a fiend would we brand any human father who treated his children like that?"

They stepped into the elevator, but Gennadi continued, "Does it make any sense to you, Josip? I say, if the suffering people of this world have anywhere to turn for help, it's their fellow man: engineers, scientists, builders, doctors, farmers. But when a disease is finally eradicated after causing untold misery for thousands of years, what do they do? They thank their God! I ask you! What did He have to do with it? Why did He make it happen in the first place?" Gennadi looked at Paula. "What I can't understand is that you're a scientist. How can you respect a government that does nothing to stop such fairy tales? Is it right that you force children to pray to this absurd God every morning in school?"

"That went away a long time ago," Paula said as the door opened and they got out. "How merciful has the god been that you force children to pray to in *your* schools?" But the answer didn't satisfy her.

They came out into the ground-level concourse of the building, where the inmates due to return to Zamork were assembling from various parts of the surrounding complex. Paula moved to the far end of the group, and to her relief Gennadi didn't stay around but left via the main entrance. She stood without speaking to anyone until the bus drew up outside the main doors to take them back. Minutes later the bus had negotiated the geometric maze out of central Turgenev and merged onto the roadway running above the monorail track in the direction of Novyi Kazan.

The galling part of it all was that the things Gennadi said mirrored her own views on religion almost perfectly. There had been many times when she had pointed out the same nonsenses to the fundamentalist fanatics she'd come across back in the States. That was why she was always so disarmed by Gennadi's arguments: she had never before been in the position of hearing virtually her own words turned back upon her, and of being able to find no way to respond.

And even more disturbing, what did it signify that he should be ascribing the same attributes to her, now, that she had always seen in people like him? She thought of Olga, and how their common appreciation of science bonded them into a global community that stood apart from superficial divisions of people into nations and creeds—meaningless divisions based not on comprehension of reality and truth, but on prejudice, myth, wishful thinking, and unreason. On both sides of the world, reason was subordinated to systems that were equally irrational, and yet were just as certain of themselves. Such systems couldn't be entrusted with the future. Now, she thought, she understood how Maurice had felt.

❖   ❖   ❖

When Paula arrived back at Zamork, she went for her evening meal—yellow-pea soup and bread, a potato, stewed pulp of cabbage leaves, and a slice of gelatinous processed meat that the cook insisted was ham—in the communal canteen of the Services Block. It was a busy time with the day workshift trickling in, but she spotted Elena, one of her companions from Hut 19, alone at one of the tables, and joined her.

Elena had somehow managed to retain her chubby build despite the unspectacular diet. She had straight brown hair, which she wore short with a fringe, ruddy cheeks, a second chin, and ample hips. Paula always pictured her as a farmer's wife, but in fact she was a sociologist, and for that reason was out of favor with the authorities who decided what the mainstream lines of learning and thinking should be. Thus, with typical topsy-turvy Communist logic, only in the society that claimed to comprehend the social struggle as a science was it study by scientific processes actively discouraged—or banned outright if the findings didn't support what doctrine said had to be true. Elena's counterparts in the West usually made prime-time TV.

"I never used to consider social science a 'science' at all," Paula confessed after they had talked for a while. "I'm not sure if I do now.

"Oh?" Elena continued eating and didn't seem perturbed.

"A science means being able to predict confidently what causes will produce what effects. It works with things like physics, but the processes that physics describes are really simple—particles and forces and how they interact. Yet it took centuries to get where it is, and we got it wrong at every opportunity. But you know, Elena, even the ecological webs that I've been working with for two months are simple compared to a nation's social system, never mind the whole world's. Nobody knows what changes will produce what results, whatever else they say to get funding. It's all still at the voodoo stage: eventually it'll rain if you dance long enough."

Elena smiled. Paula admitted inwardly that she sometimes took advantage of Elena's disposition in order to dump her own emotional charge when she was agitated about something. "I suppose you're right," Elena said. "Certainly sociology never managed to become very strong as an experimental science. You can't very well go around putting people in cages to study them. . . . But then, of course, that was mainly all you Americans' fault if anybody's." Elena's eyes were twinkling.

Paula realized that she wasn't about to be let off the hook so easily. "What do you mean?" she asked.

"If your really believe all the things you say about freedom and the rights of people to govern themselves, why didn't you allow the United States to become a huge, natural sociological laboratory?" Elena replied. "You could have let every part of the country try out whatever kind of system appealed to it—liberal or authoritarian, secular, religious, whatever—and found out from experience what worked and what didn't. Then you'd have seen which of the experts' predictions succeeded, and been able to evaluate the worth of the experts doing the predicting. Instead, you introduced those big federal programs that cost fortunes and which I'm not convinced did much good—straight from untested speculation to national law, without any experimental stage in between. And the irony is, it's exactly what you've always accused us of."

"Touche," Paula acknowledged. "I asked for that."

"But it's going to happen, nevertheless," Elena went on.

"You think so?"

"It's starting already—look at China. They've got cities that are rigidly Marxist just twenty miles from others that are totally laissez-faire. One area is run by a traditionalist religious sect that rejects technology, another has no laws at all relating to personal morality, and in another everyone carries a gun. Everyone migrates to where they think it'll suit them best, and if they find they were wrong they try somewhere else."

"It sounds like chaos."

"It is in many ways, while they're finding out how to make it work without fragmenting in all directions. But it's true evolution in action. That's why they'll lead the migration out into space when it comes. What they're doing is a foretaste of how it will be, but on a vaster scale. We haven't seen diversity yet. It will be an explosion, not a migration."

"If it happens," Paula had said before she realized it.

Elena looked at her curiously. "Naturally it will happen. Why shouldn't it?"

"Oh . . ." Paula sat back on the bench and looked around. "The way the world is. . . . Are the leaders on both sides smart enough to handle it? Take all the fuss there's been about this place, for example. You'd think it would be a simple enough matter to settle once and for all if it's a battle platform, wouldn't you? But apparently it's not so simple. Now they're saying—"

"Of course it isn't a battle platform," Elena said. Her tone of voice left no room for doubt. "I'm sorry, but that really is a figment of your Western imagination—paranoia at its worst."

"How can you be so sure?"

"Common sense tells you." Elena inclined her head to indicate a bespectacled man with a ginger beard, who was talking animatedly to a group at the next table. "Do you know who that is? Professor Valdik Palyatskin, one of the Soviet Union's authorities on low-temperature fusion. The woman across from him is a specialist in genetic diseases. The skinny man over there, in the center on the far side, is one of the engineers who built the largest aluminum refinery in Siberia. I know it's insane that such people should be in here because of their political views, but what matters for now is that they constitute a valuable potential resource to the state—in fact, if you want my opinion, I think that's the whole reason why this place was set up as it is. This is the last place anyone would concentrate them in, if it were a battle platform. It would be a prime target. They'd be much safer down underneath Siberia somewhere."

Elena pushed her plate away and looked up; but Paula's face had taken on a distant look, and she didn't answer. Of course. It was so obvious. But Western intelligence didn't know the caliber of the people who were interned up here—not to mention many of the civilian population, who had come by choice. The Russians didn't publish directories of names for anyone who might be curious. Here was something else that the intelligence advisers to the West's decision-makers needed to know about.

For a moment Paula thought of simply going to General Protbornov and telling him that she wanted to communicate with the West, and why. Surely it would be in everyone's interests. And as Olga had said when they talked about using Ivan, it would only be corroborating what the Soviets themselves had been saying publicly. But as she thought more about it, her enthusiasm waned. Coming through on an official Soviet communications channel, what would the chances be that her story would be believed? True, as was standard practice with all agents, she had memorized a coding method to indicate whether a communication was being sent freely or under coercion. But agents could be genuinely turned; the best people could be fooled and misled. And besides, the thought of cooperating with the Russians and then having to face Earnshaw later was enough to put the idea out of her head without further consideration.

But there was still Ivan.

"Are you going?" Elena asked, surprised, as Paula started to rise.

"Excuse me. Yes, I have to leave."

"Why? What's the matter?"

"I have to find Olga urgently."

CHAPTER THIRTY-SEVEN

Water pumped up by subterranean backstage machinery emerged near the top of the hill abutting the outer-hull wall to feed a stream that flowed back down to enter the reservoir at the beach. Behind the beach, the stream curved around a flat, open stretch of grass and sand that the privs used as a recreation area. Paula found Olga there, with a group of spectators who were watching some gymnasts vaulting. It seemed that Olga had been searching for her, too. Two Russian guards were looking on idly from a distance.

"Very well, I've decided," Paula said without preliminaries. "I want to try making contact with the West through Ivan." Olga opened her mouth to speak, but before she could say anything Paula went on, "I've just been talking with Elena. There are more things that they ought to know about this place—more than Maurice will tell them. When do you plan to send your next message?"

"That's what I was looking for you to tell you about," Olga said. "We already have it!"

"Already have what? I don't understand. . . . What are you talking about?"

"We have a channel to your people in the West, via Ivan."

"That's impossible. How could we?"

Olga moved her face closer to Paula's ear. "If I told you that a communication has come in over it from Tycoon, directed to Pedestal/Fox, would that mean anything to you?" She leaned closer and slipped a piece of paper into Paula's jacket pocket. "That is a copy of it."

For a few moments Paula could only stand and stare, dumbstruck. In front of them, one of the performers took a tumble, provoking derisive comments from the group watching.

"We should get some of the dirt they're sending up from Earth. Maybe it would grow better grass for you to fall on."

"Let's hope it's good, black soil from the Ukraine," another said. "I'd rather have better food."

"The whole business is so stupid," someone grumbled.

"Well, that was how a Party bureaucrat somewhere obeyed orders when he was told to send Russia into space," the first replied. The others laughed.

"Tycoon" identified Bernard Foleda in his capacity as head of the mission that had brought Paula and Earnshaw to *Valentina Tereshkova*. "Pedestal" was the code name for that mission, while "Fox" was part of the validation-coding system that labeled the message as authentic and would permit her, by her form of reply, to do likewise. "But how? . . ." she stammered.

Olga took her elbow and steered her away from the crowd, in the direction of rising terrain toward the hill. "I've learned more from Ivan since we restored the link. As was to be expected, he's been under observation by the KGB since my arrest. But with somebody of his status, they have avoided confronting him directly until they have solid evidence. Well, apparently he felt the way the wind is blowing and is looking for insurance—he's talking to the West about defecting."

"Talking? . . ." Paula checked herself and nodded. "Yes, of course. In his position it wouldn't be difficult, would it?"

"Exactly. And he'd have told your people about his position at the groundstation. My guess is that they put pressure on him to see if he could make contact, just as you wanted to."

Paula frowned. "But how could they have known about his private line to you?"

"I'm not certain that they did," Olga said. "Maybe that was just a gamble."

They sat down on a couple of rocks in a cluster that had doubtless originated from some part of the Moon. Forty years ago the material would have been priceless. Now it was used for unremarkable landscaping props—or, more likely, had simply been dumped by a construction team.

"I assume you'll want to reply," Olga said.

As things stood, Olga used any BV-15 computer to load her messages to Ivan into one of the chips that Paula had programmed—after what had happened to Ivan's original, they weren't relying on having just one—and then her undisclosed accomplice substituted the chip for a standard one contained in the encoding equipment inside the Communications Center. Although this method did not require the chip to be switched every time there was a message to go out, they had judged it safer than leaving the chip in place permanently and attempting to access it from a remote terminal, which would have left a nonstandard piece of hardware waiting to be discovered. To send a message of her own, Paula could handle the first part of the operation herself, but not the second.

"I can use the spare chip," she told Olga. "But I'll need your accomplice to switch it for me."

Olga nodded. "There should be no difficulty." Obviously it would make no difference to Olga's accomplice whose message was in the chip.

The signal that she finally composed during her next session in the graphics lab was headed TYCOON/HYPER FROM PANGOLIN/TROT, 09/22/17. It read: MESSAGE RECEIVED. PEDESTAL NEGATIVE FOLLOWING DISCOVERY/ARREST DURING ACCESS TANGERINE. CURRENTLY DETAINED MERMAID/ZAMORK. CONDITION GOOD BUT DENIED COMM'N RIGHTS. NO NEWS SEXTON BUT BELIEVED ELSEWHERE HERE. MUST CONSIDER TANGERINE LOST. HOWEVER, BELIEVE OTHER INTELLIGENCE MIGHT ASSIST EVALUATION, E.G. KEY INMATE NAME LIST. CAN SUPPLY. CONFIRM INTEREST. ENDS ENDS.

"Sexton" and "Pangolin" were Earnshaw's and her code designations respectively. Paula strung three copies end-to-end as a single data block for redundancy and tagged the message for transmission.

The validation system was based on a list of unique key words that each agent memorized, which were known to nobody else. Foleda's department kept a master file of all the lists. Each word in a list was a compound of two parts, chosen such that the first part could be combined naturally in English with many second parts to give a valid completion. For example, the word "ice" could combine with "cube," "bucket," "berg," "breaker," and many more equally valid completions. Only one, however, was correct for a particular list. Thus, whether a message originated from the agent or from the department, a correct completion from the same list confirmed both that the message was authentic, and that it was not being sent under coercion.

In the specific case of the reply sent by Paula, the "Trot" after her code name completed the compound word that Foleda had cued with "Fox." She in turn had selected the first part, "Hyper," of another compound and included it in her response. The completion "Golic" in the next message she received would confirm that it was indeed from Foleda, and not a forgery manufactured by someone with access to the communications medium.

The medical orderlies took Albrecht Haber away again halfway through the afternoon of McCain's day off. It was his second relapse in a week. An hour after the midday meal, he had gone to lie down, complaining of nausea and stomach pains, and not long after that he had become feverish.

"Barbarians, that's what they are, keeping an old man like him in a place like this," Oskar Smovak declared to the others sitting at one of the tables out in the B-Block mess area. "What harm can he be to anybody? He ought to be sent home."

"Did anybody notice what he was eating at lunch?" Luchenko asked, standing a few feet away accompanied by Kong.

"What does it matter?" Smovak replied. "With the muck they serve, it's a wonder we're not all in the infirmary." Luchenko grunted and walked back into the billet, followed by his wooden-faced shadow.

"It's your move," Leo Vorghas said.

"Oh, was it?" Smovak returned his attention to the chessboard between them.

"Charlie Chan's got a new joke about the food."

"Thanks, but I'd rather not hear it."

At the end, near Smovak, Koh turned a page of the book he was reading. McCain was sitting a couple of feet away, leaning forward with his arms folded on the edge of the table while he watched four of the Siberians rolling marbles across a pattern of chalked lines and symbols on an open area of the floor. It was a new game they had worked out with Rashazzi. As usual there was a lot of arguing and cursing, with tokens and slips of paper changing hands constantly to keep track of the scores and bets. Buried in the design were special marks that Rashazzi had made to measure accurately the trajectories of the rolling balls across the surface. But on this particular occasion he wasn't present. He had worked a series of bracelet-swapping deals and was now able to remain virtually full-time in the Crypt without interruption.

"So you really never had heard of Sam Caton, eh?"

McCain realized Smovak had moved a piece and was talking to him. He turned his head back. "Nope. Never had."

"I thought everyone in America must have heard of him. I was testing you, you see."

"I know."

"You can't be too cautious." Smovak looked at Koh. "Did you ever visit America?"

"Of course he has," Vorghas threw in without looking up from the board. "Where hasn't he visited?"

"You were in California at one time, I think you mentioned once, Mr. Earnshaw," Koh said, lifting his face toward McCain. "I know some parts of it. Where exactly did you live?"

"I was born in Iowa. But I grew up some of the time in and around Bakersfield. Went to college in L.A."

"Ah yes, Bakersfield. I have a cousin not far from there—in Fresno, as a matter of fact. He's an attorney, and he also restores antique clocks and musical machines."

"We should have guessed." Smovak shook his head disbelievingly. "He's even got a cousin in Moscow, did you know that? Has the franchise to run a Japanese restaurant there. I ask you—a Japanese restaurant in Moscow! There isn't anywhere on the planet that the Koh tribe hasn't reached."

Koh marked his place with a piece of card and set down the book. "It's just as well, too," he said. "It was mainly immigration from the East that saved the United States. Fifty years ago, everyone was being frightened by scare-stories about runaway population explosion. But even at the time, the facts were exactly opposite. It's perfectly natural and healthy that when nations industrialize and their living standards improve, their populations should grow geometrically for a while—it happened in Europe in the eighteenth century, America in the nineteenth, and is still happening to a degree in Asia. However, they level out again as lifestyles change. . . . But the wise man looks at the dry distant mountains and prepares for a drought, even while the river is in flood. The point everyone missed was that populations *decrease* geometrically too. And even while the panic was at its highest, the West's birthrate had not only declined, but fallen below the replacement level. They were facing a catastrophic population collapse. That was what almost ruined West Germany. So I'm afraid, gentlemen, that you'll have to resign yourselves to being a small minority in the world ahead. Fortunately, with the kind of civilization that I see emerging, I don't think it will matter very much."

Mungabo and Scanlon had come in from Gorky Street and sat down to catch the tail end of what Koh had been saying. Scanlon pulled a box of playing cards from his pocket and began laying out a solitaire array. "And what do you see emerging, Koh?" he inquired. "Will this be the fella to replace Western Man?"

"Maybe," Koh said.

"Got a name for him yet?" Mungabo asked.

"Next will come the Nonlinear Man—Interplanetary Man—who will emerge among the offplanet worlds that will soon take shape," Koh replied. "He will take Classical beauty, Western science, Chinese pragmatism, Japanese dedication, and maybe Russian realism, along with other stones from other rubble, but he will build them into a new edifice which will be his own. His children will accept as self-evident the concept of evolution as a succession of discontinuities, and take for granted the impossibilities of today becoming commonplace tomorrow. They will go out to populate a universe which by its very size and extent, stretching away beyond the range of the most powerful instruments, symbolizes a reality that imposes no limits on how far their civilization can grow, how much it may achieve, or what they may become." Koh looked around the table. "There are no finite resources, only finite thinking." He opened his book again, looked down, and resumed reading.

Scanlon continued moving and turning the cards. Smovak picked up a knight and thumped it back down on the board. "Check." Vorghas put his chin between his hands to study the new position.

McCain leaned forward and moved a red five onto a black six. "Busy day at the hub?" he asked Scanlon casually.

Scanlon scooped up the cards again and dealt two gin-rummy hands. McCain picked up his hand and inspected it. "As a matter of fact, I heard they had a little bit of excitement there today," Scanlon said. "A fire, no less—in the Space Environment Lab, it was. An electrical fault, by all accounts."

"That's too bad," McCain murmured. "Anyone hurt?"

"Ah, no, it was nothing serious. . . . But I'm told some things in a closet up there were burned pretty badly."

McCain sent a questioning look over the top of the fan he was holding, and Scanlon returned a faint nod. They played for a while. When they finished, Scanlon put the cards back in the box, slipped it into his jacket pocket, and rose to leave. Then, as if struck by an afterthought, he turned back, took the box from his pocket again, and handed it to McCain. "If you're going back inside the billet, do me a favor and give these back to Chan, would you? I've to meet a man in the compound in a couple of minutes."

"Sure," McCain said, dropping the box into his own pocket. But it wasn't the same box, and there weren't any playing cards inside. Instead, it held a package containing two functioning general-clearance civilian badges.

A day later, Haber had undergone an amazing recovery and was returned to the billet. With him he brought the remaining components which, together with the ones he had purloined from the pharmaceuticals lab during his previous two visits from the infirmary, enabled him and Rashazzi to construct an accurate balance scale in the Crypt workshop. They used it to measure the weights of objects at various heights in the elevator shaft that connected the Crypt deck, via the surface and Hut 8, back down to B-12 billet and gave the escape committee's "elevator route" its name.

"Things should weight less at higher levels as you get nearer to the spin axis," Rashazzi explained to McCain after the results had been compared. "And in fact they do. But the decrease is far less than it ought to be. At this level in the rim, a weight should change by two point one percent if it's moved twenty meters nearer the axis. But the amount we measured was less than half that."

Haber took off his spectacles and began polishing the lenses with a handkerchief. "The baffling thing is that once again the results are consistent with the idea of the colony's being larger than is officially stated." McCain had been thinking about that since the scientists described the results of their tests with the pendulum. He wondered if weapons could be concealed in the extra volume that seemed to be indicated. But Haber demolished the notion when he continued, "But to give these figures, the diameter of the ring would have to be something like four and a half kilometers, which is well over twice the quoted figure. I really don't know what to make of it. A discrepancy that large would have been public knowledge years ago."

Nobody could offer any satisfactory answers. But the matter was put aside for the time being when Peter Sargent and Eban Istamel brought more news from the escape committee. In the course of exploring farther down below the elevator-route shaft, they had gained entry to a tube that appeared to be part of a robot freight-transit system that possibly ran all the way around the ring. If so, then it offered not only a way out of the limits of Zamork, but a ticket to anywhere else in the colony.

So at last it looked as if McCain and his group were about to become fully mobile. Now, perhaps, they'd begin shedding light on some of the perplexing questions that had been accumulating.

CHAPTER THIRTY-EIGHT

Deep in the Pentagon's labyrinth of corridors and offices, Bernard Foleda and Gerald Kehrn came out of an elevator and turned in the direction of Foleda's office. Foleda pounded along irascibly, setting the pace. Kehrn was looking worried.

"Dirt!" Foleda snorted. "Who ever heard of shipping thousands of tons of dirt up into orbit? Not even their cloud-cuckoo-land economics could justify it. What do they take us for? It smells to high heaven, Gerry."

A lot of other people thought so, too. That was why the United States, representing a number of concerned Western nations, had demanded the USSF vessels be permitted to monitor the operations, going on in low-Earth orbit, of transferring cargo from Soviet surface shuttles into longer-range transporter ships. To everyone's surprise, the Soviets had agreed.

"Well, don't forget that their ideas on what's efficient don't exactly tally with ours," Kehrn said. "To them, efficiency is directing all the resources you've got onto whatever objective the Party says is top priority. That was how Mermaid got to be built in the first place. It isn't simply the sum total of a lot of individually profitable businesses. They wouldn't be able to see how running a pet-food factory profitably can be efficient when pet food isn't important. So maybe to them it makes sense."

"Yes, and what caused Mermaid to be their top priority?" Foleda growled. "They're up to something."

Barbara got up from a chair opposite Rose in Foleda's outer office as they appeared. Rose began leafing through a wad of papers and message slips. "It's been all hell let loose . . . Borden has called three times in the last half hour. The President's chief of staff called. The CIA director. . . . Whaley over in Defense . . ."

"Hold the trench just a little longer, Rose," Foleda said without slackening his pace. "We've got something really urgent."

"Okay, but I'm telling you, the ammunition's running low here." As she spoke, a call-tone sounded from the screen-panel beside her desk. The others went on through.

Barbara closed the door of the inner office. "What have we got?" Foleda asked her. She had beeped him via his pocket handpad a few minutes earlier and told him only that she had news from Mermaid concerning Pedestal.

Barbara opened the folder she was carrying and handed him a sheet of printout. He sat down at his desk, and Kehrn moved around to read it with him over his shoulder. "In from NSA eight minutes ago," Barbara said. "They show the time of receipt as ten-thirty-nine hours today. The validation completion is correct for Pangolin."

"My God, we did it!" Foleda breathed as his eyes read rapidly down the paper. "It's from Bryce. Our signal got through. She *is* still up there. . . . No news of Lew, though, eh?"

Kehrn nodded. "She's the communications whiz. It figures."

"Your hunch must have been right," Barbara said to

Foleda. "It must be Oshkadov that Dyashkin has been talking to."

"He did what we wanted," Kehrn said. "The guy's busting his ass over there to please. It's starting to look as if he's clean." He looked down questioningly, but Foleda was leaning back in his chair and staring at the far wall without seeming to have heard.

Kehrn was about to say something more when Foleda's desk screen began emitting its priority tone. Barbara answered it. "Yes, Rose?"

"Fix bayonets. I'm out of bullets. Borden's on his way."

Moments later the door burst open and Philip Borden strode in, looking strained. "What the hell, Bern? I've been calling you. I was told you were out."

"Sorry, Phil, I was. We only got back this second." Foleda showed him the transcript of the message from *Tereshkova*. "Take a look at this. It just came in. We've got a line to Bryce. Sounds as if Lew might be there someplace, too."

Borden took the sheet and scanned down it. "Holy cow, I don't believe this . . . a private channel to our own people inside a Soviet space station. Honestly, Bern, when you first sprung this on me I thought you'd flipped. . . . What's this bit about key inmate names?"

"I don't know. Like I said, I only saw it for the first time myself a few seconds ago."

The diversion had calmed Borden down a little from the agitated state he'd been in when he entered. He set the folder down on Foleda's desk and sighed wearily. "Well, let's hope that now you've got it, it can do some good. They sure made us look a bunch of assholes this time."

"Who did?"

"Moscow, of course. What else do you think the flap's all about out there? Don't tell me you haven't heard yet."

"I just this second got back," Foleda said again. "I've been giving a talk to that conference of Stan's all morning."

Borden waved a hand vaguely overhead. "We've sent three USSF interceptors in to monitor those Soviet transfer operations in orbit. They used X-ray detectors, magnetometer detectors, visual observation, and Christ knows what. The reports are in. They're all the same."

"What did they find?" Kehrn asked.

Borden threw up his hands. "What do you think they found? Dirt. Just lots of dirt. Nothing else. The President's mad as hell about it, we're a laughingstock, and some of the Asian states are wondering if maybe we have been crazy all along. This isn't my best day, Bern."

For once Foleda looked dumbstruck. It was he who had predicted that the Russians would never permit the payloads of the Soviet shuttles to be inspected. There was no risk that they might be decoys: the transporter ships loaded from them could be tracked clearly all the way to *Tereshkova*. Nothing could be substituted with any chance of escaping detection.

"Does that mean we've got a decision for November?" Barbara asked.

Borden nodded. "We're accepting. It hasn't been announced publicly yet, but I got it from the White House an hour or so ago. We'll be sending the Vice President and Secretary of State. The President's view is that we don't have any choice now if we want to avoid being written off by half the world as paranoids. He didn't want to force this inspection issue, and he feels that we pushed him into it. This is his way of telling us, 'screw you.' "

Foleda stared gloomily at his desk. This was what he had been fearing. In the tide of euphoria and hopes for a sudden easing of tensions that had swept the world, most of the leading European and Asian nations had already announced that they would be sending representatives. The party would travel from Earth orbit to *Valentina Tereshkova* in a neutral ship carrying a mixed United Nations crew. The President, he knew, had expressed displeasure at what he saw as the US's failure to seize an important initiative, and he held excessive caution and unwarranted suspicion on the part of the UDIA as largely to blame. "So the rest of it didn't make any difference, eh?" Foleda concluded.

Borden shook his head. "Not after this. They think we're seeing shapes in tea leaves. And to be frank, I'm half inclined to think they might be right."

"We walked right into it," Foleda said. "I was a chump. Of course there's nothing but dirt in those shuttles. Whatever they needed up there went up months ago. This dirt thing was a deliberate provocation for us to call them, and we did. Now our credibility's shot."

"You still think it's a blind for something, then," Borden said.

"No, I don't think. I'm sure of it. They wanted to make sure we'd be embarrassed enough to make amends by sending our people there, along with everyone else's."

"What for?"

Foleda looked up. "Hostages. What else? And they don't even have to hijack them—we're sending them voluntarily. Mermaid is a battle platform. Those VIPs are its protection. They guarantee we won't fire at it preemptively, and they constitute insurance against *us* having possible weapons up *our* sleeve. Hesitation and disagreement in our camp at a crucial moment could prove decisive."

Borden nodded. He had heard this before. "But aren't you overlooking one thing, Bern?" Kehrn said. "All the *Soviet* VIPs will be there too—and I mean practically *all* of them. Their tops, too: bigger than the ones everybody else will be sending. That has to count for something."

"And suppose they don't," Foleda countered. "Suppose it's all phony, and they don't send any of them up there— just empty ships for us to watch through telescopes. Do you think our people would insist on checking them out after this latest fiasco? No way. See—they've covered that base too."

Kehrn looked uneasy. "Well . . . they'd have to be there." He frowned, as if, having stated it, he wasn't sure why. "I mean, they couldn't not be there when all the rest arrive, could they? And the place will be declared open after that . . ."

Foleda looked hard at him for a few seconds, then leaned

back in his chair and shook his head. "No. They don't have to do any of that. By that time, none of it will matter. Whatever it is they're planning will have happened by November seventh. A month. That's all we've got to find out."

He sounded more certain than ever before. This time the others remained quiet and didn't argue.

CHAPTER THIRTY-NINE

Agniya left Hut 19 early in October. She had accepted an offer of a teaching position in Turgenev on condition of good behavior, and was released for a three-month probationary period to take up normal accommodations in the town.

"That's how they get you," Svetlana said to Paula as they stood watching with some other friends as Agniya sent back a final wave before disappearing into the Administration Building. The second of the two guards who had helped her carry her belongings from the hut closed the door behind. "They gave her a work assignment at the elementary school. She's always loved children. Now she'll cooperate and do what they want—and not only that, but be grateful for it, too. With you it will be computers."

"I doubt if it'll come to that," Paula said.

"We'll see."

"That's what this whole place is for," Elena said as they began retracing their steps down toward the huts. "At one time they used to punish dissenters, but it was so wasteful. Then they tried brainwashing, but it destroyed the creativity that they wanted to use. Now they rehabilitate people without losing them."

Agniya's replacement arrived that evening. A guard showed her to the hut and deposited her bags inside the door, while a second waited outside. She stepped in and looked around, nodding a greeting to Svetlana and

Elena. Then she shifted her eyes to Paula, who had risen to her feet and was staring wide-eyed. They gazed at each other in amazement for several seconds, and then hugged warmly. It was Tanya, the schoolteacher whom Paula had last seen in the infirmary, before her transfer to the surface level.

"So it was true, they did move you up here!" Tanya exclaimed. "Anastasia and I often wondered about you. You remember Anastasia?"

"Of course. How is she?"

"Up and about again. And you! You're looking so well compared to how you were. Things must really be a lot different up here."

"Yes, you'll find it quite a change. Oh, but I'm being rude—these are the other two ladies who live here." Paula introduced Svetlana and Elena. They showed Tanya the bunk that Agniya had vacated. Svetlana offered her a cigarette. She declined and began unpacking her things. Paula helped her put them away while Elena made tea.

"Is it true you have a beach up here?" Tanya asked.

"Yes—kind of," Paula said. "And more. I'll show you around before dark. But how did you get here?"

Tanya sighed. "The usual kind of deal, I suppose. There are a lot of new arrivals at *Tereshkova* these days—moving into quarters that have recently been completed at Turgenev and Landausk. They include many families with children. Apparently the place is short of teachers. I was offered a transfer up here in return for helping out at one of the schools . . . And here I am."

"You're a teacher, then?" Svetlana said.

"Yes."

"Isn't that interesting. Agniya—the woman you're replacing here—she went to teach at Turgenev, too. She was released, in fact."

"Subsurface Zamork is filling up, too," Tanya said. "New faces appearing every day."

"I wonder what's going on," Svetlana mused.

"They want the place full and bustling with people for

November seventh," Tanya said. "And this year it's going to be sun-bronzed youth and gymnastics displays. Troops and tanks are out." Potemkin villages, Paula thought. Yet at the same time the news made her stop and think. It was hardly the kind of population that anyone would want on a battle platform.

They finished getting Tanya settled in, and talked while finishing their tea, after which Paula and Tanya got up to leave for a tour of the surface level. But just as they came out of the hut, Olga appeared.

"Olga, I'd like you to meet Tanya, a friend of mine from when I was Sub. She's just moved in as Agniya's replacement. Isn't that wonderful? Tanya, this is Olga. If you really want to find out how to get anything done up here, she's the woman to know."

"A pleasure," Tanya said, extending a hand.

Olga shook it lightly and smiled, but she seemed distracted. "Paula, look, there's someone I want you to talk to. He has some news you'll be interested n."

"Now? I was just about to show Tanya around."

"It is urgent." Olga's voice was serious.

"Of course you must go," Tanya told Paula. "I'm sure everything will still be here in the morning. And to tell you the truth, I am rather tired. I'm sorry we had to meet in such a rush, Olga. We'll see each other again soon, I'm sure. Good night." And with that, Tanya turned and went back into the hut.

Olga took Paula to Hut 8, which was close to Hut 19, in the next row downhill toward the Administration Building. She tapped on the door, which was opened almost immediately by a big, heavyset man with a fleshy, smooth-skinned, olive complexion, wide eyes, and reddish curls framing a high brow. His face was familiar, but Paula had never had reason to talk to him. He had evidently been expecting them, and stepped outside. The three of them began walking slowly in the direction of the reservoir.

"Paula, this is Eban," Olga said. "You've probably seen

him around. I think Eban can help you with regard to the other American you've been asking about."

"Lewis Earnshaw? You know where he is?"

"Hmm, I've possibly heard tell of him," Eban said noncommittally. "Describe him to me."

"Oh, about six feet in height, I'd guess. One-eighty-pounds, probably—solid, lean kind of build. Black, wavy hair. It used to be short, parted on the left. Brown eyes, alert, taking things in all the time. Clean-shaven face."

"Why is he here?"

"He came here with me on May first, as a journalist for Pacific News Services of California. We were arrested on charges of espionage."

"Why did he really come here?"

"I've given you my answer."

Eban sniffed and looked at Olga questioningly. "She's reliable," Olga said. "I've worked with her for a long time now. Have you ever regretted trusting my judgment?"

"I don't like the part about showing her the Crypt and the way into it," Eban said, speaking as if Paula wasn't there. "It's not necessary for her to know of it at this stage. Why can't we bring him up here instead?"

"There are reasons, as you know," Olga replied.

"Hmm." Eban reflected for a moment longer, then nodded. "Very well. But I will need to make arrangements. Come by the hut at the same time tomorrow. Knock if a pot with yellow primroses has been put in the window by the door. Otherwise don't bother—it will mean the hut is being watched.

The next day, Olga visited the library and brought Paula the transcript of a reply from "Tycoon/Golic," addressed to "Pangolin/Hot." "Tycoon" was Foleda's code name, while "Golic" completed the compound "Hypergolic," the first half of which Paula had supplied in her transmission. It acknowledged receipt of Paula's message, asked a few specific questions, and expressed interest in the list of inmates' names that Paula had referred to. She decided to put off responding until she'd allowed some time for the promised contact with Earnshaw—which with luck might be imminent.

That evening, the flowers had been placed in the window by the door of Hut 8 when Olga and Paula approached. Paula hadn't asked how Eban knew whether or not the place was under observation. It was the kind of thing that could happen at any time for no particular reason in Zamork. Olga was carrying a book. They went up to the door and knocked, and Eban let them in. Inside was another man, late thirties or thereabouts, with flat, sandy-colored hair and a ragged mustache. He was wearing the gray uniform of regular-category inmates from the subsurface levels. Paula's first thought was to wonder how he had gotten into the hut, almost in the center of the surface level compound, without being seen. Before Paula could say anything, Eban touched his lips with a finger and shook his head as a signal for her to remain quiet.

"I've brought your book back, Eban," Olga said. "Most of it was good, but I didn't agree with the last part. Do you really go along with that?"

"Yes, but I'm not in a mood to argue about it now. Oh, did you want to hear that tape I was telling you about?"

"The American one?"

"They call it piano blues. I wonder why we never invented anything like it." Eban started a player on a shelf in one corner, and twangy music turned to high volume filled the room. Silently the mustached man handed Paula a flashlight, and then he and Eban went through to the small bathroom and shower closet at the rear of the hut, motioning for Paula to follow. Olga came after them.

The mustached man knelt down by the shower and felt with his fingertips under the edge of the lip enclosing the cubicle floor. The click of a catch sounded, and the whole square of tiling surrounding the drain hinged upward. A section of pipe below the drain had been replaced by a loop of flexible tubing to allow the trapdoor to swing free. Below was a vertical shaft, shored with strips of metal and plastic panels. It was lit by a small bulb fixed in one of the corners a short distance down. The mustached man swung his legs into the shaft and climbed down out of sight. Eban nodded for Paula to follow. She crouched down and sat on the edge of the opening. Below, the head and shoulders of the mustached man were silhouetted dimly against the light. She turned and braced her arms on the edge, and a hand from below guided her foot toward a rung fastened to the shaft wall. Paula felt with her other foot, found the next rung, and began climbing carefully down. Above her head, the trapdoor swung back over the top of the shaft and clicked shut.

They had climbed down through no more than ten feet of the surrounding soil, or whatever else lay beneath the huts, when Paula felt herself stepping out of the shaft into thin air. The hand caught her foot again and moved it onto a solid surface. She ducked out of what turned out to be an opening in a roof, and found herself standing on a steel housing of some kind, partly visible in the feeble light from a second bulb at the bottom of the shaft they had emerged from. Machinery hummed in the space she could sense around her, and there was a current of warm air smelling of oil. Then even the light from the shaft vanished, plunging the place into complete darkness. A moment later a flashlight beam appeared, illuminating the hole in the roof above them. "Give me some light there with yours," the mustached man hissed. Paula did so while he attached a panel over the opening. Then he turned back toward her.

Paula shone her lamp at his face. "We can't go on meeting like this," she said.

He grinned apologetically. "A dreadful way to introduce myself, I know." He was obviously English. "Hello. My same is Sargent—Peter Sargent. I'm taking you to Lewis Earnshaw."

"Paula Shelmer. How long has this tunnel been here?"

"Well, now, that would be telling, wouldn't it?"

They climbed down to the floor, and Sargent led the

way through a fragmented world of machines, pipes, ducting, structural supports and cable runs glimpsed briefly in the dancing flashlight beams and made all the more unreal by the suddenness of the contrast with the world they had just left. A bridge of braced girders spanning a drop into black nothingness pointed to a wall reinforced with metal ribbing, which appeared to extend beyond the containing decks above and below. Heights had never been one of Paula's strong pints, and she made the crossing with trembling legs and a dry mouth. At the far end, Sargent straddled the topmost girder and removed a section that had been cut out of the wall in front, then drew Paula close by him to look through.

She felt as if her heart had dropped down to somewhere in her stomach. The shaft she found herself staring down plunged away to lose itself in blackness beyond the range of the light from Sargent's flashlight. It was like looking down a bottomless mine."

"Down there?" Paula croaked.

"It's one of the main Core elevators," Sargent replied cheerfully. "The problem is that we're up at the top, and the place we want to get to is down near the bottom. The part that the car runs over is in between, which means we have to get underneath it."

"Wonderful."

"Nothing to worry about. First we have to get across to the other side, which we do by dropping down into that horizontal strip and following it around. There's a space across there, behind the rails the car runs on, that we can use to get down. I'll go first. If your not happy about the traverse, I can bring a line back to clip on you that'll catch you if you slip."

"No, I'll make it. Let's get it over with. But what happens if the car comes up while we're only halfway over?"

"It's all right. It doesn't come up this high But it causes quite a strong draft of air. Be ready for it."

Sargent led off, and Paula tracked him with her light. He moved surely and unhurriedly, finding his holds and shifting position with effortless catlike grace. He reached the far side in no time and lodged himself in the recess behind the vertical rails. Moments later, the beam from his lamp came on to light up the first stretch immediately below Paula. She was already wishing she'd accepted the offer of a safety line, but a streak of pride prevented her from calling out after him now. She lowered herself from the hole to the level of the horizontal strut and edged sideways onto it, feeling ahead with a hand, finding a hold, and pulling herself another step toward the first corner.

"Great stuff!" Sargent's voice called from across the shaft. "There's a plate just above your head that you can hold onto there. The next bit's a little tricky because there's nothing for your hands. Take it slowly and press your palms flat against the wall for balance." Paula looked sideways and down over her shoulder. A metal bracing strip about three inches wide ran along the wall, a short distance out from it, with nothing within reach above but smooth, featureless metal. She swallowed hard and gulped a breath. Flattening her chest and the side of her face against the wall, she moved out from the corner, her arm stretched to the side, fingertips inching their way along the surface, feeling for the first edge or crack. Her breath came in short, uneven gasps. Sargent had made it look like a stroll. Probably one of those people who relaxed by walking up walls in Yosemite, she thought savagely.

It had to happen. Just as she reached the midpoint, the cables on the far side kicked into motion with a jolt that almost caused her to fall off there and then, and suddenly the whole shaft seemed to be filled with motor noise. Paula closed her eyes and pressed herself against the wall, feeling it throb with vibrations. Air surged around her, and her fingers clawed instinctively at the cold metal. The vibrations intensified, and the terror that is triggered only by the self-preservation instinct compelled her to open her eyes and look down. The roof of the car was rushing upward at her, into the part of the shaft illuminated by the flashlight. It wasn't going to stop. She could see herself being smeared like . . .

Everything had gone quiet. She looked down and saw the top of the car just a few feet below, stationary. Then her hand gave way suddenly as the palm slipped on its own perspiration. A hand gripped her elbow and steadied her as she tottered. Sargent had moved back out of the recess and was bridging the gap that remained between her and the final corner, one hand steadying her and the other anchored on a firm hold. He drew firmly before she could panic, and seconds later she was perched next to him on a section of supporting frame, safely inside the recess.

"All right?" he asked.

Paula nodded, although she was breathing shakily. "I haven't had so much fun since my draft physical."

To get them down, Sargent produced a line that had been hidden behind a girder and uncoiled it, letting the free end drop into the darkness below. He showed her how to run it around her back and thigh to regulate her speed by friction, and then he went first again. A short while afterward, Paula felt two sharp tugs on the line to signal that the way was clear for her to follow. After her experience at the top of the main shaft, the descent seemed uneventful.

They left the elevator shaft through a maintenance hatch which Sargent replaced behind them, and came out onto a narrow steel-floored walkway leading between rows of large tanks and piping. After a short distance Sargent held a hand up for Paula to stop. "We've installed our own intruder alarms," he explained. "There's an infrared beam right here. Step over it carefully. It saves them having heart attacks in the Crypt every time someone goes down there."

"What is this Crypt? Eban mentioned it to Olga yesterday."

"You'll see."

They turned off to the side and passed by a series of

bays containing transformers and power-distribution equipment. Beyond, light showed from a space underneath an intermediate-level deck. It was so obscured by the forest of support works and engineering that Paula didn't realize its extent until they were almost on top of it. As they stepped down inside, she saw that the space had been improvised into a workshop-laboratory, with a couple of large benches, tool racks, a table covered with drawings, and all manner of components, assemblies, and devices in various stages of construction. Three figures were waiting, presumably alerted to their approach by the flashlights. The youngest was swarthy-skinned, with black hair and alert, lively eyes. The man next to him was lean in build, with sparse hair, hollowed cheeks, and protruding eyes, giving Paula an instant impression of a human weasel. The third stepped forward and stood looking her up and down for a few seconds, a grin playing at the corners of his mouth. Then he grasped her by the shoulders with both hands and stared at her face. "Hi," Earnshaw said.

"Hi." She returned his gaze for a moment, then reached up and squeezed his forearms affectionately. "So, you are here. The Russians wouldn't tell me."

"They're like that." Earnshaw looked down at her green tunic. "What's this—a priv? You're doing okay. And I was worried that you were getting a hard time."

"I was at first, but it changed. It's a long story. I have news, too. A lot's been happening." Paula waved an arm at the surroundings. "But it looks as if you haven't been exactly idle either. What's this all about?"

"Another long story. One part of it is we're fixing a laser. But we need help with the electronics.

"So that's why you finally brought me down here?"

"Of course. What else did you think?"

"Lew, you never change. You're hateful."

"A much better relationship for business," Earnshaw said. He motioned with his head to the other two men waiting behind. "This is Paula, my partner that I told you about. Paula, meet Razz and Kev, two more of the crew."

CHAPTER FORTY

McCain's brow knotted in open disbelief. "Tycoon?" he repeated. "You're in touch with Tycoon? How could you be?" They were sitting on a couple of boxes off to one side at the edge of the lighted work area and speaking in lowered voices out of earshot of the others, who were carrying on with their work. This was company business.

"It's a complicated story," Paula replied. She had anticipated problems in convincing him. "Basically it works like this. I've gotten to know a Russian woman up on the priv level called Olga. She's a scientist, too—in the nuclear field—but also a human-rights dissident. That's why she's here." McCain nodded and listened intently. Paula went on, "The point is that a colleague of hers—one of her dissident colleagues, that is—who's also one of her long-standing personal friends, happens to hold a high position in the communications ground-station in Siberia that handles the main link up to here. To cut a long story short, they found a way of sending messages to each other by concealing them in the regular traffic in a way that's transparent to the standard handling system."

"That much I can buy," McCain agreed. "But how did you get in on it?"

"They lost an electronic chip that was vital to the process, and needed somebody who could program a new one. Olga and I had gotten to know each other by then. It was in my field. She took a chance."

McCain looked derisive. "*She* took a chance? How much do you know about this Oshkadov woman?"

"Look, she's a scientist. We understand a lot of things in common. I'd still be down in that pit if it wasn't for her. She got me out."

"She needed someone to program the chip."

"Sure. So it's a selfish world. But it was still her neck."

"Okay, okay." McCain raised a hand. "So you're in the picture regarding this private line they've got. Now, how did you persuade this guy down in Siberia . . . What's his name?"

"Ivan."

"How did you persuade Ivan to send a message off to our side for you? Give me one good reason why a Soviet official in a high position—I don't care if he's a dissident or not—should agree to risk getting himself shot by sending—"

"I didn't get him to send anything," Paula said. "I thought of it, but Tycoon beat me to it. He sent a message through Ivan to me first."

McCain sat back on the box and stared at Paula incredulously. He closed his eyes momentarily, shook his head, and rubbed his brow with a knuckle. "You mean Tycoon just happens to be in touch with this Ivan, and Ivan, for no particular reason, tells him all about his secret line up to *Tereshkova*. Come on, what have they been putting in your coffee? . . . Code names get broken pretty easily—you know that. And yet somebody in a place like this shows you a message that says it's from Tycoon, and you swallow the whole—"

"It carried a correct validation-code initializer," Paula said. "I included one from my list in my response, and since then a reply has come back with the right completion. What more do you want? If we're not going to trust the code system, what's the point of setting it up in the first place?"

McCain looked nonplussed. "That's impossible," he declared. "Or else they've got your completion list. How much to do you remember from when you were interrogated?"

"You don't have to look for something like that to explain it," Paula insisted. "Ivan has approached our side with an offer to defect. Think about it. He and Olga were both mixed up in illegal goings-on together. She was discovered somehow, the KGB grabbed her, and she wound up here. Obviously Ivan could be next. He can see that as much as anybody, so the idea of him suddenly getting a divine revelation to make himself scarce would make sense. Now put yourself in Tycoon's place. To make the deal sound attractive, Ivan would have told who he is and how valuable he'd be if he came over. He's hardly in a position to refuse favors right? So if you were Tycoon, what's the first thing you might think of trying? What would there be to lose if it was Ivan's neck on the line? Wouldn't you give it a shot? Well, that's what Tycoon did."

McCain exhaled a long breath and rubbed his chin. He couldn't fault her reasoning, but he still didn't like the situation. There were coincidences involved, and he was always suspicious of coincidences. In the end he seemed to dismiss the subject for the time being, and got up from the box. "Razz will have to tell you what he wants with the laser," he said, turning toward where the others were working. "But apart from that, come and see some of the other things we've got going down here."

Rashazzi and Sargent had made a dummy head from plaster and used it as a template for various patterns of rubber headpieces, which they made by cutting and regluing sections of used inner tubes. The tubes were used on the general-purpose groundcars found all over *Tereshkova;* Sargent and Mungabo had obtained them from a recycling plant they'd discovered in the course of exploring beneath Landausk. Over the open face-section they had attached a mask assembled from stolen pieces of firefighters' breathing apparatus and experimented with ways of sealing it to contain four pounds per square inch overpressure, filling it from an improvised air pump. They had settled on a method that seemed to work acceptably, and now Sargent was donning the equipment to try it out as the first live subject.

"What about the rest of the body?" Paula asked after McCain had explained the idea of going outside using homemade spacesuits. "You'll need some kind of restraint to maintain pressure."

Rashazzi pointed at an oil drum standing by the rear wall, partly covered by a sheet of tin but emitting fumes of a not-entirely-pleasant odor. "We've found that elastic surgical bandages plasticized in the concoction that's brewing in there give the properties we need. Wrapping the body mummy-fashion would probably work, but we're going to try welding sheets of the stuff into parts of stretch-suits. Getting dressed would be a lot quicker."

Paula looked dubiously at the pump that Rashazzi was connecting to the mask over Sargent's face. "You'll need something a lot more powerful than that for a full-size vacuum chamber." A large chamber would be necessary to test the complete suits. Nobody in their right mind would try out something like that for the first time by leaping out into space and trusting to luck.

"We can rig up a natural one," Rashazzi said. Already Paula was developing the impression from listening to him that with his enthusiasm and energy, anything might be possible. "We find an outer compartment against the hull wall, drill a hole through to the outside, and fit a valve in it. Then we shut off the room and decompress it gradually by means of the valve to provide a test chamber. When we're happy the suits work, we make a hatch through with the chamber evacuated, and it becomes our airlock for getting in and out."

"How far away from the outer surface is the cosmic-ray shield?" Paula asked. An important point. The shield was a detached structure outside the hull, and since it didn't rotate with the colony, it would be moving with a relative speed of something like a hundred fifty miles per hour. That was something that McCain realized he'd forgotten in his discussions with the scientists.

"It is only a matter of feet," Rashazzi agreed. "But it's something we can only know for sure by cutting the hatch and looking out." So somebody would have to work his way across the outside skin of the structure without being thrown off, in darkness, with the inner surface of the shield flashing by probably within inches of him all the time. Paula shuddered at the thought of it. She'd done her share of heroics, she decided.

At the table near the bench, Scanlon was updating the

maps which the group was producing from information gathered in their reconnaissance expeditions carried out via the freight-transit system that the escape committee had discovered. "And 'tis fortunate lads we are, indeed," Scanlon said, looking up at her. "The traffic down there is busy these days so we've no problem getting rides to anywhere we want."

"Why's that?" Paula asked him. McCain had drifted away and was staring out into the darkness again, obviously deep in thought.

"All the good earth from Mother Russia that's coming down the spokes from the hub and having to be distributed around," Scanlon said.

"So it is true, then—they are really sending soil all the way here?"

"As true as we're here, talking." Scanlon gestured casually at a bin standing beside the plasticizing drum. "There's a pile of it in there, if you're interested. We're sick of coming back covered in the stuff."

"What did you bring it back here for?" Paula asked, walking over to the bin.

"Ah, that was Razz. It was there and it was unguarded— too much for the poor man to resist."

She stood looking down at the dark soil, then on impulse stooped and let some trickle through her fingers. It felt dry, probably partly dehydrated for shipment, but could doubtless be reconstituted on-site. "Do you need it, or can I take some?" she asked absently.

"And what would anyone be needing the likes of that for?"

"I have some friends up on the surface who might like some—real Russian soil to grow flowers in, maybe."

"Did you want it for anything in particular?" Scanlon called to Razz.

"Not really. We can get plenty more, anyway," Rashazzi answered.

Scanlon shrugged. "Help yourself. You'll find some empty cans on the shelf behind the rack there."

Paula found a can with a lid and scooped some of the soil into it. McCain came over to her as she screwed on the lid. He seemed to have arrived at some decision in his mind and drew her aside again. "There's one way I can check out this channel of yours," he said. "Can you send off a response from me to Tycoon's last message, with an initializer that *I'll* select from *my* list? If we get an answer with the right completion, I'll accept it as genuine."

It was what Paula had been expecting him to say, but as usual Earnshaw had had to check through all the alternatives and possible objections first. She nodded. "Write out what you want to send, and I'll take it back up with me."

"Exactly what do you do with it then?"

"The chip is programmed, but the transmission text has to be loaded into it. I do that on an offline system—there are several that I can get access to up there."

"Inside Zamork?"

"I'm working in a place at Turgenev in the day. Olga fixed it. That was how I got out of the kitchens."

"What kind of work?"

"Eco-modeling."

"Go on."

"Then Olga takes the chip back and passes it to an associate she's got, who substitutes it for a chip in the outgoing coding processors."

"How do you get the replies back?"

"They're encoded in statistical updates beamed up into the library. Olga transcribes them and brings me the copy."

"So Russians have access to the plaintext going both ways."

"How else could it be? Two separate systems are involved: here down to Siberia, and from there into our commnet. There has to be a conversion from one to the other."

McCain nodded reluctantly. "Okay. Let's sit down again. I won't be a second." He went over to the table where Scanlon was working, and returned with a notepad and a pencil. They sat down on the boxes again, and he handed her the pencil and pad. "What was Tycoon's last initializer?" he asked.

"Hot," she told him.

"My completion is 'Gospel,'" McCain said. Only he had known that. Paula's completion code for the same word would have been "Rod."

"Initializer?" Paula asked.

McCain thought for a second. "Trans." Paula might have chosen the same word too, for it was also on her list. *In her case only,* a valid reply from Foleda would carry the completion "Locate"; for a valid reply to McCain, however, she had no idea what the completion should be.

Paula wrote: SEXTON/GOSPEL TO TYCOON/TRANS. She waited. McCain whistled tunelessly through his teeth for a few seconds and then dictated a straightforward, innocuous statement to the effect that he was being detained on *Tereshkova,* and that he was in good shape and being treated fairly, apart from denial of communications rights.

Paula looked up questioningly. "That's it?"

"That's it."

"You're not going to say anything else?"

"What else do you want me to say?"

"Well, you could answer some of the questions that Tycoon asked in his message. We could give the names of some of the VIPs upstairs that he sounded interested in. Or mention that the place is taking in new batches of civilians with lots of children. Or that tons of soil from Earth are arriving here. Wouldn't that be considered useful intelligence material?"

McCain shook his head. "Not until I've a better idea who I'm talking to."

Paula sighed with exasperation. In her own mind she had no doubt that the link was genuine. "You're talking to Tycoon," she said. "Believe me, I *know.*"

"Let's wait and see, shall we?"

"God, why are all you intelligence people so suspicious of everything?"

"We're not. But the ones who aren't don't last too long. So your impressions end up being formed only by the rest. Scientists call it statistical bias. We call it survival. But isn't that what eco-modeling is supposed to be all about?"

On her next day at Turgenev, Paula composed the message as Earnshaw had directed. She had thought of sending a separate communication along with it under her own code to supply the additional information she had suggested, but on further reflection decided against it. It would be tantamount to a direct violation of orders, for one thing—Earnshaw was still the senior member of the mission—and for another, it would only be a matter of days at the most before Tycoon replied. Then, with Earnshaw finally reassured, all would proceed much more smoothly.

Sure enough, a couple of days later Olga brought Paula a transcript of a message from Tycoon to "Sexton/Vaal." This time Paula was spared another ordeal in the elevator shaft, for Earnshaw came up to meet her in the machinery gallery at the bottom of the shaft beneath Eban Istamel's hut. Earnshaw confirmed that "Vaal" was the correct completion for "Trans" from his own personal list. Therefore there could no longer be any doubt that the channel did connect all the way through to Foleda in Washington. To Paula's chagrin, however, he still declined to supply the information she had suggested. But he did give her a reply in which he hinted that he was in a position to enjoy virtually unlimited freedom of movement around the colony's outer ring.

The tone of the response that came back from Foleda gave the impression that he was in trouble and having credibility problems back home. Uncharacteristically throwing caution to the winds, he specified the precise locations around *Tereshkova* where weapons installations were suspected to exist, described their nature, and requested Sexton to check the sites and report as quickly as possible. The message ended, REPEAT, OBJECTIVE SUBORDINATES OTHER CONSIDERATIONS. POSSIBILITY OF COMPROMISE ACCEPTABLE. EXPEDITE BY ALL AVAILABLE MEANS.

Which meant, "Risk your ass if you have to. We need this."

CHAPTER FORTY-ONE

The two principal factors that made *Valentina Tereshkova* potentially so formidable were its distance from Earth and its sheer size. Whether driven by high-power pulsed reactors located in the hub or rim, or in the form of ejectable bomb-type devices, its weaponry would be based on transforming nuclear energy into beams of concentrated firepower traveling at the speed of light and impacting on their targets at a rate equivalent to tens or even hundreds of tons of high explosive per second. Since nuclear processes produce energy at an intensity millions of times greater than anything attainable from conventional sources, which involve only the outer electron shells of atoms, the resulting hardware would be extremely compact, and thus easily hidden in lots of unlikely places.

This had caused a lot of headaches among the Western analysts whose job was to come up with credible ways to attack the platform, should the need ever arise—the military had contingency plans filed away for just about every eventuality conceivable. True enough, a single nuclear warhead would have sufficed to destroy it totally, but missiles of any kind were ruled out. With the target at almost-lunar distance—ten times that to geosynchronous orbit—surprise would be out of the question: in the long climb from near-Earth space an attacking wave of missiles would have no hope of surviving. Yes, the West did have beam weapons of its own deployed in near Earth orbits. But this was where *Tereshkova*'s size made the telling difference. For the West's weapons were comparatively small, special-purpose types designed to attack pinpointable targets such as missiles and satellites at shorter ranges. Hence they couldn't hope to knock out the hidden weapons on something like *Tereshkova* in a surprise attack. Counterfire from *Tereshkova*, on the other hand, would be instantly devastating to clearly defined targets sitting in space. The answer, of course, would have been to build something comparable in size at the proper time, but it was a little late to catch that boat now, and the political arguing was still going on.

Also significant was *Tereshkova*'s capacity to accommodate a variety of weapons. The essence of directed-beam strategy was to be able to deliver a wide range of wavelengths from the electromagnetic and particle energy spectra, generated by a series of devices differently "tuned" to exploit the weaknesses of a given target type. Typically, hardening or protecting a target against one of the spectrum would render it more vulnerable in another part. For example, crudely focused, intense bursts of microwave energy would act by becoming trapped and concentrated, waveguide-fashion, in the structural cavities of the target, causing intense internal currents to circulate as if the target had been struck by lightning. Effective shielding against such a microwave attack could be achieved by cladding the target with an insulated metal skin. But this would make it more susceptible to pulsed diffuse X-rays, which when deposited upon an insulated metal layer induce strong electro-magnetic emissions inside the shield, fatal to electronic equipment. Heavy ions carried kinetic energy deep into solids faster than it could dissipate, causing materials to explode. Muons made lightning with two hundred times the mass of electron beams. Neutrons induced premature fission in warheads, degrading them to uselessness.

Symphony for full orchestra.

One of the suspected weapons that Foleda had communicated details of to McCain was a tunable, high-power, free-electron laser. That meant that the laser beam drew its energy from accelerated electrons that could be made to vibrate at any of a range of frequencies by a variable magnetic field. This contrasts with methods employing an excited solid, liquid, or gas medium, where the frequency is fixed and depends on the medium used. The system in question, it was claimed, operated across the optical spectrum from infrared to ultraviolet, and was aimed by the optical-mirror system located around the hub. According to the information received, it existed beneath the confused pile of buildings, tanks, conveyer ramps, and elevator machinery known as Agricultural Station 3, at the base of the minor spoke between Turgenev and Novyi Kazan.

McCain was far from certain what a tunable, high-power, free-electron laser installation ought to look like. In fact, he hadn't a clue. But as long as he was able to describe accurately what lay in there, the experts could worry about interpreting what it meant. Moreover, he had reasoned, if it existed it would be securely contained and guarded. So even if it proved impossible to actually get inside, the existence of obstacles too formidable to penetrate would say enough about the kind of place it was. And if the obstacles turned out to be no more than would allow them to simply test and withdraw? . . . Well, as Foleda had to thoughtfully reminded him, that was part of the job.

He felt the car slowing down in the darkness. Then it clattered over a series of switches before stopping for a few seconds, lurched a short distance forward, and then stopped again. From a point beside him, Scanlon's flashlight beam came on to reveal another stationary car filling the tunnel ahead, and a narrow maintenance walkway on one side, behind a handrail. It meant they were joining the line of waiting cars that often formed at the approach to the loading point below Agricultural Station 3. They had come out of the regular transit tube, and the roof here was somewhat higher.

"This will do us as good as anywhere," Scanlon's voice said from the darkness.

"Sure. Let's go."

McCain raised himself out of the hollow in the car's load of kidney beans that he had been lying in, and shone his own light while Scanlon hauled himself over the side and onto the walkway. Then McCain joined him. Even when they were heading for a destination farther on around the ring, they had learned from experience to get off the transit system here, work around the loading area on foot, and catch another car on the far side. On an earlier expedition that McCain had made with Mungabo, the load of corn they were riding had been switched up a ramp and emptied into a silo by physically inverting the car, almost suffocating both of them. McCain was beginning to feel like an unnatural denizen of some strange subterranean world of pipes, girders, ducting, and metal, whose proper inhabitants were not creatures of flesh and blood at all, but the ubiquitous, tireless machines.

An opening off the walkway brought them into an upward-sloping passage that bent through an angle to join a large compartment containing motors and winches, with cables disappearing up into the space overhead. The flashlights picked out more passages going off in other directions and walls meeting in strange combinations of angles. As with the oddly-flung-together jumbles of constructions surrounding the spoke-bases on the surface, there didn't seem to be a straight edge or surface anywhere that ran direct from one side of the torus to the other—like a bulkhead in a ship. Even Rashazzi, for all his sightings and measurements, had confessed to getting confused in the process of passing through the spoke zones, and frequently found himself coming out of them in a direction he hadn't expected. The others who had reconnoitered long-distance around *Tereshkova* had all reported similar difficulties.

They stopped here to exchange the coveralls that they had taken to wearing when riding the tubes for standard light-blue smocks and white caps, as worn by the agricultural technicians, which Koh had stolen on a work

assignment. The coveralls hadn't been really necessary
this time, as it turned out, but on other occasions they
had dropped into cars full of the earth still coming down
the spokes from transporters unloading at the hub and
come out looking like mud-wrestlers. The smocks carried
their two general-clearance badges, enabling them to
move around. Having only two badges exacerbated the
problem of limited time, and Istamel was working on a
scheme for acquiring more.

McCain unfolded a sheaf of papers containing extracts
from Foleda's instructions and sketches from previous
reconnaissances. "Section of bulkhead to the east. Inspection
ladder leading to catwalk below cable bank," he read.

Scanlon aimed his light upward and swung it from side
to side. "Well, there's what some people might call a
bulkhead, and that's a ladder. It's close to east, I'd say,
but how can a man be sure?"

"That has to be the way. Are you all set?"

"To be sure, hasn't it been me that's been waiting for
the last five minutes? So let's be off."

McCain's group had established that one of the colony's
waste-reduction and water-recycling plants was situated
in that direction, as indeed was shown in the public
information released by the Soviets. Beyond it, the official
plans showed a long space, radial to the main axis—thus
pointing, interestingly, at the mirror system surrounding
the hub—which was described vaguely as "Materials
Storage." That, according to the information that Foleda
had assembled, was where the laser emplacement was
supposed to be located.

The area they entered higher up was illuminated by
pilot lights, and on an earlier visit Sargent and another
from the escape committee had observed technicians
working there. The choice was either to move carefully
and try to stay under cover, or simply walk through brazenly
and trust in their appearance to avoid drawing attention.
Since it seemed probable that the vicinity of a high-security
installation would be under observation, acting furtively

was as likely as not to do more harm than good. Therefore they had decided on the impertinent approach.

The surroundings they passed through were reminiscent of parts of an oil refinery or chemical plant, with large domed vessels wreathed in piping and supports, pumps, compressors, and tubes zigzagging their way through heat exchangers. They passed two figures working on equipment inside a hatch they had opened on a railed platform overlooking the through-walkway. One of them raised a hand casually as McCain and Scanlon passed below. Scanlon waved back.

On Earth, the atmosphere, soil, and oceans provide huge reservoirs in which the breakdown of dead matter and wastes, the return of gases into the air, and the removal of moisture by rainfall can all proceed at a relatively leisurely pace—even slow, inefficient processes operating on a planetary scale add up at the end of a day to a lot of materials processed. But *Valentina Tereshkova* had nothing of comparable capacity. Instead, the colony relied on mechanical condensers to dehumidify the atmosphere, and the extracted water resupplied drinking, irrigation, and industrial needs. Most of the moisture came from plant and animal respiration, which was why the dehumidifiers were located by the agricultural zones. Bulk condensation of water releases large amounts of energy, and the condensation process operated in conjunction with heat exchangers which carried the excess away to be radiated into space. Wastes were broken down through a wet-oxidation process, carbon dioxide returning to the atmosphere and solid nutrients being filtered out and shipped away for incorporation into animal feed and fertilizers. The Soviets had expressed pride in the accomplishment of their designers in devising a complete recycling process that eliminated the need to transport anything away from the habitat, thereby avoiding its expensive replacement from Earth. But that had been before more recent events, of course. McCain had no idea what they were telling everyone now.

On the far side of the recycling plant they came to a sturdy-looking wall, extending up beyond the level they were in, which looked as if it was part of the main supporting structure. It emerged on one side from behind a confusion of platforms and pipes, crossed squarely across in front of them for a distance, and then angled back on a different tack through a girderwork maze. McCain and Scanlon stopped and exchanged quick glances. The line was just about where, according to the official plans, the side of the "Materials Storage" compartment ought to be.

But McCain grew puzzled as he surveyed the scene. There was nothing resembling a guardpost, no observation ports anywhere that he could detect—no warning signs, even. They moved over to a cluster of valves on some pipes coming up from below and pretended to be inspecting them. While McCain studied the wall in detail, Scanlon made notes of their route and the things they had observed, to add to their maps when they returned.

It seemed to be, for all that McCain could make of it, just a wall. Its only feature was a single, small, insignificant-looking door with the numeral "15" stenciled on it. Camouflage, McCain decided. The real installation was on the other side. He looked at Scanlon and motioned with his head to indicate approaching the door.

"It was your boss that told you to go sticking your fool neck out, not mine," Scanlon said.

"Come on, you Irish asshole."

They crossed the floor and came to the door. It looked ordinary enough, with no sign of anything suspicious close-up. Scanlon moved a pace forward and tried it. It opened. The sound of voices came from beyond, and instinctively McCain and Scanlon flattened themselves out of sight on either side. But then they realized that the voices were raised and coming from a distance. After a few seconds McCain eased himself forward and peered around the edge of the doorway. Scanlon did the same on the other side. They stared, then looked at each other perplexedly. McCain stepped out and went through. Scanlon followed.

They looked around and found themselves standing in . . . a Materials Storage warehouse.

It was certainly spacious, and reminded McCain of a walk-around contractors'-supplies yard back in the States. They had come in through a side door. Arrayed along wide aisles were stacks of all the standard structural modules used to build the apartments, public buildings, factories, and office units found all over *Tereshkova:* wallboards, floor strips, roof frames, ceiling panels; windows, doors, stairs, partitions. There were plumbing sections, electrical sections, kitchen-equipment sections, decorating sections . . . "Holy Mother of God, wouldn't Razz be in his element here!" Scanlon breathed.

A forklift truck passed, carrying a pile of metal sheeting. The voice they had heard belonged to a man with a clipboard, who was standing about ten yards away and reading a list of items to two others: "We'll need ten of those, ten of those, and twenty two-point-seven flanges . . . Now, not that kind . . . Right, those." None of them took any notice of the two newcomers.

McCain and Scanlon walked slowly on through. There were ceramic bricks, blocks, tiles, and slabs; metal strips, rods, bars, and sheets; piles of sand, grit, chips, and gravel; wire in coils; paint in drums. None of it suggested a high-power, tunable, free-electron laser.

"Are you two looking for something?" a voice asked.

They turned and found a broad, bearded man in a brown workcoat standing at an intersection of two of the aisles.

"Er, just looking around," Scanlon said.

"Which unit are you with?"

McCain remembered what Paula had told him about new arrivals, and gambled on a bluff. "We're not, yet. We've only just shipped up from Earth. Trying to get our bearings. It's very confusing."

"I see. Well, glad to have you here. Look around if you want." The man turned to carry on in the direction he had been heading.

"One moment," McCain called.

"Yes?"

McCain gestured toward the far side of the warehouse, opposite where they had entered. "What lies that way, behind there?" According to the official plans, it should have been a crop-drying plant.

"A crop-drying plant," the man said.

"Thank you."

When the man had gone on his way, they continued on to the far side of the warehouse, which was formed by two walls meeting asymmetrically at an angle a third or so of the way along. They went through another open door, crossed an alley behind it, and came to a steel structure supporting a complex of large hoppers and interconnecting conveyors. "What place is this?" McCain asked one of the two women they found monitoring panels in a control room nearby.

"Number-Three Crop-Drying Plant," she told him.

"What's above?"

"Hydroponic recirculators and a crushing mill."

"And below?"

The woman laughed. "Oh, that's a long drop. There's nothing until you get to Earth, Moon, or somewhere else, depending on which way we're turned at the moment. Are you lost?"

"Er, yes, I suppose we are. New arrivals. . . . Thank you."

"And I think it's about time we were trying to find our way back," Scanlon said. "There's nothing more to interest us down here."

"No . . ." McCain sounded bemused. "No, Kev, I guess you're right."

CHAPTER FORTY-TWO

When the reports were in, every one of the specific reconnaissance objectives listed by Foleda had yielded similar results. Gonares had seen nothing at the hub resembling the launching guns for ejectable, fission-pumped, X-ray laser modules that McCain had described. Rashazzi and Sargent had penetrated into where the aluminum-smelting plant was supposed to be below Landausk and found no sign of a nuclear-driven microwave projector there; instead, they had found aluminum-smelting furnaces. And McCain himself had verified that there were no particle accelerator tubes running deep down in the ring at Novyi Kazan, and others had confirmed it at two other places. Yes, it was inevitable that in a volume as large as that of *Valentina Tereshkova*, there were still a lot of places they hadn't seen. A complete search would take months. But the fact remained that without exception, *all* of the findings prophesied by Western intelligence had turned out dead wrong.

"So what does that tell you about all the other suspicions and delusions you people have been suffering from for years? Oh, I don't mean just on our side—the same mentalities exist on both sides. The whole problem with the world has always been the kinds of people who end up running it. It never mattered so much in the past, because they could always go off to fight in out-of-the-way places and keep it between themselves and anyone stupid enough to follow them. But that started to change when we" —Paula was referring to the general category of scientists— "gave them knowledge that allowed them to fly, and they used it to bomb cities. Now things have gone way past that and it affects everybody. You want to play at being scientific, and test the hypothesis. Okay, it's tested. Now we have to tell the people who matter what the results are. There isn't any choice, morally, or whatever other way you want to think of it." She pushed her hair from her brow and turned to face Earnshaw, who was standing impassively on the other side of the Crypt, his arms folded across his chest. For the moment they were alone. Paula was tired, and her voice had been rising with emotion and exasperation.

Earnshaw breathed in heavily and shook his head. "I still don't like it. I say no."

Paula stared disbelievingly. "Why, for Christ's sake? You can't give me one single reason . . ."

"So I'm pulling rank. That means I don't need a reason."

"Beliefs without evidence . . . No, not even that. In the face of evidence."

"Call it uncertainty and caution."

"How can there by any uncertainty? Look, you can't argue with facts. Why do so many people act as if refusing to accept facts that don't conform to their preconceptions can change reality? Reality doesn't care about anyone's preconceptions. The only way to learn anything is by allowing facts to shape beliefs. Aren't you doing just the opposite by letting preexisting beliefs decide what you're prepared to accept as fact? That's called prejudice and superstition."

"I call it gut-feel."

"It's the same difference."

Earnshaw sighed and turned away for a moment. His voice grated, as if he was managing to control his patience only with an effort. "What happened to probability in this all-very-scientific analysis of yours? There are too many facts that look suspiciously to me like unlikely coincidences . . ."

"Suspiciously, suspiciously. See, there you go again. Is there anything you're not suspicious about?"

"And I don't like the thought of having to communicate everything openly through Russians."

"You're obsessed with Russians. Because this place doesn't match your preconceptions about Russian prisons, you're convinced it has to be a cover for something. You never stop to think it might be *you* that's wrong—that your whole set of ideas about their prisons and everything else might be behind the times. Maybe they *are* changing, and people like you just haven't woken up to it yet."

"It's a nice thought," Earnshaw agreed. "But it could turn out to be wrong. What makes you as confident as you sound?"

"Gut-feel." Paula smiled icily and turned away.

"Well, maybe now you're not being so smart. Gut-feel might not be a strong point in your department. What do you know about Olga, apart from that after they'd given you a hard time and kept you on your own for a while, she showed up friendly and understanding just when you needed someone to talk to. Did you ever wonder about that?"

"That's not the way it was. *I* approached *her*—in the infirmary. I'd only seen her for a few seconds before that, by chance."

"By chance. And she just happened to walk through the infirmary."

"Oh, Jesus Christ, don't you ever quit? . . ."

"Look," Earnshaw said, finally sounding sharp. "I've never disputed that you're good at what you do. Don't start trying to tell me how to do what *I* do. That's my job. Okay?"

Paula glared back at him. "Okay. But isn't the main part of that job to communicate back what you find out? We've got information. There are lots of civilians arriving here, lots of children, lots of dirt, and no weapons. Doesn't it occur to you that sending that information back might be a duty?"

Earnshaw held her gaze long and steadily. When he spoke, his voice had returned to normal. "And hasn't it occurred to *you* that *that* might be exactly what somebody somewhere wants us to do?" he asked.

McCain should have been out with a labor detail assigned to soil spreading and planting, but he had used Rashazzi's bracelet-insert-swapping trick to buy enough free time from a couple of Siberians and a Japanese in A Block, a Russian and an Arab in E Block, and a Finn in F Block to be virtually free of work commitments. He had also made it worth Luchenko's while not to notice. For the rest of the day, he prowled around Gorky Street and the general compound alone, reflecting on all the impressions and oddities that he had registered since his coming to

Zamork, and seeing if he could fit them into a different pattern from the one that had taken root in his head.

For one of the things that Paula had said was true: the way the place was run was unlike any Russian prison system that he had ever heard of, and was out of character with the mentalities of totalitarian bureaucrats. It was too free and easy, too unrestrained: prisoners from different nations and backgrounds, convicted for different reasons, mixed and moved around inside Zamork with minimal supervision; there was too much lenience toward things like alcohol, Rashazzi's wire-stripping mice, stealing, and absconding. Then there was the Exchange system, which made bribery and corruption rampant— yet surely it could have been curbed had there existed a will to do so—and the distinctly un-Russian practice of operating by incentives rather than by fear and intimidation. Paula thought it was all just part of the Russians' catching up with the times at last. McCain wasn't so sure.

Naturally, others had noticed this, too. Some of the inmates argued that it simply reflected the pointlessness of having Earth-style security in a space colony; others saw it as consistent with a purpose of rehabilitation and reeducation, not punishment; while McCain for his part had come to the conclusion that the Russians had cultivated these impressions deliberately to camouflage the real purpose of Zamork, which he had described as an "information mine." It was all designed to *encourage* people to mix freely, and therefore talk. And there were many people around who would have much to talk about that the Russians would be very interested to hear. Oh, true, the Russians did go through the motions of interrogations, searches, punishments for infractions, and the like, but with time it had all come to strike McCain more and more as not quite genuine—a charade to dull critical examination by satisfying expectations.

Very clever, McCain had conceded. Everything operated at a double level. There were the apparent reasons for things being as they were, which most people worked out for themselves and were happy with, as they were meant to. And then there was the real reason, which only a few, such as he, had fathomed. And taking advantage of that insight, he had turned the Russians' own tactic back on them by exploiting the very freedoms that they had built into the system—for their own purposes—to set up and run his own miniature espionage operation. Even cleverer.

Now he was beginning to suspect there had been not two, but three levels to the deception all along. And far from being cleverer, he had been duped all the way down the line.

For the same facts that had led him to the information-mine explanation were also consistent with the supposition that he had been meant to believe just that, and that the actions he'd imagined himself to be carrying out freely had in reality all been part of the same plan. In other words, what he'd been doing was exactly what the Soviets had wanted him to do. And now it all made sense why prisoners inside Zamork should have found all the resources they needed to organize themselves as they had, why the security system had turned out to be ridden with loopholes, and why Paula had just happened to gain access to a supposedly secret communications channel back to Western intelligence at the same time: The weapons did exist. The information that Foleda had supplied regarding their locations, however, was false—planted over a period of several years though phony defectors and leaks. The whole thing had been staged to feed misinformation to the West from a source they would believe: their own, trusted agents on the inside. The real weapons were in the places that McCain and his people had never been able to get into.

McCain stopped suddenly, staring at the compound wall in front of him, as the full implication of that line of thought became clear. If Magician had been a double agent and part of that same stratagem, then the Tangerine file had never existed. The whole story had been fabricated to lure the US into doing exactly what it had done: send somebody after it. That explained his and Paula's capture. They hadn't goofed somehow. The Soviets had set the whole thing up from the beginning, specifically so that the agents the US sent would be captured. That was how they had obtained the "inside people" whom Western intelligence would trust. It wasn't an information mine at all; it was a misinformation factory.

He sought out Rashazzi. "Razz, have you ever gotten the feeling that everything we've been doing has been steered?"

One thing McCain had noticed over the months was that Rashazzi was never surprised by anything. "I'm listening," was all Rashazzi said.

McCain went on to summarize his latest thoughts. The young Israeli listened intently, nodding and agreeing occasionally, but without interrupting. "Just for two people?" he queried dubiously when McCain had finished. "They would set up a deception as elaborate as that, just for two people?"

McCain shook his head. "I never said that. My guess is that they've been grabbing all kinds of different candidates and shipping them up to Zamork on one pretext or another for a long time—people like Peter Sargent, for example, who I'm sure is from British intelligence. You might have been on the list, even. The Russians have been auditioning for months before they made a final choice of which ones to use."

"And these weapons we've been looking for. You think they really are here, but in the places we haven't been to."

"The places we haven't been *steered* to," McCain said. "Our side was fed faked information to make us look in the wrong places."

"So where ought we to start looking?"

"In the places we've been steered away *from*."

"For example?"

"Underneath Zamork, for a start."

Rashazzi frowned, trying to follow what McCain meant. "Explain," he invited finally.

"Think back nine weeks to when you and I found the original route, underneath B-three. One level down, in the first machinery space, the floorpanels were spot-welded—which we could have cut around with the tool you'd made. But just in case we didn't have anything like that, there was also an easy way down through the lighting panel, and we took it. Our original intention was to keep on going down. But the floor of the pump bay below was solid and seam-welded. Yes? That was why we started exploring outward at that point. Doesn't that say to you that perhaps we were deliberately headed off in that direction? And what do you think we might find if we went back now and carried on going straight down?"

"But . . . Are you saying we were *meant* to find that route down from under B-three? Wouldn't that mean that the Russians knew all along that we'd set up the Crypt?"

"Or something like it, somewhere down there." McCain nodded. "Sure. That's what I think. It was essential to their plan. Without some of the stuff that we thought we were making secretly, we wouldn't have been able to get out and about. And that would explain why they put scientists like you and Albrecht in with us, too. The effort had to be real to make the setup look genuine." Rashazzi cupped a hand over his mouth as he strove to assimilate the torrent of new suggestions. He shook his head wonderingly. McCain stared at him expectantly. "Well, what do you think it would take to cut down through the floor of the pump bay? Could we do it?"

"Would we be allowed to?" Rashazzi asked. "From what you've just said, mightn't that whole area—the Crypt, all of it—have been under surveillance all along? I know we've checked it enough times and never found anything, but still . . ."

"I've got a hunch that it really might be clean," McCain

said. "If there were bugs and we discovered them, the whole game would be up. So maybe the Russians wouldn't risk it."

"You mean they'd rely on stooges to know what's going on down there?"

"Exactly."

Rashazzi's eyes flickered over McCain's face. "Any guesses who?"

"Any of the escape committee, maybe. I've never trusted that Indian, Chakattar. Then there's our bunch . . . Who knows?"

"Albrecht is okay," Rashazzi said.

"I guessed that." McCain nodded. "Okay, so how about that floor? Let's assume that whatever's down there, nobody will be expecting anyone to be coming through that way."

Rashazzi thought for a while before replying. "With a slow drill and plenty of lubrication, we could bore a pilot hole through quietly, with a good chance of not attracting attention. Then we could push a fiber-optic pipe down for a look around. We've got a good range of tools now. The only real limit on how long a man-size hole would take is the amount of noise we could afford to risk. That would depend on what we find down there."

"Then, let's start right away," McCain said.

Rashazzi nodded. "I assume this like the geometric anomalies—we keep it to ourselves?"

"Absolutely." McCain nodded emphatically. "And one more thing. Obviously we can't trust any method of communication out of here that's controlled by the Russians. That means we'll want the laser. How's it going? Has Paula finished what you wanted on the power supply?"

"Yes, just about."

"So you and Albrecht can do the rest?"

"I think so."

"Good. I want to have it operating ASAP."

CHAPTER FORTY-THREE

It was late morning. In Hut 8 on the surface level, Eban Istamel had connected the output from a cassette player to the wire that had been uncovered from the bug hidden in the ceiling vent, in order to confound any unwelcome listeners. Two of the hut's other occupants were on work assignments at Turgenev and one of the agricultural stations, and the third was away in the Services Block library. Paula stat staring wearily across the table at the electronic chip that Olga was showing in the palm of her hand.

Olga's voice was appealing but firm. "There isn't a lot of time, Paula. The bus will be leaving soon, and I'm due to be back at work in Turgenev for the rest of the day. From the way you described it, the situation sounds serious. Nobody could blame you for deciding to act on your own initiative. So I did take it upon myself to preload the message that I asked you to draft this morning. It's in this chip now, ready to be sent." She gestured toward the sheet of paper lying by Paula's elbow. The message Olga had written was directed to Tycoon/ from Pangolin/ in the standard format that Paula used, but had blank spaces after the slashes.

The text listed the hub X-ray-module emplacement, the Agricultural Station 3 laser, the Landausk microwave projector, and the other installations that Tycoon had specified in his request to Sexton. Along with each item was a summary of what had been found there and a terse concluding assessment: FINDINGS NEGATIVE—SOURCE INVALIDATED. FINDINGS NEGATIVE—SOURCE INVALIDATED. . . FINDINGS NEGATIVE—SOURCE INVALIDATED. "All I need from you now," Olga said, "is your completion code for Moon and a new initializer." "Moon" had been the initializer in Foleda's last incoming communication.

Paula got up and crossed the room to stare out through the window. The Polish historian from the hut in the next row higher up the slope was out fussing with his tomato plants again. Paula crossed her arms in front of her and rubbed her shoulders as if she were cold. They had been through all this earlier, before Olga went to Turgenev. Although Paula was surer than ever of the stand she had taken with Earnshaw, her anger had abated. Now she just felt tired of it all.

"If the information is true, what harm can it do to set the West's suspicions at rest?" Istamel asked from where he had been leaning by the side of the washroom door, listening. "They're always telling everybody about how incurably suspicious *Russians* are, after all. And don't get me wrong—I've got no reason to feel especially friendly toward Russians. But I've always said American propaganda exaggerates everything just as much. They're all as bad as each other. It's the line of work that does it. Which side they're on doesn't make any difference."

Olga had told Istamel simply that they had a way of communicating secretly with one of the American intelligence services. She hadn't said how. Paula would have been happier if Olga hadn't said anything at all, but Olga evidently regarded the whole business as sufficiently serious to warrant his involvement and advice. Paula wasn't sure what position or influence the Turk had that should cause Olga to value his opinion in this way—but people didn't ask unnecessary questions in Zamork. And besides, Olga must have had good reason to consider him reliable, for they were talking about her own channel to Ivan, too.

"Look, I'm not sure you quite understand," Paula said. "What my opinions might be as an individual, and my capacity in the mission that I came here on, are not the same thing. Intelligence work isn't what I do. I'm a scientist. I was only in a technical-support role."

"But you came on an intelligence mission, all the same," Olga said. "Doesn't that make it just as much your duty to report back what you can?"

Paula drew a deep breath. "I still don't like the thought of deciding something like this on my own. Why can't we get Lew Earnshaw up here? Maybe if you two tried talking to him, it might make him see sense. Couldn't we at least give it a try first?"

"The Crypt is cut off," Istamel reminded her. "We can't get him up here."

"Is that maintenance crew still working down the shaft?"

"It's worse than it was this morning. They've got half the wall opened up and cables everywhere. It could go on for days."

"And do you have days?" Olga asked. "Remember how urgent Tycoon's last message sounded. We don't know what might be going on down there. A crucial situation may have developed, and its outcome could depend on what we know. Nobody's going to hold anything against you for doing what you thought might help prevent a war."

"Yes, it might prevent a war," Eban repeated, nodding gravely as if the realization had only just struck him. "A war that would affect everybody in the world, wherever they are, whatever side they are on, and even if they're not interested in either side. Perhaps this is a situation where it is not possible to permit the luxury of thinking like an American. You must try to think just as a member of humanity—of a community that knows no frontiers, whose only interest lies in truth."

"Like a *scientist!*" Olga said.

A long silence followed. Paula continued staring out the window. The scene outside hadn't changed, and wouldn't change. Neither would her predicament. The decision had to be faced. There was no escaping it. She turned. Olga and Istamel were waiting silently, she at the table, he still leaning by the far door. Paula looked at them for a moment longer, but capitulation was already written in her eyes. She came back to the table, sat down heavily, looked across to Olga, and nodded. "The completion for 'Moon' is 'Rise,'" she said.

Olga drew the sheet of paper over and wrote the word in the first of the blank spaces. She looked up. "And a new initiation word from your list?"

There was a silence. Olga and Eban remained motionless while moments passed that seemed to drag like hours. A woman's voice called out to somebody on the pathway between the huts outside.

" 'Pin,' " Paula answered.

They had cut a section out of the floorplating, guided by the small test holes that Rashazzi had drilled to keep them inside the square of underfloor ribbing. Below was an interdeck space one to feet deep. McCain sat by the edge and watched, while Rashazzi used a holder fashioned from stiff wire to push the fiber-optic cable down into the hole they had drilled through the lower surface at one of the corners. Rashazzi peered into the viewing piece attached to the other end of the cable, and after a few seconds began rotating the top of the holder for an all-round view of whatever was below.

"See anything?" McCain asked.

"Nothing. It's all dark." Rashazzi passed the viewer to McCain. McCain hunched forward and lifted it to his eyes. The entire field of view was pitch black. He spent longer than Rashazzi had, panning slowly through a full circle, but there wasn't a glimmer of anything. McCain withdrew the holder and held it up over his head while he looked into the viewer again. A fuzzy but discernible image of the shapes and shadows produced in the pump bay around them by the lamp that Rashazzi had hung overhead marched across his field of vision. The fiber optic was working okay.

"We could drill a second pilot hole and put a light down," Rashazzi suggested.

"We could fart around like this for weeks, too," McCain said.

"You want to carry on?"

"It looks dead enough down there to me, Razz. Hell, we've gotten this far. Sure, let's go the rest."

Rashazzi probed with a gauge to assess the thickness of the panel, and selected a sawblade with the pitch he estimated would work the most quietly. He fitted it into the handle and began cutting two-handed with slow, deliberate motions, using the hole to gain a start. They had experimented with a power saw in the Crypt, but rejected it as too noisy. After a few minutes, Rashazzi rested his hands and McCain took over.

"I've been thinking about something," Rashazzi said after a while as he watched.

"So what's new? You're always thinking about something."

"About the laser."

"What about it?"

Rashazzi reached up and moved the lamp to illuminate better the area that McCain had cut to. "You don't trust this communications channel that they've got upstairs . . . because it goes through Russian intermediaries."

"Damn right."

"Just because they're Russians? The fact that they are dissidents doesn't carry any weight?"

"I don't *know* that. I've only been told it—secondhand, thirdhand, who-knows-how-many-times-hand. Who can believe anything they're told in this place?"

"You think the KGB might be reading it?"

"Let's just say it wouldn't be on the list of things I'd be most surprised to learn about the world."

Rashazzi rubbed the tip of his nose with a knuckle, as if pondering how to put what was on his mind. Finally he said, "But you wouldn't be any better off with the laser, even if you did get it talking straight into the US military network. You'd have to use the existing channel to advise them what frequency they should watch for, the code you plan to use, and so on. If the KGB get that information too, they'll be able to intercept anything that comes or goes over the laser, just as easily. You won't have gained anything."

McCain sat back and returned the saw to Rashazzi. "True," he agreed.

"But you must have figured that out already."

"Yes, I had."

Rashazzi looked up and frowned. "So, what use is it?"

"Camouflage," McCain said. "If we've got informers

around, I wouldn't want word to get back that we've stopped working on the laser. It would be too much of a giveaway that we're suspicious. Also, my partner from upstairs is in on it, and I don't like the sound of the people around her up there. It reeks of a setup. I don't want her carrying back an impression that anything's changed down here. We carry on with the laser as planned." Rashazzi nodded in a way that said it made sense, and resumed cutting.

When the panel was fully cut, they lifted it clear and lodged it to one side. The beams from their flashlights failed to reveal anything significant in the darkness below. The space seemed to be quite large and open. McCain lowered a weighted line, which bottomed at ten feet or so. He swung his legs down and let himself down hand over hand, and Rashazzi followed.

This was not another machinery compartment. They were in a long, bare room, entirely without furnishings or contents of any kind. And yet, strangely, there seemed to be something familiar about it as they probed upward and around with the beams from their lamps. They were near one end of the room, and in the middle of the end wall was a doorway. Rashazzi directed his lamp along the length of the room and picked out the shape of another door at the far end. And then McCain realized why it looked familiar: it was a standard Zamork-style billet, without partitions or any of the fittings, but the same shape and size. Rashazzi had noticed it too. He moved toward the door and hesitated, but there was no bracelet-interrogation signal from above. He tried the lights, but they were dead. The door opened when he pushed it. He went through, and McCain joined him outside.

They were looking down into a larger space now, from a railed walkway. There was a similar door behind them to the left of the one they had come out of, and another to the right. There was a whole row of them they saw, no longer with surprise, as they proceeded along the walkway.

"We're not going to find any weapons down here, Razz," McCain said.

"I know."

"You know what this is?"

"Yes. What's it doing down here?"

"I don't know. Are they planning to turn the whole place into a prison?"

For they were in a standard Zamork billet block. They had come down through the ceiling of one of the upper-level billets, and knew where the stairs down to the lower level would be even before they saw them. They went down, moved out into the central mess area, and sure enough, there were the two levels of billets facing them from the other side. All empty and silent. They walked to the end of the mess area, but instead of the bars and gate as existed in all of the blocks above, they found a solid wall with ordinary-looking double doors. McCain tried one of them, found it unlocked, and eased it open an inch, then instantly caught Rashazzi's shoulder as a signal to keep back and stay quiet. There was light outside, and the sounds of voices and movement. They moved closer to the crack to peer through.

Outside was a broad thoroughfare which in every way resembled Gorky Street. The layout was the same, the directions were the same, and there was another set of large double doors farther on and across the corner, just where the next block would be. They seemed to have emerged inside a whole, new, unsuspected level of Zamork that existed deeper down beneath the regular complex, except it wasn't fitted out in the fashion of a detention facility. It seemed more like a normal residential complex. The large double doors that they could see were open, and inside them—in the mess area of the block they opened into—a work crew was unloading furniture from a truck. Whatever the place was, it was evidently being prepared for occupation. Suddenly McCain remembered all the bedframes that he and Scanlon had made when they were in the metalworking shops in the Core.

"What do you make of it?" Rashazzi whispered.

McCain watched through the crack and shook his head.

"I don't know what to think. But it looks as if they're expecting more guests. That means this block we're in could be next. We'll have to patch up that hole we made in the ceiling back there."

"No problem. It'll fix so that nothing will show unless you're looking for it," Rashazzi said.

"But while we're here, I want to measure the layout," McCain muttered. "We need to make another hole to get down into here, but in another place—somewhere concealed—that won't be right in the middle of someone's ceiling."

"One of the service ducts, maybe . . . or through the utilities bay?"

"Yes." McCain eased the door shut again and turned to face Rashazzi.

"That should be easy enough," Rashazzi agreed. "But what for? Why do you want to be able to get in and out of here?"

"Because," McCain said, "it looks as if it's being fitted out for civilians. In other words, this place must connect out to the rest of the colony."

"Of course. That truck got down here somehow."

McCain nodded. "Exactly. And if we were *meant* to get out and about to collect wrong information on all those weapons installations, then the Russians know all about our freight-line route out of Zamork, too." He gestured over his shoulder with a thumb at the doors behind them. "Well, maybe here's a way out for us that they won't know about."

CHAPTER FORTY-FOUR

It was not customary for the deputy director of the UDIA to attend the meetings of the National Security Council, normally held in Washington's Old Executive Building. Nor for that matter the UDIA director, since intelligence matters were usually covered by the director of the CIA, who presented the findings and recommendations of all departments. But Borden had been called in to this session because of the importance that the link into *Valentina Tereshkova* was assuming, and he had brought Foleda with him to permit Foleda to voice his disagreement for himself. Foleda felt privately that Borden's dissociating himself from Foleda's view in this way was uncalled for and fell short of the degree of reciprocation that Foleda's support on previous occasions warranted—but that was the way of politics. For his part, he had decided the situation justified stating his opinions bluntly, without making concessions to anyone's sensibilities.

President Warren Austin gestured at the report lying on the table in front of him, with its appended sheaf of Pedestal-Sunflower transcripts. "Sunflower" was the new code designation for the complete link from Foleda, through Cabman, to the Pedestal-mission operatives up in the Soviet space colony. "And that covers all the weapons installations that we've compiled from various sources— Magician and the rest?" he said.

"The main ones that we specified," Borden confirmed. "Every one that our people penetrated has turned out to be negative. In each case, what was found conformed to published Soviet information."

"Hmm, so when this gets to be made public, we'll all look like bozos again," the President murmured. Borden shifted uncomfortably in his chair. Apparently UDIA wasn't among the President's favorite outfits again today.

At the far end of the table, General Thomas Snell of the Army, chairman of the Joint Chiefs of Staff, looked up from contemplating his fingers. "One question," he said. "All we know for sure is that this information is coming into our network from Cabman in Siberia. How certain are we that he is in fact getting it from where he says he's getting it from? Could the Soviets be managing the operation?"

"We know from the validation codes that it is coming from our agents," Borden said.

Snell nodded. "I know that, but agents have been turned before."

"True," Frank Collins, the CIA director, agreed. "But on top of that, NSA has intercepted Teepee-Blueprint transmissions that correlate with every Sunflower message. So we have confirmation that it's coming down from Mermaid." In fact, they no longer really needed Cabman's transmissions from Siberia, since NSA could read the signals coming down to him from Mermaid before he relayed them on to the West. But to reveal that to Cabman would have been giving away too much.

The President looked at Foleda. Other eyes followed forbearingly, with okay-Foleda-let's-hear-it-for-the-record expressions. Borden stared down at the table.

Foleda returned the President's stare directly. "I don't trust the Sunflower transcripts. Our agent on Pedestal has the code designation 'Sexton.' Sexton is an experienced operative whom I've known personally for years, whose judgment I trust, and whose reliability I wouldn't question. But the messages we've seen from Sexton have all been neutral, with no content of any substance. The reports pertaining to weapons are from Pangolin *only*—a technical-support person, not of the department. I move that all incoming Sunflower material not validated by Sexton be discounted." That was out of order. In the chair next to Foleda, Borden winced.

Robert Uhl, the defense secretary tossed out a hand. "We have to make allowances . . . They're in a *prison* up there. I don't know exactly what the conditions are, but does it seem reasonable to *expect* that Sexton is even able to be present all the time? They might have all kinds of problems getting together to collaborate. Pangolin could well be doing the best job that's possible."

Collins shrugged. "I could buy that." Beside him the secretary of state, Joseph Myers, nodded agreement.

"Motion denied," the President ruled. He reached for a file in front of him.

"I haven't finished," Foleda said.

"Shut up, Bern," Borden hissed. "This is an NSC meeting. There are recognized procedures . . ."

"I'm saving you from having to say it," Foleda muttered back. "That's why I'm here, isn't it?"

"Go ahead, Mr. Foleda," the President invited.

"We're continuing to get reports from all sources of ominous developments throughout the Soviet-bloc nations. The number of warships at sea is unprecedented. Military-communications traffic in all bands has been abnormally heavy for days." Foleda gestured toward a folder on the table. "A new item in yesterday of food-canning plants switching to three-shift working a month ago. It can all be construed as indicative of hostile intentions. In such a climate we can't afford to dismiss anything that casts doubts on the reliability of Sunflower material. I repeat my previous motion. I would also recommend that we consider raising the readiness level of our armed forces until Mermaid has been opened to international inspection and cleared."

The secretary of state heaved himself restlessly forward in his chair and shuffled about among some papers. "Look, we know it's your people's job to worry, but I think this is going too far. We've wanted a breakthrough for years to relax the tension. I'll put my money on this being it. I say we have to try for it." Interestingly, he directed his words at Borden, not Foleda.

General Snell rubbed his chin hesitantly. "Although, I don't know . . . Maybe there could be something to it . . ."

"We've been through all this," the defense secretary said. He nodded toward Foleda to concede the point. "Yes, I agree with Mr. Foleda; under normal circumstances all the things he's reminded us of would constitute grounds for concern—serious concern. But there is one fact that outweighs those considerations: virtually the entire Soviet leadership—its top leadership, including the First Secretary of the Party, chairman of the Council of Ministers, chiefs of the KGB and the military—are either there already, or will be within the next couple of days. We've asked ourselves, Is that where anyone in their right mind would concentrate the brain of the entire national organism at a time of intended conflict? On a battle station out in space that would be bound to be a first target? Of course not. It just wouldn't make sense. A more plausible explanation for all the Soviet military activity we're seeing is that since they won't be having their big parade this year, they're organizing exercises instead."

It was the first week of November, and Soviet television was already broadcasting live coverage into the world news grid of the first groups of Soviet leaders arriving inside *Valentina Tereshkova*. More transporters were en route, and others, including the UN vessel with the Western VIPs, would be departing from Earth orbit in the next day or so. As the defense secretary had pointed out, they would all be very vulnerable if there were hostilities.

The factors that made *Valentina Tereshkova* a virtually unassailable weapons platform didn't make it automatically a safe haven for people. The reason was that to disable its weapons effectively, the West's orbiting lasers and other beam projectors would have to knock them all out simultaneously with a first shot. With the devastating and instantaneous return-fire that *Tereshkova*—if the rumors were true—could bring to bear, there would never be a chance for a second shot. But such a first-shot knockout would be impossible for the simple reason that the West's weaponry was designed to attack pinpoint targets in space; without knowing exactly where to aim, it would have no chance of surviving long enough to find a few compact, hardened spots on a structure measuring miles around.

But for people loose in the general volume of the main torus, the situation was different. A salvo from all the West's orbiting beam weapons fired in unison could blow away enough of the relatively thin skin to decompress the whole ring in seconds. Even if the Soviet weapons operators were protected inside their hardened emplacements, the chances for survival of anyone out in the general colony areas would be slim. That was why the consensus had gone the way it had, leaving Foleda out on his own. If there was anything to what he said, nobody for a moment could see the Soviets acting the way they had.

The large screen at one end of the room was showing a still picture of the Soviet chairman of the Council of Ministers standing on a rostrum, a garland of flowers hanging down over the front of his suit, addressing a crowd in the main square of Turgenev, inside *Tereshkova*, minutes after his party had descended from the docking facilities at the hub. It was from a clip of the latest Soviet news bulletin, which the people at the meeting had watched earlier and not bothered to turn off. Behind the crowd were glimpses of *Tereshkova*'s bewildering, Oz-like architecture, and above, the strange curving sky with its elongated suns.

Foleda leaned back and extended a hand briefly to indicate the screen. "Just suppose," he suggested, "that what we saw there a little while ago isn't happening at all. Wouldn't that make a difference?"

The President shook his head and pinched the bridge of his nose. "What do you mean, not happening, Mr. Foleda? I'm not sure I follow."

"Of course it's happening," the secretary of state muttered impatiently. "I'm starting to wonder if this is happening."

"We know the transmission is coming in from the Soviet news service, that's all," Foleda said. "But how do we know that the events it's showing are happening *now*—up there inside Mermaid, right at this moment?"

"NASA's picking up the TV transmissions from Mermaid independently of the Soviet news broadcasts down here," Collins said. "There's no question that's where it's coming from, if that's what you mean."

"Look at the screen," the secretary of state said, gesturing. "You can see where it is."

"That only demonstrates that a signal is being transmitted down from Mermaid," Foleda persisted. "No, that wasn't my question. What I said was, how do we *know* that the events that it depicts are actually taking place right now?" He looked around the table. Nobody seemed to be quite with him. He drew a breath. "How do we know that it isn't all something they did months ago—that what they're transmitting isn't a recording, just like what we're looking at on the screen here?"

"We can see the ships arriving up there . . ." the secretary of state started to answer automatically, but then his voice trailed away as he realized that it didn't mean very much. Everyone else saw it too, and Foleda didn't bother pointing out the obvious.

"That has to be ridiculous," the defense secretary declared, sitting back abruptly.

Collins looked at Foleda, frowned, then looked away again. Borden had half-turned and was sitting with his face propped on a hand, staring as if Foleda had just grown another head. The President was shooting looks all around the table to get someone to respond. Everyone seemed to be thinking that someone ought to say why the idea was crazy, but no one wanted to say it first.

"Well?" Foleda challenged. "Okay, I agree I'm suspicious, but that's what you pay me to be. Our job is to make worst-case assumptions. I've made one. Show me I'm wrong."

The secretary of state spread his hands. "There have to be some things you can't always prove. Some things you just have to take on trust and hope you're right. It's possible that anyone in this room could be a KGB spy. We don't *know* it isn't true. We just have to carry on and hope it isn't. If everyone waited for everything to be proved, they'd never do anything. Who was the general who said that if you wait until all the information's in, you'll be bound to be too late?"

"I'm not so sure, Joe." General Snell was leaning back, rubbing his chin thoughtfully. "Maybe there is a way we can find out if those Russians are really where they say they are."

"How?" the President asked them from the end of the table.

"We've got agents up there, right now. And we've got a means of communicating with them. We don't have to rely on what the Soviet news service says. Can't we ask our own people if they can see with their own eyes the same things we're seeing on screens down here? If they say they can, that would be good enough for me."

The heads turned back toward Foleda. Foleda blinked. He had discredited Sunflower so much in his own mind, he realized, that the possibility of using the link for this purpose hadn't occurred to him. An unskilled agent's failing to find weapons that might be there was one thing—negative evidence was always questionable. But confirmation of something taking place right in front of one's eyes constituted positive evidence. That was a different matter.

"What do you say, Mr. Foleda?" the President asked. "You have expressed the greatest skepticism toward Sunflower. If we took up General Snell's suggestion and got confirmation from our own agents there, would that satisfy you?"

Foleda's brow creased into a frown. The truth was that he didn't trust the Soviets an inch, and didn't like the West in general—and the US in particular—were dancing eagerly to the Soviet tune to demonstrate their inoffensiveness. But those were prejudices pure and simple, and there was no way to defend them now. He looked up and nodded.

"Yes, Mr. President, I guess that would change the picture a whole lot," he agreed unhappily.

CHAPTER FORTY-FIVE

In the background, the large screen in the graphics lab at Turgenev still displayed the exchange cycle of gases between soil bacteria and the atmosphere. But Paula and Olga were more interested in the smaller deskscreen pivoted to face them on the console below, which was showing on a local channel the crowd gathering in the square outside the building. The second transporter bringing Soviet government and Party officials had arrived at the hub twenty minutes previously, and they were expected to emerge from the spoke at any time. There was considerable excitement among the privileged-category inmates back at Zamork, too. Rumors had been circulating of large-scale amnesties to be announced during the November 7 celebrations, and the compound was alive with speculations about whose names might have been chosen.

"But why?" Olga asked again. She shook her head and moved over to a worktop at the side of the room and stared down again at the transcript of the latest request to come in from Tycoon. "They can see on the public television channels that there are important people arriving here. Why should they want corroboration from you? And why does it matter so much, anyway?"

"It's strange . . ." Paula answered in a faraway voice, leaning back and staring at the large screen but not seeing it. They had established some time ago now that since it was part of the Environmental Department, which was classed as a normal civilian work area, the graphics lab was not wired for surveillance. Therefore they could speak freely there.

Olga turned and came back to stand behind Paula's chair. "Why should the Americans doubt it? Do they think that what they're watching down there might be recordings or something? Maybe they still believe this is a war platform." She tapped her lips with her fingertip for a moment. "Could they be afraid that the Russians might be planning to hijack the Western VIPs who are on their way here? You know them better than I do. Are they capable of dreaming up something like that?" Paula didn't answer. Olga waited, then looked at her. "What are you thinking?"

Paula swiveled the chair slowly, her elbow resting on the armrest, and looked up over her loosely closed fist. "I think it's worse than that," she said.

Olga frowned. "Worse?"

"A lot."

"What do you mean?"

Paula pushed herself up from the chair, paused to choose her words, and then turned to stand with her back to the console, resting herself against the edge. "We don't know what's been going on down on Earth between your side and mine over the past few months. But we do know they're run by some people who can be pretty irrational."

Olga nodded. "Yes, I would agree with that. So?"

"Well, if you were the Americans," Paula said, "what would the fact that practically the entire Soviet leadership had gone up to *Valentina Tereshkova* for the November seventh celebrations say to you?"

"Why . . . that they were taking time off to go away and enjoy themselves for once, I suppose. And since a potential target would be the last place they'd pick, I'd be pretty happy that they weren't planning to—" Olga broke off and turned her head toward Paula quizzically as she saw what Paula was implying.

"Yes," Paula said. "And what would it say if they hadn't gone there at all, but wanted you to think the things you've just said?"

Olga stared incredulously. "No!"

"I think so." Paula nodded somberly. She met Olga's eyes fully. "I think the Americans believe you're about to launch." Olga sat down weakly and shook her head. "And worse," Paula said. "What if the West decides to preempt?"

"Oh, God . . ." Olga licked her lips and turned her head first one way and then the other. She seemed to be having trouble coming to terms with the enormity of it. Paula watched silently. At last Olga gestured at the transcript, then indicated the BV-15 terminal standing in a corner. "We must do something . . ." Her voice choked. She waved a hand again. "The channel. We must send them an answer."

"Yes, I know." Paula straightened up from the console,

gathered the transcript, and sat down at the terminal. Her movements were purposeful and resolute, as if she had been giving Olga time to catch up with the conclusion she had already recognized in her own mind as inevitable. Paula took a screwdriver from a drawer and removed the BV-15's cover. Then she reached in her pocket, took out a small plastic box containing one of the preprogrammed chips, and plugged the chip into the socket that it was coded to work in. Then she replaced the cover, sat down, and activated the screen. Olga moved her chair closer to watch.

Then a frown crossed Paula's face. She sat back uncertainly and turned her head to glance at the small screen showing the scene outside the building. The crowd was denser now, and officials were buzzing excitedly around the doors that opened from the concourse outside the spoke elevators. Paula looked back at the terminal again with a suddenly numb expression. "I can't do this," she said.

"What's the matter?" Olga asked. She sounded alarmed.

"This message. I can't send it. I *can't* tell them those leaders are arriving here."

"But why not?"

"Because I don't *know* that they are." Paula turned her head and looked at Olga oddly. "Am I being paranoid too, now? But don't you see? All I have to go by is a TV picture, just like the people down there in America. I can't tell if it's real any more than they can."

Olga was shaking her head. "But . . . but that's ridiculous. You're *here*. They're not." She waved frantically at the deskscreen. "That's all happening right outside the building we're in." They couldn't simply walk out and look, of course, because their Zamork bracelets would trigger alarms if they tried leaving their authorized working vicinity, which would achieve nothing but get them spells in solitary.

Paula was adamant. "If I sound silly, I'm sorry, but I think it's important. You're always reminding me that we're scientists. Well, this would be confirming reported data that we haven't observed for ourselves. Scientists can't do that."

Olga was looking dazed. "But . . . we're talking about possibly averting *war!*" she insisted. Her voice was pleading, her face strained. "Global war. How many times we've talked about this, what it would mean . . . You can't stop because of something like this." She got up from her chair and stood with her hands pressed flat together against her face. Her eyes darted this way and that, as if seeking answers on the walls. "I can show you. . . . Yes, look, wait there. I'll go and get Gennadi."

Paula turned her head and watched, puzzled, as Olga hurried across the room and opened the door. She went out into the corridor and her footsteps retreated. Then Paula heard her say, "Oh, Dr. Brusikov, are you leaving?"

Brusikov's voice answered, sounding surprised. "I was going out to watch the arrival of the foreign minister and his party, and then have lunch. Why?"

"Oh, good. Then, you are going out into the square?"

"Yes." The voices were right outside the door now.

"Could I ask a favor?" Olga ushered Brusikov into the room. He nodded perfunctorily to acknowledge Paula's presence. Olga glanced quickly around the lab and took a bright-blue cylindrical cardboard container, three feet or so long, from a stack lying on a shelf—the kind commonly used for carrying things like rolled technical drawings. "I promised these to somebody urgently, but missed him. He's outside in the square now, but I can't go out there. I wonder if you'd be so kind . . ."

"Oh, I see." Brusikov nodded. "Very well. But how will I know him?"

Olga turned to the screen showing the scene outside and pointed to a man in a yellow jacket and green hat, standing on the edge of the crowd, near the main door of the Government Building. "That's him. He's very distinctive. His name is Zavdat."

Paula had stood up from her chair behind them. As Brusikov turned to leave, she said suddenly, "No, that's the wrong one."

He stopped and looked back questioningly. Paula held

Olga's eyes steadily while she drew a red cylinder off the shelf. "I put them in *this* one."

Olga didn't falter. "Oh yes, that's right . . . I must have got them mixed up." She took the red cylinder and exchanged it for the blue one that Brusikov was holding. He nodded and left, closing the door.

A strained silence descended while the two women watched the screen, Paula looked remorseful now, Olga tight-lipped and flushed. After a minute or so the figure of Dr. Brusikov came out of the Government Building entrance, carrying the red cylinder. He stopped and looked about for a few seconds, then approached the man in the yellow coat and green hat. Brusikov said something and offered the cylinder. The man in the yellow coat shook his head, shrugged, and waved a hand. Brusikov remonstrated and pointed back at the Government Building. The man shook his head again. Finally Brusikov, looking disgruntled and not a little mystified, moved away to find a different spot in the crowd.

Paula turned away but avoided facing Olga directly. "I'm sorry," she whispered.

Olga shook her head. She was her usual calm self once again. "No, you were quite right," she said. "Neither of us knew for sure. It is I who should apologize."

"For a moment I didn't trust you."

"At times like these, it's a wonder anyone trusts anybody."

On the screen the doors on the raised level above the square opened and a group of smiling figures came out to be greeted by cheers and applause. Paula sat down at the terminal again and pushed the curl from her forehead. "Then, let's get on with the job," she said.

Dressed in a selection from the civilian attire accumulated in the Crypt, Rashazzi took the laser outside to repeat over longer ranges some tests that he and Haber had conducted inside the structure which had yielded odd results. He emerged at the surface in a ventilator outlet above some apartments on the far side of the reservoir, and spent more than an hour surreptitiously aiming pulses at parts of the buildings of central Novyi Kazan and timing the returns on an electronic interferometer that Paula had built. He explained the results to McCain later, after returning to the Crypt. Haber was with them.

"Since we are on the inside of a cylinder, the verticals of buildings converge toward the center, like the spokes of a wheel. And since we know the size of *Valentina Tereshkova*, it's easy to calculate how much the convergence ought to be: verticals spaced two hundred meters apart at the base ought to converge by about three meters through a fifteen-meter difference in height."

McCain nodded. That much was straightforward enough. "Okay."

"But they don't," Rashazzi said. "It works out at closer to one point three meters. So what's happened to the difference?"

McCain could only shake his head. "It fits with this idea that keeps coming up, of the whole place being bigger than it's supposed to, doesn't it," he said.

"Yes," Haber agreed. "And not only that. To give the amount of convergence that Razz had measured, the colony would have to be just the diameter that was indicated by the experiments we did with the balance scale: almost four and a half kilometers instead of less than two kilometers."

McCain made a face. "I hate coincidences."

"Oh, I don't think this could properly be called a coincidence," Haber said.

"Probably not. But we still don't have any explanations, huh?"

Rashazzi looked at McCain with a strange, unsmiling expression for a second. Then he picked up a sheet of paper that he and Haber had been poring over when McCain arrived. "Yes," he replied in a curious voice. "As a matter of fact, Lew, this time I believe we do have an explanation. . . ."

❖   ❖   ❖

Brusikov came in again on his way back from lunch to return the cylinder and ask what the hell Olga had been playing at. Paula apologized and explained that Olga had been fooled by the yellow coat and green hat—hardly the most common of outfits to be seen around *Tereshkova*, she pointed out with as much charm as she could muster—and had not paid enough attention to the face. It wasn't the right man. Brusikov went away grumbling about being made to feel a fool, but accepted it.

Paula remained, staring at the work she had been doing on the larger screen, but no longer interested in it. How was anybody supposed to care about the flatulence of microbes when the world might be about to cremate itself?

She thought about the message she had composed for Foleda, and how inadequate it seemed compared to the scale of what was at stake. Her conviction grew that the nature of *Valentina Tereshkova* had become a major factor in the equations being juggled in Washington and in Moscow. Here she was, not only present at that fulcrum of events, but singled out through a strange series of twists of fate for a unique perspective that should surely be crucial to any decisions embarked on at such a moment. She remembered reading somewhere that Napoleon scoffed at the notion of luck. "Lucky" people, he maintained, were the ones who put themselves in the right place and at the right time for the right things to happen.

In other words, they rose to the occasion. Here was an occasion that surely beckoned.

She was still feeling despondent when Olga returned. The Russian woman slipped in without knocking, and closed the door behind her.

"Did the message go off all right?" Paula asked.

Olga nodded and stood leaning against the door with her eyes closed for a moment, as if allowing tension to drain away. "Top priority, so Ivan will send it straight on." She went over to the empty chair in front of the console and sat down, noticing as she did so the red cylinder, which Paula had put back on the shelf. "Has Brusikov been back?"

"Yes. He wasn't very amused."

"What did you tell him?"

"That it was the wrong man. You were misled by the hat and the coat—an unlikely similarity in appearance."

Olga nodded, and sat staring at the console for what seemed a long time. Paula watched her but had nothing to say. Eventually Olga turned her chair to face across the room. They looked at each other. At last Olga said, "It doesn't seem enough, somehow."

Paula nodded in a way that said Olga didn't have to elaborate. "I've been thinking the same thing. And on reflection I'm not even sure they'll believe that much."

"Why shouldn't they?"

"Who am I? Just the support half of the team." Olga gave the impression that she had expected the reply but had allowed Paula to make it all the same, just to be sure they both understood the same things. Paula got the feeling that Olga's thoughts had been running parallel to her own. Olga hesitated visibly. "Yes?" Paula prompted.

Olga looked up. "There is another way."

"What way?"

"Ask the Russians to connect you to America via one of their regular channels—it could be a private military link, not public TV. Show yourself here, in *Valentina Tereshkova,* alongside the Soviet leaders. Let your own people talk with you over the link, ask questions, and observe you responding and interacting. That way they will know that the Soviet leaders are here, and that they are here now." Paula was so surprised by the proposal that for a moment she could only shake her head and stare incredulously. "Say you wish to talk with General Protbornov urgently, and tell him everything," Olga urged. "He has access to the people who can arrange it."

"But . . . everything? We'd have to reveal the channel. You'd lose your communications to Ivan. Ivan would be exposed."

"I know. I've already thought of all that. What do things like that matter now? If there's a war it will all be lost anyway."

Paula swallowed hard. "That's . . . that's some decision you're asking."

"Is it? What is the alternative?"

A good point, Paula conceded. For when she thought about it, the only alternative to trying was to live the rest of her life, irrespective of the outcome, with the knowledge that she hadn't tried. Put that way, it didn't really leave much of a choice.

CHAPTER FORTY-SIX

Major General Protbornov stared back across the desk in his office at the Internal Security Headquarters in Turgenev. For several seconds his rugged, heavy-jowled face was completely blank, as if it had just been solidly punched. Then he blinked and raised a hand to rub the corner of his eye. "Communications?" The heavy, rumbling voice assembled the word slowly, a syllable at a time, as if they were steps he was having to mount to overcome his disbelief. "Communications into American intelligence, from inside Zamork? How could this be possible?" Beneath their puffy lids, his eyes had taken on a bleak expression that already seemed to be looking into the face of demotion, arrest, and possibly even a firing squad.

Uskayev—the same blond, gray-eyed major whom Paula had last seen with Protbornov in the infirmary—drew a notepad closer across the top of his desk, which stood by the window to one side of the office. "Describe the mechanism of this communications method," he said. "What form does it take?"

Olga sighed in the chair beside Paula. "We possess an electronic chip that is programmed to insert encoded text into the random-number-group fillers in the regular message stream to Earth," she replied, speaking in a tired voice. "The chip is substituted for the standard one in the outgoing encryption processor located in the Communications Center."

"How do you gain access to the Communications Center?"

"I don't. I have an associate."

"The name?"

Olga hesitated. Uskayev looked up sharply. Clearly if she'd come here asking for favors, she couldn't expect to hold anything back. "Andrei Ogovoy, an engineer at the Communications Center," she said. Uskayev wrote rapidly on his pad.

"Go on," Protbornov said.

Olga described her channel down to the groundstation at Sokhotsk and the technique of disguising encoded replies as statistical data. She said that the channel had been extended to connect into the US military and intelligence communications system, but insisted, correctly, that she didn't know how the link from Sokhotsk to the US operated.

"You say this person at Sokhotsk was communicating with you privately before there was any contact with the Americans," Protbornov said when she had finished.

"Yes."

"So this person must have set up the link to the Americans, and managed the transfer of messages after it was established. Who was this person who commanded such extraordinary opportunities?"

"The name?" Uskayev said, pen poised.

Paula stared woodenly ahead and heard Olga take in a long breath beside her. "Professor Igor Dyashkin," Olga said. "Director of the operational facility at Sokhotsk." Despite herself, Paula raised her eyebrows. Protbornov and Uskayev exchanged ominous glances.

Protbornov stared down at his hands in a way that said the sky might as well fall now, for all the surprises life had left to offer. He looked up. "So, you have your channel to the professor. And how did you progress from there to initiating contact with the Americans?"

"We didn't," Olga said. "They initiated contact with us." Protbornov stared at her incredulously.

That had been expected. Paula explained, "I'm not a

journalist with Pacific News Services. My companion and I came here on a mission for US military intelligence. It was our people. A message came over the channel from them, to us." She looked at Uskayev and nodded resignedly before he could say it. "Bryce, Paula M., second lieutenant, United States Air Force, serial number AO 20188813, temporarily attached to the Unified Defense Intelligence Agency."

"And your colleague?" Protbornov clearly wasn't going to quit while he was on a roll.

"I only know him as Lewis Earnshaw. He's with the UDIA. That's all I know."

Protbornov nodded, having disposed of those preliminaries, and clasped his hands. "So, you say the UDIA contacted you here, using the link through Professor Dyashkin. But how could they possibly have known about it?"

"I don't know," Paula replied.

"You can't expect us to believe that," Protbornov scoffed.

"She's telling the truth," Olga said. "We are both scientists. We don't know what kinds of intrigues go on among you people. But that's all immaterial now, compared to the reason why we've decided to come here and reveal everything." She paused to let the point sink in. Protbornov waited. Olga went on, "To us, the messages we have been receiving indicate that the West believes the Soviet Union is about to launch a first strike. We think there's a strong possibility that the West will decide to attack preemptively. Preventing such a catastrophe must take priority over other considerations—that is why we have been frank. We think there is a way it can be prevented, but we will need your help."

Protbornov was looking astounded. "A first strike . . . by us? Preemptive attack? But this is ludicrous. Our whole leadership is up here, practically on vacation. Tomorrow we will be declaring *Valentina Tereshkova* open to international visitors. The ship bringing the first representatives from all nations, including the United States, is on its way here at this very moment. There will be celebrations, games, amnesties . . . Why would anyone be worrying about a strike at *this* of all times? Have they all gone mad down there?"

Olga was nodding. "I know, I know. It sounds insane. The irony is that those very things are what has caused the concern. It's all a misunderstanding, and it mustn't be allowed to lead to a calamity. But since the problem is one that stems from misinformation, it can be rectified by correct information. That is what we need you to help us do."

Uskayev had put his pen down and was listening with a dazed look on his face. Protbornov moistened his lips and nodded curtly without change of expression. "Explain what it is you wish us to do," he said.

Olga told him about the reconnaissance expeditions by Zamork prisoners to investigate alleged weapons installations around the colony. The muscles in Protbornov's throat convulsed in spasms as one revelation followed another, but he heard her through without interrupting. "But from the tone of their responses, the Americans didn't seem satisfied by the negative findings," Olga concluded. "We think they suspect that false information concerning the locations was planted to mislead them." She described the Americans' latest request for confirmation that Soviet leaders were in fact at *Tereshkova*, and interpreted it as indicating Western suspicions that the Soviet broadcasts might be prerecordings made months ago. If the West so concluded, then the only motivation they'd be able to deduce would be that the Soviets were about to launch a strike. Olga ended, "The only way to eliminate that risk is to convince them of their mistake. Paula has agreed to talk to her own people over a live connection into the US communications network is one can be set up. If she's seen here, alongside the arriving leaders and conducting a responsive dialogue with Washington, all doubts would be dispelled. Can you do it?"

Protbornov's bushy eyebrows knotted. "What you're

asking, and in so little time . . . It would require the highest authority. And with all of them so preoccupied at this time . . ."

"This is a state emergency," Olga said. "I know the procedures exist. We have volunteered everything. Will you try?"

The general sat immobile for almost a minute, staring at the desk, his expression unchanging. Finally he spread his hands wide along the edge of the desk and stood up. "Wait here," he instructed, and left the room.

Major Uskayev busied himself with completing his notes and then entering them into a terminal by his desk. Paula and Olga waited without speaking. There was a tap on the door, and a woman in uniform entered to deposit some papers in a basket by the door. She took more papers from another basket and left. Paula thought of all the effort, ingenuity, perseverance, and courage that had gone into setting up Olga's channel to Ivan—now revealed as Dyashkin—the link to Foleda, the secret workshop below Zamork, and Earnshaw's private espionage operation. Now that she had a moment to reflect, she was horrified at how much would be lost because of what she and Olga were saying here today. But if they were right, all that and infinitely more would otherwise have been lost anyway. She tried not to dwell on what it meant if they were wrong. . . . No, that wasn't possible. They *had* to be right. She convinced herself with the certainty that comes only with the knowledge that being wrong would be to lose everything.

Protbornov returned twenty minutes later with a captain and four armed guards. The entire party, including Uskayev, took an elevator down inside Security Headquarters and followed a series of passages that took them underneath the Government Building. Here they ascended again and came to a corridor, where the escort conducted them to one of the doors and took up positions outside. Inside was a conference room, where two men were waiting. One was in his early forties, short, with thick black hair and bushy brows. Protbornov introduced him as Comrade Kirilikhov from the Party's Central Committee. The other was older, with thinning hair and a sallow, tired complexion; his name was Sepelyan, and he was from the Soviet Ministry of Defense. An orderly brought in tea. Protbornov said that Turgenev was keeping a channel open to Moscow, where the appropriate people to take the matter higher were being sought.

Step by step and in greater detail, the two women went through the whole story again. Kirilikhov expressed amusement at the suggestion of Western doubts about Soviet leaders really coming to *Tereshkova*, since he himself had arrived from Earth a mere twelve hours previously. Protbornov listened glumly while Olga described once more how prisoners inside Zamork had talked with American military intelligence in Washington, and Paula told how they had been burrowing around the whole colony like rabbits. She listed the locations that they had checked, and summarized the findings she had communicated to Washington. "It was hardly something that could be called espionage," Olga pointed out. "She simply confirmed what the Soviet government itself had been saying publicly for years."

"Yes, that point has not been missed," Kirilikhov said, nodding. He shifted his gaze to Paula. "But you say you have reason to believe that the credibility of your reports was not rated highly in Washington?"

"From the tone of the responses, yes," Paula said. "Probably because of my position."

"As a support specialist, not a trained agent," Olga explained.

"Ah." Kirilikhov nodded.

Sepelyan studied his fingers while he weighed up the things that had been said. "So why should they believe you any the more if we put you on a line to Earth? You could have been turned—brainwashed. They still think we do things like that, don't they? Or maybe we have somebody standing off-camera, pointing a gun at your head. After what you've told us, would it be enough to convince them?"

There was a short silence. Protbornov shrugged. "What else can we do?"

"It's something, at least," Kirilikhov said.

Sepelyan sat forward to the table. "I was thinking about this other agent that came with you, this . . ."

"Lewis Earnshaw," Uskayev supplied.

"This Mr. Earnshaw. He is the professional, you say, yes? Experienced. Believable. If we could get *him* to appear on the line also and confirm the story, might that do the trick? Those who know him, his own boss, maybe . . . Would they believe their own man?"

"I've interrogated him many times," Protbornov said. "Yes, professional. Impossible to intimidate or persuade. You get nothing from him, nothing. If he were *my* man, I would believe him. Unquestionably, I would believe him."

"He couldn't have been brainwashed?" Kirilikhov inquired.

Protbornov shook his head emphatically. "Him? Never."

"Why couldn't he have a gun pointing at him too, then?"

"He'd tell you to pull the trigger and be damned. He wouldn't compromise."

The Russians began warming to the idea, but then noticed that Paula had sat back and was shaking her head. "What is wrong?" Protbornov asked her.

Paula sighed hopelessly. "I just can't see him agreeing to it. . . . You have to understand what he's like: stubborn, antagonistic, indoctrinated with fixed views. He won't even consider the possibility that there might be alternatives to the way he thinks." She raised her opened hands. "He abhors everything about the Soviet system. The general said it—he wouldn't compromise. As a matter of principle, he'd never be seen going on television, public or private, and voluntarily cooperating with Russians. That's the way he is. It won't work. Forget it."

Protbornov pulled a face. "On reflection, I have to admit

that she's probably right," he said. "That does sound like him."

"It was just an idea," Sepelyan said.

"A pity," Kirilikhov murmured.

Silence fell. Then Olga, who had been sitting and thinking to herself in silence, said, "I don't know . . . perhaps there is a way in which we could get him to do it." She glanced at Paula. "Or maybe you could."

"How?" Paula asked.

"The laser that they've got," Olga said. "Wasn't that the idea of it in the first place? And you said it's working now. Well, maybe he won't go on a live TV transmission with Russians—but he might say the same thing privately, over his own personal link. Might he be persuaded to do that?"

Protbornov was looking bewildered. "Laser? What laser? What are you two women talking about now?"

They told him about Earnshaw's laser and its intended use for communicating with Earth. Protbornov sat looking stunned. The two men from Moscow glanced at him from time to time like officials from the head office of a bank with a branch manager whose staff had been giving away notes on the street. If Earnshaw believed he was acting independently, possibly he could be induced to send a personal confirmation from *Tereshkova* of what his own eyes were seeing there, Olga said. All Protbornov would need to do was make sure the guards stayed out of the way.

Paula thought it was worth a try, but she pointed out a problem that still remained. Communications only work when the person on the receiving end is listening. For a signal from the laser to get through, somebody down on Earth would have to be expecting it, and know what frequency and code to look for. Furthermore, in view of the minuscule amount of energy that would actually reach Earth, they would need to be using more than just any equipment for the looking.

Olga was aware of that. "But I understand that you helped them build the electronics," she said to Paula.

"Could you provide the operating frequency and whatever else somebody would need to know to set a receiver up?"

"Sure—actually there isn't that much," Paula said. "What have you got in mind?"

"We use the existing channel through Sokhotsk to give that information to the Americans," Olga replied. "We're here now, in Turgenev. We can send it off right away. You can tell Earnshaw it was your idea—that you did it in anticipation, hoping he would agree. We will have to hope that the Americans can arrange a suitable method for reception in time. It might take, what . . . a day, maybe?"

"A lot less is they use emergency procedures," Paula replied. "But that only applies to relaying a signal through the communications net. I don't know how they'd pick it up in the first place."

"We can only leave that side to them," Olga said. "Once they're set up, then all Earnshaw would need to do is get himself to a place where he can witness what's happening here, and point the laser at the roof. That shouldn't be too difficult if the guards stay away from him—but nobody tells him that, of course."

"Will he know if he's getting through?" Sepelyan asked. "Does this device receive also?"

"Yes," Paula said. "A reply signal comes back along the same path in the opposite direction."

"Along with the sunshine? Wouldn't the signal get lost in it?"

"It shouldn't. We picked the operating frequency to coincide with one of the dark absorption lines in the solar spectrum. And at the Earth end, they'll be able to use a powerful transmitter, don't forget."

Sepelyan nodded in a way which said that was all right with him, whatever it meant. Everyone looked at everyone else. Evidently there was nothing more to be said.

"Then, we seem to be agreed to give this suggestion a try," Protbornov announced. "We have little time. Therefore I propose that Lieutenant Bryce be taken back to Zamork at once to contact Mr. Earnshaw and explain the situation. Comrade Oshkadov goes downstairs to the Communications Center to send the message to the Americans via the Sokhotsk channel, advising the laser frequency and other details. Lieutenant Bryce can write them down before she leaves."

"Very well," Olga agreed.

Protbornov looked inquiringly at Kirilikhov and Sepelyan. They returned nods that said they were satisfied. "I'd better go and check on what's happening in Moscow," Kirilikhov said. He gave Protbornov a withering look as he rose from his chair. "After the present situation is resolved, we can discuss Zamork and the effectiveness of its security measures. Out of curiosity, have you ever been down a salt mine in Siberia, General?"

CHAPTER FORTY-SEVEN

Inquisitive visitors waiting to board the spoke elevators after their arrival at *Valentina Tereshkova* had always been told that behind the bulkhead facing the boarding area at the hub were storage tanks for water and liquid chemicals, as the official plans showed. In fact there were no storage tanks there. The small amount of agriculture and industrial processing that had been staged purely for show had never required much in the way of chemicals. And neither were there any manufacturing facilities worth speaking of next to the hub nuclear reactors behind the docking ports. The dummy bulkhead with its pipes, and the rest of the facade, had been dismantled now. What the reactors actually powered were capacitor banks feeding a battery of electromagnetic coil guns capable of imparting an acceleration of hundreds of g's into their drum-shaped projectiles to hurl them miles clear of the platform in seconds. Each projectile consisted of a fission bomb contained in an ellipsoidal cavity shaped to feed a configuration of lasing material that would transform a large proportion of the detonation energy into fifty independently amiable beams of high-density X-rays.

Field Marshal Vladislav Kyrenko, Commander in chief of "Anvil"—the designation of the entire space bombardment system that the superficialities of *Valentina Tereshkova* had disguised—steadied himself against a handrail while the general in charge of Battle Station 2 at the hub finished his report. One of the things the planners of space warfare hadn't taken into account was the difficulty of maintaining dignity under conditions of negligible weight.

"All mechanical and hydraulic systems tested and functional. Registration computers have been tracking assigned targets for twelve hours and check positively. All projectile onboard computers have been updating continuously without errors. Power-plant and launch systems are fully operational."

"Sounds good," Kyrenko said. "So what odds should I bet on our zapping every American lasersat with the first salvo?"

The general smiled faintly. "Oh, pretty good, I'd say."

"And the morale of the crew?"

"Just waiting to go for it."

Kyrenko nodded. "Good. Carry on." He watched as the general went back into the armored fire-control center from which the hub batteries would be directed. Inside, through the opening next to the massive door that would be closed before the action commenced, he could see technicians and operators busy at their rows of consoles. And that was merely the inner defense. The space between the inner and outer skins held a layer of pulverized moonrock several feet thick at the strongpoints.

That completed the hub part of the inspection. Kyrenko turned to Lt. General Churenev, his principal aide, who was standing with the party of officers waiting behind. "Everything looks fine here. Let's move on down."

They bobbed and pulled themselves across the deck and entered the elevator waiting at the top of one of the shafts from the Turgenev spoke. The doors closed, and moments later they were descending toward the ring. The outer tube of the spoke was armored, too; but since it was more exposed than the hardened battle stations at the hub and various locations around the rim, it would not be used while combat conditions prevailed. Once hostilities commenced, the garrison at the hub would be sealed in there for the duration.

At Turgenev they came out of the elevator into the main concourse of the skeleton that had once been the Government Building and crossed the dusty, derelict space to come out onto the raised terrace bordering the main square, where two staff cars were waiting. All was darkness, broken only by pools of light from the floodlamps set up at ground level by the military. The lines of reflecting slats in the roof had been closed to prevent their directing hostile laserfire into the interior. Kyrenko halted with his party, and stood for a while staring out at the black, empty shapes of the deserted ghost city. On the far side, the bones of what had been Internal Security Headquarters stood silhouetted against one of the lamps, picked clean by an army-engineer squad collecting materials for a piece of last-minute improvised construction. A row of groundcars stood silent and abandoned in the shadows beneath.

"It's hard to imagine it the way it was," Churenev commented. "With light, color, people, children . . ."

Kyrenko nodded distantly. "The day has come at last, Oleg. For a hundred years we have been treated like lepers. The capitalists sent Lenin back from Switzerland because they thought his Revolution would destroy Russia. When that failed, they set up Hitler and the Nazis, and sent them against us, but we destroyed them. Then they encircled us with guns and bases and missile sites, as if we were a disease that had to be contained. They spread lies, waiting . . . thinking they could wear us down by siege. But they forgot the Mongols, Napoleon, Hitler—how many times Russia has come back to bury those who thought they had destroyed her. And so it will be again. They say we are on the verge of collapse. But soon they will learn." He turned his head. "Am I not right?"

Churenev sighed. "If that is how it must be . . ."

The party descended the steps to the square, climbed into the cars, and left Turgenev. For a little over a quarter mile they drove through a desolation of bare metal terraces and piles of rotting vegetation that had been one of the agricultural sectors. In fact, only the crops along the valley center, lining the route along which visitors had been taken, had ever been real. The wheat, sorghum, vegetables, and rice terraces higher up the sides, which foreign observers had admired so enthusiastically from afar—apart from one show-piece section that they climbed laboriously to inspect more closely for themselves—had been planted with plastic imitations.

They came to Agricultural Station 3 and parked outside the waste-recycling plant that consisted mainly of dummy tanks, pipes, and reactor vessels. Its processing capacity was only a fraction of the publicized value—for the simple reason that there had never been that much waste to process. The field marshal and his aides walked through an opening in the side of an armored enclosure and entered the space that the public plans described as "Materials Storage." The commander of Battle Station 4, free-electron-laser emplacement, was waiting with his senior officers.

The party moved through the bays of windings and super-conducting magnets, the linac tunnel, and the control room. Accelerator potentials and field frequencies had been tuned to take out the West's communications and instrumentation satellites, checks were positive, and there were no problems to report. Emergency generators, local backup life-support systems, and escape chute down to the armored ring-transit tunnel were all operational. The men were in good shape.

"Very good, General," Kyrenko approved. "First-rate. So, we will meet in Washington, eh?"

"Yes, sir—to help burn down the Pentagon." Everyone laughed.

Kyrenko turned to Churenev and the others. "Very well,

gentlemen. That completes the tour. My compliments to all of you. Let us return to HQ."

They reembarked in their vehicles and drove the remaining distance to Novyi Kazan, climbing the ramp by the emptied reservoir to the main entrance. On the way in, Kyrenko stopped in the upper-level communications room to send a signal to Moscow. It read: ANVIL AT BATTLE READINESS, CONDITION ORANGE 1. ALL UNITS OPERATIONAL. COUNTDOWN STATUS TO PLAN IS CONFIRMED.

Then he continued on down into the hardened zone containing the command center from which he and his staff would direct and coordinate all the battle stations. It was a place that had never been included in the official tours. On the publicly released plans, however, it was described as a detention and rehabilitation facility. Its name was Zamork.

CHAPTER FORTY-EIGHT

The speeches were over, but the main square in Turgenev was still alive with people when Paula came out from the main concourse of the Government Building, accompanied by Major Uskayev, the captain, and two guards. The sight of a woman in a plain green tunic under armed escort contrasted with the colorful, holidaylike atmosphere that had taken over, and heads turned to watch them curiously as they crossed the terrace outside the main doors and descended the steps to the square, where a security-police van was waiting.

As the van entered an underpass, changed direction, and emerged again to negotiate the tortuous route out of the town, Paula saw that the bridges and pedestrian ways were bustling with people. Many of them were acting like tourists, rubbernecking at the sights and posing for pictures—no doubt recent arrivals out viewing their new home, she thought. On the edge of town they passed a large, open area of grass, where teams of children in white and red outfits were putting final touches to their gymnastics routines for the celebrations. For a moment the brightly lit tunnel of the colony's valley curved upward before them, with the green and yellow arms of the agricultural terraces spreading upward on either side, and then the van entered another tunnel to descend from town-center level to the valley floor.

The agricultural sector looked presentable again after the heroic efforts that had gone into saving its face—not to mention those of the Soviet leaders—and terraces of grain, fruit, and vegetables, and pastures with reasonably contented-looking cows lined the route beneath the inverted blue-yellow skybowl all the way past Agricultural Station 3 to Novyi Kazan. Here, they exited from the throughway by the reservoir, where a couple of boats were out sailing, and ascended the ramp to the gate in front of the surface buildings of Zamork. They passed through the checkpoint into the outer yard, where they disembarked from the van and entered the Administration Building.

A few minutes later, Paula came out on her own through the rear guardpost into the surface-level compound. In talking the situation over, she had agreed with Olga and Protbornov that the best chance of succeeding with Earnshaw lay in sustaining an appearance of everything's being normal, which meant he couldn't be allowed to know that the Russians were involved. Obviously the days of the elaborate clandestine operation that had run from B-3 were now over. But before they intervened to close it down, the authorities would permit it to serve this one final purpose.

Istamel was reading on his bunk in Hut 8 when Paula arrived. Seeing from her face that something urgent was afoot, he got up and went over to the cassette player. For some time now the occupants of Hut 8 and the regular visitors to it had been recording assorted conversation, usually arranged to be as boring as possible, between different individuals for occasions like these. Istamel selected one that featured just the two of them talking interminably about medieval Turkish poetry, dropped it into the player, and connected the output into the microphone circuit. That way the conversation would correlate with who had been seen entering the hut, if it happened to be under observation.

Paula had decided during the drive from Turgenev that there wasn't time to go through the whole thing again to let Istamel know what had happened. Besides, the whole ploy was to tell Earnshaw only that Olga had sent a message alerting the West to receive the laser signal, and to make him believe everything beyond that was normal. Istamel would play his part better if that was as much as he knew, too—and he could find out when she told Earnshaw. "I have to go down to the Crypt immediately," she said. "Do you know if Lew is there?"

"He should be. I was there earlier and left him with Razz and Albrecht. They seemed busy. Where's Olga? I thought you'd both be back together."

"A lot has happened. Look, it's too much to explain now. Come back down and hear it with the others."

Istamel nodded and asked no more. They went through to the shower and opened the hatch in the cubicle floor. Istamel went down first, and Paula followed, closing the hatch over them. They came out of the roof where the ladder ended, threaded their way through the machinery compartment, and crossed the girder bridge to the outside of the elevator shaft. Paula had been over this route many times now, and the traverse across the shaft to the recess on the far side no long troubled her. On the next two crossings after her first introduction by Peter Sargent, she had balanced with the help of a handrope that was stowed nearby to be temporarily strung across if needed, but now she could manage without. Istamel still used the rope, which inwardly gave her a certain satisfaction. They completed the descent, left the shaft through the maintenance hatch at the lower level, and made their way between the lines of tanks toward the Crypt, taking care not to trigger Rashazzi's alarm system on the way.

As they came within sight of the Crypt's lights, they caught the sound of raised voices arguing excitedly. That in itself was unusual. Paula pursed her mouth determinedly and steeled herself for the coming confrontation.

Earnshaw was with Rashazzi and Haber, as Istamel had said. In addition, Koh had appeared. They were standing around the large table, which was strewn with pieces of paper, and they continued gesticulating and making sketches even while Paula and Istamel were climbing down into the workspace, as if unaware of their approach. Then Earnshaw turned his head to acknowledge their presence, and the others fell silent.

It wasn't a time for observing niceties. Paula drew up facing the group and moved her arm in a brief gesture that took in the whole of the workshop and its contents. "All of this can wait for a while," she told them. "I've just come from Turgenev. Olga is there, sending off a message. It's an important message. A lot of things have been happening that you don't know about down here." Haber motioned to one of the sheets of paper that he and the others had been talking over and started to say something, but Paula cut him off with a wave of her hand. "We received a message from Tycoon this morning which said, in effect, that the West believes the Soviets are about to launch a first strike. I mean, they're not fooling. This is *it!*"

Istamel was staring at her incredulously. "But you never mentioned anything about this . . ."

"There wasn't time up there. I'm mentioning it now."

"But what did it say? Why should they think the Russians would attack now, with all their leaders here? It doesn't—"

"That's the whole point," Paula said. "They don't believe the Russian leaders are here. They're suspicious that the TV broadcasts going out might be recordings—in other words, a deception concocted to cover a strike. Anyhow, Olga and I have already sent a signal back confirming that the leaders are up here. That was as much as we

could do right away. But we don't think it's enough. What
we want you to—"

"Shut up." Earnshaw's voice wasn't loud, but it carried
such an unexpected whiplike snap that Paula did shut
up. He acknowledged with a nod. "Now, run that by me
again." Paula was too taken aback to reply. He said it
for her. "Our side has reasons for thinking the Soviets
might be about to strike if their leaders aren't really up
in *Tereshkova*—is that right? But you know it's all a
mistake, because the leaders really are here. And that's
what you've told Tycoon."

Paula nodded and returned a puzzled look. When he
didn't respond immediately, she collected herself together
again and got back into stride. "We did what we could,
but the signal only had my validation code. I'm not sure
that would carry enough weight in Washington. To really
convince them . . ." Her voice trailed away as she saw that
Earnshaw and the two scientists were not listening, but
exchanging ominous looks among themselves. Koh had
backed inconspicuously into the shadows, but Paula's
confusion just at that moment was such that she didn't
notice.

"It fits," Earnshaw murmured. "They've put them all
down a big hole, somewhere out of the way. Jesus, they
are about to launch a strike. They're on their countdown
right now!"

"The whole thing is a super-battlestation," Rashazzi
whispered. "They're probably only waiting for that UN
ship to arrive."

"About sixteen hours from now," Haber said numbly.

It was dawning on Paula that she'd been running off
the tracks since somewhere way back up the line. She
sent an uncomprehending look from one to another. "I . . .
don't understand what you're talking about. What's going
on?"

Earnshaw exhaled a long sigh and turned away, as if
needing a moment longer to integrate the new information
into his thinking. Rashazzi turned absently away toward

the bench, lost in a world of his own and thinking furiously. Haber still looked thunderstruck. Paula looked around for Koh and noticed for the first time that he had disappeared. Earnshaw saw the question forming on her face and stepped forward, cutting her off before she could speak. "Maybe there are a few things that *you* ought to know before you do any more talking," he said. Just for an instant, Paula sensed the tenseness in his voice, an urgency to divert her attention.

Without warning Earnshaw whirled round and his fist streaked out in the same movement, bunched karate-style to deliver a devastating blow to the V below Istamel's ribs. The Turk emitted a strained gurgling sound and dropped to his knees as his legs buckled. In the same instant Koh materialized from the darkness behind and slid his right arm around Istamel's neck to seize the jacket collar high on the opposite side below the ear, while his left arm came round from the other side to grasp the right lapel. Koh drove his knee into the Turk's back, gaining leverage to tighten his arms scissor-fashion in a way that slid aside the muscle covering the carotid artery and exposed it to the full pressure of the bony edge of Koh's forearm— cutting off the brain's blood supply brings unconsciousness much faster than strangulation. Rashazzi turned from the bench with a heavy metal bar in his hand, ready to help out if needed. Istamel tried to struggle, but the blow from Earnshaw had paralyzed his breathing. His efforts became feeble, then his eyes rolled upward and he went limp. Koh sustained the pressure for a few seconds longer and shook his head regretfully. "Something like this seems to happen whenever you two meet," he commented to Earnshaw as he released the body and let it crumple to the floor.

Earnshaw squatted down and opened Istamel's jacket. He undid the shirt and uncovered a Soviet communicator pad secured on a waistband. A quick but thorough search added a .45 automatic in an underarm sling, some extra clips of ammunition, and a general-clearance badge. Haber produced some cord, and Earnshaw helped him truss up the Turk out of the way in a sitting position with his back to one of the supporting pillars. Rashazzi tied a gag around his mouth.

Paula could only shake her head in helpless bewilderment as she watched. Earnshaw straightened up and turned back toward her. "You pick nice friends," he commented.

"What is this?" Paula mumbled. "Will somebody tell me what's going on? How did you know he was a plant?"

Rashazzi, Haber, and Koh moved back around the table. "He said he went to the hub on one of our missions," Earnshaw said.

Paula still hadn't fully accommodated to what had just happened. "So?"

"There isn't any hub," Rashazzi said.

Paula shifted her gaze uncertainly from one to another of them, finally letting it come to rest on Earnshaw. His face had an odd, challenging expression. "Suppose we told you that this place we're in is not *Valentina Tereshkova*," he said. "In fact, it isn't even in space at all."

The statement was so preposterous that for a moment it didn't register and Paula answered mechanically. "That's crazy. Of course it's in space. Go to one of the ag sectors and look up through a window. Everyone knows they came here from Earth, don't they? I know that you and I did."

"Do you?" Rashazzi's quietly reasonable tone broke her stupor and made her look away from Earnshaw. Only now did her face show its first sign of any willingness to try to understand. Rashazzi went on, "You may know that you were taken out to *Tereshkova* on a transporter from Earth over six months ago, but that's not quite the same thing. A lot has happened since then."

"Just out of curiosity . . ." Earnshaw said. Paula's head jerked back to face him. "Were you taken sick soon after we were arrested?" Her expression supplied the answer. He nodded. "So was I. And when you came round, did a doctor tell you you'd been out for a couple of days? These guys had similar experiences, too. Now, isn't that strange?

What do you think might have happened during that couple of days?"

"That's . . . absurd," Paula said. This time, however, her voice had lost its earlier conviction. Instead it was asking how what they were saying could be possible.

Rashazzi stepped over to the table and picked up a pencil. Paula moved forward, while the others closed around. Taking a blank sheet of paper, Rashazzi sketched a shallow, truncated, inverted cone—a circular strip, banked all the way round, like a racetrack.

"Suppose this were a large platform, miles in circumference, with miniature cities, agricultural sectors, and landscaping on it, all contained in a big, donut-shaped tunnel deep underground somewhere," he said. "Now support the entire platform on a system of superconducting magnetic fields and rotate it at such speed that the force vectors of gravity and centrifugal force combine into a single resultant perpendicular to the floor. If you want some specific numbers, from the tests we've conducted I'd estimate a banking angle of twenty-five degrees and a rotation period of ninety seconds, which implies a radius of a little under a kilometer, or about six tenths of a mile."

Paula shook her head in the way of somebody trying to wake up. "It can't be . . . I mean, adding the vectors like that . . . Everything would weigh more."

"By about ten percent, with the figures I've just quoted," Rashazzi agreed. "Which is about the most you could expect people to adjust to reasonably quickly, and why you couldn't go to a larger banking angle. And in fact, the gravitational acceleration as measured in Zamork is ten percent greater than Earth-normal. A strange way to design a space colony, wouldn't you think?

"And incidentally, the scales they weigh you on in the infirmary are calibrated to read ten percent light," Haber interjected. "That is very interesting, yes?"

"Do you remember feeling weak and heavy in the limbs when you woke up?" Earnshaw asked her. "We did, too. It wore off after a few days."

FIGURE 1

Paula was looking at Rashazzi's sketch with a changed expression, as if she wanted to be convinced. But now the scientist in her asserted itself, searching for the flaws. "Why rotate it at all?" she asked. "If it's on Earth and in a gravity field to begin with, why bother?"

"Because of the curvature that can be built into the structure," Rashazzi answered. "A static platform would have to be flat, like a washer. It could never support the illusion of being the inside of a big hamsterwheel, as it would have to do to look real. But banking it introduces a vertical component of curvature and gives you a floor that does indeed bend upward as it recedes."

Paula stared down at Rashazzi's sketch dubiously. She thought for a while, then took the pencil and on another sheet drew a pair of curves coming inward from the sides as if from behind an observer, and then retreating and converging to one side. It was a representation of Rashazzi's racetrack as seen by somebody standing on it. She added a series of radial lines sloping down at intervals from its higher, outer edge to the inner, and then some crude human figures at varying distances.

She inspected the result critically, tipping her head first to one side, then to the other. The others remained silent.

Finally she said, "No, I still can't buy this. However much you try and disguise it, it's still going to look like a banked racetrack. The people will start to lean over as they get farther away. It won't look anything like this." Beside it she drew another perspective view, this time with the two curves converging upward and away directly in front of the observer, and with the cross-lines appearing as horizontal rungs. It was a hamster's view of the inside of its wheel. Again she added some human figures.

"See, they're nothing like each other. The people should stay vertical, and foreshorten." Paula gestured back at her first sketch. "If you blocked off all the long sight lines, then maybe you could get away with it. But this place isn't built like that. I've just driven from Turgenev, and everyone here's been outside. You can see all the way from Novyi Kazan to the edge of Ag Station Three. It's the same everywhere. Long lines of sight aren't obstructed around the colony, yet you don't see a banked racetrack. So how could it be the way you're saying?"

Rashazzi took back the pencil. "That was something that puzzled us for a long time, and why we at first rejected the racetrack explanation," he said. "This is how you do it." He drew an imitation of Paula's first sketch and superimposed on it a pair of lines cutting across the curve of the track and forming a section of straight strip, as would the edges of a piece of ribbon laid flat along the sloping rim of a dinner plate. Then he added a series of verticals along the lines, connected them with horizontals to complete the illusion, and added a couple of figures as Paula had done.

Rashazzi covered the parts outside the walls with his hands to leave just the view looking along between them. The result came uncannily close to the second sketch that Paula had made. "You build walls," he said. "The colony we are inside is a replica of the real *Tereshkova*— the one you were taken to in May. But it is a replica with a difference. Instead of being circular, it consists of a series of straight segments with sides that don't veer

FIGURE 2

off laterally, just like the real one, and by the geometry I've described, with floors and roofs that curve and yet possess perpendicular gravity everywhere, just like the real one. There are six long segments, running between the bases of the spokes. In addition there are what amount to another six short segments that form the complexes around the spoke-bases themselves—three towns and the three agricultural stations." Rashazzi rummaged through some of the papers that he and the others had been discussing when Paula and Istamel arrived, and produced a plan view to show what he meant.

"That means you'd have to turn through a thirty-degree angle between segments," Paula commented. "Then—" She broke off as the further implication struck her.

"The architect who designed the towns wasn't a nut," Earnshaw supplied, as if reading her mind. "They're that

FIGURE 3

way on purpose, to make you lose your sense of direction."

"Or at least, sufficiently mislead you into not realizing that you're coming out thirty degrees off from the direction you went in," Rashazzi said.

And that explained why the towns and the agricultural stations forming the intersection zones were all built high: to obscure the views to the far side. From relatively close distances the rising structures formed a screen, while from

FIGURE 4

farther back the dip of the roof interceded before it was possible to see over the top of any of the zones and into the next long, straight section.

"The odd bits of sky that you think you see behind the intersection zones from some places are no doubt optical images projected onto screens built in among the higher levels of the architecture," Haber said. "from even a short

FIGURE 5

distance away, the difference would be impossible to distinguish. The overhead views of the hub and the stars at some places are also graphics simulations,"

"And so there isn't any hub, and that's why he couldn't have gone there," Earnshaw said, gesturing at Istamel's inert form. And why security is so tight around the spokes."

Paula looked back at the papers on the table, accepting what was on them now, but still needing time to absorb it fully. "And suggestion did the rest," Earnshaw said. "There is some residual distortion, but the unevenness of the valley-sides hides it—you won't see it if you're not looking for it. The gravity does vary a bit from the centers of the long sections to the ends, and the banking angle increases slightly toward the outside. . . . But what dominates everything else is that you *know* you came here physically through space, and that knowledge shapes your perceptions—it was your own first reaction. And being surrounded by people who reinforce the belief . . ." He shrugged. "What reason would there be to question it?"

"Why did *you* question it?" Paula asked.

"Me? I didn't. Ask these guys. They were being scientists while you were saving the world."

Paula had asked for that, and let the remark go. There were so many questions bubbling in her head now that she didn't know where to begin. "*All* the people out there? Surely they couldn't all have been through the same treatment. Not on that scale."

"The Russians officers and so on are no doubt just playing parts," Earnshaw said. "And probably a lot of the prisoners are, too. But some are genuine, like us—probably to give us an authentic layer of immediate contacts to interact with."

"I meant the inhabitants of the colony generally," Paula said.

"I don't know. They could have been told they were taking part in a simulation experiment, and have a taboo about mentioning it—to preserve the realism. On the other hand, I've talked to some people who don't seem to have any clear recollection of how they got here. They think they do, until you question them about details. Then you find it's all vague and muddy."

"Drugs," Haber said. "It would be possible to transport many people on a simulated two-day flight under the influence of sense-disorienting substances that would dull memory and increase suggestibility."

"A weightless flight?" Paula queried.

"Later, they wouldn't remember," Haber said. "They could recall it as having been weightless if that was suggested to them."

Paula closed her eyes and nodded that she was finally persuaded. "Why?" She asked in a voice that sounded suddenly tired. "What would be worth so much effort . . . the cost of it all?"

"The world," Earnshaw said simply. "They saw years ago which way the game was going for them, and this was their last-ditch gamble. They built a weapons platform in space, thinly disguised as a colony—enough to fool visitors on the guided tours. At the same time they built this replica, with all the trappings of the complete colony. Then they hatched a scheme to get people inside the replica whose credibility the West would trust, and allowed them to set up supposedly secret communications channels to report back through. They staged this stunt with the November celebrations and the leaders to put everyone off guard. Sure there were people on the dummy we went to months ago, but they'll have been taken off since."

Now a lot of things were becoming clearer. "The dirt," Paula said slowly. "That's what that business was all about. Those ships didn't come here . . . go there to take dirt *up*. They went there to bring the people *down*."

Earnshaw nodded. "Sure. And where have the Russians *really* been putting their leaders in the meantime—with all their families, generals, Party hacks, and lots of people who'd be too useful to risk losing if there was a lot of rebuilding to do afterward? Down here, wherever here is—in a self-contained world with its own industry, agriculture, life-support, and a population ready-installed to keep it running for years, if need be, if the predictions turn out wrong and bad conditions on the surface last for a long time. What we're in is a giant-size bomb shelter."

Paula went very quiet as the full extent of how completely she had been taken in and how willingly she had fallen for it all became sickeningly clear to her. It must have shown on her face, she realized when she looked up and found Earnshaw watching her. "Oh, don't worry too much," he said. "You weren't the only one. They were thorough. They even stripped the fittings from the cells they put us in after we were arrested up in the real *Tereshkova,* and transferred them down here with us to the cells in the replica. I remember a vent in the ceiling of mine that had the same scratch in it. And don't think you were the only one they managed to hang a stooge on, either." He indicated Istamel with a turn of his head. "He wasn't the only one who was supposed to have been to the hub. I had my own Olga, too, and I fell for it."

Paula looked at him uncertainly. "Scanlon," Rashazzi said. It was the first time that Paula had ever heard a note of hopelessness in the Israeli's voice. "He's known everything, right from the start. They've been playing us like fishes all the time."

Paula stared back, horrified. She looked across at the bench and the things around it that had been constructed with so much effort: the laser, to signal across a void that wasn't out there; the survival suits—four of them—to get to a hub that didn't exist; the detectors, circuit-test meters, RF monitors, IR sensors, badges, bracelet solvents, and all the other paraphernalia devised to evade a surveillance system that had never been intended to contain them. She shook her head in mute protest, struggling to take in the full magnitude of the disaster.

And then a new voice spoke softly from the shadows in an Irish brogue. "Is that a fact, now?" They turned as Scanlon moved out into the light. Earnshaw started forward, then froze as he saw the automatic in Scanlon's hand. The others remained motionless on either side of him. Scanlon stopped far enough back from them not to be rushed. "No, to give credit where credit's due, Lew never told me that you were on your way to working out where we really are." He looked around the circle of grim faces. "My compliments, gentlemen. As the barmaid told the parson, 'It gets more interesting as you uncover more of it.' Wouldn't you agree?"

CHAPTER FORTY-NINE

"Now what?" Scanlon asked them. "It was an interesting conversation and I'm impressed by your ingenuity, but what did you imagine you were going to do next? There wasn't so much of a mention of any suggestion, unless I'm mistaken."

McCain didn't bother replying, but continued staring back woodenly. It was true. There was no way out, and the Russians controlled all the communications—as they had done all along. Scanlon doubtless had a communicator like Istamel's and would have summoned for help before revealing himself. Now he was simply waiting for it to arrive. Although Paula hadn't had a chance to say so, McCain guessed that the errand she'd come here on after sending the message to Foleda had been to try getting him to endorse it personally. Scanlon had waited long enough to see if she would succeed. Now the whole sorry charade was over. There was nothing left to do but await the appearance of the show's stagehands and producers from the wings.

A whole pattern now became clear, which McCain could have kicked himself for not having spotted earlier. Of course the Russians would have ensured that there was always somebody at his elbow to steer and prompt him, making sure he played his part according to the design. Scanlon had ingratiated himself with McCain from the beginning, by arranging—so he'd said—for McCain to get news of Paula via the library from the phantom Russian officer, who probably didn't exist. It was Scanlon who had urged him to take on Maiskevik, which McCain could see now had been intended to equip him in the eyes of the billet with the image his role would require. Scanlon had steered McCain's group to Istamel's escape committee, and the committee had steered them to the freight system, which had doubtless been monitored all along by the Russians. McCain burned inwardly with anger at his own failing as much as at Scanlon's duplicity. He stared at the gun in Scanlon's hand, judging the distance and weighing up the chances—if everything was lost anyway—of taking the Irishman with him.

And then Scanlon did something very strange. He checked that the gun's safety catch was on, reversed it, and tossed it to McCain. McCain caught it reflexively but was too astonished to do anything more than blink. "I didn't want to risk you fellas being too impetuous," Scanlon said with a shrug. "Not after watching what happened to the sleeping beauty over there." Everybody was still too dazed to move or say anything. Scanlon regarded them all quizzically for a few seconds more, like a professor waiting for a class of slow students to catch on. "Well?" he asked them. "Doesn't a man have a right to change his mind?"

For once, Rashazzi could do no more than stammer. "Change? . . . Change how? Are you saying you're with us?"

"To be sure, what else do you think I'm saying?"

"But why?" Haber was shaking his head, equally bemused.

"I found the way I thought about things and people changing as time went by," Scanlon said. "Being among the likes of yourselves had a lot to do with it. But there isn't the time now to be going off into grand speeches. The fact of the matter is that you're stuck with me. And you'd be best advised to trust me whether you like it or not, because I'm the one chance you've got of getting out of here. And that's the only way you'll ever tell anyone what you know."

Haber looked baffled. "Get out of here? Tell what we know? How could anything like that be possible now? The Russians know everything."

"Ah well, that's not quite so," Scanlon said. "Aren't I

just after saying that the way I see things has been changing for a while now? There are some things they don't know about. For one thing, they don't know you've worked out that the place we're in isn't in space—for haven't I only this minute found out that you know that much meself? And they don't know that you've burrowed your way into the civilian levels underneath Zamork that have just been opened up. You were supposed to find the freight system and go joyriding around, but you weren't supposed to go that deep."

"Who are the other informers?" McCain asked, finding his voice at last. "They wouldn't rely on just one."

"You've already got him," Scanlon said, nodding toward Istamel. "But he never got to know that you'd found the deep levels. You did a good job of covering up. You were supposed to include more plants in your team than you did. Maybe you've a nose for sniffing them out."

"Chakattar?" McCain said.

Scanlon nodded. "All the escape-committee crowd, except Sargent. He's straight."

"I was never happy about them," McCain said. The way they'd gotten hold of the wiring diagrams had seemed too easy in retrospect. "What about in our billet? Gonares was supposed to have been at the hub, too, so we know about him. What about Mungabo? He's been down in the deeper levels."

While McCain was speaking, Rashazzi went over to check on Istamel, whose breathing was more regular again now. Rashazzi poured an ethery-smelling liquid onto a gauze pad and applied it to the Turk's nose. "This will keep him out of it for a while," he said. "He might be a bit sick when he comes round."

"Mungabo's okay," Scanlon said. "I was the only plant in the front section. Nolan, Andreyov, Borowski, Irzan, and Charlie Chan are clean. The rest are fakes."

McCain looked genuinely surprised. "Smovak? Vorghas?"

"Both with Czech political intelligence. Luchenko is a KGB colonel. The other Asiatics are with GRU."

"So Creeping Jesus isn't in on it, eh—a true disciple?"

"Do me a favor. Who in their right mind would depend on the likes of him? He was put there to be a source of provocation to draw you out, and it worked like a charm."

"What about Maiskevik?" McCain asked. That was something he'd often wondered about. "Was that for real, or did he take a dive?"

"Oh, you clobbered him all right," Scanlon said, grinning. "It was real enough—part of the test, you might say. They wanted a man with fight in him, to be sure he'd hit back at the system when he got the chance. And they made sure the only chance he got would be by setting up a spy operation. They had about a dozen or more people they might have used, scattered around in Zamork. But not all of them managed to set up a communications link back to wherever it was they came from, and others didn't measure up in other ways." Scanlon looked at Paula. "That was why the Russians waited until the Earth-end connection into Washington—the end they couldn't control—was working before they involved you. If that had failed, they'd have concentrated on one of their other candidates."

"Where is this place?" Rashazzi said. "Where are we all?"

"Underneath some hills near a place called Sokhotsk, in Siberia—where the groundstation is located that handles communications to the real *Tereshkova*," Scanlon replied. "There's been a genuine exchange of message traffic with the real *Tereshkova* for your people to follow, to keep up appearances. The Russian code name for this place is 'Potemkin.' How's that for being appropriate? Or maybe there's someone in the Kremlin with a sense of humor, after all. Now, if—"

"Why?" McCain demanded. He had recovered from the shock, and his mind was starting to work again. "Why are you doing this? It's not exactly a job they'd have picked anybody for. You must have been pretty hot. What happened?"

Scanlon scratched the side of his sparse head of hair and sighed. "Yes, it's true that at one time I was mixed up with the IRA. But when I got to thinking about it I found meself asking, Are these really the kind of people I'd like to see running Ireland if the Brits left and they did win? They were not. And they're not the kind of people you stay around for very long if you've crossed them, either. I decided I'd be safer heading East. But I found myself asking the same question about the Russians and the world as I'd asked about the Provos and Ireland: Are these really the kind of people I'd like to see in charge of it? And the answer came out the same." Scanlon tossed out an arm to dismiss the subject. "But are we to be getting on with what needs to be done, or stand here prattling like old women all day? Olga and the general are waiting in Turgenev for Paula to get back and make her TV debut, and I've decided to take my chances with the rest o' ye and have a shot at getting us out."

"What's this about TV?" McCain asked, giving Paula a mystified look.

She avoided his gaze, feeling sheepish now. "Olga and Protbornov asked me to appear on a connection to Washington to back up the signal that we sent. I agreed. They wanted me to try and persuade you to do the same thing—because you'd have better credentials."

"Some goddam hope! And you actually—"

"No, that's what I told them . . . really. Then Olga had this idea that maybe you'd confirm the message if you thought you were doing it independently—using the laser. I came here to try and sell you on that." Paula exhaled a sharp breath and showed her empty hands. The gesture said that that was the way it was, that she couldn't change it now, that he could think whatever he liked.

McCain stared at her for a second, then nodded. It was all under the bridge now. "That would have been their trump. Well, at least we didn't . . ." He looked at her again, frowning. "Olga suggested that?"

"Yes."

"But she knows this place isn't in space. The laser couldn't communicate out. Why would she come up with a damn fool idea like that?"

Paula bit her lip awkwardly. "I've been wondering the same thing," she said. "It had to be part of what they'd set up all along, too. They could intercept the laser signal at the roof, relay it up to *Tereshkova,* and repeat it on another laser set up inside. They could handle replies from Earth in the same way. That was how they planned to involve *you.* And I walked straight into it."

McCain shook his head. "Surely not. That has to be too—"

"She's right," Scanlon said. "That's exactly how it was. Don't you remember back in June, it was *me* who put you onto the idea for the laser. And it was me who found the broken one that's now fixed and lying on the bench there—but it wasn't *too* broken. And it's me who's supposed to go with you to Turgenev now, to make sure it's aimed at the right place on the roof—where the detector to relay the signal up to the groundstation has been fixed."

McCain stared as if he was having a hard time believing it. "That far back? It was all planned that far back? We were *supposed* to build the laser for this all along? . . . Jesus Christ!"

"And we thought we were being so cunning," Rashazzi muttered despondently.

Paula sat down on one of the stools. "My God, and it came so close . . ." She looked at McCain. "Would you have? If I'd told you the story and you went to Turgenev to see the VIPs for yourself, would you have confirmed it to Washington with the laser?"

McCain turned his face toward her, thought about the question, and then nodded with a strange, glassy-eyed expression. "Yes," he told her. "To be frank, I think I might."

"And perhaps we won't disappoint them yet," Scanlon said. Everyone turned to look back at him curiously. He nodded, satisfied that he had all their attention again. "Right, are we through with the talking now?" he asked.

There was silence. "Good. Now, they say the best way to catch a thief is with a thief. It might be, I'm thinking, that the best way to outwit deceivers is with deception. And there's something all the more poetic when it's by turning their own deception around on them, which has a natural appeal to an Irishman. The first thing we have to do is collect Sargent and Mungabo. And let's get Charlie Chan and Borowski down here, too, since they're okay and we'll need all the help we can get. After that, this is what I'm proposing . . ."

CHAPTER FIFTY

The Infra-Red Orbiting Observatory (IROO) was a permanently manned astronomical space observation platform operated jointly by the Jet Propulsion Laboratory in California, NASA, and the East Asiatic Scientific Research Council. Designed for studying the universe at high resolution in the longer-than-optical wavelengths that the Earths atmosphere blocks almost completely, it boasted a main telescope built around a 200-centimeter diameter primary mirror, which was cooled with liquid helium to avoid polluting its sensitive detectors with heat radiated from the structure. Since becoming fully operational five years previously, the observatory had penetrated the screening dust clouds that attend both the births and deaths of stars, bringing a new understanding of stellar evolution; it had mapped the inner regions of the Milky Way and pinpointed the supermassive black hole centered there; and it helped reveal the dynamics of energetic distant galaxies. Its instruments were sensitive enough to detect a speck of dust thirty miles away by its heat radiation alone; also, it was in an almost-polar orbit oriented such that for the next several days it would be able to train those instruments on *Valentina Tereshkova* continuously.

"We're keeping a line open to Tokyo," Kay Olson, a special assistant at the State Department, said from one of the screens in Foleda's outer office. "The Japanese prime minister is talking to Professor Kobasuka at this moment. Meanwhile the IROO crew have been alerted via JPL to stand by for a special operational directive. The President has asked to be kept informed, and we'll advise you of further developments at they happen." Kobasuka was chairman of the committee that selected the program of objectives for IROO to study from proposals submitted by scientists all over the world.

"Fine," Foleda acknowledged. He turned his head toward Barbara, who was waiting for a response from a man looking offscreen on another display. "How's it going?"

"Defsec C-three-I has ordered an emergency-band connection into MILCOM from the NASA tracking net. They're testing it now. JPL has confirmed that the IROO high-power signal-laser can be tuned to the frequency specified in Pangolin's message."

"Anything on Sunflower from Sexton?"

"No."

Foleda grunted. "Stay with it and let us know straightaway when anything new comes up."

"Will do."

Foleda walked back to the interview room next door to his office, where Philip Borden and Anita Dorkas were sitting at the table with a heavily built, bearded man. Foleda waited inside the door without interrupting. "You're certain," Borden was saying to Anita. "You arrived that morning and were transferred to low-security work without explanation, and Colonel Felyakin talked to you the same day. What did he say, exactly? It's important."

"He told me to reschedule the day's leave I had listed for the next day, because some people were due to arrive from Moscow to straighten out an administrative mixup. He said it involved the durations of some of the postings in England, and asked me to be there at ten o'clock with Enriko, and to make sure we had our passports."

Borden nodded. "And Enriko came home drunk that same night?"

"I don't know that I'd say drunk. He had been drinking."

"With the Line KR chief, Colonel Shepanov."

"Yes."

"And what did Enriko say?"

Anita sipped from a glass of water on the table. "He was very quiet and preoccupied—not the way he usually was when he and Shepanov got together . . ."

"Go on."

"He mentioned that Shepanov had been having personal problems and sometimes talked too much. Then, quite suddenly, he asked about the scientist from Novosibirsk that my ex-husband went off with seven years ago. Shepanov had let slip that she'd been arrested for dissident activities."

"Did he say when she was arrested?" the bearded man interjected. He had a strong East European accent.

"About three months previously—that would have been April—May, I'd guess."

The bearded man nodded. "And you assumed that your ex-husband had been under investigation, too, and that as a matter of standard KGB procedure all his close relatives and associates would be suspect, including you."

Anita nodded. "Yes, exactly."

"And what was your reaction?" Borden asked her.

"I was terrified, naturally, because of the work I'd been doing for the British. From the other things that had happened that day it seemed likely that I'd been found out already, that Enriko was under suspicion, too, and that the people from Moscow were coming to take us both back."

"So you ran away, and sought asylum with the British."

"Yes."

"Leaving your husband?" the bearded man queried, raising his eyebrows.

"There was no love in our relationship. He was pure KGB. His postings abroad were useful to my own work."

"That never struck you as just too convenient?" Foleda asked, still near the door, and speaking for the first time.

Anita looked uncomfortable. "Not at the time . . . although since you mentioned it, I've been wondering."

Borden looked inquiringly across the table. He had been through this many times, but wanted the bearded man to hear it firsthand for himself. Voldemar Zatin, former chief of the KGB's training academy at Bykovo, forty miles north of Moscow, whose defection to the West five years previously had been a minor sensation, leaned back in his chair and thought for a few moments over the things that had been said. Then he looked at Borden and gave his opinion.

"The business at the London Residency—that is not how they would do it. You would never be permitted to leave the building in a situation like that. The first thing you know is when the KGB men from Moscow come in, and then you stay there in the embassy until you leave for the airport. Complete surprise. No opportunity to suspect or do anything. The passports? Bah!" Zatin waved a hand in front of his face. "They send someone to your apartment for them, if that is where they are."

"All a setup, then, you think?" Borden said.

"I'm certain of it. It was all so that she would bring a story to the West that would make them believe that Dyashkin was genuine and had a legitimate reason to defect. He was part of it from the start. His dissident activities—all part of his cover."

Anita stared in astonishment. "But that was over seven years ago."

Zatin pulled a face and tilted his head indifferently. "Seven years, ten years—what of it? Some operations they plan twenty years ahead. Thirty years, even. The husband was another part of it—from the beginning. They allowed the marriage to happen, exactly so she would get into compromising situations on foreign postings, from which she could defect easily. She was allowed to believe she was using him; in reality, they were using her. I have seen similar schemes."

Stunned, Anita stared down at the table. Borden looked

over at Foleda and exhaled a long breath. "You were right all down the line, Bern. . . . Look, it's kinda late in the day to say so, I know, but—" Foleda waved his hand in a way that said it was okay, save it till later. Borden nodded. "So what's the situation out front?" he inquired, nodding toward the door.

"Technically it looks good," Foleda said. "State is talking to the Japanese now, and we've got an emergency military hookup through NASA. The President's being kept posted, and the defense secretary and Chiefs of Staff are standing by."

Borden got up from his chair. "Then, let's get on down and see what comes in," he said. And to Anita and Zatin, "You've helped a lot. Thanks. We'd like you to stay around for a while."

As they passed by Foleda's outer office, Foleda stopped to poke his head in. "Have Security send someone to take care of the visitors while they're in the building," he said to Barbara. "We're going on down to Communications. Anything new here?"

"The Japanese want to know if we're willing to underwrite the cost of lost research time on IROO if they reassign it to Mermaid," she told him.

"Shit," Foleda said over his shoulder as he turned to follow Borden again. "Tell 'em I'll write a personal check."

CHAPTER FIFTY-ONE

Paula's feelings as she drove back to Turgenev in the security police van with Major Uskayev and their escort were very different from the zeal that had carried her in the opposite direction just a few hours earlier. Although it was a source of wonder to think that the valley packed with buildings and trees beyond the roadway, the Russian television crews filming decorations being set up for tomorrow's celebrations, and the panoramic view of the hub and starfield overhead in the agricultural sector were all parts of an illusion manufactured underground in Siberia, she remained quiet and subdued.

Thinking back over everything that had happened in the six months since it had all begun, she could see now how systematically and ruthlessly she had been deceived. And what had made the deception possible was her own intellectual conceit and a conviction of infallibility that it had never crossed her mind to question. The irony was that it was she, the scientist, who had taken her assumptions for granted; Earnshaw, the cavalier, had questioned every assumption. That, of course, was the way the Russians had set it up. That, precisely, had been their whole intention.

The Tangerine file had never existed. The story had been planted on Western intelligence as the irresistible lure that it had turned out to be, guaranteeing they would send somebody to try and retrieve it. Depicting it as a computer file—but one held inside a low-security maintenance computer, and hence not impossible to extract—ensured they would send somebody expert in Soviet computer techniques, and hence qualified to be duped into setting up the communications channel later.

What stung most of all was the realization that the long period of isolation and interrogation after her arrest had constituted an elaborate process of observation and testing by the Russians to find the right combination of vanity, stubbornness, exaggerated self-confidence, and political naivete that they needed for their purpose. And out of all the candidates who had been brought to *Tereshkova* in various ways during the past year or so, hers was the dubious distinction of having passed every test with honors. "The whole problem with the world is that fools and fanatics are always so certain of themselves, but wiser people are full of doubts," she remembered quoting pompously to Earnshaw on their voyage up. "How come he didn't add, 'I think'?" Earnshaw had asked. It had taken her this long to understand what he'd meant.

A lot of things were painfully clear with hindsight. The

women who had been such obvious plants in her cell during the initial interrogation period had been meant to be obvious—to entice her into a mood of self-congratulation for having spotted them, and contempt toward those whom she had mistaken for fools. Thus they had established in her a conviction based on false security that *she* couldn't be fooled; or, if she was more honest with herself, they had simply built upon the belief they found existing there already. She remembered a stage magician she met at a party once, who had talked about how easily some scientists were fooled by claims of paranormal phenomena. "Basically it plays upon conceit," the conjurer had said. "They don't like to think they can be taken in by 'mere entertainers.' Therefore their subconscious thinking runs something like: If *I* can't spot the trick, then there can't be a trick. The only choice they've got left then is to accept what they think they've seen as genuine."

The spell in the kitchens, the environment she'd been put in, the degradations she'd been subjected to—all calculated to create a readiness born of desperation to throw herself at the first promise of escape back to anything resembling her kind of world, with her kind of people. And so they'd drugged her food to make her sick, and that had gotten her into the infirmary, ready for Olga's appearance, staged after their "coincidental" encounter in the corridor outside Protbornov's office. That, of course, had been to make sure that Paula would approach Olga first, thus avoiding any of the suspicions that might have been caused by Olga's coming to her. The position in the Environmental Department, the link to "Ivan" that had needed a technical expert to restore it, and the manipulation to make her believe that extending the link to the West had been her own idea— all parts of the plan. And then, playing on the personality traits that she recalled snatches of having revealed during the drugged, hazy period of her early interrogation, there had been Svetlana, Elena, Gennadi, and others —all acting out roles calculated to echo and amplify her own prejudices and perceptions, and reinforce her private self-image.

The hardest part of all to swallow was Olga's treachery. Paula had not only trusted her, but had admired and accepted her as sharing a common ethic based on truth, honor, and integrity that put them above the irrationalities of a lesser world. Truth, honor, integrity! Olga had baited her line with those very sentiments. As Scanlon had said, the thought of turning their own deceptions back on them by continuing to play their own game had a very sweet, poetic appeal to it.

They arrived at the Government Center in Turgenev and went straight up to a room full of maps, screens, and communications equipment, where Olga and Protbornov were waiting. Some other officials and officers were doing a good job of pretending to be anxious. Olga played her part with nauseating perfection. "Thank heavens you're all right, Paula. You were gone a long time. I was beginning to worry. Did you speak to Earnshaw? What did he say? Will he do it?"

Paula looked Olga straight in the eye and nodded. "Yes, he's convinced. He'll do it. He and Scanlon are going to try getting up onto the roof of the air-processing plant next to the Security Headquarters building, where they can observe the main square and operate the laser." Despite himself, Protbornov was unable to suppress a triumphant gleam in his eyes at Paula's confirmation that Scanlon would be accompanying Earnshaw. This was the last of the possible problems that the Russians had anticipated. It was important that Scanlon go too. He knew where on the roof to point the laser.

"Which route will they be taking?" Protbornov asked.

"Up from the freight line through the terminal below Turgenev center," Paula replied. "From there they'll come into the square through the shops on the north side disguised as civilians, with the laser and spectrometer dismantled, rolled up inside bundles that look like parade banners. With the square crowded, they figure on slipping in to the garage below the air-processing plant, finding a way up to the roof, and tapping into a power line somewhere to run the equipment."

"When will they be coming?"

"Three hours from now—when the crowd starts getting big for the First Secretary's arrival." The final shipload of Soviet VIPs, including the First Secretary of the Communist Party, Chairman of the Supreme Soviet, and the whole of the top cadre of government, would arrive in time for its passengers to rest and freshen up before welcoming the UN ship bringing the rest of the world's delegates twelve hours later.

Protbornov looked over at Major Uskayev. "Did you get that? Get on to Security control and make sure they have the details. Under no circumstances are any of the police to interfere. Make sure Earnshaw and Scanlon have an unobstructed route up to the roof, and clear any watchmen, or anyone else who might interfere, off the premises."

"Right away, sir," Uskayev said, and left the room.

"And for you, we have something special," Protbornov told Paula. He slipped an arm around her shoulder in an almost fatherly fashion and steered her over to two men in suits who were waiting nearby. "Here are the engineers who will brief you. You came here as a television journalist, yes? Well, now we are going to make you into a real one. Very appropriate, don't you think? Would an American find it funny?" His eyes twinkled, and the craggy, heavy-jowled face actually contorted itself into a laugh. "But not public television, of course—as we promised. Just a private transmission to your own people. Our embassy in Washington is making the arrangements now." He presented her to the two men. "This is the American lady who might save the world." They smiled dutifully and said it was a pleasure to meet her. Olga, who was on Paula's other side, actually had the nerve to turn and kiss her on the cheek. At least the ecstatic shine in Olga's eyes was genuine.

"No, the pleasure's mine," Paula told them. And that statement was quite genuine, too.

Meanwhile, in a compartment in the deeper levels below Zamork, McCain, Scanlon, Koh, and Rashazzi, assisted by Mungabo, Charlie Chan, and Borowski, had finished their preparations and were almost ready to begin cutting through the outer hull wall. . . .

CHAPTER FIFTY-TWO

The tank was made of heavy-gauge steel sheet, solidly riveted. Before they drained it, it had contained fresh water and been one of a row of several such tanks in a compartment on the service deck beneath the recently opened civilian level below Zamork. Then they had cut off the top five-foot section with an acetylene torch from the engineers' stores they had broken into, lifted it off, and turned it on its side to form an open box, with the inspection hatch that had been on top now in the side opposite the open one. Getting down into the service deck had proved easier than expected—the place was virtually deserted, no doubt because of the holiday and the celebrations commencing up on the surface.

Rashazzi had guessed, and Scanlon had confirmed, that even though the structure they were in was not in space, nevertheless it was rotating in a vacuum—in fact, inside an evacuated toroidal tunnel. Besides reducing power requirements, the vacuum would eliminate wind noise from the outside—a strange thing for people to hear who were supposed to think they were in space—and it would insulate the structure from the surroundings, avoiding the risk of unusual heat patterns on the surface that might arouse the curiosity of Western surveillance satellites. Hence a breakout party would still need the survival suits, and it would need an airlock. However, they hadn't been able to find a chamber small enough and strong enough, adjacent to the outer wall, to use as one. The compartment holding the water tanks and associated pumping machinery came closest, but its volume was still much too large to evacuate in a reasonable time—other than explosively. And even if they did evacuate it, Rashazzi was doubtful that the walls could withstand the load that would have resulted from the normal pressure in the rooms surrounding it.

Therefore they had improvised their own airlock. The section of tank now stood with its open side butted up against the outer wall and secured by crude welds to the reinforcing ribs. Rolls of rubber padding and thick plastic sheet, stiffened by metal plates and heavy with "Razzgoo," were wedged all around the joint, which had then been heavily dusted with powdered chalk. The packing would be sucked in tighter when the box was evacuated, and the seal didn't have to be a perfect seal anyway—moderate leakage from the huge volume outside the tank would be of no consequence.

Mungabo, with Charlie Chan and Borowski, now recovered from their initial amazement at what had been going on not so far beneath their feet, had finished cutting away a section of the inner wall—Scanlon had confirmed that the outer wall was also a pressure vessel and would be able to take the load. The tank would be evacuated by the simple expedient of drilling holes through the final skin to the vacuum outside, and then cutting away the entire section as soon as the pressure had fallen low enough. A thick steel plate over the inspection hatch on the other side of the tank would be adequate to close it off, since the pressure of the air outside would keep the plate in place.

Suited up already, McCain, Scanlon, Rashazzi, and Koh had spent the last hour sitting against a step in the floor, resting and breathing oxygen, to denitrogenate their body tissues, from a large cylinder connected to the four hoses. McCain found the garment heavy and constricting, like a stiff scuba wetsuit, and it seemed to stick to itself and everything else where the sealing compound that Rashazzi had concocted oozed from the joints. In front of them, Mungabo climbed out of the hatch in the side of the box and began passing items of equipment that Borowski checked off against a list to Charlie Chan, who was still inside. There were two battery-operated inspection lamps and a regular flashlight apiece, for there was no reason to expect the outside to be lit—Scanlon didn't think it was; four heavy-duty electric hand-drills, and a reel carrying hundreds of feet of cable connecting back through a packed hole in the side of the tank to an electrical junction box; two satchels full of large aluminum eyebolts, S hooks, snaplinks, and miscellaneous lines and slings accumulated during the two months since they'd had the idea of crossing over the outside to get to the spokes; a hundred-foot rope ladder formed by making loops at intervals along a nylon line and tying them to a second line; spare oxygen bottles; two bags containing clothes to change into when they got out; and a bag of assorted tools.

Borowski checked the final items and Mungabo passed them inside. Then Chan climbed out. The four figures on the floor stood up awkwardly, and working in pairs— McCain and Scanlon, Rashazzi and Koh—checked each other's face seals one more time. The other three helped them fix webbing harnesses over the suits to carry the equipment, and switched their oxygen hoses to the smaller bottles they would be taking with them. At last all was ready. The four who were going and the three who would be staying behind exchanged final handshakes.

"You'll do just great, guys," Mungabo said, talking loudly to be heard through their head coverings. "Don't forget to send us a card, huh?" McCain nodded and made a female shape in the air with his hands. Mungabo laughed and slapped him on the shoulder.

Borowski checked each one's oxygen valve and connections as they stepped up to the hatch, where Charlie Chan helped them through. "Good luck. I'm only sorry that you didn't bring us in on this sooner. We would have liked to help more." Rashazzi made a palms-up gesture. Borowski nodded. "It was never possible to be sure who you could trust, eh? Well, a pity all the same."

Charlie Chan was looking somber. "Let's hope that you can manage to do something out there, if you make it. This time I don't have a joke."

The four squeezed into the box, wedging themselves into the corners to avoid sticking together when they bumped. Rashazzi nodded, and the others outside lifted the coverplate into position over the hatch. The box was lit by an inspection lamp the others had used while cutting through the wall's inner skin. McCain concentrated on his breathing. It felt smooth and trouble-free, and he had no sensations of light-headedness or reduced vision. He recited a list of arithmetic multiplications in his head, and judged his faculties to be unimpaired. When Rashazzi looked at him questioningly, he returned a nod with a thumb-up sign. Scanlon and Koh did likewise. Scanlon pulled the gas cylinders connected to the cutting torch toward him to make room, and Rashazzi drilled a close pattern of holes through the exposed wall of outer skin facing them.

Rashazzi watched a pressure gauge as plumes of white dust began appearing around the wall joint at places where air was being drawn in from the outside. Koh at one end, and Scanlon at the other, signaled to the three outside where the worst leaks were by tapping on the sides, and after some minutes the currents had diminished. Even so, it was not long before the total flow into the tank balanced the flow out, and the pressure stabilized. Rashazzi drilled more holes to increase the outflow, and the pressure dropped farther. Everyone checked their respirators and seals again, and waited for more leaks to be plugged. Because of the lack of time, the whole business was going to be riskier than it would have been with the kind of airlock they had envisaged originally: the lock they had been forced to improvise would only work one way. Had an emergency developed up to this point, they could have aborted the operation by covering the drilled holes with rubber pads and steel plates, which had been brought into the tank for the purpose, and repressurized the box by opening the large oxygen cylinder. But once they cut away the final wall and opened the box completely to the vacuum, the air pressing on the hatch coverplate would exert a force of over three tons. After that, there could be no going back.

A strange stillness came over McCain as the pressure continued falling and the world of all the sounds that he had been registering unconsciously receded. He felt completely isolated now, cut off from the light, air, and the life of Zamork, and already a part of whatever existed on the outside. Rashazzi turned out the light for a second, and a crushing, total darkness added its weight to the silence. As they had guessed, no light showed through the holes from the far side. Rashazzi turned the light on again and continued drilling. Nobody indicated experiencing any ill effects, and when the pressure had fallen to a level where the flow to the outside was diminishing, McCain began using another drill to speed things up. At the joint, the remaining leaks showed as fast, fine jets now, accompanied by faint vaporlike fans where the cooling of rapidly expanding air turned its moisture content into ice. Then Rashazzi pointed to the gauge, made an O with his thumb and forefinger to indicate zero pressure. The others acknowledged that they were okay. Rashazzi nodded, lit the torch, and began cutting away a small rectangle of metal.

When the section broke free, Koh lifted it clear and Scanlon directed one of the inspection lamps outward to reveal a vast, dark void, and on the far side of it an immense gray wall, broken at intervals by vertical supports, rushing past at what Rashazzi and Haber had calculated would be a hundred fifty miles per hour. Rashazzi commenced cutting an enlargement of the hole for them to climb through. Because of the confined space he was only able to cut half the rectangle they needed, and then he passed the torch to McCain to finish it on his side. McCain did so, but the section refused to budge. He looked out through the small hole and found that the piece he had been trying to move was attached to a diagonal rib running across a corner on the outside. He made a new cut following the line of the rib, and the section came free, leaving behind a triangular corner piece. But the hole was large enough for their purpose.

Scanlon leaned out and pointed the lamp sideways, down, and up. McCain peered out with him and found himself staring out of the sheer face of a monstrous precipice of metal. The wall was reinforced by a square grid of heavy stiffening members spaced ten feet or so apart horizontally and vertically, with thinner tension bars running diagonally and crossing at riveted gussets in the centers—one of these diagonals partly crossed the section that McCain had tried to cut first, which was why he had been unable to move it. Rashazzi had estimated that above them this wall would extend at least two hundred fifty feet vertically before it began curving over to form the roof.

Looking down, they were about forty feet above the platform supporting the colony, which, McCain recalled from Rashazzi's sketches, was in the form of a tilted circular track, like the rim of a dinner plate. The wall they were looking out of, however, was straight, cutting across an arc of the platform's circumference like the outer edge of a strip of ribbon laid along the dinner-plate rim—in fact it was one of the long sections connecting the spoke-base zones. Hence the floor at the base of the wall was an exposed part of a circle, with the enclosing tunnel forming the far side and roof. To the left, the floor narrowed toward tunnel-side; immediately below them it was about a hundred feet wide; and to the right it continued to broaden beyond the range of their lamps as the tunnel-side receded. According to Rashazzi's drawings, the exposed arc of floor would reach a maximum width of about two hundred feet at its midpoint.

McCain had to force himself to remember that since the supporting platform was banked at twenty-five degrees and they had emerged at its upper edge, the wall they were looking out of was in reality tilted back from vertical by that amount, with respect to the Earth's surface. But the combination of gravity and centrifugal force generated a "local vertical" within the spinning reference frame of the colony, and that was what the senses responded to— as indeed they had been doing for six months on what was, after all, simply the other side of the same wall.

Scanlon was to lead the first pitch of the climb. He attached one of the lines to a snaplink on his harness, and McCain ran the line around his shoulder and back, bracing himself to be ready should Scanlon fall. Scanlon clipped a satchel to his harness at one hip, one of the drills to the other, then turned around on the edge of the drop and leaned back the length of his arms to inspect the area overhead. Then he selected one of the S hooks, attached a sling to it, and stretched to reach sideways along the outside. One foot remained visible, and the fingers of his other hand curled around the edge of the opening. The foot vanished, then the fingers, and he was gone. Koh stood by, ready to pay out the cable of the drill, and Rashazzi moved into the now-vacated opening to shine a light upward for Scanlon.

The line moved intermittently through McCain's hands and around his body. He could read Scanlon's progress from its motion: stationary while he worked at preparing holds, then moving up onto them, then stopping again to survey the next part. When about twenty-five feet had run out, there was another halt. Then the line went taut, and after a short pause, jerked three times. Scanlon was signaling that he had anchored himself to the structure and wanted to bring McCain up—they had decided to move in short pitches if they found the outside in darkness, to stay within range of each other's lamps. McCain gathered a coil of extra line and the second satchel, and Rashazzi squeezed out of the way to let him move forward. McCain tugged twice on the safety line, and Scanlon drew in the slack from above. Then McCain turned around, grasped the sides of the opening, and backed himself out.

Scanlon's lamp was sending down enough light from above to show the first sling, which he had hung as a stirrup from one of the gussets where the diagonal ribs crossed. McCain leaned sideways as Scanlon had done, leaving one foot in the opening and a hand gripping the edge, and stretched out his other leg to find the stirrup with his foot. He grasped the gusset and pulled himself across, transferring his weight slowly until he could crouch in the stirrup. A moment later Rashazzi reappeared in the opening behind him with another light. Scanlon had drilled a hole into the skin above the crossover and hung the next sling from an eyebolt. A snaplink was also attached to the eyebolt, with the safety line and drill cable running up through it. Scanlon would have placed "runners" like this at intervals as a safeguard. Thus, had he fallen, he would only have dropped through twice his height above his last runner before McCain checked the fall from below. Without threading the line through the runners, he would have dropped through twice his height above McCain before the line tightened.

McCain slipped the lines out of the snaplink—if *he* fell, Scanlon would catch him from above, now—and grasped the higher sling to straighten himself up, which brought his face level with the first of the horizontal ribs. There was a bolt inserted immediately below this rib, attached to a short loop of rope threaded through another snaplink. The end of a longer sling hung down from above the rib. Scanlon must have stood in the sling that McCain was clutching and clipped the loop above it to his waist to hold him while he leaned out around the overhanging rib to attach the sling above. McCain pulled himself up as high as he could using the loop, then stepped out into the long sling, found another one above as he had expected, and moved up to stand on the rib itself, where he could reach the next diagonal crossover. From there the sequence of movements repeated itself. After the next panel, the light from above showed him he was getting close to Scanlon, and one more panel later they were side by side.

Scanlon was standing on a horizontal rib with his harness fastened to two separate bolts. He passed the drill across and McCain took over the lead, now threading the line as Scanlon had done on the previous pitch, since his protection was now from below and no longer from above. The psychological effect was to make him feel less secure, and as soon as he was more than a few feet above Scanlon, he found himself perspiring and breathing heavily. Physically he was beginning to feel the strain, too. The routine became a torment of forcing aching muscles to stretch and pull, fighting to gain every inch of movement against the drag of the suit. Fatigue dulled his mind and sapped his concentration. He placed the next bolt and attached a sling, but even as he began hauling himself up on it, he remembered too late that he hadn't tested it before trusting his weight. The thought had barely formed in his mind when the wall and the surrounding void merged into a blur. There was a sensation of falling, then a jolt as if he were being cut in half, and almost simultaneously he felt a painful blow to his shoulder and a crack on the head that set lights exploding before his eyes . . . and the next he knew, he was hanging limply in his harness against the wall, his ears ringing.

He stirred, and looked about him in a daze. His lamp was hanging a couple of feet below him on the loop of line attached to his harness, still lit. He pulled it in and shone it upward. From him the line went up about five feet to the runner that had caught him, and from there back down past him again to where Scanlon was. So he'd fallen about ten feet. He hung for a few more seconds to regain his breath, then pulled himself back into the nearest sling and climbed laboriously back to the place where he had fallen from. He replaced the bolt that had come out, testing it thoroughly this time, and carried on. And then, when he stretched up to start on the next hole, the drill seized up with a burned-out motor.

They had expected it. The drills were designed to be air-cooled, and hence overheated rapidly in the vacuum. That was why they had brought several spares and why McCain had brought an extra line. He tied the drill and lowered it to Scanlon, who in turn lowered it on down to Rashazzi at the opening. One drill gone in less than fifty feet, McCain reflected as he waited for a tug on the line to tell him that a replacement was ready for him to pull up. They had over two hundred feet to go, and only three more drills. The odds weren't reassuring.

The next drill did even worse. McCain continued to the end of his pitch after the replacement came up, and anchored himself as Scanlon had done; then Scanlon came on up and took the drill to leapfrog as McCain had before and lead the next pitch. He was halfway up it when the second drill burned out. They had planned on getting both of them a full hundred feet above the opening before Rashazzi and Koh moved up to join them—that was how long the rope ladder was. The seriousness of the situation was enough to change that, however, and a series of violent tugs on the line from below told them that Rashazzi wanted them to hold everything right there and to come up himself, now.

A cardinal rule of roped climbing is that only one person moves at a time. Unable to progress farther, Scanlon secured himself where he was above McCain and lowered the auxiliary line again, this time to pull up the coiled rope ladder. Scanlon secured the top of it at the high point where he was, McCain guided the rest down as it unrolled, and Koh climbed right on past him to join Scanlon, carrying one of the remaining two drills, plus some of the extra gas cylinders and bags. Finally Rashazzi came up, similarly loaded. He stopped when he reached McCain, and, standing on the rope ladder, beckoned urgently for McCain to follow what he was doing. Rashazzi pointed at the vent inlets on the drill he had with him, then held the nozzle from one of the gas cylinders close and with his other hand made the motion of opening the valve. McCain understood. Rashazzi was telling him to use the cooling effect of high-pressure gas expanding into a vacuum. Rashazzi jabbed a finger at the wall, then held it up. Cool the drill after every hole. McCain nodded that he understood. Rashazzi resumed climbing, and vanished around the next horizontal rib above.

McCain stayed in that position for some time. When he finally got a signal to follow, he moved quickly on the ladder, past Scanlon, who was still just a short distance above, and on to where Rashazzi and Koh had pushed while Scanlon and McCain rested, a hundred feet or so from the top. And they were still using the third drill. From there Scanlon led off again, and McCain followed through. Only fifty feet to go.

Topmost on the rope once again, McCain anchored himself and took up position with the line around him in preparation to bring Scanlon up. He noticed with a feeling of vague detachment that he seemed to be running in slow motion, like an action replay: leadenly deliberating every movement, and then having to exercise inordinate concentration to execute it. He hung, staring out into the void, and the realization slowly came to him that everything was going to be fine. Not jut fine, but—wonderful! The certainty washed over him in a wave, sweeping away his discomfort and bringing, instead, relief. Suddenly all their worries seemed comical through being so trivial. He began giggling behind his facepiece at the thought. The world was going to be just fine. War? There wasn't going to be a war. . . . He realized that somebody below was trying to pull him off. They were jerking on the line and trying to pull him off. That wasn't very friendly. . . . Why would anybody want to be unfriendly on a day like this? He let the slack of the line fall away from him. Scanlon didn't need the protection, anyway—nobody was going to fall. He hung in his harness, laughing into the dark around him, then singing. "Home, home at Lagrange . . ." The world was beautiful, and everybody in it wonderful. . . .

After that he remembered nothing until a light shone straight into his facepiece from immediately outside, blinding him. Scanlon must have arrived. McCain grinned back into the light and waved.

Scanlon caught McCain's body as it slumped down in the harness, and clipped on an extra sling to hold the inert form fast to the wall. Then he dropped the auxiliary line for the others to send up the ladder, signalling frantically for them to move fast.

CHAPTER FIFTY-THREE

They took Paula down to a room looking out over the main square of Turgenev, where a standard two-way videophone was connected through to Washington via Moscow and the regular international telecommunications system. Olga, Protbornov, and a group of others crowded in to witness the proceedings. A technician in contact with the Russian embassy in Washington on an adjacent panel announced that they were through, and moments later Bernard Foleda, poker-faced, was looking at her from the screen.

" 'Micro,' " he said.

" 'Phone,' " she responded.

There was a short delay. The transmission time to *Tereshkova* was a little over a second each way, the engineers had reminded Paula. Also, Soviet censors would be monitoring the broadcast to delete any undesirable material before it went out, which would introduce an additional short delay—Americans did the same thing on most of their "live" TV shows. Also, of course, it masked the additional turn-around time of the transmission's being sent up from Earth before it was relayed back again.

Foleda nodded. "Glad to see you're looking okay. It's been qute a while. People here were getting worried. There's a lot been going on back here to try and get you out."

"I guessed."

Again there was a delay before the image of Foleda responded. "Do you have any news of Sexton?" He was playing his part straight, not knowing what the score was.

"He's here, and they know I know he's here. I assume you received the previous message that I sent, validation initializer 'Pin.' " That had been the message confirming the presence of the Soviet leaders.

A flicker of genuine surprise crossed Foleda's face. "They've found out about that?"

"I revealed it," Paula told him.

Foleda drew in a long breath, containing his emotions with obvious effort. "Go on," he said curtly.

"You wanted confirmation that the Soviet leaders are really here. The tone of your request implied that if the facts were otherwise, you had reason to believe that the Soviets were intending attack. You suspected that the broadcasts you're receiving might be recordings. Obviously a mistaken impression couldn't be risked. I *know* their leaders are up here, because I'm up here and I've seen them. I sent the 'Pin' message to say so. But I wasn't sure that it would carry enough weight in itself. The accomplices I have here, who helped me operate the channel that we've been communicating over, convinced me that the situation was serious enough to go to the Russians and get them to let me talk direct to you, to do whatever I have to do to make sure there's no misunderstanding." Following cues from one of the Russians across the room, Paula walked across to the window. A technician followed her with a camera. "This is the central square of Turgenev, in *Valentina Tereshkova*," Paula said. "I'm in a building looking down over it. The people you can see down there are waiting for the arrival of the Soviet First Secretary and his party. If you're getting Russian news coverage of this, compare what they're showing yo with what I'm seeing. What I'm offering to do is go down into the square and describe the scene from there as the first Secretary actually arrives. I have approval from the Russian authorities here to talk with some of his party on-camera, if you request it. They're all extremely concerned here."

"If they're so concerned, why don't they let Sexton come on with you?" Foleda asked.

"I tried to get him to do just that, but he refused. He wouldn't cooperate with Russians in any way."

Back across the room, Foleda's face stared out of the videophone screen for a long time, unmoving and unblinking. Paula hadn't said anything about a message giving the laser frequency, and neither had he. That, of course, was still supposed to be a secret. Suddenly, Foleda seemed to arrive at a decision. "Wait," he said. "There are other people that I have to bring in on this." With that he stood up abruptly and disappeared from the picture.

Mutters of approval came from the audience that had been watching from around the room. In the midst of the hubbub, Major Uskayev came in and drew Protbornov over to the window. He pointed down at the far side of the square outside, where two figures were working their way along the edge of the crowd. One was wearing a knee-length tan coat with a black hat; the other had workman's coveralls and a floppy brown peaked cap. Both were carrying long, rolled bundles. They looked casual, but were moving closer to the doors of the garage underneath the air-processing plant. Protbornov pointed them out to Paula. "Those are Earnshaw and Scanlon?" he asked.

She nodded. "Yes, that's them."

"Is their way clear?" Protbornov asked Uskayev.

"Yes, sir. All police have been moved back from that side of the square. The building is cleared but under observation."

"Excellent." Protbornov raised a pair of binoculars and gazed down through them. "My word, what theatricals!" he commented. "One has put on a beard. The other has a beard and spectacles."

"They believe in being thorough," Olga said, next to him.

Paula watched the two figures saunter to the back of the crowd, stand looking around them for a few seconds, and then vanish quickly inside one of the garage doors. For an instant no one was looking at her, and she smiled to herself. "Yes, very thorough," she agreed.

Then, Foleda reappeared and stated that the transmission from *Tereshkova* was being put onto a conference circuit to involve other US officials also. He requested live coverage from the square outside as Paula had offered. Accordingly, she went on down and out of the building with a party that included a number of Russian officers, engineers, and the camera and sound operators. Protbornov, Olga, and the remainder of his group went back upstairs to follow the exchange from the control room that Paula had been taken to on her return from Zamork. A number of screens had been hooked into the conference circuit by the time they arrived. On them, the Russians had so far identified Foleda's chief, Philip Borden, the director of the CIA and his deputy, two senior military assistants to the defense secretary, a White House presidential aide, and several faces from the offices of the Joint Chiefs of Staff. Protbornov was radiating triumph, and Olga looked coolly pleased with herself.

Then a thunderous applause went up from the crowd on the screen showing Paula in the square outside, as the doors at the rear of the terrace in the background opened. The dignitaries who were already gathered parted to make way for the familiar stock figure of First Secretary Vladimir Petrokhov, flanked by his most senior ministers and key Party members. "Describe what's happening now," Foleda said from one of the screens.

"Petrokhov and his group are coming out onto the terrace in front of me now," Paula replied on the other screen.

At that instant one of the engineers at the consoles on the other side of the room looked up sharply. "Laser contact! We're picking up a laser transmission from the roof. Positive acknowledgment from Sokhotsk. It's relaying out to *Tereshkova* now."

"Text?" Protbornov snapped.

"Just a call for acknowledgment, sir, coded 'Tycoon/High from Sexton.' "

Absolute silence descended on the room. Even while the operator was speaking, the signal had been repeated on a portable laser set up by the military inside Anvil two hundred thousand miles away, and transmitted back out in the direction of Earth. Now everything depended on whether the Americans had managed to organize some means of receiving it. Tension mounted as the dialogue between Paula and Foleda, continued on the screens. Then, on the screen showing Foleda, a woman approached him from behind, caught his shoulder, and whispered something urgently in his ear. He promptly excused himself and left. In the Russian command room, the suspense became agonizing. Shortly afterward, Borden was summoned away, too. More minutes of agony dragged by. And then the engineer who had spoken previously shouted out in jubilation, "Acknowledgment! A response is coming in from the Americans, via Anvil!"

"Source identification?" another general, who was with Protbornov, queried.

Another of the engineers consulted readouts and tapped keys. "First report indicates they're using the IROO observatory, sir."

"As we expected," the general said, sounding satisfied.

"Text?" Protbornov called.

"Text from Tycoon reads, 'Sexton/Two from Tycoon/Ball. Signal received. Reading clear. Standing by. Over.' "

"By the czars, we've done it!" Protbornov breathed.

"Response intercepted from Sexton," the first engineer sang out again. "Text reads, 'Consider it imperative that arrival Soviet VIP cadre Mermaid be confirmed. Voluntary cooperation via Soviet TV judged inappropriate. Am occupying position affording direct visual observation Turgenev center. Personal positive identifications confirmed, list of names follows: Petrokhov, Kavansky, Sanyiroky, Vlasov—' "

Whoops and shouts of jubilation broke out all around the command room. Protbornov emitted a loud belly laugh and slapped Olga heartily on the back, causing her to gasp, while the other senior officers crowded round to pump his hand and offer congratulations. Across the room, on the far side of it all, Major Uskayev smiled as he watched on one of the screens the view being picked up through a telescopic lens by one of the KGB teams posted among the roofs surrounding the air-processing-plant building. It showed the hatless head of whoever was wearing the sandy-colored beard—with the heavy-rimmed spectacles and hair tinted to match the beard, it could have been McCain or Scanlon—peering down from behind a cowling at the edge of the roof, then turning to say something, presumably to the one who was operating the laser. Then the head withdrew from view.

"How are we doing here?" Protbornov asked, having moved across the room.

"They're like puppets dancing on our strings," Uskayev said. "And they tried so hard. . . . It's almost possible to feel sorry for them."

Behind the cover of the parapet of the air-processing-plant roof, Peter Sargent unstuck his beard for a second to scratch underneath his chin. A few feet back, sitting comfortably in the recess between a ventilator housing and a stanchion supporting some pipes, Albrecht Haber finished tapping a sequence into the keyboard connected to the laser.

"Bloody stuff makes you itch," Sargent said. "Where did Razz get it—off a horse or something?"

"Who knows?" Haber answered. "That's the last of the names. What do you have now?"

Sargent consulted the list of information that he'd compiled in a notebook. "Ah yes, this should take a while. Ready? Message begins: 'Previously advised data confirmed as follows . . .' " Sargent started working through the list of weapons emplacements that Paula had described before, going into greater detail about how they had been penetrated and reiterating that the weapons didn't exist.

"Let's hope that Protbornov's people leave us alone for a while," Haber said as he worked.

"Oh, I think they will," Sargent replied breezily. He stretched back and looked up at the sky. "As long as we find things to say, we're doing a great job of distracting the opposition for them. That means they'll be perfectly happy to let us stay up here all day if we choose—certainly until their zero hour, anyway. . . . Care to pass the coffee and one of those sandwiches, old chap?"

CHAPTER FIFTY-FOUR

Many airplane pilots have crashed to their deaths singing and laughing in their last moments before losing consciousness. What makes hypoxia, or oxygen starvation, so dangerous is its insidious onset and the delirious sense of euphoria that comes just before total collapse, which makes the victim the least qualified to judge the seriousness of the situation.

McCain felt anything but euphoric when he came round. His head felt as if it had been split with a butcher's cleaver, everything spun nauseatingly, his throat was raw, and his lips stung. He was lying back and being supported, but he couldn't see anything and was aware only of the pressure against his face. He tried to move his arms to push it off, but had no strength. Pressure around his middle forced him to exhale, then release. He breathed in again.

Where was this? Had he been in an accident? . . . The fragments of his mind slowly came back together and started functioning again. He was lying on his back, which meant they were off the wall. The others must have gotten him to the top. He couldn't remember anything of what had happened. Then sudden light blinded him. He tried to turn his head away, but the pressure around his face remained. Someone was shining a lamp in through his facepiece, but the facepiece was being forced down. The urge to struggle welled up, but he didn't have the strength. After a few seconds it subsided, and he lay with his eyes closed.

He understood now. They had turned his oxygen pressure up and were holding his facepiece down against the seal to stop it from being blown off. Everything was starting to feel quite warm and pleasant. He settled back to doze. Somebody struck him a couple of sharp blows on the side of the head. Now someone was pinching his upper arm through his sleeve—with pliers or something. Jesus—it *hurt!* He shook it off angrily . . . but the effort had started him moving again. He felt himself being hauled into a sitting position, and opened his eyes to see just a confusion of shapes, lights, and forms. Dizziness swept over him again, and he fought not to vomit inside his mask. The feeling gradually passed.

Now they were tapping him insistently on the shoulder. He opened his eyes again and saw they were on what looked like the same wall of metal panels contained behind reinforcing girders, except that the pattern was now sloping instead of vertical. It curved over and fell away steeply to the right, but seemed to level out above them to the left, like the ridge of a hill. Ahead, the whole ridge curved up and away. Somebody swung a lamp to illuminate a figure standing in front of him, and McCain caught a glimpse of a roof flying by not far above their heads. The figure—McCain wasn't sure who it was—gestured urgently for him to stand up, and at the same time the two who were supporting him pulled at his arms. They carried him the first few yards with his legs trailing and feet bumping over the metal ribs. Then his legs began working again, feebly at first but improving quickly as blood brought oxygen to his starved muscles.

They continued edging upward to the left as they followed the ridge, and continued crossing its flat top when it leveled out. In the center they came to a ready-made metal walkway, and continued along it without having to step over ribs and gussets every few feet. The tunnel roof curved upward ahead of them as it receded, paralleling the top of the structure they were on—although they had no more uphill work to do, since the geometry ahead became "level" as fast as they moved onto it. Nevertheless, McCain was exhausted and had to be helped all the way. But the two who were supporting him urged him on relentlessly and permitted no rest.

They reached the end of the long section they had been following, which meant they were over Novyi Kazan. Here, unlike the situation inside the colony, the sudden leftward change in direction to the next section was unmasked, although the stretch ahead seemed to continue curving upward. The walkway brought them to the side of a rounded, turretlike structure that was just about in the position of the spoke elevator at the center of Novyi Kazan. They followed around it to the left, and the surface they were on began sloping downward noticeably again, but in the opposite direction from before; this meant that they had crossed over the center of the roof and were approaching the inner edge of the racetrack. A bridge from the turret projected out horizontally, with the colony's inner wall falling away below on the near side. The others sat McCain down at the base of the turret's side and shone their lamps outward.

The chasm facing them was difficult to judge because of the unfamiliar scale of everything and the feebleness of their lamps in the great void of darkness. The outward curve of the ridge-side below them prevented their seeing to the bottom. On the far side, the chasm ended at a sheer wall that moved with the tunnel roof. The wall carried a horizontal groove which the bridge from their side disappeared into. According to Scanlon, the far end of the bridge was supported by a wheeled cradle running on rails. The rails formed a circular track inside the racetrack's nonrotating core—the solid hole in the middle of the empty donut.

Unlike the real *Valentina Tereshkova*, Potemkin—the

replica beneath Siberia—didn't possess a hub. The main reason was the impossibility of engineering a cavern over a mile in diameter with an unsupported roof—as would have been necessary, since spokes connecting a hub to the rim would have swept through that whole volume; another reason was that a hub couldn't have contributed to the deception: it would have had to exhibit reduced gravity, which couldn't be reproduced on Earth. The elevators that departed from the spoke-bases at Turgenev and elsewhere stopped inside turrets protruding above the roof like the one McCain was sitting outside, and then engaged a horizontal drive to travel inward through the bridges—of which there were six in all, one for each spoke. Thus, to return to terra firma, the escapees would have to get across the bridge. However, that promised to be simpler now, with the guards on the inside and them on the outside; furthermore, they could see a railed catwalk running the full length of the outside of the bridge, which they could reach from a steel ladder not far from where they were standing. . . . But making this part of the task easier had been the whole point of breaking through to the outside in the first place, after all—before anyone had known that there wasn't a hub out there to get to.

The others came back to McCain and changed his oxygen bottle and their own for the spares they had brought. Then they climbed the ladder to the catwalk, Scanlon going first, with Rashazzi and Koh still assisting McCain behind. McCain had recovered his senses sufficiently by now to know he'd gone down with hypoxia. Probably the fall that he'd taken earlier had loosened his facepiece or breathing tube. The trouble, he recalled vaguely, was that the physical and mental disablement following acute hypoxia could persist for hours. And he couldn't really remember, he realized, why it was so important for them to get out at all.

As they moved out onto the bridge, they could look down into the chasm and see they were high above an exposed arc of the racetrack platform once again, but

Gondolas
(1) On nternal track
(2) Hauled up guides off track mating with terminal

Tilted platform — "racetrack"

Tunnel Wall

Turret

Escape Route

Side loop

Inner well of gallery

Horizontal Grove — "gallery"

Terminal

Bridge

an inner arc this time, not an outside one as they had looked down over from the wall. Far below, they could make out jumbles of pipework, cabling, and gigantic windings in the space enclosed by the platform, while ahead of them the curve of the wall they were approaching grew more apparent as they got closer. Behind, they could trace out with their lightbeams the full height of the wall enclosing the dummy colony, from its base far below on the supporting racetrack, up through tier after tier of diagonally-crossed square lattice, until it curved to become the flat roof that they had so recently been walking along. Except, it wasn't flat anymore. Looking back along the bridge, they could see its lines to be curved concavely upward; and the farther along it they moved, the more the angle of the far end that they had come from increased. By the time they were almost across the chasm and nearing its inner wall, the distant end of the bridge, and with it the ridgetop that it projected from, had taken on a distinct tilt toward them. What was happening was that since they were moving inward along a radius, the centrifugal force they were experiencing was getting less. This in turn required a progressively smaller banking angle to compensate, and the architecture curved accordingly. Nevertheless, when they entered the groove which they had seen from the far side—now revealed as a deep gallery twenty feet high at least, cut into the cylinder forming the tunnel's inner wall—the floor below and the roof above were still racing by at well over a hundred miles per hour.

Inside this gallery, the bridge ended in a large boxlike construction cluttered with cables, motor housings, and catwalks, supported by a set of wheeled bogies. Scanlon had described this assembly as a "terminal." The bogies ran on four rails, which the escapees could see flashing by below as they reached the end of the bridge and clambered across the outside of the terminal to reach its inward-facing side. Here, a mating port, set above a system of guides and lifting gear, faced another pair of rails that ran alongside the ones the terminal rolled upon, thus tracing a smaller circle inside. The port mated with airtight vehicles called gondolas, which accelerated along the inner track until their speed matched the terminal's—that was how transfers of people and materials in and out of Potemkin were effected. In itself, this arrangement would have permitted the use of one gondola only—obviously, since having more than one speeding up and slowing down on the same track would have been unworkable—and with six terminals to service, would have been inadequate. The problem had been solved by having a gondola, after it had matched speed with a terminal, physically lifted from the track and up onto the guides to mate with the port, which immediately freed the track for other traffic. Similarly, after a gondola had slowed down from Potemkin's speed, it exited from the ring formed by the through-track to come to a halt in a side loop.

With the current level of traffic between the "hub" and rim, the escape party hadn't anticipated difficulty in finding a ride to hitch. Sure enough, the port of the terminal they had arrived at had a gondola already docked. They worked their way over the port and across onto the gondola's roof. After a wait that seemed interminable but in fact had probably been less than ten minutes, the gondola detached from the port. A pair of hydraulic rams pushed it down the guides and set it on the inner track. The rams disengaged, and the entire, uncannily silent rolling assembly of terminal box, port, lifting gear, and bogies moved away into the darkness as the gondola began shedding speed.

Shortly afterward, another, identical terminal appeared from the other direction as the spoke that had been following behind them—the one that connected to Agricultural Station 3, if McCain had been visualizing things correctly in his muddled condition—caught up and then overtook them. The strange thing now was that the whole terminal was tilting down at them. The body of the gondola pivoted about its long axis, McCain realized—like some carnival rides. As the gondola slowed down, its body was returning to Earth's horizontal from the banking angle it had assumed while at the terminal's speed. When the next spoke passed them, moving much faster this time, its tilt was noticeably greater, and the next raced by tipped at what must have been almost the full angle corresponding to terminal-radius speed.

The roof and inner wall of the gallery moved by very slowly in the flashlight beams now. Then the gondola exited into a side tunnel and came to rest at a port similar to the one it had docked with at the terminal, but on the opposite side. While whatever transfer it had come to make was in progress inside, the four men lowered themselves down from its roof. The first thing McCain noticed on regaining his feet, despite his condition, was how light he felt. He looked down and stamped one foot, then the other. It was elating to stand on real, solid ground once again— even Siberian. The others seemed to be having a similar reaction. But there was little time for celebrating just now. The next job was to get out of the vacuum.

This part had been taken care of for them by safety-conscious Soviet design engineers, and involved procedures that Scanlon had been familiarized with during his training after being posted to Potemkin. Maintenance workers sometimes needed to come out and work in the transfer bay where the gondolas docked. Since the bay contained a hard vacuum, that meant putting on suits and going out through airlocks. To prevent anyone's getting trapped out there, the airlocks could be opened from the outside; Scanlon, moreover, knew where they were located and how to open them. The only problem was that opening an airlock would trigger an indicator in the maintenance control room.

Scanlon had selected an airlock situated at a remote end of the transfer bay—unlikely, therefore, to have many people in its vicinity inside. A line of small orange lights in the bay led the party to it, and a larger external light above, showing green, marked its location. Lower down, beside the outer door of the lock, was an illuminated panel with several buttons. Scanlon pressed one of the buttons and the door opened, bathing them in sudden light that dazzled them after the hours of working in blackness. They crowded through, shielding their faces with their hands, and Scanlon used an inner panel to close and pressurize the lock.

Sound!

McCain wanted to shout out with sheer joy and relief as the world of sound re-formed itself around them. There was humming and vibration that seemed like a hurricane, hissing from the air system, rustling and movement from the bodies around him . . . and yelling and laughing! Rashazzi had warned them against the risks of aching ears and sinuses from repressurizing too quickly, but nobody cared. Scanlon pulled away his facepiece, drew in a chestful of air, and whooped. Rashazzi and Koh helped each other, then both of them removed McCain's. The rush of cool, fresh air after hours of claustrophobic confinement made all the more isolating by the silence was overwhelming. He stood and gulped, and sucked it into his lungs.

"Does it taste good?" Rashazzi asked them, grinning.

"It beats even Dublin Guinness," Scanlon sighed, pausing for just a moment.

"Definitely one of life's more . . . memorable moments," Koh said, savoring.

McCain didn't care at the moment whether the Russians appeared or not.

But Scanlon cared. He had already opened the control box of the airlock doors and was detaching a wire that would make it appear that the control-room indicator had been triggered by a fault. Then he opened the inner door. On the far side was an anteroom with rows of steel closets and some seats, and behind that a corridor, many doors, and a steel-railed stairwell visible at the far end beside an elevator.

Scanlon led the way along the corridor to the stairs, hustling the others along after him. They went down a level to an intersection of two more corridors, with a well opening down onto a maze of piping on one side, and then through one of the doors into a cluttered machinery compartment reminiscent of the ones they had known below Zamork. It was warm and smelled oily, and the noise inside sounded to McCain like Niagara. But it was deserted, and it promised rest. . . .

McCain eased himself painfully down against a wall. Rashazzi had already flopped out on an open expanse of floor and was lying with his eyes closed and his mouth wide open gulping in air, but also with a smile of weary triumph on his face. Koh collapsed next to him with a barely audible, grateful moan. Scanlon closed the door quietly, turned on a light, and looked at McCain. "Will you be staying with us in the land of the living for a little longer, then?" he inquired. McCain nodded but didn't reply. "Ah, sure, that's a good thing to be knowing. As the strip dancer said to the reverend's wife . . ."

But McCain had slumped back and was out of it before he heard the rest.

CHAPTER FIFTY-FIVE

Americans sometimes described things as being almost crazy enough to work. And Lt. General Vladimir Fedorov's initial reaction to the proposal for replicating a two-kilometer-diameter space colony underground and using it as the basis of such a deception had certainly been that it was crazy. In fact, that was the one time when he'd found himself wondering if the leaders of his country had gone collectively insane, and had seriously contemplated defecting to the West. Now, as he stood with his adjutant, Colonel Menikin, and several aides, watching the activity in the mess area of B Block, after two years as the governor of Zamork, he had to admit that it all seemed to have been sufficiently crazy to have worked.

The atmosphere was abuzz with excited murmurings as guards shepherded the prisoners out of the billets and down from the upper level to be formed into ranks for general assembly on the mess-area floor. Work assignments had been canceled, and more prisoners were coming in from the compound, Gorky Street, and the Core. There were rumors of mass amnesties about to be announced, that the Moscow government had fallen, and that war had broken out back on Earth. One squad of guards was particularly busy in billet B-3, which had been cleared out. Outside its door the block commandant, Major Bachayvin, and several officers were talking with the block supervisor, Supeyev, and the billet foreman, Luchenko.

Zamork had served its purpose. The things that mattered now were happening outside its boundaries, and whichever way the outcome of it all went, the charade inside was over. It was time to reestablish proper discipline and security, and to commence sorting out form the individuals who had been brought here as inmates those who showed the most promise and willingness to be useful in the new era of the regime. Fedorov wondered what kind of place the new era would have for him.

A communicator beeped on the belt of one of the aides standing near him. The aide answered it, listened for a moment, and passed the unit to Colonel Minikin. "From Colonel Gadzhovsky, sir."

"Very good," Menikin acknowledged. Gadzhovsky was in command of the guard detail that had been sent to open up the supposedly secret workshop that the prisoners had set up in the machinery deck below. Menikin talked to Gadzhovsky, then reported to Fedorov. "Three prisoners were apprehended down there, all members of McCain's billet: the Zigandan Mungabo, the Pole Borowski, and the Buryat. They're being brought up now."

Fedorov nodded. "Good. You'd better go and inform Major Bachayvin." He watched as Menikin walked over and said something to the group outside the door of billet B-3. Then his brow furrowed. Bachayvin, Supeyev, and Luchenko were gesticulating vigorously as they answered, and seemed agitated. A few moments later, a foreman from one of the upper-level billets came hurrying across the floor, went over to join them, and started saying something to Supeyev. Fedorov cast a general eye around the rest of the mess area, and when he looked back again, Menikin, Bachayvin, and Supeyev were coming toward him. The expressions on their faces gave him his first inkling that something was wrong.

"There are still three prisoners from B-three unaccounted for," Menikin said. He looked inquiringly at Supeyev.

"The two scientists, Rashazzi and Haber, and the Asiatic, Nakajima-Lin," Supeyev said. "Also the Englishman, Sargent, is not present with the contingent from B-twelve."

Fedorov frowned uncertainly. "They can't be out in the colony somewhere. We've been covering their access to the freight line at all times. They must be loose somewhere down in that machinery deck." He turned to Menikin. "Have Gadzhovsky seal all exits down there, and send Major Kavolev down with his men to help with a search. The whole place is to be combed—every inch of it."

"Yes, sir." Menikin took his own communicator, contacted Gadzhovsky again, and began speaking.

"I never did like this policy of relying on informers to tell us what was going on down there," Fedorov growled to Bachayvin. "The whole place should have been wired so tight that a bug couldn't have moved without our knowing."

"But if the prisoners had discovered it, sir? . . ."

"Bah! It could have been done invisibly. Everyone must take risks sometimes."

Menikin looked up from the communicator to interrupt. He looked concerned. "There's more from Major Gadzhovsky."

"Well?"

"We know now why Istamel failed to report in on time. He's just been found unconscious in the elevator shaft. They're taking him to the infirmary now. There as a piece of broken rope near him. The three prisoners who were detained down there say that he fell, and that they were on their way up to report it."

"Any sign yet of the four others who are missing?"

"Negative, sir."

Fedorov didn't like it. He turned away and stared morosely out at the lines of prisoners and guard details now coming to order. If he waited a few more minutes and the four were found, nothing more would come of it. But if he delayed and they weren't found, the consequences for him would be worse. Such was the justice of life that withholders of bad news could lose their heads just as easily as the bearers. Americans called it "Catch-22" for some reason he'd never understood.

He turned back toward Colonel Minikin. "Call General Protbornov's office in Turgenev," he ordered.

CHAPTER FIFTY-SIX

The human body is a continuous liquid system. Blood must flow to and from every part of it to bring oxygen to its cells and remove the waste products of metabolism from them, and the intercellular volume supporting this flow is connected throughout. Hence, if pressure differences exist between parts of the body, blood, like any other fluid, will migrate from high-pressure regions to lower-pressure ones, and the delicate skin capillaries will rupture if the pressure across them exceeds their strength.

When, after resting for some time in the machinery compartment, the four escapees cut and peeled away the survival skins they had used to make the crossing through the vacuum, they found their bodies covered with long, painfully swollen, black and purple weals. The worst were around their waists and major limb joints. Inevitably, the stretching and exertion of climbing the first wall had opened cracks in their suiting despite the improvised seals, into which the flesh had literally been sucked in elongated blood blisters that only the inner clothing had contained. The middle of Rashazzi's back looked as if it had been beaten with a rubber hose, Scanlon's left wrist was swollen into a balloon that practically immobilized the hand, and Koh had the same trouble with an elbow and a knee. Between them, a pretty sorry team, all in all, McCain thought. In addition to a collection of blemishes pretty much the same as the others', he had two hideous black eyes.

"I feel like I've been breathing powdered glass," he said as they sat cleaning the worst of the goo from themselves and putting on the clothes they had brought to change into. "What happened back there?"

"Your face seal had been knocked crooked on one side and had started leaking," Rashazzi told him. "I had to lift part of it away briefly to fix it."

"You mean my whole face was open?"

"Yes . . ."

"Holy shit!"

"For about five seconds, maybe. The reason you feel all dried up is that gas and moisture poured out of your lungs and mucous tissues into the vacuum. It's possible that the evaporative cooling caused ice to form on your tongue."

"It feels like I've been eating ashes."

"Be thankful it's us and not you who have to look at that face of yours," Scanlon said. "You look like me uncle Mick, the morning after a night out enjoying himself."

"Be thankful there aren't any gas pockets behind the eyes," Rashazzi said matter-of-factly. "Otherwise they'd have blown out like champagne corks."

Scanlon had stayed by the door to peep out from time to time, but had seen no signs of excitement or searching. They concluded, therefore, that if the opening of the airlock had triggered an indicator, either it hadn't been noticed, or it hadn't been deemed serious enough to investigate yet, or it had been put down to a wiring fault as they'd intended. Whichever, it seemed they were in no immediate danger. But they had far from unlimited time.

McCain winced as he stretched an arm up into the sleeve of the baggy gray sweater that he'd unrolled. "So what are the possibilities now?" he said to the company in general. "Where do we go from here?" He pulled the sweater down over himself and pushed his head through. "Which one said that—the bishop to the barmaid?"

"Do we all feel up to surprising a guardpost full of KGB and overpowering them, stealing their uniforms, and bluffing our way through in disguise?" Scanlon asked. The looks from the others answered the question and said they weren't in a mood for Irish humor just then.

"How far above us is Sokhotsk?" McCain asked.

"We're under a range of hills to the northwest," Scanlon answered. "Elevator systems from here go up five hundred feet to Potemkin's transportation and control center. From there, Sokhotsk is about three miles away, connected by a road and rail tunnel. The tunnel comes out in a staging area below the main Sokhotsk administrative complex."

"Which is presumably in a high-security area," Rashazzi said.

"The whole place is a high-security area," Scanlon replied.

"Against outside penetration, anyhow?" Rashazzi suggested. "But in a way, we're already on the inside."

"It doesn't make any difference," Scanlon said. For once he sounded pessimistic. "The security is as strict every way. Let's face it, getting into Sokhotsk isn't going to be a piece of cake by anybody's definition."

There was a glum silence. Then McCain said, "What about the rest? You said something about mining and some kind of industrial center."

"Scientists, VIPs, and the like—small numbers of people—they come and go through Sokhotsk," Scanlon said. "But building and operating Potemkin meant moving materials and people on a scale that would never be seen going in and out of a research establishment. So some industry was sited nearby as a cover. There's a bauxite-mining operation on the other side of the hills from Sokhotsk, and an aluminum-smelting plant and rolling mill at a new town called Nizhni Zaliski, about five miles away from it—places where trains and trucks don't attract attention."

That sounded closer to what McCain had in mind. "So Potemkin, the place we're at, connects to the mining operation, and to Sokhotsk," he concluded.

"That's right," Scanlon said. "But the mining side doesn't connect direct to Sokhotsk. The only way into Sokhotsk is from where we are, and getting in will be the devil of a job that I'm already after telling you."

"Hmm . . ." McCain sat back, rubbing his chin.

"What about other ways in?" Rashazzi asked Scanlon. "Pipes, ducts, drains . . . How tight is the protection on things like that?"

"As tight as the arse on a fish, and that's watertight," Scanlon said.

McCain finished dressing. He tried stooping to pull on the canvas shoes that he'd brought, but the soreness around his waist prevented him from bending. Rashazzi put them on and laced them for him. "Well, that's just great, Kev," McCain couldn't stop himself from saying. "Why couldn't you have thought of all that before we bothered coming this far?"

"There wasn't a hell of a lot of time for speculating, for one thing, if you remember," Scanlon said. "And for another, I assumed your interests would lie in getting away from the Russians—it never occurred to me that anyone would want to get closer to them. And for another, if you want me to be honest, I never thought we'd make it this far."

Koh had been sitting quietly and staring into space while he listened. When silence fell again, he remarked, "You know, the deviousness of the Western mind will never cease to mystify me. Why do you always look for the most difficult way of doing everything? Does it have something to do with inscrutable Puritans and their unfathomable work ethic?"

"What are you talking about?" McCain asked.

"Why do you imagine that you must get into Sokhotsk?"

McCain looked nonplussed for a moment, then shrugged as if dismissing the obvious. "There might be a war about to start out there. We know something that nobody else on our side knows, which might be vital. We have to try to communicate that information back if there's any possibility at all for doing so, no matter how slim the chances."

Koh looked back unblinkingly in a way which said that whatever was obvious to McCain wasn't obvious at all to him. "Well?"

McCain shrugged again, started to speak, then looked at Rashazzi. "It is a communications establishment," Rashazzi said. "We're in the middle of Siberia, and we need to communicate with the West." He spread his hands briefly, in the manner of a person not wishing to offend someone who was being obtuse. "We'll need access to the kind of equipment that's inside Sokhotsk."

Koh looked unimpressed. "And what will you do with it?" he asked. "Could any of you operate sophisticated Russian equipment that you haven't been trained to use, even if you knew the right access codes? I certainly couldn't. So what else do you think we'll do—sneak in somehow, just happen to find somebody who knows how everything works, hold a gun to his head, and make him do as we say?"

"Maybe," McCain mumbled, taken aback slightly by the realization that he hadn't thought it through. "Who knows?"

Koh snorted. "Very derring-do. And the type of people you'll find in there will probably tell you to go ahead and shoot. So what good would it do?"

Koh was right, but McCain couldn't let himself concede defeat now. "We won't know until we get in there." He sat back wearily against the wall. "Like I said, however slim the chances . . ."

"Zero is a pretty slim number," Koh agreed. "Taking on those chances would be the same as throwing your vital information away."

"What else can we do?" Rashazzi asked. "We can't just sit here without trying anything."

"Why do you insist that you have to use sophisticated equipment in a top-security Soviet research establishment at all?" Koh asked. "What's wrong with simply picking up a phone?" The others all started to speak, then stopped again at the same instant. They looked at each other, each waiting for one of the other two to tell Koh why it was crazy. "Scientists!" Koh sighed, shook his head, and continued looking distant while he waited for them to get there in their own time.

"What phone?" Scanlon asked at last.

"You're all asking how to get *into* Sokhotsk," Koh said. "I'm saying let's thing about going the other way. You said this place connects out through the bauxite-mining complex to Nizhni Zaliski, an industrial town. Well, a town ought to have phones in it. And very possibly the freight going out that way isn't checked as thoroughly as anything going into a place like Sokhotsk. If anything's worth a try, surely this is."

The others exchanged looks again, but with more interest this time. "You know, it might just be crazy enough to work," McCain murmured, half to himself.

Scanlon had steepled his hands in front of his nose and was staring wide-eyed over them, thinking furiously all of a sudden. He stood up, walked a few paces stiffly toward the far wall, then turned to face the others again. "The containers," he said. "All those containers full of soil that have been coming down the spokes . . . they're the kind that deep-space transporters use—designed for automatic handling. That means they probably came in by rail through Nizhni Zaliski to the transportation center upstairs, and were offloaded into the elevators, transferred via the gondolas, and sent down the spokes without any unloading."

"So?" McCain asked.

"They'll be going back the same way, empty," Scanlon said. "They're probably still going back now, because there were a lot of them. And if I'm right in what I'm thinking, I know where they'll be collected together to go onto the trains. If we could get into one of those, we might find ourselves with a clear run out to Nizhni Zaliski. . . . Koh's right. We were all talking about going the wrong way."

McCain was frowning, however, as he considered the implications. "What's up, Lew?" Rashazzi asked. "Is there something wrong with it?"

"Not as far as it goes," McCain said. "But what then? Okay, so we find a phone. Exactly who are we intending to call with it? An international call to Washington— from here, at a time like this? No way. What else is there? The US embassy? Sure, they're in radio contact with Washington all the time, but what about a line to their number in Moscow? Don't tell me the KGB won't be monitoring it twenty-four hours a day. We'd never get through, and we'd be picked up in minutes."

Scanlon nodded resignedly. "Lew's right."

"We call my cousin in Moscow," Koh said simply. "The KGB aren't interested in his number."

McCain blinked. "Who?"

"My cousin—the one who has the restaurant franchise in Moscow. I told you about him once. He's only a fifteen-minute walk from the American embassy. I'll call him, and he can go there and tell them whatever you want him to say."

For several seconds there was one of those sudden silences that descends when everybody realizes that there's nothing left to say. McCain stared at Koh disbelievingly, and shook his head—but still couldn't fault it. They got up and gathered together the rest of the things that were worth taking. Then Scanlon turned off the light, opened the door a fraction, and brought an eye close to the crack. "It looks clear," he hissed. "Lew and I'll go first. The other two of you follow when we've made it to the top of those stairs."

"Then, let's go," McCain said.

"Just a minute," Rashazzi's voice whispered from the shadows behind.

McCain turned his head. "What?"

"I don't have any money for the phone. Does anyone else?"

"Holy Mother of God," Scanlon breathed disbelievingly.

"Scientists!" Koh muttered at the rear.

"Razz, let's worry about that after we get out of this goddam place," McCain groaned tiredly.

CHAPTER FIFTY-SEVEN

President Warren Austin of the United States stood in the center of the Pentagon War Room floor, looking grimly up at the situation displays. General Snell, other senior officers of the Joint Chiefs of Staff, and advisers watched from one side as Borden summarized the latest analysis. "What it boils down to is that our agents there are telling us it's not a weapons platform and that the top Soviet leaders are arriving, and at the same time not to believe what they're telling us—Pangolin and the sender designating himself Sexton have both returned incorrect validation codes."

Defense Secretary Robert Uhl, who had only recently arrived, shook his head and hesitated. Nothing was making any sense. He gestured at one of the screens monitoring the Soviet TV connection from Paula, who at that moment was talking to others in another part of the Pentagon. "How can they be telling us not to believe what they're saying? They're telling us they're up there where the Russian leaders are, and we can see it with our own eyes."

"We think it could be for the Russians' benefit rather than ours," Foleda said from beside Borden. "Somehow they're controlling all the communications, in and out. Sexton—if it is Sexton—seems to be letting them hear what they want to hear."

"But how could it not mean what it says when we can see that what it's saying is right?" Uhl asked again.

"Could that TV transmission with the woman in it be recorded?" an aide asked.

Somebody else shook his head. "No. 'We're interacting with her live."

"So what does it mean?" Uhl asked.

Borden could only shake his head. "We don't know. There are all kinds of theories . . ."

"Theories!" Uhl snorted and turned away, rubbing his hands together nervously.

The President stared up at the displays again. "If Mermaid is a weapons platform as we've been fearing, its mission will be to take out our spacebased systems from long range in an opening strike," he said slowly. "That would deprive us of two things: our Starshield defense against a strategic attack down on the surface, and our ability to knock out their shield. Agreed?"

"That's the way we see it," General Snell confirmed. In other words, the Soviets would be able to launch virtually unopposed from behind a now-immune defensive screen that would reduce any retaliatory strike from the West down to ineffective proportions.

"Would we accept the odds under those conditions, or would we back down without a fight?" Austin asked. "Could that have been their aim all along?"

"It would make a lot of sense," Uhl agreed. Who wouldn't have liked an intact global economy to dictate terms to, rather than a mess that would take fifty years to rebuild?

Austin paced a yard or two with his hands clasped behind him. "So what are our options?" he asked the room in general.

"Well, as long as those Soviet leaders are walking around out in the towns up there, they're vulnerable," Snell said. True, US weapons firing from Earth orbit could blow away the roof and wipe out everybody unprotected, even if they couldn't damage hardened weapons emplacements. But this was really ruling out an option rather than offering one. It would be unacceptable morally to resort to anything that drastic purely as a precautionary measure—and the consequences if the fears subsequently turned out to be unfounded would be unthinkable. As a retaliation, yes. But the problem there was that if the fears were well grounded and *Tereshkova* was permitted to fire its weaponry first, the US would have nothing left to retaliate with.

Uhl chewed unhappily on his lip for a moment. "I wish I had something else to offer, but I don't. I have to agree with the intelligence people." He glanced quickly in Borden and Foleda's direction. "We eliminate part of Mermaid's advantage by a preemptive strike against the Soviet shield, and hope we can take out a large part of it before Mermaid replies. That would leave them exposed—partially, anyhow—to our missiles. Then, after Mermaid takes out our shield—which we can't stop it from doing, anyway— we'd be left set for a slugging match, eighties-style."

"In that case, they might end up being the ones who back down," somebody suggested.

Snell shook his head. "They'd still have the edge. Besides, they're desperate; we're not. Time isn't on their side."

Uhl accepted the statement with a heavy nod. "What about the UN ship?" he asked, looking at the President. "There's still time to try and get it diverted."

Austin thought for a while. "I'm not sure we should try," he said at length. "If we're likely to end up depending on surprise, it might be the wrong thing to do. The Soviets would be alerted through their UN people." Snell nodded his agreement without saying anything. "I'm afraid they'll have to take their chances with everyone else," Austin said. He turned to take in the whole of the waiting assembly. "We go to General Readiness Orange, and Red Standby One for the spacebased orbital systems. Send it out right away. And find out how we're doing with that conference hookup to the Europeans."

CHAPTER FIFTY-EIGHT

"Yes, hello? This is the Tunguska Cement Works. . . . Comrade Gorzchenko? One moment." Mariana Porechny plugged a line into a socket on the switchboard in front of her and keyed in an extension number. "So I told her not to be stupid," she continued saying to Eugenia, her only companion in the exchange. "If you can't keep your boy from climbing over fences, I said, it's not my fault if he goes and cuts his leg. I mean, the nerve of the woman—complaining about us leaving *our* tools out in our *own* yard. You'd think it was your job to mind everybody else from their own stupidity, wouldn't you. And it's not as if it was the first time, either. And her husband's always blocking our gate in that wreck they drive around in. And then there was the time when— No, he isn't answering. . . . The works manager? Wait, I'll try it. . . ."

"I tried to call my son in Moscow yesterday," Eugenia said distantly. "He said it's like a graveyard there. They're having rallies outside the city this year because there's no parade. The funny thing is, he said they were on alert for civil-defense drill. Did you ever hear of anything like that before? It gets worse. What a thing to go and do on a holiday. I sometimes think they haven't got anything worthwhile to do at all—any of them."

"Nasty kids they've got—especially him, that one. That day there was paint all over our window and down the wall, they tried to say it was the two little Bryokov boys from round the corner—and they're no angels, mind—but I knew straightaway it was them. I even saw the tin—it was the one her creepy-crawly husband had the day before, when he painted their door. A real mess he made of it, too. You've never seen such an ugly color. Kind of purple, like the stuff that tart across the street plasters all round her eyes when she goes out, wobbling along on those heels with her skirt up the top of her legs—you can tell she's up to no good. And do you know what time she comes prancing back, brassy as you please? And then her mother told me one day— Hello? The general manager? . . . Well, that's not my fault, is it? . . . Yes, wait a minute. I'll try it. . . . No patience, some people. They're the kind who make the world what it is—never a good word to say for anyone. I can't understand them at all."

"He sounded as if he'd caught a cold," Eugenia said absently.

Neither of them noticed the door inching inward until it opened all the way suddenly. A tall, heftily built man in a gray sweater, followed instantly by another one, scrawnier, with bulging eyes, came though so swiftly that the two women found hands clamped over their mouths before they'd had a chance to react or make a sound. Another man, younger than the other two, and swarthy-skinned, with wavy black hair—definitely a killer, from the intense look in his eyes—moved in between them and the switchboard, while a fourth closed the door softly and bolted it.

Mariana quivered with terror. The four intruders looked mean and desperate, with blotchy, unshaven faces, disheveled hair, and scruffy, grease-stained clothes— escaped convicts if she'd ever seen one. The face of the man staring down at her was grotesque: wild eyes staring from a mask of bloated purple. Psychotic murderers were often physically deformed or mutilated, and they killed compulsively to get revenge on the society they felt rejected by—she'd read it in a magazine somewhere. Eugenia had slumped over in her chair and seemed to be in a swoon. The man at the door turned, revealing cruel, slant-eyed, Oriental features. That meant for a certainty they'd be raped. Mariana's chest pounded, and every reflex drove her to struggle and scream in mindless panic. But the two killers were holding her so tightly that she couldn't move, and the hand over her mouth stifled her shouting.

"We don't want to hurt you," the big man said slowly. His voice had a foreign accent. "There's no need to be afraid. All we need is your cooperation. Nod your head if you understand me." They held her until her strength was exhausted. "There is no danger. Do you understand?" At last the meaning sank in. She nodded her head twice. "I'm going to let go so that you can breathe. Please do not make any noise."

The hand on her mouth loosened, and she gasped in air gratefully. The hand drew away. "Who are you?" she asked fearfully. "What do you want?"

The Oriental wrote something on her notepad and pushed it across the console. "Merely your help, if you would be so kind, madam," he said. "Please call that number in Moscow for us. It is extremely urgent."

"That's all?"

"Please. It is urgent."

Mariana nodded. She indicated a handset on the console, and the Oriental picked it up. Then she looked at the notebook and keyed in the number with trembling fingers. It rang for four or five seconds. Then a voice answered, "Willow Garden restaurant."

"I—I have a call for you," Mariana said in a shaking voice. The Oriental began chattering excitedly in a strange tongue. It sounded to Mariana like an obscure dialect of Chinese.

General Snell listened while the two Defense Department scientists explained the figures being displayed on one of the War Room consoles. Snell nodded, and turned back to the President and his group. "The next thirty minutes will be the crucial period. Three of our biggest space lasers will come out from eclipse behind Earth during that time. If Mermaid is going to take out our system with a surprise strike, it will be in that time frame." Austin nodded somberly.

"We have to go for the Soviet shield, now," Uhl implored. "Okay, so it's an act of war. But if that colony really is clean, they should have been open about it from the beginning. If it isn't clean, we've got a good reason. The world will understand that."

"If it leads to an all-out exchange, the world will

remember that it was us who struck first. Will it understand that?" Austin asked.

"They haven't left us with a choice," Uhl said. "It wouldn't be striking first. It would simply be getting us back toward more of a balance. We hold right there. The next step would be up to them."

"God, I don't know . . ." Austin stared up at the situation displays again.

On one side of the room, an aide approached Foleda, who was standing with Borden. "You have an urgent call from your office," he said in a low voice.

"Where do I take it?" Foleda asked.

"Follow me." The aide led Foleda into a side room, packed with consoles and operators, off the central floor near the main door. Barbara's face was waiting on one of the screens.

"What is it?" Foleda asked.

"A call's come in for you from the Moscow embassy. It—"

"At a time like this?" For an instant Foleda had trouble keeping his voice down. "What do they want, for chrissakes?"

"Apparently somebody who runs a Japanese restaurant there walked in off the street and said he got a phone call from Siberia . . ." Barbara's voice faltered at the look on Foleda's face.

"Are you serious? We've got a war about to—"

"The call was to 'Tycoon/Shot/Line/Rise/Glove' from Sexton."

Foleda blinked, frowned, and shook his head bemusedly. "Those codes check?"

"All of them. 'Glove' is Sexton's exceptional-status verifier."

"From Siberia? How the hell can he be calling from Siberia?"

"You'd better hear the text. . . ."

Footsteps pounded in the corridor outside Lt. General Fedorov's office in the administrative sector of Zamork.

Moments later, a major strode in, followed by several guards who between them were hustling the three prisoners Mungabo, Borowski, and the unpronounceable Asiatic. "Block Supervisor Supeyev and Foreman Lunchenko are here also," the major reported.

Fedorov gave a curt nod. "Have them wait outside." He licked his lips nervously and surveyed the three prisoners as they were lined up before his desk. They stared back at him impassively. "This is urgent, and I have no time for politeness," he said. "You understand? The Turk, Istamel, who was taken to the infirmary." There was no response. "You know who I'm talking about?" he demanded in a louder voice.

The major punched Mungabo in the stomach. "Yes, sir," Mungabo wheezed.

"Then say so when I ask you," Fedorov shouted at him. "The doctor says he has no broken bones, no bruises, and shows no signs of having fallen. He does show symptoms of being drugged. What do you know about this?"

"Nothing . . . sir," Mungabo replied. The major drew back his fist. Mungabo braced himself.

Then a tone sounded from the terminal next to Colonel Menikin, who was looking on. Fedorov held up a hand and turned to watch while Menikin took the call. It was from Major Gadzhovsky, who was commanding the search of the lower levels. Alarm was showing on his face. "Yes?" Menikin snapped at the screen.

"Still no sign of the four missing prisoners," Gadzhovsky reported. "But we have found an additional hole cut through into the public levels below Zamork. Major Kavolev and his section have already left and are on their way down there now. Also, we can find no trace of the escape suits that the prisoners are known to have been manufacturing." Istamel had been keeping the Russians updated on the progress of the suits. Since the proposed date for the prisoners' ridiculous intended attempt at breaking out had been given by Istamel as weeks after November 7, the authorities had seen no harm in allowing them to carry on distracting themselves with the idea.

Menikin swallowed hard and flashed an apprehensive glance at Fedorov. "They can't have done anything with them," he protested. "They haven't even begun work on an airlock." Just then, another call came in on an adjacent screen. "It's Kavolev," Menikin said.

"Major Kavolev reporting from Level Four-H in the public sector. We've discovered an engineers' store that's been broken into. I'm having the engineering supervisor brought here to give us a list of what has been taken. From a screenview of the interior that we sent him, he says there's an acetylene torch missing and a number of gas cylinders."

There was a long silence when Kavolev had finished. "We just collect things," Mungabo offered, and shrugged.

The color was draining from Fedorov's face. "Get me a line to Turgenev," he said in a suddenly weak voice.

The senior Russian leaders had withdrawn, and the speeches being given now were from secondary officials. The crowd had thinned somewhat. On the roof of the air-processing plant above the square, Albrecht Haber sat forward suddenly and gave the laser terminal a couple of raps. Then he picked it up and shook it. "Something wrong?" Peter Sargent asked from his vantage point by the edge.

"The screen just went blank. I don't think we're getting anything."

"Oh-oh. Do you think it spells trouble?"

"I'm not sure." Haber tried tapping in some test codes, and fiddled with a control. "It's dead. I suspect they've cut us off."

Sargent looked out over Haber's head, and his eyes took on a sober expression. "Yes, you're right. I rather think the show's over, old boy."

Haber looked up, and Sargent nodded to indicate the direction behind him. Several figures in KGB uniforms were scrambling frantically across the rooftop toward them. "So it would appear," Haber agreed, nodding. "I would say that we put on an acceptable performance, wouldn't you?"

"Absolutely. I see no bouquets, though. But we should go out in style nevertheless, don't you think?"

Haber nodded solemnly. "Yes indeed," he agreed. "In a manner that befits gentlemen of the acting profession."

So saying, the German and the Englishman stood up in full view to face the windows of the Government Building opposite. They took off their beards and hats, and extending their arms wide, bowed as if acknowledging applause. They were still taking encores when the first KGB arrived and dragged them away out of sight.

Confusion had taken over the command center in the Government Building. One of the console operators was yelling something, Uskayev was trying to make sense out of what the KGB squad commander was saying via a handpad from the rooftop opposite, and Fedorov was babbling something else from Zamork. What was clear was that the faces of the two men being held up on the roof were not those of Scanlon and McCain. Major Uskayev used another screen to call up shots of the prisoners who had been reported missing. "The German, Haber, is one," he announced. "The other is Sargent."

Protbornov was wearing the expression of a skydiver who had just realized he'd forgotten something important before he jumped. On another screen to the side, Fedorov at Zamork waited for orders but was now forgotten. "What . . . What does this mean?" Protbornov choked. "Where is the American? If those two have returned wrong codes . . ."

Olga was gaping, horrified, as she took in what it meant. The color drained from her cheeks, and her face became a strained, pallid mask of wax. She turned her head slowly and found Paula watching her with a quiet, satisfied expression. "You betrayed me!" Olga whispered.

Paula almost burst out laughing. "*Me?* You wanted me to try to stop a war. Well, that's what I've been doing—

what *you* wanted, in *your* way. So screw you, too, lady."

Total shock had seized the room. Seconds ticked by with nobody speaking or moving. Protbornov stared fixedly ahead of him, heedless of his surroundings as the full enormity of the catastrophe unfolded. In the background, the faces on the screens continued making noises but were no longer saying anything.

Then the shrill tone of a priority call broke the silence. Major Uskayev answered it woodenly. It was from the duty controller in the Strategic Headquarters located beneath the Government Building, which was where the Soviet leaders had withdrawn to direct the forthcoming operations. He looked dazed. "Please advise General Protbornov that American battle lasers have just fired without warning on our spacebased missile defenses," the controller said. "The whole shield has been crippled."

"Down below, inside Strategic Headquarters, the First Secretary of the Communist Party and his immediate circle were staring dumbfounded at a message appearing on one of the main display screens. It had started coming in over a priority link from Moscow just as the Soviet supreme commander was about to send the order for Anvil to commence return-fire.

The message, signed by President Warren Austin of the United States and endorsed by all the Western European and East Asian premiers, was addressed to the First Secretary personally. But instead of being addressed to him at the *Valentina Tereshkova* space colony, it was addressed to him at "Potemkin, Ground Zero," and specified correctly the latitude and longitude coordinates of the replica beneath Siberia.

The West, the message said, had retargeted three thousand of its strategic warheads on those coordinates. The final move of the endgame was up to him.

EPILOGUE

"Good evening, Mr. McCain."

"Hi, Jerry. That light seems to be fine."

"Yes, the maintenance man said it should be okay now. Your cab's waiting out front." Jerry took in the dark suit, crisp white shirt, and tie with jeweled clip beneath the overcoat as McCain crossed the rooftop lobby to the main doors. "Going to a party tonight?"

"No, just a quiet dinner with an old friend."

"Have a nice evening."

"I'll try."

McCain went out and found the cab waiting on the pad in front of the doors. "Is it the Milburn Towers, sir?" the cabbie checked as McCain climbed in.

"That's right. We've plenty of time." The engine note rose, and McCain settled back in the comfortable leather upholstery of the rear seat. Moments later, the brightly lit roof of the apartment building with its garden and pool was falling away below. Lights were coming on in the twilight, and as the cab's nose swung around, the glow of the Washington, D.C., area moved into the frame of the windshield against the darker sky on the horizon to the east.

So, the war that would end wars had done precisely that—by never happening. With an entire strategic arsenal ready to rain down on the very point where they had concentrated everyone they had judged as worth the most to preserve—including themselves—what else could the Soviet leaders have done but capitulate? The hills overhead would have made little difference to the size of the hole that would have been made in Siberia.

Thus in a position to dictate terms, the West had obtained a reconnection to its agents and allies inside Potemkin, and used them to ensure that the Soviets stayed put while an international inspection force was dispatched to *Valentina Tereshkova*. What they found there, with the world looking on, was enough to topple the Soviet empire, and a modern democratic state eventually emerged from the ensuing internal chaos. Some observers described the process as "1917 played backward."

It was November 7 again, and on that date McCain usually found his mind going back to the events that had culminated on that day in 2017. It was customary when thinking over things like that to say that it didn't seem like ten years, he reflected as he looked up through the cab roof at the stars that were starting to come out—some of them were the artificial worlds being built out there, which at certain times were visible to the eye; he'd seen all he wanted to of artificial worlds and was content to make the best of the real one. But the truth was, it did seem like ten years. A lot of things had happened in that time.

With the big standoff between the giants at last resolved, the world had been left with little more than local squabbles and police actions to occupy its military minds while it completed its process of growing up. Defense institutions had shrunk accordingly, and the release of creativity and resources from all nations into more productive enterprises had made visible already the beginnings of a social and economic upheaval that promised to dwarf the Agricultural, Industrial, and Information Revolutions put together. The human race would soon explode outward across the Solar System. Real colonies were taking shape in the Earth-Moon vicinity now—in fact, the interior of *Valentina Tereshkova* had been rebuilt, and it was now one of them. There was a permanent base on Mars, which was mushrooming as new arrivals poured in. Gigantic manned ships for voyaging to the outer planets were under construction in lunar orbit, and robot starprobes were at the design stage. And the underground space colony that had been called Potemkin was still there and working underneath Siberia, as a familiarization and training simulator for would-be colonists. Earth's population was plateauing out; that of the Solar System, the experts said, was about to take off. The late twentieth century of McCain's boyhood, with its endless pessimisms about imminent doom and declining everything, seemed a long way away.

The cab joined one of the traffic corridors into the city, and minutes later was over the rainbow-lit heights and glass canyons of the metropolis. It singled out the blue-frosted pinnacle of the Milburn Towers, circled into its descent, and let McCain off outside the doors leading in from the roof-level parking area, where other vehicles were discharging their loads of evening diners, hotel guests, and revelers. McCain walked through the lobby to the Orchid Lounge adjoining the restaurant, checked his coat, and gave his name to the host, who showed him through to the booth where he was expected.

The figure that rose to greet him was wearing a dark gray suit, maroon tie, and matching handkerchief protruding from the breast pocket. The face had filled out a little since McCain had last seen it, although the eyes still had a noticeable bulge. It showed the lines of ten additional years, but at the same time had mellowed out and lost the tenseness it had once radiated. It was a face that seemed more at peace with itself and the world now.

"Hello, Mr. Earnshaw, journalist," Scanlon said. "It's been a long time. Your face has undergone some improvement, I see."

McCain grinned. "You're not looking so bad yourself."

They shook hands warmly, and Scanlon dropped the act. "Lew, I'm glad to see you so well. This is a fine place you picked."

"One of the best in town. Have you been here before?"

"I can't say that I have. Washington isn't a place I've ever had an opportunity to get to know."

"The restaurant's beautiful—looks right down over the center of the city. You'll like it."

The cocktail waiter appeared at the booth. He was Oriental in appearance. McCain ordered a Napoleon cocktail, and Scanlon took a refill of Bushmill's Irish with a touch of water. It was getting on near ten years since they'd last seen each other at the end of the winding-down after it all, when Scanlon had disappeared to pursue his own life. Then, a month or so ago, he had called out of the blue to say he would be in Washington in early November. November 7 had seemed a good day to choose for getting together.

"So, this is one of your regular haunts, eh?" Scanlon said, raising his glass.

"Oh, I wouldn't say regular. Once in a while, maybe. . . ."

"And a fine place for charming the ladies out of their wherewithals, too, I wouldn't wonder. 'Tis a grand view out there on that side. Do you live near here?"

"No, not in the city. I've got a place at Warrenton, in Virginia—west from here."

"How far would that be?"

"Oh, about thirty miles."

Scanlon sat back and looked McCain up and down. "And speaking of ladies, do you ever see the blond partner in crime that you had back then? A bit skinny if I remember, but not bad-looking for that. She had a temper on her, too, that'd put many a man to shame."

McCain shook his head. "Not these days. We were just doing a job, that's all. She got together with Razz in the end. I guess they had some things in common. . . . At least he could hold his own with her. They both went off on one of the lunar projects."

"Is that a fact, now?"

"Something to do with beaming power out to spaceships."

"Since you're still in the area, I suppose you keep in touch with your pals from your old firm," Scanlon said.

"I still see Bernard Foleda and his family from time to time," McCain replied. "You remember him from all the debriefings—the guy I worked for."

"I liked him. He said what he had to, without any frills or fancy airs and graces. How's he doing?"

"He retired after they started closing chunks of the Pentagon down and the excitement went out of life. Myra—

that's his wife—told me once that he couldn't get used to not having the KGB tailing him to work every morning. It was as if he'd lost old friends. So he quit. He does things with his grandchildren and drinks with old cronies from the Pentagon Mafia." McCain made a brief openhanded gesture. "I do see Koh every now and again. He's into big-time politics in Asia again, and travels backward and forward to Washington. He's always on a tight schedule, but he makes time if he can."

The drinks arrived. McCain looked across, hesitated for a moment, then raised his glass in a toast. "Well . . . to old times, I guess."

"And old friends." They drank, and stayed silent for a few seconds. "And what about yourself?" Scanlon asked at last. "Is the world managing to keep you well enough supplied with mischief?"

McCain set his glass down and shrugged. "Oh, they gave me an allowance that'll see me okay permanently, so money's no problem. I fly a plane and keep pretty active. There's a woman called Donna that I stay friendly with—I am a one-at-a-time kind of guy, whether you believe it or not. She's a lawyer and doesn't need full-time entanglements either, so it suits both of us. Politics and history still interest me—I read a lot." He sipped his drink again. "And I'm collecting information on the history of espionage technology. I'm thinking maybe I'll try writing a book about it one day." He smiled wryly. "The only problem is, I'm not sure if there are many people left who'd have any use for it these days. Maybe commercial espionage is the only field left that pays."

"Try writing one on mountaineering, then. Ye've some experience of that, too."

McCain grinned. "Anyhow, what about you? When you called, you said something about teaching? You? Surely not."

Scanlon looked upward and rubbed his neck in a guilty kind of way with his fingertips. "Ah, well now, it's teaching of a kind, all right—'security adviser,' I suppose you might call it. Some of these new nations that are appearing in Asia and all over . . . the people who are mixed up in the jockeyings to run them tend to worry about their safety and such, you understand. They'll pay well for good instructors to teach their bodyguards the business, if you follow my meaning."

McCain nodded in a resigned kind of way. "I might have guessed: know-how for sale, eh? Homicide, mayhem, explosives, booby-traps . . ."

"A man has to make a living," Scanlon said, using a phrase from the past. "And besides, hasn't anyone a right to sleep easy in their own beds?"

McCain fell silent and studied his glass for a while. When he finally looked up, his face was more serious. "Kev, there's one thing I always wanted to ask you about. What did make you switch sides back in Zamork?"

Scanlon shrugged. "Ah well, now, the KGB were never happy about having to use a foreigner for a job like that. But then, they could hardly have used a Russian with a fella like you, could they? So they took the risk and lost. I think maybe the let themselves believe too much of their own propaganda on Irish-English-American relationships. . . . And then, who ever understood how the Irish tick, anyhow?"

McCain drank, thought, and shook his head. "That was what you said at the debriefings and interrogations, but it never rang true—not to me. What was the real reason?"

Scanlon looked across, not answering at once, but his expression showed no surprise. Finally he said, simply, "It was Koh that did it."

"Koh?" McCain looked genuinely astonished.

Scanlon turned his head away to gaze out through the glass wall that formed the far side of the lounge. "It was them things he used to say about civilizations: Greeks, Romans, Europe, America . . . even the Brits. How they all were born suddenly like living things, grew and flourished and expressed what they were in everything they did . . . and then they died. A few stones from the rubble are picked up by the next one and built into something better, but the race as a whole moves on and that's what matters." He gestured up at the darkening sky outside. "And that's what's going on out there, right now. Wouldn't anyone like to think that what he did helped make a brick or two of what went into it? And when I got to thinking about it that way, how could I carry on working for the crowd I was with? Everything about that system represented where the rest of the world that mattered had come from, not where it was going to."

McCain leaned back and looked at him wonderingly. "So it was all those hours you used to spend talking to him. Koh did it, eh? He sweet-talked an Irishman around. I wonder if he knew what he was doing."

"Ah, to be sure he knew. . . . And it was watching the likes of yourself, and Razz, and the rest, and thinking what it all stood for," Scanlon said. "I'd seen a regime that could only survive through fear—that destroyed people's minds. And then I saw the power of the human mind, and people who would survive through overcoming fear. And I made my choice."

McCain drained his glass, then nodded. "Poetic, and philosophical," he complimented.

"And isn't that what you'd expect from the Irish?"

McCain looked across the booth. "I never had any quarrel with the people, you know, Kev," he said. "It was only the system. Look how well they're doing now. . . . Oh, and guess who I got a letter from a little while ago—Andreyov. Remember him?"

"The old fella, with the white hair."

"Yes, him. He's back in the Ukraine."

"Did you know that his father was there—in Germany in 1945, with Konev's army?" Scanlon asked. They both laughed.

"He mentioned the first Russian Disney World that's opened up outside Moscow," McCain said. "He says

Protbornov's running it. I couldn't make out if he was being serious or not."

At that moment the host came back to the table and announced, "More of your party have arrived, gentlemen." McCain looked up, puzzled, just in time to catch Scanlon giving the host a wink.

Then a woman's voice said from behind him, "I thought you'd have picked a Japanese restaurant, Lew."

McCain turned disbelievingly. She still had the obstinate curl of hair on her forehead that said so much about her personality, but her figure was more full now. He half-rose to his feet, speechless.

Rashazzi was behind her, grinning from ear to ear. "It's our first Earthside leave for eighteen months," he explained. "We couldn't let it go by without looking you up. And the timing was perfect." McCain shook Rashazzi's hand, then gave Paula a warm hug.

"It was her idea," Scanlon said. "She tracked me down and called me from the Moon six weeks ago."

"So we're a little late," Rashazzi said. "You know how it is—women . . ."

"Er, your table is ready," the host informed them. "But if you'd like a cocktail first, we can get you another one later. Mr. Nakajima-Lin called a few minutes ago to say he'd been detained slightly, and for you to go ahead. He'll join the party shortly."

"No, let's wait for him," Rashazzi said. "I'm not starving yet."

"We're in Washington for a week," Paula told McCain. "Why hurry?" Paula and Rashazzi sat down.

McCain was looking astounded. "Koh? Koh's coming here too?"

"One of his little jaunts that you mentioned," Scanlon aid. "Just between the four of us, I think the tribe is planning on colonizing the United States."

"So, what's it like being scientists on the Moon?" McCain asked.

"Indescribable," Rashazzi said. "Exhilarating. The sense

of vastness, the sheer rawness of nature up there . . . You can't imagine it."

"You're sure that's where you really are?" McCain said over the top of his glass. "It couldn't be down underneath Brooklyn or somewhere?" Rashazzi laughed.

"And being a scientist . . ." Paula said. She gave McCain a long look that was suddenly serious, just for the moment. "You had a lot to do with that, you know, Lew. I learned a lot about people, yes . . . But I learned what *real* science means, too."

"How d'you mean?" he asked.

"You know what I mean. Science is realism—eliminating wishful thinking. If you can't do that, you can't begin. You'll never know what truth is. You can make your own Potemkin in your head. And sometimes it can be just as difficult to break out of. But when you do, and you look back at the prison you were living a whole make-believe life in and mistaking it for reality, it's the same feeling of release and endless room to grow."

"Just like Koh's ideas about evolution," Scanlon commented.

"They're the same thing," Rashazzi said.

The Oriental cocktail waiter came back to the booth, and McCain stared up at him while he took Paula's and Rashazzi's order. His features seemed to be a mixture of Japanese and Chinese, with neither predominating— McCain had learned to distinguish them during his earlier years in the East. Then he frowned uneasily as a new thought struck him. "Your name wouldn't be Nakajima-Lin by any chance, would it?" he asked the waiter.

"No, sir. It's Jones."

McCain sat back with a sigh of relief. "That's good to know, anyway."

"Why do you want to know?" the waiter inquired curiously.

McCain looked out at the stars beyond the far wall. "Oh, that's a long, long story. Let's just say that it would have been a coincidence. I've never been very comfortable with coincidences."

The other smiled. Scanlon and McCain ordered refills.

Meanwhile, high in the sky outside, a particular pinpoint of light was just becoming visible, close to the Moon.